The WidowMaker

R.A. CONSTIBLE

ISBN 978-1-957956-08-4 (Paperback)
ISBN 978-1-957956-09-1 (Ebook)

Inquiries and Book Orders should be addressed to:

Leavitt Peak Press
17901 Pioneer Blvd Ste L #298, Artesia, California 90701
Phone #: 2092191548

This story is dedicated to Martin Pelichaty, a friend whose spirit now wanders the high plains country he embraced and loved so dearly. I miss his kind words and encouragement.

BOOK 1:

In the last years of our lives,
it comes to pass, the one love we seek —
all encompassing, filling needs and wants
and desires.

Reaching out, seeking to touch
the love we crave, searching for the immutable
haven, basking in the wellspring of strength
flowing from within, and peace, and security.

Concealed emotions, rising from obscurity:
a phoenix with no beginning and no end;
love eternal, buried within the heart,
Unexplained. Undefinable.
Forevermore.

ONE

McPherson sat astride the grey buckskin, one leg hooked loosely around the saddle horn as he allowed his horse to graze while he watched for signs of life in the cabin across the field. Nestled in the shadows of the Cumberland Mountains of East Tennessee, the cabin was the end of a journey that began a month before in East Texas.

It was well into the spring of 1885. Warm weather had been late arriving across the South, and even now, patches of snow remained within the dense forest that covered the ridges and mountainside, the after- effect of a winter of heavy snows and deep cold. But the pockets of mist McPherson encountered since leaving the campsite below Winter's Gap were a sure sign that spring had arrived.

Starting before dawn that day, he had pushed his horse to complete a journey to deliver the words of a dying man. And as the horse continued to forage on the new grass, McPherson gazed at the thin ribbon of smoke spiraling from the cabin's chimney, wondering again why he agreed to make this ride. He certainly owed nothing to Picquett; the man had tried to kill him. That he survived was less good fortune than skill with a gun, a skill that condemned Picquett to an early grave. But there was an inner sense of responsibil- ity, an obligation to honor the man's last request; and now that he had arrived at his destination, it was time to take stock of the situation before passing on the message.

McPherson sat motionless for better than an hour, watching the cabin with calm detachment, waiting for any indication of move- ment. He reacted with a grunt as his patience was finally rewarded. A woman came out of the cabin carrying a milk pail in one hand and a rifle in the other. He gathered up the reins and started down across the field toward the cabin, wondering how he was going to explain her husband's death…

For three long months, McPherson had spent the better part of each day sitting at a table near the back of the River's Edge Saloon in Texarkana, playing cards and waiting out a winter that seemed determined to go on forever. Seven years past, he succumbed to the lure of the West, and since then, had time and again crisscrossed most of the states and territories west of the Mississippi, following an inborn need to wander. But the weariness of the trail was beginning to weigh him down, draining him of the constant vigilance that had been his companion for almost as long.

"Mista McPherson!"

McPherson glanced up from the hand of cards he had been staring at. Standing in front and to one side of the table was a sorry excuse for a man. Unshaven and reeking of stale whiskey, his eyes bloodshot, he was dressed in the remnants of the attire of a fancy man. In his hands was a Winchester, pointed at the middle of McPherson's chest.

"Git up, McPherson."

McPherson calmly laid his cards face down on the table and sat back in his chair. "I know you, sir?" "No suh, you don't know me. But you know'd my wife." The last words were spat out. He waved the gun barrel. "Now, git up."

"You have me at a disadvantage, Mister…?" McPherson accentuated his query with a show of empty hands.

"Name's Picquett. Thet mean anythin' to ya?"

"No, I'm sorry." McPherson replied after a moment of reflection. "The name's unfamiliar."

"James Picquett…from Tennessee." His voice went up in pitch, his agitation underscoring the fact of the rifle in his hands.

"A lot of people are from Tennessee, Mister Picquett, myself included." "Don't fence with me, McPherson. I been afollowin' you fer months."

Maintaining as calm an exterior as he could manage, McPherson slowly edged his left hand toward the Peacemaker resting on his thigh, "Mister Picquett, why would you be following me?"

"'Cause I'm gonna kill ya." The gathering around the poker table reacted as one and moved ner- vously away.

"And why would you want to do that?" McPherson asked.

"You was with my wife. I seen ya ride away. Thet grey buckskin o'yourn was easy enough to foller." McPherson let out a sigh, relaxing. "Mister Picquett, you can rest easy. I was in the Montana Territory last summer. I haven't been this far East in over seven years."

"Yore lyin', McPherson. Now stand up, or I'm gonna shoot ya where you sit."

Resigned that there was no way out, McPherson kicked the chair back and sprang to his feet, draw- ing and firing his pistol in the same motion. His intention was to wound—he'd had enough killing to last a lifetime—but Picquett turned into the bullet, the force of it spinning him around and slamming him against the bar. The rifle slipped from Picquett's grip as he slumped to the floor.

• • •

As was her custom each morning upon rising, Hatty Picquett dressed quickly and built a fire to make coffee. Glancing out the window to see what weather awaited her for the morning chores, she saw the horse and rider on the knoll overlooking the farm. She took little notice; a rider pausing there to look around was not unusual given that the hill was close to the road and the highest point around.

A few minutes later, she glanced out the window a second time toward the hill. The stranger hadn't moved more than a few feet, but his interest in the cabin was evident. As she stepped onto the porch with a milk pail in one hand and the rifle she kept by the door in the other, she wasn't really surprised to see him start across the open field that lay between them. She continued walking toward the barn, all the while watching the rider's movement out of the corner of her eye, noting that he seemed to be in no great hurry. One thing was sure: the milking would have to wait. She was about to have a visitor, the first in more than a month.

Setting the milk pail inside the barn, she went out a side door and circled down behind the cabin. From there, she could follow his progress without being seen, and at the same time, decide how to deal with him. As the rider neared the gate, she got her first clear look at him. He sat upright in the saddle, and appeared to be a tall man. He worn his blondish hair long, and although his rough-hewn complexion indicated that he spent much of his time in the outdoors, she surmised he was her own age, or perhaps a year or two older.

Dressed in a tan buckskin shirt and well-worn denim pants, he wore a red bandanna tied loosely about his neck, and sported a dust-covered black hat with a low crown and a brim turned down in front; a pistol was tied low on his left thigh. But it was the horse that unsettled her. Her instincts told her the sudden appearance of this stranger on a grey buckskin had something to do with her husband's departure the previ- ous summer.

From behind the cabin, she watched as he as he rode up to the fence and stepped down from his horse in order to open the gate. Once inside the gate, his back was to her while he tied the horse to the fence. She moved quickly, leveling the cocked Winchester at his midsection.

"Something I can help you with, Mister?" "You Miz Picquett?" he asked.

"That's right. Who might you be?"

"My name's Jess McPherson, Miz Picquett. Fraid I'm the bearer of bad news. Your husband was killed about a month ago."

For a brief moment, her mind raced frantically to make sense of the news, but she never allowed the rifle leveled at his chest to waver. "Where… How?"

"Over to Texarkana. He got into a gunfight."

"And how is it you're here to tell me this, Mister McPherson?" She was a little surprised that her vis- itor continued to ignore the rifle, acting as if guns were pointed at him every day.

"I was with him when he died. He asked me to look in on you and I said I would."

"All right, Mister McPherson, you've looked in on me. Now please get on your horse and ride out." "Excuse me, Miz Picquett," he asked, his forehead furrowed. "you don't seem too grievous about your husband."

"Mister McPherson, my husband's whole life was affected by only two things: his inability to recog- nize the truth and his foul temper. It would seem that one of those particulars has gotten him killed."

As soon as the words were out of her mouth, she wished she hadn't been so flippant, but McPherson's comment had struck home. She sensed…knew she should be overwhelmed with grief, but she felt little anguish. Her early enthusiasm for wedded bliss had worn off quickly. Nevertheless, she found the news of his death disturbing.

"Actually, it was a misunderstanding," McPherson responded.

"I'm sure it was. James Picquett had a real problem with mis- understandings. Was it you that shot him?" The look on McPherson's face answered her question. "Your horse, Mister McPherson. My husband left here last summer following a man on a horse just like yours. Another misunderstanding."

She allowed the gun barrel to drop and turned away as the tears began to flow. Her husband was dead. And this stranger had ridden a great distance just to communicate his last words.

"Ma'am?" McPherson appeared confused.

Hatty took a deep breath and turned back to face him; her eyes were red, but she was no longer cry- ing. She knew she had to make him understand that he had done the right thing by coming there.

"I've forgotten my manners, Mister McPherson. Have you eaten this morning?"

"No, ma'am. But I don't want to put you to any bother. I'll just ride on out, like you said."

"You won't be putting me out. Take your horse out to the barn. There's oats there. Then wash up and come to the house. I'll put on some coffee."

• • •

McPherson's mystification grew as he watched Hatty to the cabin. *How could this woman have been married to the wretch he shot in Texarkana?* Given the unkempt appearance of the man, the farm— and his wife—were totally out of character.

Besides the cabin, there was a roughed-log barn with a small fenced corral located off to one side. Two smaller out buildings which evidently served as a chicken coop and a tool shed were situated near the barn. Like the barn, the cabin was also constructed of logs, but they had been smoothed down, the cracks between the logs filled with caulking, and then white-washed. A front porch ran the full length of the cabin, serving as a platform for two rocking chairs and a long-eared hound that had noted McPherson's approach and then went back to sleep. A waist high split rail fence completed the scene, encircling the cabin and main yard, each end butted against the barn. A water trough was nested just to the right of the doors.

After allowing the horse to drink, McPherson stepped inside the barn, and his wonderment contin- ued—it was as neat and tidy as the yard. He unsaddled the horse and led him into a stall, found the oats she had mentioned, and doled out a healthy couple of scoops which the grey acknowledged with a snort. Out- side the barn, McPherson cut across the yard to the washstand near the cabin and filled a wash-basin with water from the hand pump. He hung his hat on the pump and splashed water liberally on his face and hair, tossed the water and refilled the basin, repeating the process. She walked up and handed him a towel just as he finished.

"Coffee's ready," she announced and returned to the cabin, McPherson trailing close behind.

"You can hang your gun and hat there," she gestured, smiling at his hesitation. "It's alright, Mister McPherson. You're safe here."

Untying the leather thong around his left thigh, he unbuckled the gun belt and draped the gun and holster across the chair next to the door, hanging his hat next to them. At the table, he made short order of the food she put in front of him—he was obviously much hungrier than he had let on—while she carried on a one-sided conversation. But in spite of her efforts to make him feel welcome, his discomfort at being inside the cabin was quite apparent. It was only with a lot of encouragement that she was finally able to get him talking about his travels, but it wasn't until he openly admitted the incident in Texarkana that he finally relaxed.

"I appreciate that talking about this makes you uncomfortable, Mister McPherson, but I'd like to know about my husband's death."

"He didn't give me a lot of choice in the matter, Miz Picquett," he answered softly. "I would have been surprised if he had. My husband was not a fair-minded man." "You said something about my horse and a misunderstanding?"

"I did," she nodded. "One morning last summer, a traveler come through here riding a horse the same color as yours. He stopped just long enough to ask for directions and some water." She paused momentarily, uncertain if she should continue. "My husband happened to be returning from Knoxville about the time the man rode off. He assumed the worst. When I denied any wrongdoing, he became hateful and left that afternoon to find the man."

McPherson picked up his coffee cup and leaned back, amazed that she would talk of such things. But he could understand her husband's feelings. Hatty Picquett was a pleasant sight to McPherson's weary eyes after years of dust-choked trails and look alike dance-hall girls. She fit no image he could conjure up of a farm woman. Obviously, she worked hard—the farm presented ample evidence of her efforts—but she didn't seem to suffer physically from the labors of farm life. If anything, the work had enhanced her appearance, and from the moment he first laid eyes on her, something reached inside him and grabbed hold.

"I gather he thought the man was me…"

"So it seems," she acknowledged, getting to her feet.

McPherson's eyes followed her as she walked over to the cook stove to retrieve the coffee pot. She stood a good head shorter than McPherson, her shoulders and hips gently mocking her slenderness. She had small delicate hands that belied the long hours spent in the sun. Her features were exotic: high cheek bones and lush green eyes framed by auburn hair that cascaded in soft waves across and below her shoul- ders, reaching almost to her waist; a mouth that was inviting and alive. She dressed simply, wearing a long calico dress that had seen better days, faded from the sun and washings too numerous to count.

Her eyes radiated a softness and warmth that countered the severity of her cheekbones, and spoke of a knowledge far beyond her years. There was something about her calmness in the face of what he had thought would be disaster, an unpretentious manner that bespoke of self-assurance, of a certainty in her convictions.

Her surroundings were just as intriguing. The farm had a rough hewn symmetry about it and she took obvious pride in how it looked. And there were the books, piles of them, stacked high against the walls of the cabin. He had never seen so many books in one place. Whether or not she had actually read them was immaterial; that she had them at all put her into a unique category.

He found it hard to believe that an hour before, she had been pointing a rifle at him and was ready to shoot. He finally decided it was the hair. Outside, she had worn her hair in a single braid, but she had obvi- ously undone it while he was in the barn, because now it was loose and flowing, and the effect was dra- matic.

"Did he suffer?" she asked.

"No ma'am. I don't believe he did."

"You're a kind person, Mister McPherson. Most people wouldn't of ridden this far just to deliver a message."

Embarrassed, he quietly sipped the coffee, occasionally glancing at her when he thought she wasn't paying him any attention. Finally, he stood and picked up his gunbelt, methodically adjusting the belt around his waist until it was comfortable before tying the leather thong.

"I best be going, Miz Picquett." She nodded and walked out with him. "Where's your home, Mister McPherson?"

"My folks live up near the Gap, leastwise they did when I left. I haven't seen them in seven years." "You should visit them," she advised solemnly.

"Yes, ma'am," he agreed. "I'm heading that way when I leave here."

"Will you be coming back through, Mister McPherson?" she asked as they walked toward the barn. "Don't know, Miz Picquett," he answered, surprised at the question. "Hadn't thought that far ahead."

She quietly speculated about McPherson as he saddled the buckskin, noting that his movements were unwasted, precise, and sure. She recognized that McPherson was a different sort of man from any she had ever met before, and was the direct opposite of her late husband. Cooking for him had been a pleasure, and he had obviously enjoyed the food, but it was his sidelong glances in her direction when he thought she wasn't looking that quickened her blood and entranced her. When he suddenly announced he'd be on his way, she knew without hesitation that she wanted to find out more about him…that she wanted to see him again.

"Well, I hope you won't be afraid to drop by if'n you're back this way." "No ma'am," he replied. "I'd like that very much."

"Then please do."

He untied the reins and led the animal out of the barn, pausing while she closed the barn door. Hatty walked beside him to the gate, holding it open while he led the horse through.

"I'm real sorry we had to meet this way, Miz Picquett," he said across the fence. "And I thank you for the breakfast. Don't think I remembered to eat much the last couple of days."

"There's still some coffee, if you'd like some…" she offered.

"I appreciate that, but I best go. Is there anything I can do before I leave?" "I don't think so, Mister McPherson," she answered, "Then I'll be on my way. Goodbye, Miz Picquett." "Goodbye, Mister McPherson."

Leaning against the gate, she followed his progress as he rode away from the farm until he crested the hill. Her breath caught when he stopped for a moment and looked back at the farm, acknowledging the fact that she was still standing at the gate. He sat unmoving for a moment, gave a slight wave of the hand and spurred the horse to a slow gallop toward the Cumberland Gap.

• • •

McPherson rode northeast out of Clinton, planning to follow the trail that paced the north side of the Clinch River. Seven years back, he paid little attention when he traversed the state—he was focused on covering as much ground as fast as he could. But as he rode along now, he was overwhelmed by the multi- tudes of people. Folks appeared to be everywhere, and they seemed to have fenced in most of the land, forcing him to detour around farms again and again.

He expected to take no more than a couple of days to reach the gap, but the two days turned into three, and then four, giving him ample opportunity to speculate about seeing his family. The Widow Pic- quett, however, dominated his thoughts. He was captivated by her open friendliness, and fascinated by her candid invitation to stop by again. He concluded that he wanted to see her again, but apart from the circum- stances that had initially brought him there; if events permitted, he would make every effort to return to the farm for another visit.

His first priority, however, was his family. The pull of home had been tugging at him for months. His abrupt departure from the farm had left an emptiness inside him that continuously ate at his resolve. He never intended to stay away so long, but he needed to grow up— and growing up can take a long time. The gunfight in Texarkana gave him the excuse he needed to at last face his father again. He could no longer pretend there was yet another trail to follow.

Two

It was midday when McPherson reined up in sight of the farm where he had spent most of his life. At first glance, the farm looked pretty much as it had when he left, but there were differences. The home place had grown in size and seemed to have a fresh coat of white-wash. A new barn had been built a little nearer to the cabin and a couple of lean-tos added to the old one. Nonetheless, just as he had done four days ear- lier at the Picquett farm, he took time to look the place over before heading in. The years spent in the West had taught him prudence; he had learned that familiarity with a situation was no reason to throw caution to the winds.

He nudged the horse forward, following the familiar road that skirted the land he had spent so much time on as a boy, all the while, taking in the changes. The road led in a relatively straight line across the hill where he had been sitting, down to a small creek that flowed along the valley floor. Once across the creek, the road wandered back uphill, curving to the left around a stand of trees and then back to the right before making a final jog toward the cabin.

The land below the cabin had been recently worked in prepa-ration for spring planting. On the slope above the barns, McPherson could see a small herd of cattle grazing. And everywhere was the fenc-ing his father had hated. What disturbed McPherson at that moment, though, was the number of horses and wag- ons tied in front of the cabin and the fact that he could see no people. The farm should have been a beehive of activity, but nothing was moving and to his mind, that meant trouble.

As McPherson cleared the last of the trees, a young man, a stranger dressed in black, came out of the cabin to stand on the porch. The stranger watched him as he covered the last hundred yards to the cabin, then stuck his head inside to announce his arrival. McPherson dismounted and tied the horse to a hitching post standing just outside the split rail fence enclosing the cabin and yard as the young man was joined by an even younger woman, also dressed in black. The somber couple stood with their arms around each other, obviously mystified as to who the person was that had ridden so boldly onto the farm. McPherson looked at her and then at the young man, equally mystified, before the woman's hand flew to her mouth in recognition.

"Jess… Jesse? Is it really you?" She ran to him and threw her arms around him. "I'm Maggie, Jess." "You're Maggie?" He held her at arm's length. "Well, I'll be damned. The last time I saw you, you weren't any bigger than…"

"I'm all grown up, Jess. I been married for three years now." She hugged him again with even greater enthusiasm, oblivious to everything around her, until the young man cleared his throat. "Oh, my goodness, Jonathan. I'm sorry." She took each of them by the hand, introducing them in an almost formal manner. "Jonathan, this is my long lost brother, Jesse. Jesse, my husband of three years, Jonathan Morgan."

The two men shook hands. "Heard a lot about you, Mister McPherson," Morgan said with some ner- vousness.

"I trust it wasn't all bad, Mister Morgan," he replied dryly, before turning back to his sister. "What's going on, Maggie? Why the black?"

Her eyes filled with tears. "We buried Aaron this morning. He took sick with fever back in the win- ter, and just never come out of it."

The news of his brother's death shook McPherson's composure, but the anguish he felt was all but imperceptible to his sister. "Where's Pa?"

"He's dead too, Jess, just after we got married. We tried to find you…" McPherson nodded, stoically accepting what he had already sensed. "And Jacob?" "He's out back at the grave site."

"Who belongs to all these horses?" he asked.

"Friends, neighbors." She took him by the hand and led him toward the rear of the cabin. "Come on.

They'll want to see you."

McPherson followed his sister around the perimeter of the fence and down the sloping ground behind the cabin to the family burial plot. The half dozen men who were filling in the grave looked up as they approached, all but one returning to their work after a cursory look. But the sixth one leaned on his shovel and continued to stare until they had reached the site.

"Well, well, well. Would you look who's here. The prodigal son returneth. You remember my way- ward brother," he said, addressing the others, "Jesse McPherson, last of the breed."

"Jacob." McPherson said, nodding.

"Y'all might not know it, but ol' Jess here was our Paw's favorite son. He was the one picked to carry on the family name. But brother Jess wasn't content with that. No sirree. He turned his back on the family and the farm and went out west. And he broke Paw's heart." Jacob's voice took on a mocking tone as he continued his diatribe. "Tell me somethin', Jess. What brings you back? Come to lay claim to the spoils now that most of us're dead?"

McPherson turned on his heels and headed back to the cabin without bothering to reply.

"How could you, Jacob?" Maggie cried out, tears streaming down her face. "He's our brother!"

Jacob ignored her and returned to the task of filling in the grave. Maggie stared at her older brother a moment longer before running after Jesse. By the time she caught up with him, he had reached his horse.

"Don't leave, Jesse, he didn't mean it."

"That's where you're wrong, Maggie. He meant every word. Besides, some of it's true."

Yes, McPherson thought bitterly, *some of what Jacob said rang true. But it was the things he left out, things he didn't realize that make the difference.* The last two days he spent on the farm came back as if it were yesterday…

"Time you got this wanderin' foolishness outta your head, boy. We got a farm to tend to." Zebadiah McPherson had spent the entire meal lecturing his youngest son.

"Don't know if I can, Pa," Jesse answered, unconsciously stirring the beans on his plate. "Something out there's calling to me. I got to go see what it is."

"I be damned if I understand you, Jesse," his father said angrily. "Your brothers and sisters don't have no problem with being here. They're a part of this place. And you are too, even if you don't want to admit it. But all you think about is followin' some damn fool notion you got in the back of your head about goin' out west. They ain't nothin' out there but desert and hostile Injuns."

Jesse looked around the dinner table in the faint hope that he would get moral support from someone, but his brothers and sisters seemed determined to stay out of the discussion. Better their father's wrath be directed at Jesse than at one of them. Jess decided to try a different tack.

"Didn't you ever want to travel, Pa, to go somewhere new?"

"Wasn't no need to," his father declared. "I was born on this farm. I fought the damn Yankees *and* the Johnny Rebs to keep it. Plan to die here." Although he had heard the assertion a hundred times or more, Jesse bridled at his father's matter-of-fact declaration.

"All of us were born here, Pa. Does that mean we're supposed to die here too?" His father said noth- ing, but Jess wouldn't let it drop and continued trying to reason with him. "Look, Pa. Jacob and Aaron both want to live here, and maybe someday I will too. But I ain't ready to settle down yet."

"He's right, Pa," Aaron spoke up. "Give him your blessing and let him go." Zeb turned his attention to his middle son. "And why should I do that, Aaron?"

"Cause he won't be any use to us long as he's got the wanderlust. Jacob'n me'll take care of the place 'til he gets back."

"And what about you?" Zeb glanced toward Jacob. "You hold an opinion?"

"Let him go." Jacob stared directly at Jesse. "He ain't part of the family, nohow." "I'm as much a part of this family as you'll ever be, big brother," Jesse snapped. "You don't know the meanin' of the word, Jess," Jacob sneered.

"Well, thank you, Jacob. And I suppose you do?"

"I know a lot more than you give me credit for, little brother. And I don't need a bunch of book learnin' to prove it."

"Ain't my fault you can't read, Jacob." Jesse gave his brother a triumphant smile.

"I ain't got time for readin'. I work around here, which is somethin' you might try sometime."

Jesse ignored the remark, redirecting his attention toward his father in an attempt to make peace. "Look, Pa. I don't want to go against your wishes, and I don't want to fight with you. But with or without your blessing, I'm gonna go."

"I know that, boy," he conceded, laying down his fork and knife. "And for what it's worth, you can have my blessin', as long as you understand that if you leave, there'll be nothin' for you to come back to."

Jesse sighed. "If that's how you want it, Pa."

"Ain't what I want, boy," he countered as he wiped his mouth. "Just the way it has to be."

The next afternoon, while Jesse was packing his few personal belongings in a bedroll, his brother Aaron walked into the room carrying a worn leather holster and belt wrapped around a Colt .44 Peace- maker. "I got this off a traveler a couple of years ago, Jess. Might as well take it with you. You might need it." Jess took the pistol from his brother with a nod of his head. "It's pretty accurate up to twenty yards, but past that it shoots high and left."

"You'd think he'd understand," Jesse protested, unable to forget the previous night's conversation. "Oh, he understands, little brother," Aaron said wistfully. "If'n it was Jacob or me that was taking off, it wouldn't be any problem. But you've always been special to him, so it ain't easy for him to watch you leave."

Jess untied the bedroll and wrapped the pistol into it. "I just hate to see him so unhappy."

"He'll survive." Aaron picked up the bedroll. "Come on. I got something else for you." Jesse fol- lowed Aaron out of the cabin and walked silently beside him toward the barn. "Get your saddle and come out back." Aaron went around back of the barn while Jesse went inside and retrieved his saddle and blan- ket. He continued on through the barn to the rear door to find his older brother holding the reins of a light grey buckskin horse and grinning from ear to ear.

"Well, what do you think, little brother?"

"He's beautiful." Jesse acknowledged. "Who's he belong to?"

"He's yours. Pa and me figured that horse you been riding wouldn't last a month." Aaron's grin took on a more serious note. "I told you Pa understood, Jess. Now quit standing there with your mouth open and saddle up. You got a long ride ahead of you."

Jesse nodded and threw the blanket and then the saddle over the horse's back. The horse reacted with a snort, but stood quietly while he tightened the cinch. Aaron helped him tie on the bedroll and saddle bags and stuck out his hand. "All right, little brother, take care, and don't forget us. He's all yours, Pa."

Jess turned to see his father standing behind him holding a shiny new carbine and a small leather sack. He tossed the rifle to Jesse, then handed him the sack. "Hundred dollars there, boy. Keep you goin' for a while."

"Don't know what to say, Pa."

"Then don't say nothin'. Just make damn sure when you come back here you're ready to stay." "Yes sir."

"Now go on afore I change my mind." Jesse shook his father's hand and then quite unexpectedly, Zebadiah threw his arms around the boy's shoulders. Embarrassed by the sudden gesture, the boy tensed and pulled away.

"Don't worry about me, Pa," he said as he climbed on the horse, "I'll be back."

Zebadiah opened the corral gate and slapped the grey across the rump, startling both the horse and his son.

"Git."

Jesse nodded a final goodbye and spurred the animal into move- ment. Twice before he reached the trees beyond the barn, he started to pull up, but forced himself to keep going. Even though he had made the decision to leave and was finally on his way, he was still afraid that some last minute hitch would jump up to stop him from leaving. But his fears were unsubstantiated. There was no last minute interference, no final plea from his father to change his mind. And the possibility that he wouldn't see him again was far from his mind…

McPherson knew he should have turned and left the minute Jacob started in on him at the grave site. Instead, he listened to Maggie's pleas and stayed the night, and paid a heavy price for doing so. Over the years, Jacob had become even more cynical about his leaving, and he made no bones about it throughout the evening and into the next morning. He seemed determined to pick a fight over long dead issues. In a vain attempt to calm the flaring tempers, Maggie tried to intervene, and Jacob turned his rage on her. Eventually, Jesse could stand no more.

"You've said just about enough, Jacob."

"Enough?" he roared angrily. "I ain't hardly started."

"Maybe not," Jesse countered, "but you got no reason to be picking on Maggie."

"Who are you to be dictatin' anythin', little brother? You left, remember? This farm is mine now, and I'll thank you to stay the hell outta my way."

"That's not true," Maggie objected. "Pa left the farm to all of us, Jess included, and you know it." "She telling it straight, Jacob?" Jess asked softly.

Jacob's face reddened as the rage built up inside him. "While you was gallivantin' around the coun- tryside, I worked this place. *I* worked it, and as far as I'm concerned, it's mine."

"Was there a will, Maggie?"

"No, when Pa knew he was dying, he just gathered us around and told us. I don't think anything was written down."

"Then it's your word against Jacob's. And since he's the oldest son, he'll win." "But that's not right," she cried.

"Don't matter, Sis. He'll still win."

"We'll see about that," she said defiantly. "What about the rest of it, Jacob?" "The rest of what?"

"Pa's watch. And that fiddle of Aaron's. They both belong to Jesse."

"Nothing belongs to Jesse, sweet sister," Jacob gloated. "When he left, Pa said there'd be nothin' for him to come back to, and that's what he's gettin'. Nothin'."

"Well, Jacob," Jesse mused, "I'll say one thing for you: your greed seems to be boundless." McPher- son crossed the room to where his pistol belt was hanging on a coat hook and took it down, buckling it around his hips. After he tied the leather thongs at the bottom of the holster around his thigh, he pulled the Peacemaker and checked the load before returning it to his hip. "I'll tell you what. I'll take the watch and fiddle and you can keep the farm, that is if Maggie agrees. How about it, Sis?"

"I s'pose, but it don't seem right. Pa give it to us all." "And if I don't go along?" Jacob snarled.

"Then there stands a good chance you won't survive 'til your next birthday." "You threatenin' me, Jess?" Jacob's face was etched with raw hatred.

"Nope." Jesse stood facing his brother, arms loosely folded across his chest. "One thing I learned in the last seven years, Jacob. Never threaten. Now just how greedy are you?"

The two brothers stared at each other for what seemed an eternity, before Jacob turned on his heel and walked into one of the back rooms. A minute later, he came back out carrying a wooden case and a pocket watch. Tossing them down on the table, he gestured at them and snapped at McPherson. "Take 'em and get out."

"All right, Jacob." McPherson picked up the watch and fiddle. "You heard Maggie. The farm is yours 'til the day you die. But I'm warning you. Don't try to sell this place. I would take that to mean you didn't really want it, and that all this was just to get at me. Is that clear?" When Jacob didn't bother to answer, McPherson turned on his heels. "Mister Morgan, I apologize for my brother's lack of hospitality. May I escort you and my sister home? I believe we've worn out our welcome here."

THREE

McPherson stood on the front porch of his sister's home, his arm curled about her waist as he said his goodbyes. He was tired, not so much from the confrontation with Jacob, but from trying to keep up with the constant chatter of his sister. For two solid days and nights, Maggie had talked non-stop, asking an unending string of questions about his travels and periodically dredging up much more of the past than he would have preferred to talk about or thought necessary.

Even so, the time spent with the Morgans had been pleasant. His little sister had chosen well. Jona- than Morgan was a person-able young man, and obviously cared deeply for her. But now the visit was over, and all McPherson felt was a need for the peacefulness and solitude of the trail. This time at least, he felt no regret at leaving. Both he and Maggie knew his future lay somewhere other than Cumberland Gap. So it was one last round of hugs and kisses and promises to keep in touch, and no looking back.

With no real destination in mind, McPherson decided to head south into Knoxville along the May- nardville Pike and restock his dwindling supplies before turning toward the west. He made good time and by late morning two days later, he was sitting in a Halls Crossroads roadhouse on the outskirts of the city, savoring a cup of hot coffee and reflecting at length on his ill-fated homecoming. His thoughts drifted to the Widow Picquett and for a brief moment, his mood brightened as he recalled the sight of Hatty Picquett standing at the gate as he had ridden off.

But as he continued to dwell over the coffee, his mood unexpect-edly deteriorated, his thoughts filled with a foreboding. He couldn't put a finger on his sudden uneasiness—it had no source or direc-tion— except for the disquieting feeling that it somehow involved

Hatty Picquett. Finishing his coffee, he spoke to the proprietor as to the shortest way back to Wolf Valley and the Picquett farm.

Mounting up, McPherson turned the buckskin southwest along Emery Road and picked up the pace. The sooner he got there, the better he would feel. Just before sunset, he topped the rise overlooking the farm. Hatty was standing on the porch, looking expectantly in his direction. After a quick glance born of caution, he rode straight in. She met him at the gate.

"Good evening, Mister McPherson."

"Miz Picquett," McPherson nodded as he dismounted. "What brings you this way, Mister McPherson?"

"Can't rightly answer that, Miz Picquett," he answered softly. "Seemed like the right thing to do." "Will you be staying long, Mister McPherson?" she asked, suddenly unsettled.

"Haven't given it much thought."

"Then maybe you best put up your horse while you do."

Jesse walked the horse toward the barn, Hatty by his side. Inside the barn, McPherson tied the reins to a crossbeam and after hooking one stirrup on the saddle horn, loosened the cinch, pulled the saddle and blanket off and set them over a sawhorse next to the stall. Picking up a brush, he began grooming the horse, working methodically along the animal's length. Hatty watched in silence for a couple of moments before going to one of the bins near the back of the barn and filling a small bucket with oats. Setting a flat pan at the buckskin's head, she poured the oats into the pan and gave the horse a playful scratch between his ears.

"Best not do that too much, Miz Picquett. He'll get to expecting it on a regular basis." "Come to the house and wash up when you're finished, Mister McPherson."

"Yes ma'am," McPherson answered to her back as she left the barn, continuing to brush the animal until he was satisfied the task was completed. Turning the horse into the corral, McPherson untied the sad- dlebags and threw them across his shoulder before heading for the cabin.

From inside the cabin, Hatty followed McPherson's progress as he walked across the yard toward the pump located at the side of the cabin and drew water into the basin sitting on the stand next to it. She watched as he untied the leather thongs around his left thigh and unbuckled the gunbelt; watched as he stripped off his shirt, lathered his face and body, and rinsed the soap off; watched him empty the basin and refill it, rinsing the last of the soap residue away; watched as he took a straight razor and a small mirror from the saddlebags, relathered his face, and shaved off the two days of growth that had accumulated. Mesmerized as McPherson shaved in the fading light, she allowed her thoughts to drift to the nights that had passed since she last saw him, centering on the emotional journey she had been through since first meeting James Picquett. She wondered whether McPherson would be the gentle man she had dreamed of, the man Mister Picquett should have been…

One of a dozen children, Hatty Morgan's world was a circle of overlapping chores. There was always something that needed doing, be it tending to her younger brothers and sisters or helping her father in the fields. The few brief respites from the work were taken up by her mother's attempts at teaching the children reading and writing. Her mother had insisted that they all have schooling, and had set about to ensure they would. But Hatty's enlightenment went beyond basic learning. She immersed herself in books, and with the knowledge she gained from reading, she flourished, the books providing a gateway to the world. Hatty used them to escape from the daily drudgery of the farm, and they became her life. When James Picquett of Virginia appeared on her family's front porch one Sunday afternoon, she perceived in him a world traveler from that exotic life she read about. When he presented himself as a suitor, she jumped at the chance.

But the image that Picquett tendered to Hatty and her family was a concoction of shrewd chicanery and wily bluster. He led them to believe that his family was one of the landed gentry of Virginia, that his purpose in Tennessee was to purchase land to expand his family's interests in the raising of tobacco; and while he was at it, he would be most pleased to take the hand of Hatty Morgan in matrimony. In truth, James Picquett was a charlatan, and once he had taken her away from the family, Hatty discovered that with the exception of his being from Virginia and having purchased a small farm, everything he had told them was a lie.

Picquett had left Virginia under a cloud, disowned by his family because of gambling debts and a concerted effort on his part to drag the family name through every roadhouse and brothel in Eastern Virginia. As for tobacco farming, his knowledge was limited to avoiding it. He possessed a violent temper, often flying into a rage over small details and then taking out his wrath on her. She discovered quickly that he preferred the associations found in saloons and whorehouses to her company, and he seldom spent more than a day or two with her before disappearing for two and three weeks at a stretch.

Even so, Hatty clung to the belief that things would change. In the first two years of their marriage, she gave birth to a son and a daughter, much to her delight and Mister Picquett's displeasure. Instead of moderating their father's temper, however, their presence only seemed to add to his malevolence…

"I tol' you to keep them away from me, Hatty!"

"They was no call to hit him, James. He was just trying to tell you he loved you."

"Time you understand somethin', woman. Them kids was yore idea, not mine. I din't want 'em afore you had 'em, I don't want 'em now."

She made every effort to placate and please him in an attempt to win him over, but he took to stray- ing even further from the farm, staying away for months at a time, leaving her to focus all her emotions on the children. But even that small pleasure was taken away when influenza took the children from her. Hatty's world crashed around her, and the only sensations left for her were those of numbing pain and the barely consoling thought that their suffering was over.

In the aftermath of her loss, she redirected her attention and energies toward the farm, turning it into a reflection of her own temperament, a personality fashioned by the basic education her mother had insisted on and heavily influenced by her reading. Drummers passing by the farm left her books—all kinds of books—often detouring miles out of their way to drop off their latest find. The books comforted her, much as they did in her childhood, and pro-vided her relief from the loneliness. Her isolation became com- plete, and remained that way until the morning she saw the horse and rider up on the knoll.

For a brief time, a few short hours, Jesse McPherson revived her appetite for another person and then with a wave of his hand, he rode off, and she was once again alone…and more than a little unsettled. She stood by the gate long after he had disappeared from sight, won-dering what forces had caused this man to come into her life. Of all the travelers that had passed through her life since she was a child, she couldn't remember ever meeting anyone quite like him.

In McPherson, Hatty recognized qualities that most men aspire to and never seem to achieve. She saw a steadfast courage and a sim-ple honesty, but there was also an indefinable shyness that made her want to reach out to him and take him in her arms and protect him. She had read of such sensations, and calling to mind some of the things she had read sent shivers of anticipation through her body. But the thought of actually experiencing those emotions frightened and at the same time fascinated her. No one, not Mister Picquett nor anyone else, had ever aroused such feelings in her before.

She'd continued to gaze in the direction he had ridden, won-dering if she would ever see him again, wondering why she had so openly extended an invitation for him to return, especially since he was respon- sible for her husband's recent death. Admittedly, she felt no for Mister Picquett's demise. Plain and simple, he was an adven-ture that went bad. But her instincts told her that Jesse McPherson represented far more than an adventure.

She'd passed the remainder of that day and the days that fol-lowed doing the things that had seen her through the long periods of loneliness when her husband was off on one of his excursions: keep-ing busy with the many chores that the farm required, and reading one of the many books she had accumulated. Her evenings, however, took on new meaning. They became a time for reflection, and a time for thinking about Jesse McPherson.

Slowly but surely, McPherson became the central focus of her thoughts, overriding the other inter- ests that kept her occupied.

That he hadn't spent more than a couple of hours with her was unimportant. He had disturbed the peace and calm surrounding her, had reminded her that she was first and foremost alive, and not meant to live out her life in solitude.

Eventually, her musings became dreams, and the dreams fantasies, escalating in intensity until she ached with raw hunger. Each night she imagined his presence beside her, felt his lips on hers. Each night the intensity grew, her own hands playing the role she imagined Jesse's would, cupping her breasts, caress- ing her body. Slowly the fantasies became an obsession, dominating her thoughts, over-shadowing percep- tions of common sense. Now, as she watched him rinse the last of the soap from his face, the uncertainty and anticipation she had sensed after his departure returned with a vengeance, and she knew that whatever the consequences, he would share her bed.

McPherson pulled a fresh shirt from the saddlebags and dressed before walking around to the front porch. Hatty met him at the door, took the saddlebags from him and draped them across the back of a chair. Nothing was said as she reached up, running her fingers along the edge of his jaw, at last brushing his lips with her fingertips. Hesitantly, he duplicated the gesture, gently following the line of her chin and the out- line of her lips, at last touching her cheek with an innocent caress. She covered his hand with her own, holding it against her face, finally wrapping her arms around his waist and laying her head on his chest.

Their lips brushed as he returned the embrace she so openly offered, enveloping her in his arms, holding her tightly against his chest. His hands moved behind her head to pull her even closer, the long strands of her hair wrapped around and between his fingers. She responded in kind, kissing him with a ferocity bordering on wanton abandon, her calm demeanor suddenly a distant memory.

"I apologize for my forwardness, Mister McPherson." Hatty smiled self-consciously, as surprised as McPherson was by the sudden outpouring of her own emotions. "I've thought of little else since you rode off."

"Miz Picquett..." Jesse started to say, obviously uneasy about the circumstances of their being together and the suddenness of her embrace.

"Please, Mister McPherson, I know what you're going to say and it ain't necessary... Just hold me close."

As McPherson relaxed, Hatty slowly unbuttoned his shirt, pulling it open until it hung loosely around his hips before beginning to undo the buttons running down the front of her dress. She shivered involuntarily as he reached out and grasped her wrists, taking over the task to undo the remaining buttons, kneeing at her feet to release the last of them just below her waist. With great effort, she urged him to his feet and led him into the large alcove at the rear of the cabin. Sitting him in a chair next to the bed, she helped him remove his boots and stood in front of him as he peeled the dress off her shoulders and arms, dropping it in a heap around her ankles.

Hatty reclined on top of the rumpled quilts of her bed, watching intently as he unbuckled his belt and removed his pants. Fighting the ache to hurry, she pulled him onto the bed, giving in to the urgency of the moment. With her hand guiding him, he plunged deep into her center, moving with deliberate speed, never losing contact, matching the rhythm of her undulating hips. He refused her time to catch her breath, push- ing her senses past all reason, until he could no longer hold back, erupting, filling her with his seed.

•　•　•

"Who are you? Really." She asked as she traced random patterns in the hair on his chest. "Your destiny?"

"Ummm... Don't believe in destiny. But you're what I've waited for all my life." "I find that hard to believe."

"Perhaps, but it's true." She reached up to caress his face, running her hand into and through his hair.

He took her hand in his and brought it to his mouth, softly biting the soft mound of flesh at the base of the thumb, then kissing the fingertips, taking them one by one into his mouth. "You're different from...other women I've known."

"I hope for the better." Her words came out as intakes of breath as she reacted to his touch. "Something about you, something that says you're full of life."

"I'm pleased you think so, Mister McPherson."

Again she ran her fingers into his hair as he ran a hand across her breasts, sliding it around behind her back and down along the length of her body. Hatty tensed, wondering where he would touch her next, feeling his hand move to her abdomen and into the dark triangle that guarded the entrance to her sexual being, sending chills through her, renewing the level of tension between them. A warmth radiating from his touch began to spread throughout her body.

She shifted until she was poised above him, once more guiding him until he was buried within, the heat searing her sensibilities, her body racked with a rush of adrenalin as she rocked on her knees. She took his hands, placing them on either side of her hips, resisting the tendency of her movement to separate their bodies. When at last he exploded inside her, she collapsed onto his body, no longer able to support herself. As her spasms ebbed and his hardness slowly diminished, she held him against her, and spoke of love…and the missed yesterdays…and the shared tomorrows.

• • •

Sleep was long in coming for McPherson as he lay quietly in the darkened cabin. Hatty was curled up in his arms, one arm thrown across his chest, a leg nested between his. The past few hours were, to say the least, unexpected. He had had every intention of looking in on Hatty Picquett almost from the moment he had ridden away— her invitation to return ensured that he would. He assumed they would visit for a while and he would go on his way and that would be the end of it. But sharing her bed wasn't part of his figuring.

Now, however, he was at a loss as to what to do. The ill-defined apprehensions he had felt earlier in the day were still there, still unexplained and unresolved. Under normal circumstances, he wouldn't have been overly troubled—he had learned to survive in spite of himself. But nothing about this situation was normal. And therein lay his confusion…

BOOK 2:

Alone within the crowd,
Searching for happiness
Existing only in the mind;
Facing emptiness of purpose;
Crying for that which was lost.

Desolation strikes deeply;
Moving the soul to seek
Reassurance within;
Venturing forth to satiate
Ambient convictions of worth.

FOUR

Zebadiah McPherson was typical of the people that lived in East Tennessee in the late 1800s: a God- fearing, fiercely independent thinker of Scotch-Irish extraction who didn't take kindly to interference by outsiders of any persuasion. Born in the days when a good portion of East Tennessee was still wild and uncleared, Zeb McPherson spent his early years watching his father work himself into an early grave trans- forming a homestead he had carved out of the wilderness south of the Cumberland Gap into a working farm. By the time Zeb reached his thirteenth birthday, his father's failing health had placed most of the workload squarely on his young shoulders. Zeb willingly accepted the challenge and responsibility, dealing each day with the necessities of running the homestead, while at the same time helping care for his father. Most evenings he spent teaching himself to read and write, fully aware he would need the knowledge in the future. His efforts were slow and laborious, but they were more than compensated.

Five years of working the homestead transformed Zebadiah McPherson from a gangling youth into a man. In the process, he established the personal characteristics he would eventually pass on to his off- spring. Those years also witnessed a final changing of the guard: his parents gone, he took a wife, and they were blessed with a child they would call Jacob. Times were good for the family of Zeb McPherson, despite persistent rumors of war, and with the good times came other children. Jacob was joined by a brother named Aaron, a sister given the name of her mother, Kathleen, and a second brother who would be called Jesse.

However, the tranquility that surrounded the McPherson family was deceptive. Rumors of an impending war increased, a part of conversations at every gathering, and Zebadiah and his neighbors were being pushed slowly and surely into the unenviable position of having to choose sides. But they were all in the same basic predicament: their loyalties were first and foremost to their families and farms, and thereaf- ter to East Tennessee. They had little personal interest in what was happening outside their own sphere of influence, even though they took pride in the fact that their forebearers had played an integral part in the creation of the Union. Nevertheless, the subject wouldn't go away, and in fact came to dominate most of McPherson's exchanges with his neighbors.

So after uncounted nights of reflection, Zebadiah McPherson resolved to steer away from taking sides, and was quick to justify his decision by saying that he was just a farmer, not a slave owner. If pressed on the issue, he quietly explained that while he could see both sides of the issue, his friends and neighbors were too important to him to side with one or the other; and for a time, his stand on the issue was respected. However, the firing on Fort Sumter and President Lincoln's subsequent request for volunteers to help put down the rebellion heightened emotions, and therein lay the seeds of mistrust. Tennessee's secession from the Union added to the apprehensions, and eventually, it set neighbor against neighbor...

The Cumberland Gap had served as a conduit for more than a hundred years, funneling settlers into the western frontiers of what would become Tennessee and Kentucky. Both factions—Northern and South- ern—believed that if war became a reality, control of the Gap to a great extent meant control of East Ten- nessee. As such, it was a point to be defended by one side and coveted by the other. Zeb McPherson, for his part, maintained his neutrality, insisting that he had no argument with either side. Without exception, he steadfastly refused to quarter troops on his land, and refused them supplies unless given no choice.

The convictions of his neighbors weren't so impartial. In spite of the preponderance of soldiers in the area being Southern, the majority of McPherson's neighbors supported the Northern cause, and they paid dearly for their decisions. They were often beaten, their crops stolen or destroyed, their property confis- cated by Rebel troops. Southern sympathizers fared little better, and unfortunately for the McPherson fam- ily, respect for anyone claiming neutrality slowly disappeared.

The final two years of the war saw almost daily troop movements around and through Cumberland Gap, and in a couple of instances, the McPherson family was caught on the edge of skirmishes when Northern and Southern troops passed too close to each other. For the most part, however, their losses were limited to the crops and some animals. And after five years of blue or grey clad soldiers stopping at the farm, peace of a sort returned to East Tennessee and the Cumberland Gap.

The peace, however, was short lived, and Zeb McPherson was confronted with a new enemy and a different kind of struggle: keeping the farm out of the hands of carpetbaggers. But keep it he did. With a good deal of determination and hard work, Zeb and his family slowly returned the farm to its pre-war con- dition. Little time was wasted on worrying about what the family had lost, or what they were facing. No effort was spared, no person exempt from the work. As a result, each day witnessed an ongoing transfor- mation: new crops were planted; fences were rebuilt; a new milk cow was bartered for. From early spring until the crops were harvested in fall, each and every morning for the McPherson family was a routine of rising at sunrise, eating a large breakfast, and working until the heat of the day prevailed. The labor was often hard, and being young wasn't seen as a drawback.

Nevertheless, there was little doubt that Zeb cared for his children. When the day was finished and supper was over, the evenings were spent teaching the children to read and write, and with the exception of Jacob, they responded with enthusiasm. Jacob showed no interest in book learning, preferring to put in his time working the farm. Eventually, Jacob's preference for physical work was accepted as being right for him, and he was often left to his own devices while the others were given basic schooling.

Given a second chance, and having the advantage of precognition, Zebadiah McPherson might have chosen differently, but it was his youngest son that received the bulk of his attention. From the day the boy took his first steps, Jesse became Zebadiah's particular pride and joy, and the child responded in kind.

He tagged along behind his father, attempting to emulate his every move. Zeb doted on the boy, often speaking of him to his wife and neighbors in terms never accorded any of the older children. In his mind, it was Jesse who was predestined to run the farm after he passed on. For Aaron and Kathleen, the added attention given Jesse by their father was taken in stride: Jesse was the baby of the family. But Jacob saw the preferential treatment as an affront to his position as the oldest child, and he took his resentment out on his youngest brother at every opportunity, which meant any time Zebadiah wasn't around. Jesse dealt with his circumstance as best he could. When his father or brother Aaron wasn't able to intercede, he either took whatever Jacob handed out, or sidestepped him until the threat diminished.

Eventually, his older brother's abusive streak extended into the farm work, with Jacob taking out his bitterness in more subtle ways. Jacob wanted the cows fed; Jesse preferred to go fishing. Jacob wanted the stalls in the barn cleaned out; Jesse wanted to go swimming. In short, Jacob wanted things done exactly as he specified, when he specified. Each day, Jesse was given two choices: finish the chores, or forget about spending any time on his own, and from Jesse's viewpoint, the chores were endless. No matter how long he worked, or how much he did, there was always somehing else to be done. So he tended to take short cuts— do as little as possible and still get it over and done with—a decision which often turned into a David and Goliath confrontation, except that Goliath always won. Jacob was quick to lose his temper and lash out at his younger brother. If he wasn't physically beating him, he was threatening to do so at the next excuse that came along, and from Jesse's point of view, there seemed to be no shortage of excuses.

Over time, the ongoing conflicts with Jacob created a strength within Jesse, and a stubborn resolve that until he was old enough to defend himself, he would not give Jacob an excuse to pick on him. When- ever possible, he avoided his older brother and the seemingly endless chores, spending as much time as possible with his father or with Aaron. And those moments away from the daily grind of doing chores were times of learning, especially when a traveler stopped in on his way south...or north...or west. He would lis- ten in rapture to the tales woven for his wide-eyed benefit. And when the traveler moved on, he would tackle his chores in the hopes of finishing quickly and being able to chase his own dreams.

On the day preceding Jesse's tenth birthday, the last of the McPherson children came into the world. Named Margaret, which quickly became Maggie, she was the object of Jesse's adoration, and although it was unintentional, she would eventually provide Jesse with the excuse he needed to avoid his oldest brother. He would spend hours with her, filling her head with elaborations of the same stories he had lis- tened to and taken such joy in. As she grew older, he passed on many of the lessons he had learned from Aaron: teaching her to ride a horse, to fish and swim; and they formed a bond that would stand them in good stead throughout their lives.

The years following Maggie's birth were also an unsettling combination of exhilaration and pure unadulterated hell for Jesse. All too often, the contrasts of his emotions were so interwoven that he was often unsure of which way was up...or down. But early on, Zebadiah McPherson recognized his son's uneasiness for what it was—wanderlust.

The wanderlust was strong in the McPherson blood. Even though his own father had succumbed in his younger years to the seduction of the unknown that was always across the next mountain, Zeb himself had fought the enticement off, but not without considerable struggle. Even so, he hadn't given much thought to it affecting his own children, at least not until Jesse came along.

In those early days following the war, Zeb had noticed some indefinable characterisic in Jesse that set him apart. The other children were much like their mother: they believed that the farm was enough. There was no evidence of an impulse to travel in either of them. Jesse was another matter—Zeb had seen himself in his youngest son; moreover, he had seen in him his own father. He knew the wanderlust was full-blown, that Jesse wouldn't—couldn't be satisfied with just living and working on the farm and eventu- ally dying there without looking beyond. But to Zeb's way of thinking, the wanderlust was an affliction—a torment that had to be overcome.

Admittedly, acknowledging the wanderlust within himself had never been easy for Zeb. Neverthe- less, time and circumstance, beginning with his own father's deteriorating health, gave him the perspec- tives he needed to conquer his wanderlust. With Jesse, however, no such circumstance existed. Zeb knew that unless he could find a way to blunt Jesse's oncoming appetite, preventing him from following the enticements that continuously streamed from the other side of the mountain was nigh on impossible. But Zebadiah McPherson was a stubborn man. He believed that if he was able to instill solid moral values in his son, the boy would be strong enough to withstand the lures that could destroy him.

From the time his first child was born, Zeb had used himself as a model for raising his children. He willingly acknowledged that his own father's methods, strict as they were, had played a major part in his being able to take over the responsibilities of the farm at such an early age—the homestead was near wil- derness back then; there was little room for weakness or sentimentality. His father had believed in a philos- ophy of hard work and strict devotion to the Ten Commandments, strong values to Zeb's way of thinking, teachings worthy of passing on to his own children.

Their lessons, however, were an odd amalgamation of a strict adherence to the law of the land and a skirting of the very same laws if they went against the basic tenets of the Bible. Certainly, the `Good Book' held a prominent place in the McPherson home, and was quoted from on a regular basis. Yet Zebadiah McPherson maintained a healthy cynicism about religion. On the one hand, he seemed to believe in a lit- eral interpretation of the Bible, and used it constantly to support his beliefs; but he continually argued with a local preacher over details of scripture that contradicted his matter-of-fact accep- tance. He wouldn't set foot in a church except for marriages and funerals and even then, he did so only out of politeness. He fre- quently stated his conviction that churches were nothing more than gatherings of hypocrites, that praying and talking to God was a per- sonal matter, not something to be shared with anyone.

Such was the atmosphere that Jesse grew up in. Besides living with Jacob's constant mistreatment— a situation Zeb quietly tolerated out of a belief that it would make the boy stronger—the boy was faced with growing up hearing many sides to the same argument, and while he thought he believed wholeheart- edly in the Bible, in reality, he was given little choice in the matter. He lived with the demons of hellfire and damnation being tossed around most every Sunday morning and quite often, on other days as well. But the effect on his son was not what Zeb would have expected. Resolute in his conviction that his methods were the only way to help his son survive, he failed to take into consideration the possibility that his per- sistent determination would accomplish the opposite of what he wanted for his son.

Undeniably, Zebadiah's approach provided the beginnings of Jesse's transformation into an adult, but it also obliged Jesse to bury his sentiments within himself. Zeb disregarded the boy's growing fascination with the occasional visitor, paying him little attention when he asked questions. But as time passed, Zeb realized his tactics had misfired, that the wanderlust he had attempted to contain had won out. Increasingly, heading West and seeing what was beyond the horizons became Jesse's chosen topic of conversation. Zeb knew that his only option was to delay, that the day was nearing when he would run out of reasons to pre- vent the boy from following the sun…

Jess McPherson rode southwest from Cumberland Gap in the fall of 1878, his father's final words tumbling over and over in his head to the rhythm of the buckskin's hooves. "…Come back when you're ready to stay …Come back when you're ready to stay." The remark was confusing—he had been told in front of the entire family there'd be nothing for him to return to if he left—yet there his father was, telling him just the opposite as he mounted up to ride out. It just made no sense, and he concluded that for the time being, it would serve no purpose to worry about it.

He rode hard for the first couple of days, cutting along a seldom used trail that more or less paral leled the north bank of Powell's River and then followed the Clinch, ending in the thriving community of Clinton. After stopping there overnight, he continued south-west at a more leisurely pace until he reached the main east-west road coming out of Knoxville and turned toward Winter's Gap.

In his eagerness to travel, he had paid little attention to the surrounding countryside northeast of Clinton, and even less to the few people he met in the short time since starting out. But in the week it took to reach Nashville, he began to go through a meta-morphosis of sorts. He started looking around, taking stock of the incredible beauty which surrounded him, basking in the array of fall colors, marveling at the precipitous escarpment of Walden's Ridge as he rode into the depth of the Cumberland Mountains. He men-tally registered the name of each town he passed through, names like Wartburg, Standing Stone, and Carthage, and noted the destruction that was still very much in evidence fourteen years after the end of the war. Most of all, he started letting time take care of itself, and when the opportunity arose, he sat and talked to whomever he happened to meet.

By the time he was approaching the outskirts of Nashville, he considered spending a week or two there. The realization that he had indeed left home and could very well never see it again was finally begin- ning to penetrate the fervor which pushed him westward. As such, he suddenly found himself having sec- ond thoughts about his family and the magnitude of the adventure that lay ahead. He wanted to go west, but leaving his family was a most unpleasant part of doing that. On the other hand, the thought of constant ridicule by Jacob if he failed was a far worse fate than leaving Tennessee. The enthu-siasm he met each time he explained where he was going, however, was enough to dismiss those thoughts, and the misgivings quickly evaporated. The frontier was waiting and he was getting anxious to see what all the fuss was about. So after stopping just long enough to replenish his supplies, McPherson turned toward Memphis and the Mississippi…

FIVE

McPherson's eagerness to get to Memphis and beyond hit a snag. Along with descriptions of a boom- ing, vibrant, city overlooking the Mississippi, he heard rumors that ranged from Memphis being quaran- tined, to the city having been deserted—all stemming from a severe outbreak of yellow fever. He paid little attention to the stories. The lure of the west in him was growing in intensity, and the dangers presented by the disease meant little. But the nearer to Memphis he got, the more people he saw, and he found the amount of traffic on the road puzzling. By the time he reached Jackson, he had his answer.

The outbreak had reached such epidemic proportions that people were leaving Memphis in droves, abandoning everything to escape, some unknowingly already infected, or at the very least carrying the dis- ease. As a result, many of the small towns east of Memphis had established quarantines of their own, and were enforc- ing them at gunpoint. Memphis was isolated from the world, and his idyllic ride was for the moment over. But McPherson was trapped by his own desires. He wanted to continue west, but his chosen path was blocked. The alternative was to bypass Memphis, which meant swinging either north or south.

After a short consideration, the decision was simple: cut south of Memphis and follow the Missis- sippi River into New Orleans. If he listened to the advice of the people that had already warned him away from Memphis, however, going south might well be a worse decision: New Orleans was no place for a decent God-fearing soul. The delta city had a reputation for wickedness and depravity; maybe even worse than the stories told about the Natchez Trace. And truthfully, the stories he heard about the Trace seemed somewhat far fetched.

The Trace had been the primary overland trail between Natchez and Nashville for the better part of fifty years, falling into disuse once the Mississippi river boat became commonplace. During its heyday, thousands of travelers who had worked the flatboats down the Mississippi made their way back north from New Orleans, cutting northeast along the Trace to return home. But the Trace provided more than a short- cut home: it was a sanctuary for enterprising highwaymen who terrorized the travelers, brutalizing and kill- ing men, women, and children alike. Names bandied about by those that survived the attacks, names like Micajah and Wiley Harpe, Samuel Mason, and John Murrel, were intertwined with the normal hardships experienced along the Trace, and in time, became part and parcel of the evil incarnate attributed to New Orleans. 'Forget about New Orleans and cut straight west,' they said, 'or better yet, turn around and go home to your family.' But they were talking of a time forty years past, and he figured that things had to have changed for the better somewhere along the way. And in a way, McPherson was right, things had changed. But after spending a week in the Crescent City, he almost conceded that he should have listened.

Seen by many as the Sodom and Gomorrah of the South, New Orleans was a polyglot of people and cultures found nowhere else, a city at once a mixture of old world and new frontier. To a naive young man fresh out of the hills of Tennessee, the city was both fascinating and not a little unsettling. McPherson had been taught that such places should be avoided, but the city's enticements outweighed any warnings of fire and brimstone: New Orleans captivated McPherson, beguiled him, and provided him with a taste of the forbidden.

For the first day or so after arriving, he walked up and down the streets, taking in the sights and sam- pling the exotic foods available along Tchoupitoulas Street. But an early afternoon stroll through the French Quarter and into Jackson Square proved to be his undoing. She was petite and delicate, with a tawny complexion and dark hair that flowed in a tangled mass of curls to the middle of her back. She was quite simply the most beautiful woman he had ever seen…

Jackson Square is a small quadrangle of ground on the river side of the French Quarter. Originally called *Plaza de Alma* in the days of the Spanish, it had been transformed into the garden showpiece of the French Quarter, with an impressive statue of Andrew Jackson astride a charging horse as the centerpiece. Titled *Chalmette's Hero*, the statue glorified Jackson, who to many was the savior of New Orleans. The statue caused a swelling pride in the breast of a Tennessean who was seeing it for the first time, so much so he didn't notice the young woman strolling along the circular path until he turned into her, almost knocking her from her feet.

"*Tordieu!*"

"Excuse me, ma'am," McPherson exclaimed, reaching out to steady her. "I didn't see you. I was look- ing at the…"

"I can very well see what you were doing, *m'sieur*," she replied haughtily. "Is it your intention to allow me to pass, or will you continue to stare?"

"No… Yes… I mean…" he sputtered, stumbling over his words. McPherson stepped aside to allow her passage, continuing to stare in open-mouthed bewilderment. After a moment's hesitation, he walked quickly in the same direction, slowing only when he had reached her side.

"Pardon me, ma'am, may I walk with you?"

"*Non*, I think not, *m'sieur*," she answered, pausing momentarily to ponder his request. "I do not know you."

"My name's Jesse McPherson," he said, hastily introducing himself. "I'm from Tennessee."

"Ah, the home of the *grand général Jackson*. Now I understand your intrigue with *Chalmette*. And are you also here to rescue *New Orléans* from the British, *m'sieur?*"

"No, ma'am. But you are walking alone. Perhaps I could protect you from the evil I hear about in your city."

"*Oh la la*," she teased, "I would not expect such *galanterie* from the *Américain*. Do you really think I am in danger?"

McPherson grinned. "Prob'ly not, ma'am. But," he hastened to add, "you can't be too careful."

Nodding her head, she replied with mock seriousness. "Perhaps you are right. I would be foolish to take risks on such a fine afternoon as this." She placed her hand in the crook of his left arm. "Come, *M'sieur Jessé McPherson*. Let us adjourn from the eyes of *général Jackson* and I will tell you of *mon Vieux Carré* and you can regale me with stories of Tennessee..."

McPherson stood expectantly at the foot of *Chalmette's Hero*, alternately watching the two entrances leading from the Quarter into the park, wondering if Angéline DuBois would indeed appear as she had promised she would the previous afternoon. The wonders of New Orleans paled in her presence, and while he knew she was humoring his impromptu attempt at chivalry, he wasn't about to let that awareness get in the way. He had never before experienced such excitement and he eagerly awaited the return of the exhila- ration.

He smiled at the image they must have presented to the citizens of New Orleans as they strolled along Tchoupitoulas Street. He was a farm boy that looked the part: he was wearing homespun, a hat that had seen better days, and hobnailed boots that were more appropri- ate behind a plow. In outright contrast, Angéline was dressed in her Sunday best. She wore a light blue dress and white lace gloves, and carried a matching blue parasol. Interwoven in her hair was a ribbon that also matched her dress, framing a face that hinted at other than a French origin. She wore no jewelry other than a thin gold bracelet, her only other adornment a second ribbon worn around her neck as a choker.

She was beautiful. But in his eyes, Angéline was more than just beautiful: she had about her an angelic glow, yet her green eyes spar- kled with mischief. What McPherson didn't see, however, was that her eyes also spoke of a knowledge reaching far beyond his own experiences.

Now the sun was low in the sky, and his wait had become inter- minable. In truth, she had not said she would be there for sure, only if circumstances permitted. And since he did not know the location of her home, he could not call on her. But at the point when he started to leave, a soft caressing voice addressed his back.

"Bonsoir, M'sieur McPherson."

He spun on his heels, the elation of the previous day returning in force. She stood a few paces from him, her mouth pursed with concern. The smile she remembered reappeared, turning quickly into an open grin.

"I'd given up on seeing you. I been here since noon."

She nodded, savoring his desire to be with her. "I know. I saw you." His brow furrowed, he shook his head. "I don't understand."

"Let us walk for a moment, *m'sieur*," she said taking his arm. Passing through one of the gates McPherson had watched for the better part of the afternoon, the two made their way silently along Chartres Street and then up St. Philip. "I envy you, *m'sieur*," she with regret. "You `ave freedom. Innocence. I do not wish to take them from you."

"What are you talking about?" he asked.

"You do not know me, *m'sieur*. You do not know what I am." "No, don't suppose I do," he agreed. "But I'm willing to learn."

"Ahhh, I should imagine you are. But you must see that the learning is easy. It is the teaching that presents the problem."

McPherson digested her words, hearing only that she was avoiding telling him something. "What is there that I would find so terrible about you?"

"I do not know `ow to explain," she cried. "But I know it is better that we should part now." "You telling me to leave?"

"No, *mon chéri*," her voice anguished, "as much as I should, that I cannot do. It is a decision you must make."

"That may eventually be the case, Angeline, but my brother Aaron taught me that running from the unknown ain't the McPherson way. So unless you're married, or promised to someone, I'll take my chances." Stopping, he faced her. "You aren't, are you…married, or anything like that?"

"No, *m'sieur*," she answered in a whisper.

"Fine," he declared, jubilant. "Then it's time for you to stop this m'sieur stuff and start calling me Jesse."

"*Oui, m'sieur… Jessé*. It will be as you say. But there is something you must know." "And what is that, Angeline?" Jesse asked, hearing the inflection in her voice.

"I am..." McPherson was oblivious to the hurt in her words. "Ah, *chéri*, I cannot say it. I must show you."

They continued north on St. Philip, turning east on Burgundy and then north again to Ramparts Street. Two doors from the intersection, Angéline led him through an iron latticework gate into a large, square courtyard dominated by a centrally-located fountain, hanging ferns, and an enormous and very old moss-covered tree. On either side of the open-air atrium, latticed stairs led to each corner of a narrow bal- cony. In the fading light, the glow of lamps could be seen through a few of the windows looking out on the balcony. Beneath the overhang, the darkness in the corners was more complete, disturbed only by light cast through the pair of glass doors at the rear of the courtyard. As McPherson took in the surroundings, passen- gers alit from a carriage outside the iron gate and entered the courtyard, greeting Angéline as they passed before continuing on through the glass doors. He heard music as the doors were momentarily opened. Occasional laughter drifted down from one of the upstairs rooms.

"What is this place, Angeline? It's beautiful."

"This is where I live, *Jessé...*" she answered, adding with emphatic seriousness, "where I work." "I don't understand."

"Come sit with me for a moment, *Jessé*." Angéline steered him to a bench near the fountain. "I meant it when I said I envied you. You are a free spirit. You still believe that the world is good. Only someone like you would not recognize this `ouse for what it is." She pressed her fingertips to his lips to stop his objec- tions. "Shhh, *mon ami*, it is not wrong to be ignorant of these things. I `ave often wished to be just so. But painful as it will be to tell you, you must know the *vérité*, the truth. I am *une fille de joie*, what some in *New Orléans* would call *une putain*, a whore. It is what my mother did, and I `ave known no other life. And now you must go from `ere."

Six

"There's only one way to deal with it," McPherson declared with conviction, "I'll take you with me." "*Pardon?*"

"You don't have to stay here. I'll take you with me out west. Or better yet, we'll go back to Tennessee."

"I think you mean it," she exclaimed. "Course I mean it."

Angéline was fortunate the darkness obscured her face. McPherson's avowals had triggered a euphoria within her, yet the emotions she was experiencing were contrary to what she felt she must do: send him away. "That is very sweet of you, *Jessé*, but I cannot change what I am."

"No, I s'pose you can't, but it don't matter anyhow. You *can* change what you do."

"But it *will* matter," she countered, at a loss as to how to break through his stubborn refusal to see the truth. "It will..."

They sat together in the dark, silent, each lost in thought, until a voice called from inside. "*Angéline?*"

"*Oui, Madame,*" she answered. Touching his sleeve, she told McPherson to wait. A few minutes later, she returned. "I `ave told *Madame* I will be with you tonight. But tomorrow, you must continue on your journey...and you must forget me." She took him by the hand and led him up one of the stairs to the apartment above the front gate. "Come..."

For more than three quarters of a century, prostitution and its associate evils had flourished in the Crescent City. Despite the half-hearted efforts of a few well intended city fathers, corruption was a way of life in an area picturesquely labeled 'The Swamp', far outweighing any stand that moralistic citizens might take. The inhabitants amply demonstrated the depths of depravity to which men and women could aspire. Drunken debauchery, beatings, and robberies were a daily part of living. Murder was common, and people often disappeared without a trace. Prostitution just happened to be the most visible.

The aftermath of the war—and the subsequent appearance of carpetbaggers from the north—altered the picture considerably. While the demise of the Swamp became inevitable, prostitution in New Orleans continued to be on the rise, tenaciously expanding outward from Girod and Gallatin Streets until every street and avenue spawned at least one bawdyhouse and quite often more. Nowhere was this more obvious than that area on the north side of Ramparts Street, a district that became known as Storyville.

The bordellos located in and around Storyville quite literally embraced the art of indulging prurient desires. Many of the houses were two and three story mansions, lavishly furnished, and extravagantly dec- adent. They provided entertainment in the form of food and drink, music, dance, and women, who were mostly young, often beautiful, and almost always high priced. But even though the class of the bordellos— and their clientele—was improving, very few of them were able to avoid the violence that dogged their very existence. And if the violence didn't involve the clientele, it involved the madams. While not an everyday occurrence, duels between potential customers happened frequently. In a few instances, madams themselves got involved by eliminating their lovers—literally. But there were exceptions to the rule, and the house where Angéline DuBois lived and worked fell into that category.

La Maison des Deux Soeurs stood apart from many of the post civil war bagnios of New Orleans. It too offered the diversions many of the others did, but there were also unspoken rules that elevated it above the rest. Formal attire was required for all occasions, not only of the *filles de joie*, but of the men they ser- viced. Each of the women was expected to be conversant with interests of the day as well as being knowl- edgeable in the language of love. In return, the women were provided with the necessities of life, including a room of their own to live and work in. But Jesse McPherson knew none of this as he followed Angéline up the stairs. His only thought was that he wanted to be with this woman.

At the top of the stairs, Angéline wrapped her arms about McPherson's waist, laying her head against his chest. Leaning back, she reached up and caressed his face, gently mocking his light growth of beard. She then pulled his head down and standing on the tip of her toes, kissed him for the first time. He returned the kiss, roughly pulling her against him in his eagerness.

"There is no rush, *M'sieur Jessé*. We 'ave the night." "I'm sorry. I…"

"Shhh," she touched his lips to reassure him. "And no need to apologize."

As they started to enter the apartment, McPherson hesitated, then sheepishly followed her in. "I never been with a woman before."

Angéline smiled at his confession. Gesturing around the room, she tried to ease his discomfort. "This is where I live. Do you like it?"

Encouraged by the momentary reprieve, Jesse quickly explored the room with his eyes, noting the strong and functional simplicity of the furnishings, the soft shadows cast by the oil lamps, at last coming to rest on the double bed, nodding by way of answering.

"*Bon*. Are you 'ungry?" When he shook his head, she continued. "Then we shall eat later." Sitting him down in a chair next to the window, she knelt at his feet and began removing his boots, ignoring his protests that he could do it himself. "Please, *Jessé*, let me 'elp." A knock came from a second door he hadn't noticed when he looked the room over. Angéline opened the door to a young girl.

"*Le bain est prêt, mam'selle.*"

"*Merci, ma petite. Nous dinerons dans deux heures.*" "*Oui, mam'selle.*"

Leaving the door ajar, Angéline returned to her attempts at undressing McPherson, speaking softly of what lay ahead. She peeled his galluses from his shoulders, running her hands down and around his sides. Again taking his hand, she led him through the door into the other room. A pair of porcelain tubs stood side by side, the heads at opposite ends, both filled with steaming water. "Your bath, *M'sieur McPherson*… And mine."

Angéline began unbuttoning his shirt, kissing the newly bared skin after each button was released. At the last button, she roughly yanked the shirt from his pants. At that point, McPherson was truly embar- rassed, his reddened face quite visible even in the dimness of the lamp. Muttering something to the effect that he wasn't helpless, he unbuckled the belt and finished removing his clothes. Still fully clothed, Angéline reached up to cup his face, gently encourag- ing him to return her kisses. That kiss turned into a second, and then a third as she ran her hands over his bared skin, ignoring the growing presence between them.

She stepped back and turned away from him, lifting her hair from the back of her neck and instruct- ing him to open the hooks down the back of her dress. He fumbled awkwardly with the hooks, eventually getting them open to her waist before she freed him from his discomfort and pointed him toward one of the tubs. Once he was immersed in the water, she continued removing her dress in a slow tease, until she wore nothing more than a lacy shirt that only hinted at covering her breasts, silk stockings, and bloomers reach- ing to just above the knees.

McPherson's eyes never strayed as she lifted the shirt over her head, revealing breasts just matured, rose-tipped and firm, but not so large as to detract from her beauty. His eyes widened as she slid the bloom- ers over her hips and let them drop to the floor, exposing the small triangle of black curls at the vee of her legs, widened again as she placed a foot on the edge of his tub and slowly rolled the knee-length stocking over her calf, then repeating the process with the other foot. McPherson stared in open lust as she now stood before him, wearing nothing but the ribbons around her neck and in her hair.

"Am I pleasing to your eyes, *Jesse*?" she asked, already knowing the answer, but wanting to hear him say it. "Very much," he replied, his words coming in a hoarse whisper. Angéline leaned over the tub and kissed him, her lips lingering on his. Reaching into the water, she lifted his hand to a breast, encouraging him to cup the firmness. As his hand responded to the hardening nipple, she ran her fingertips into the fine curls on his chest, following the line of hair leading down to his navel and below, lightly touching and then grasping him, sending a shockwave through his body. Leaning forward, he cupped the other breast.

"Bite it, *Jessé*," she gasped with a sudden intake of air. "Make it 'ard…" He reacted without thinking, taking her in his mouth, suckling as would an infant. Her urgings overcame any remnants of shyness, the physical hunger of a man newly grown dominating his whole being.

"We… We should complete our bathing," she murmured. The words came out haltingly between gulps of air.

Angéline pulled away with great difficulty, not wanting to break the contact; she was trying to main- tain a semblance of control… and failing. She climbed into the other tub and made an effort to attend to her bath, but McPherson's steady gaze was like a magnet, drawing her eyes to his. Jesse watched closely as she finished her bath and toweled herself dry. And then the roles were reversed: Angéline was the observer as he stood in the tub and began wiping the excess water from his body. He stepped out of the tub onto a large cloth she had placed on the floor, where she started vigorously scrubbing the moisture from his skin until he would have no more of it. Still damp from the bath, he gathered her up in his arms and carried her into the other room, stopping every few paces to kiss her, at last laying her in the center of the bed.

Kneeling beside her, he let his eyes wander from the droplets of water still in her pubes down to her feet and back, until their eyes met, their senses flowing together in an unspoken understanding, intertwined in a bonding uncommon to first time lovers. Angéline wantonly parted her legs, spreading them like a bird in flight, teasing, inviting, guiding him until they peaked together. Only then did the intensity subside, and it was but a momentary pause.

She gazed steadily at the young face of the man who was suspended above her, wishing for a brief moment that she had never met him, had not brought him to the house. Once before a man had awakened the ecstasy within her. That had led to a killing in an argument over who would possess her. Now she was faced with the possibility of history repeating itself. But as McPherson once again began to move inside her, any thoughts or fears about the past disappeared in the pleasure she was experiencing.

• • •

They sat across a small table, feasting on steaming rice-laden gumbo, and making small talk into the late hours of the night. The faint sounds of men and women making love drifted through the open window from other rooms, sporadically broken up by a louder, raucous laughter. Angéline had covered her naked- ness with a cotton chemise, but the image of her body was imprinted into McPherson's mind.

"I love you, Angeline." McPherson expressed his feelings with great seriousness. "I want you to come with me."

"Ahhh, *Jessé,* if love is possible for me, then I love you also. But leaving 'ere cannot be. You must understand that."

"All I understand is that you haven't told me anything that would make me change my mind." "You are a very stubborn man, *Jessé.*"

"I'll take that as a compliment," he replied with a laugh. "Say you'll come with me. Please."

Angéline looked deeply into McPherson's eyes, trying to read his thoughts, looking for the answers that were eluding her, searching for an explanation that would alter his thinking. "Nothing would make me happier at this moment than to say yes, but it would be a mistake. There are things about me you do not know, things which I cannot change."

"You're talkin' in circles. Your past is just that—past."

"*Jessé…*" She shook her head in despair. "The girl that prepared our baths, and brought us our food—she is the child of a whore. She lives and works 'ere because 'er *maman* is dead and she knows not 'er *papa.* One day, she will become one of us. It is 'ow she will pay for living 'ere."

"What's that got to do with you?"

"Because it is very much my own story. I grew up 'ere. And I too must pay my debt." "But that's no different than slavery," he protested.

Angéline's face brightened somewhat, encouraged by McPherson's reaction. "*Oui, mon amour,* but slavery is also a part of my past."

"What are you talkin' about?"

She rose from the table and removed the chemise, once again standing naked in front of him. "*Jessé,* if this feeling of yours is truly love, then you are living proof that love is blind. But you must now open your eyes and look at me."

"Gladly," he said, reaching for her.

"*Mon Dieu,*" she exclaimed. Yielding to the pressure of his hands, she sat straddling his legs, her arms wrapped behind his neck. "You are impossible."

"Angeline, I was never taught to hate or fear the black man." "You know?" she asked incredulously.

He nodded. "More of a guess, really. And the fact that your blood isn't 'pure' don't change a thing. I don't even know what that means. What I do know is that you're beautiful, and I want you with me."

"Ohhh," she cooed, reaching between her legs to caress him. "It's my *beauté* you love."

"Yes…" he answered, reacting to the playful manipulations of her hand. "I love your eyes… And your mouth…" pausing with each declaration to kiss that particular feature.

Standing on the side rungs of the chair, Angéline lifted her bottom just enough to allow him to nest there, then buried its length within. A moan escaped from her as she slowly rocked back and forth.

"You feel so good in me, *Jessé,*" she whispered, "So good…"

Clawing and scratching McPherson's back and shoulders, she gripped his hips with her legs, locking him inside as he cradled her behind and carried her to the bed. Her moaning increased, competing with the creaking of the bed, increasingly loud as McPherson escalated the tempo, each thrust more forceful than the last, until at last she could no longer contain her passion. They now moved as one, each feedingoff the energies of the other, giving, taking, building peak upon peak, rushing forward in a torrent of joy, at last exploding in a final exhilaration.

Afterward, they lay quietly in each other's arms, satiated, their stamina spent, whispering the endear- ments of lovers. Finally, unable to remain awake, she nested in his embrace, her back against him, his arms around her breasts. Sleep came quickly to both of them, and the light of dawn found them still cradled together, unmoving.

McPherson woke to the smell of coffee heavily laced with chicory and the sight of Angéline sitting on the balcony overlooking Ramparts Street. She was attired in a simple red blouse and skirt, with her hair brushed down on her shoulders, adorned by a ribbon that matched her clothes. But her attention was not on the activity of the street. She was sitting with her bare feet propped up on a chair, facing into the room: she had been watching him as he slept. Dressing quickly, he joined her on the balcony, exchanging pleasantries more common to long time lovers. After sipping on the coffee for a few minutes, he looked straight into her eyes with the awareness of the previous night heavy between them and renewed his request that she join him on his journey.

"I 'ave not changed my mind that going with you would be a mistake," she explained. "You may truly believe that my color is meaningless; or that my being a *fille de joie* is unimportant. But one day it will matter…" Getting to her feet, Angéline leaned over the balcony railing and looked up and down the street, gesturing, "These are my family."

"Angeline…"

"Please, *chéri*," she said pensively. "I 'ave lived on this street all my life. It will not be easy to say goodby."

"Wha…" he exclaimed, not believing his ears.

"I cannot see beyond this moment, *Jessé McPherson*. But we dream, you and I. So I will go with you, and may God ride with us."

SEVEN

McPherson rode into Mesquite, Texas, dusty, hot, and decidedly irritable. Back when he was listen- ing to all the talk about the West, someone had forgotten to mention the fact that the weather in Texas could be oppressive. The main street, which ran alongside the railroad, was for the most part empty, not surpris- ing considering the heat. Reining up in front of a watering trough located near the center of town, he stepped down and gave the buckskin his head. After splashing handfuls of the tepid water on his face and neck in a vain attempt at washing off some of the dust caked on his skin, McPherson looked the town square over, noting the general store that served as the train station, at last pausing on the tell-tale batwing doors of a nameless saloon.

While the grey drank its fill, McPherson followed the movement of a mangy old dog as it looked for cooler shade beneath one of the mesquite trees spotted around the square, openly sympathizing with its plight. Not bothering to remount, McPherson led his horse to the hitching post nearest the saloon and looped the reins around before going inside. The saloon was deserted except for three men sitting at a table near the rear. They looked up at McPherson as he came through the doors, concluded he was of no interest to them and returned to their card game. The only other person in evidence was a barkeep who was dozing at the far end of the bar, having succumbed to the heat. Jess stepped up to the middle of the bar and waited patiently for a moment before clearing his throat to announce his presence. The sound startled the bar- tender, snapping him out of his lethargy. He took a moment to get his bearings and get to his feet.

"Afternoon, Mister. You look thirsty. What'll you have?"

"Anything wet," McPherson replied. The bartender set a glass and a half-empty bottle in front of McPherson and returned to his perch at the end of the bar. Jess picked the bottle up and splashed a brown liquid that passed as whiskey into the glass, taking a couple of sips before tossing the remainder of it back. Refilling his glass, McPherson glanced around the room.

The saloon was like twenty others he had been in over the past few months: a dozen tables with at least one of them occupied by old men playing cards; a bar worn from spilled whiskey and frequent clean- ing; a Rubenesque painting hanging behind the bar, yellowed by years of smoke. In one corner of the room stood the standard pot-bellied stove, though its presence seemed absurd in the heat. The other corner was occupied by stairs that led to rooms where dance hall girls enticed drunken cowboys to spend the last of their hard earned dollars, although there was no visible evidence that such crea- tures actually existed in this place.

McPherson poured a third drink and pushed the bottle back. He was ready to concede one thing to his father: there was an awful lot of desert in the West. His wanderings had taken him as far west as Santa Fe and as far south as Corpus Christi and the vast emptiness outside the towns astounded him. But he had seen very few Indians, and those he had seen were far from being hostile. However, a few of the cowboys he had run into were an entirely different species. They were ill-tempered, pushy, and ready to fight at the drop of a hat.

The first time it happened was as clear as yesterday. He had stopped at The Longbranch Saloon— didn't matter which one—it seemed that half the towns he passed through had a saloon by that name. What did matter was that in every damn one of them, there was some cowboy ready to throw down on him because of his accent, or because he was just past being a kid, or for any number of other half-baked rea- sons they didn't bother to explain. For the most part, he had talked his way out, but one dusty afternoon that changed...

"Well, well, well. Looky what we got here. What farm you off of, boy?" A cowboy had wandered in off the street and was standing a few feet away. McPherson looked up from the beer he was sipping, unaware the man was trying to pick a fight with him.

"Sir?"

"Sir? Who you callin' sir? You tryin' to be a smart ass, boy?" The cowboy was drunk and spoiling for a fight. McPherson wanted nothing to do with it.

"Look, Mister…" He started to speak and instantly realized that it was the wrong thing to do.

"I don't like smart asses, boy." He hit McPherson in the chest with the flat of his hand, shoving him off balance. "You need to be taken down a notch or two."

Recovering his balance, Jess looked around, noticing that the other people in the saloon had moved back from the sudden violence, giving them plenty of room. "Got no argument with you, Mister."

"Well I got one with you, boy." The cowboy grabbed for the gun hanging on his hip. "Now fill your hand."

McPherson hesitated for an instant. Even though he had seen meaningless showdowns like this, common sense and good fortune had kept him clear of all but the most innocent squabbles. But when it was over, he realized that the only thing that had saved him was the cowboy's drunken stupor. He had time to draw and fire the Peacemaker his brother had given him before the cowboy's gun completely cleared the holster. The bullet hit the cowboy's chest dead center. The cowboy stared at McPherson in amazement, then at the spreading stain of red on his chest, before slumping to the floor, dead. Jess McPherson returned the smoking pistol to his hip and turned back to the bar. McPherson's luck continued to hold—one of the witnesses was the town's sheriff.

The sheriff stepped up beside him and after verifying that the cowboy was dead, commandeered two men to carry the body to the undertaker's. That dealt with, he asked the bartender for a bottle, filling two glasses with the amber liquid, and pushing one in front of McPherson. Hand shaking, Jess picked up the glass and downed the whiskey, oblivious to the burning as it coursed its way into his stomach. The sheriff leaned on the bar beside McPherson and sipped his whiskey, for the moment seemingly lost in his thoughts. He refilled the glass in front of McPherson as well as his own.

"New at gunfightin', son?" The question was more of a announcement, and it startled McPherson. "Why do you ask?"

"Huh. Look at your hands, boy. Yer shakin' like a leaf." McPherson gripped the whiskey glass tighter in an attempt to control the tremor.

"I didn't even know the man."

"Uh huh. And if he has any friends or relatives, you won't know them either. But that won't stop 'em from tryin' to put you into the same condition. Hope you know how close you come to dyin', boy." McPherson bit his lip and nodded his head in agreement. "Yer slow with that piece yer wearin'."

McPherson nodded again. He was slow, and even though his shot was accurate, he knew if the man had been sober, he would've have been the one they carted out. The sheriff nodded toward some of the men who were keeping a wary eye on the conversation. "And they all know it."

"I didn't want to kill him."

"Well now, I know that, but they don't. All they know is what they saw, and from their way of seein' things, yer a lucky man." McPherson knew the sheriff was right.

"All right, sheriff. What do you suggest?"

"Either take the gun off and go home, or get some practice usin' it. Strappin' that Peacemaker on yer hip is just asking somebody that's spoilin' for a fight to pick one."

Well, McPherson wryly mused as he continued to sip the whiskey, that old sheriff had been right. For some reason he still couldn't fathom, the pistol was a source of aggravation for every would-be fast draw artist he met. Had he not spent countless hours practicing, he would not have survived. Not that he was in a lot of gunfights. The half dozen he took part in, however, were enough to press home the point that he was a person to steer clear of. But his ability with a gun was only a part of his education in surviving the West. It was the other point the sheriff made that was to be his real salvation, the one about being prepared to deal with indignant friends and relatives. His advice had been simple. Recognize the underlying motives of peo- ple in general, and understand their rationale for doing things. Not appreciating the reasons behind some- one's actions was a quick invitation to trouble.

Words of wisdom, and none he hadn't heard before. His father had tried to tell him much the same thing, but back then he hadn't paid that much attention. Then again, if he discounted the poundings he took from Jacob, people weren't trying to kill him at the drop of a hat either. Thinking back, he couldn't remem- ber any of the travelers that had passed by the farm mentioning the extent of the violence that seemed to permeate the West. As far as he could tell, the majority of people in the West had enough to do just to stay alive; but a large number of them seemed bent on living off the avails of others, and took exception if their victim objected to being robbed or cheated. Back home, thieves and cheats were quite often strung up to a handy oak tree, but he had found out all too quickly that west of the Mississippi, anyone with a fast gun had easy pickings. The first time he had run into problems he had been fortunate—a kindly stranger had sided with him, and probably saved his life. Since that time, he had lost count of the number of times he was forced into compromising situations, but he was fully aware of the price paid in blood to settle them, and that was something else his father had failed to mention before his leaving. Truth was, there were a lot of things he failed to mention.

McPherson picked up the bottle and his glass and weaved his way to one of the unoccupied tables against the wall. He parked in a chair that allowed him to face the room and not have to watch his back, a direct result of being involved in too many disputes not of his own making, of being hit from behind and having to defend him- self out of sheer self preservation. And while this particular saloon seemed calm enough and showed no evidence of any such need, bet- ter he should be prepared now than have to fight his way out later in the evening. He once again surveyed the barroom, at last centering on the stairs leading to the upstairs rooms, rememering the court- yard at the House of Two Sisters, the climb up the stairs and all that transpired that night and the days that followed with utmost clarity.

McPherson had to stifle a laugh. Nothing he had been taught as a child prepared him for the moment when Angéline announced that she was a prostitute. She had taken him by surprise, but then, she fit no image he could dredge from the past. McPherson unconsciously reached for the bottle and refilled his glass. The lesson he had learned in New Orleans reminded him in a strange sort of way of the first time he had ridden a horse. He had been clamoring for days to ride Ol' Charlie all by himself, and his father had at last given in. He had sat up on that horse for about two minutes, just filled with pride. Then the animal walked under a tree branch low enough to sweep him off, and he was so wrapped up in trying to get that fool horse to obey that he forgot to duck. That experience was a hard one, felt mostly on the back of his head. But just as it had been with wanting to ride that horse, his stubbornness about Angéline overwhelmed common sense, except that the pain was more in the vicinity of the heart. He should have listened to her and walked away, but he thought he was in love—a possibility he still couldn't discount completely—and the small technicality that she might have bedded half the men in New Orleans wasn't a consideration.

EIGHT

The first McPherson was aware of the fading daylight was a dim realization that the bartender was methodically working his way around
the saloon, lifting the glass chimney of each lamp and adjusting the
wicks as he lit them. But it was the low voice of a woman standing
beside his table that startled him, momentarily snapping him out of
his growing melancholy and back to the present.

"You lost yer woman, no?"

He looked at her through eyes bleary from the whiskey, and
from the tears of remembering the last few hours spent in New
Orleans. He stared at the woman, straining through his drunken
haze to make sense of what she was saying, yet trying to shut out
her words. Jesse McPherson was remembering the exhilara- tion he
felt that late fall morning in New Orleans, sitting on the balcony
overlooking Ramparts Street. His eyes were filled with the sight of
Angéline, his heart overflowing with the love he felt for her; and this
woman, this stranger, was trying to violate that memory.

"Go away," he mumbled.

"You jest a boy. It ain't good, bein' like this, cryin' over some
woman." "I said get away from me," his tone now threatening.

"And if'n I don't?" she asked, hands braced arrogantly on her
hips.

McPherson tensed his body in an effort to stand, but realized
the exertion would be more than it was worth. He shook his head
violently, trying in vain to clear the effects of the cheap whiskey he
had been consuming for the past few hours. Alert now to her lack of
fear, he inspected the woman more closely, wondering why she was
bothering to badger him.

She was a tall woman, at least a head taller than Angéline, and by all appearances seemed to be the one part of the saloon that had been missing since he had first walked through the swinging doors. Over- dressed to McPherson's thinking, she was wearing a costume that might have been appropriate for a fancy ball in the old South, but seemed totally out of place in a whistle-stop like Mesquite. As his eyes focused more closely on her, however, he saw that the dress was threadbare, the gilt worn off. And like the dress, her face was also worn, the powder and rouge applied in a vain attempt to hide the effects of too many years spent in grubby saloons drinking bad whiskey and offering her body to every range rider that had two dollars. But for all that, he could see a strength within her that suggested more than her current circum- stances.

"Well?" she asked again.

Feeling helpless to argue, he gestured toward one of the chairs. "Help yourself. You're goin' to any-

how."

"I'll take that as an invite," she said as she perched on the edge of the chair. "But yer wrong. I don't make a habit of sittin' with men what don't want me to."

"Huh," he mumbled wanly. "Coulda fooled me."

Ignoring his half-hearted attempt at sarcasm, she looked him straight in the eye. "My name's Reba, short for Rebecca. What's yorn?"

"Jess… Jesse McPherson."

"Well, Mista Jess McPherson, will ya be buyin' me a drink…?"

"I don't make it a habit of buyin' drinks for a…" The palm of her hand smacked the table top with a loud crack that resounded in the empty confines of the saloon.

"Don't say it! Whatever I am, it ain't fer you to be passin' judgment." "I didn't mean…"

"Course not," her voice softening. "But this ain't Tennessee, and I ain't been a lady for a long while." "You're from Tennessee?"

"Sometimes, it seems like half of Texas is," she nodded, a gentle smile returning to her lips. "I was mostly raised up on a farm in the

Cumberlands, but after the war, I come out to Texas, and jest never went back."

"How come?"

"Cause none of the menfolk in my family had a lick of sense. My Pa and my brothers, they went cha- sin' off after the war started. Lookin' fer adventure, they said. My brothers was both killed at Shiloh, and we heard lots of stories 'bout Pa, but they was prob'ly jest that. Eventually, Ma jest give in an' died from despair'n loneliness, and you kin see the rest. Now you gonna buy me that drink?"

McPherson nodded at the bartender to bring a second glass and another bottle, pouring the whiskey for her as soon as it was placed it on the table. Looking in his eyes, she picked up the glass and slowly sipped the liquid, savoring it, allowing it to linger on her tongue before swallowing. She watched as he began to withdraw back into his shell, his eyes glazing over with a film of moisture.

"Jess?" His head snapped up. "Ain't nothin' to be shamed about, losin' a woman. It's part o' growin' up."

"Don't want to talk about it."

"All right." She reached for the bottle and refilled both glasses. "But talkin' might help."

McPherson knew that she was right, and he wanted desperately to tell someone, anyone that would listen, of the weight he carried on his shoulders. But he also knew it wasn't simply a matter of reeling out a fanciful story to a stranger. This woman was too much like Angéline, operating under very different cir- cumstances perhaps, but in essence the same. And telling her about New Orleans meant baring his soul.

•　•　•

As the darkness settled in and the light cast by the lamps took over, they sat across the table from one another, neither of them speaking, but one or the other refilling the glasses as soon as they were empty. The air about them was charged with electricity as he fought to keep the remnants of New Orleans inside. But the continuing silence proved to be the catalyst, and the battle was lost. McPherson talked about Tennes- see, and about his family, trying to overcome the effects of the alcohol and articulate the difficulty he had going against his father's expressed wishes.

He described his excitement in being away from home for the first time, of his arrival in the Crescent City, eventually focusing on Angéline and the *Maison des Deux Soeurs*; and despite the continued intake of alcohol, McPherson was now alert, and the anger he had subdued for months was starting to build. But the perceptive whore from the Cumberlands recognized more in his torrent of words than anger: there were indications of pain which only someone in love could experience, a pain which she had often witnessed, but had never experienced herself.

What Reba was feeling at that moment, however, was another part of life she had never experienced: the need to mother. But the maternal instincts were put on hold at the sounds of riders reining up in front of the saloon. Moments later, a half dozen cowboys came through the doors, boisterous and in the mood to drink. First glancing at the table where the old men were playing cards, they also took notice of McPherson and the woman before lining up the length of the bar and taking up the glasses the barkeep had filled as they came in. And although McPherson continued relating the events of New Orleans, she sensed an almost imperceptible shift in his mood.

"They be local ranch hands, Jesse," enlightening him. He acknowledged her information, watching them out of the corner of his eye.

"They usually are," he said bitterly. "Don't stop 'em from givin' me grief."

McPherson's remark was prophetic. One of the cowboys leaned his elbows on the bar facing McPherson and the woman and made a quick assessment of their relationship. As he locked eyes with Jesse, the others broke out in raucous laughter at something he said.

"And this time ain't gonna be any different," McPherson muttered under his breath.

The cowboy turned to pick up one of the bottles sitting on the bar and wandered over to the table. "Hey, Reba, how come you sittin' here with this plowboy when you could be drinkin' with us?" McPherson bridled at the slur.

"Din't know I had to get yore permission to sit with a customer, Clay."

"Well now, Reba, what kinda talk's that? Hell, it ain't like we don't know each other."

"Clay, this ain't the time nor the place. Now why don't you go on back over there'n leave us be." "What you been tellin' this boy, Reba? It sure as hell *is* the place, and I never knowed you to worry about the time. How 'bout it, plowboy?" he said, for the first time addressing McPherson. "Reba offer you a poke?"

Reba looked at McPherson with alarm. His face had taken on a stony cast, the emotion she had sensed building in him now a distant memory. She tried to shake her head, to tell him that she could control things, but seeing that it was a waste of time, turned her attention back to the cowboy, and promptly made the situation worse.

"Leave him be, Clay. He's jest passin' through."

"That so? Maybe he shoulda kept right on goin'." McPherson's voice was so quiet, it took the cowboy a moment to realize he was speaking to him. "You gonna have to speak up, boy. You in Texas now."

"I said, 'Why don't you do what the lady asked?'"

"Hey boys, hear that. The plowboy called Reba a lady." He leaned his hands on the edge of the table, and stared into McPherson's eyes. "And why would I want to listen to a whore?"

"Because if you don't, this piece of iron in my hand is gonna go off, and you're gonna become a part of Texas history." The cowboy snapped upright, his hand inching toward the holster sitting on his right hip, but the faint sound of a hammer being thumbed back was enough to freeze it in mid-motion. "Not a smart move, mister. You're right about me bein' young. But I wouldn't suggest you confuse bein' right with bein' stupid. Your hand gets any closer to that holster, you ain't gonna have to fret."

Clay glanced over his shoulder at the men standing at the bar. "You a dead man, plowboy," he growled.

"Maybe. But look at it my way. You keep callin' me names, I'm gonna be real tempted to just shoot you and take my chances with your friends. So how 'bout you unbuckle the gunbelt and put it on the table nice and easy." With his left hand, the cowboy untied the thongs around his thigh, and then unbuckled the belt, laying it on the table in front of McPherson.

"Reba, you go tell his friends that I want no grief, that I'll be out of here at first light." Once Reba had gone over to the bar, McPherson turned his attention back to the cowboy. "So what's it gonna be? Does it end now, or you gonna push your luck in the hopes I'm a bad shot?"

The cowhand considered his predicament, catching McPherson by surprise by changing the subject. "Reba's not yore woman."

McPherson laughed in spite of himself. "The impression I get, she's not anybody's woman." "I don't see nothin' funny," Clay retorted, caught between anger and chagrin.

"No, I s'pose you don't. Look," McPherson said, attempting to put him at ease. "I'm headin' north in the mornin'—alone."

"My gun?"

"It'll be behind the bar," Jesse answered, continuing, "you understand, it's nothin' personal. I just ain't partial to bein' backshot."

Clay spun on his heels and trod heavy-footed back to the bar, muttering under his breath. McPherson watched as he grabbed a second bottle and stomped out the doors, slamming them open with obvious anger. The others tossed back whatever remained in their glasses and followed close behind. But it wasn't until McPherson heard the thundering hooves fading into the night that he relaxed. Reba reclaimed her chair, staring at McPherson with new respect.

"He ain't happy."

"Guess not, but when he wakes up tomorrow, he'll still be alive."

She tried to gauge what he was saying against what she believed to be the truth. "Somehow, I don't think you'd really shot him."

McPherson shrugged. "*He* was convinced I would and that's all that mattered."

Reba shook her head in amazement. "You are somethin', Jess McPherson. I ain't seen the likes of you for a long time. What *did* happen in New Orleans? That girl was a fool to let you go."

"She didn't let me go. She was…" McPherson's thoughts drifted back, remembering Angéline, all decked out in red and glowing in the first rays of the bright morning sunlight. Her voice was clear, saying what he wanted to hear. *We dream, you and I...I will go with you, and may God ride with us.* Except that the ride was short, and God didn't bother to show up...

NINE

An oppressive heat had settled over the Quarter by late afternoon, escalating the tension surrounding the young lovers. Angéline's decision to leave with McPherson was heavy with the potential for disaster. He may have been older in years, but he knew little about the ways of the world; Angéline on the other hand was more than familiar with most of them. Nevertheless, McPherson's enthusiasm was infectious, and any thoughts of adversity, once mentioned, were either brushed aside or ignored. Even so, his enthusi- asm was tempered by the seemingly endless preparations that had to be attended to before they departed for Texas. While she packed and said her goodbyes, he had to find another horse; but finding the horse proved to be the easy part.

The madam of *La Maison des Deux Soeurs* didn't take kindly to the prospect of one of her girls up and leaving without so much as a fare-thee-well, especially since in her opinion, Angéline was still in her debt. So when McPherson returned to gather up his new-found love, he was met in the courtyard by a weeping Angéline, and a woman uncompromising in her insistence that he would be traveling alone.

"I am sorry, *m'sieur,*" she said in a gesture of helplessness. "We in *New Orléans* are not unsympa- thetic to the ways of the heart; but there is an obligation. Angéline explained this to you, no?"

"She explained it, but it sounded an awful lot like slavery to me." "It is the way we do things here, *m'sieur.*"

"Then maybe it's time to change your ways, ma'am," McPherson said resolutely. "Angeline has agreed to go with me and I aim to see she has the chance."

"I think not, *m'sieur.*" A third person butted into the conversation. "If *Madame* says *Angéline* stays, then she stays." McPherson had not noticed the slight, foppish man standing to one side—he had been focusing on the woman that operated the house—but the man's interference alerted him to the crowd gath- ering around them.

"Mister, I don't know what your stake is in this, but she *is* coming with me. I intend to make her my wife."

"Your wife?" The man laughed contemptuously. "You are even more stupid than I thought, *m'sieur.*

She is *une putain*; she will always be *une putain.*"

Events blurred as McPherson's anger boiled to the surface, urging him to silence the one who would tarnish the woman he loved, blinding him to the flashing knife that suddenly appeared in the man's hand. A cry of anguish filled the air as Angéline jumped between them in an attempt to protect him, catching the brunt of the knife thrust intended for him, collapsing at his feet.

"Angeline!" McPherson's anger turned to shock and then to agonizing sorrow as he cradled her in his arms, unable to stop her life from fading away. "Angeline…"

McPherson anxiously scanned the crowd, searching for the miracle that would restore her life, know- ing there would be no miracles. Now grown to more than a hundred, the faceless throng met his grief with stoic silence, moving back as he got slowly to his feet, still holding her in his arms. Pausing long enough to get his bearings, he carried her lifeless body up the stairs and back to the room they had shared the previous night.

Gently laying her on the bed, he tentatively positioned a strand of hair that seemed out of place and caressed her lips with his own, marveling at the serenity of her face. After a few moments, he wiped the tears from his eyes and told her he'd be back, closing the door as he left. Back on the ground floor, he asked the madam as to the whereabouts of Angéline's killer.

"Where is he," he whispered, gripping her arms and shaking her violently, screaming when she refused to answer. "Where is he?"

"*M'sieur McPherson!*" McPherson spun at the sound. Standing behind him was a man about his size, dressed in a white linen suit and wearing a low-crowned white hat with a wide brim. The man was calmly pointing a revolver at his midsection. "Leave 'er alone, *m'sieur*. Please." McPherson let his hands drop to his sides, an emptiness pervading his heart.

"My name is *René d'Iberville, m'sieur*. I too am saddened by the death of *Angéline DuBois*; she was my friend. But it is not *Madame's* fault. You cannot take out your pain on her."

"She tried to protect me… She saved my life."

"*Oui,* and you must never forget that. But you cannot remain in *New Orléans* any longer. *Raymond Baptiste* has many friends and they will see this as your fault."

"I will not leave until I bury Angeline and kill that bastard."

"I understand how you feel," he replied, trying to comfort McPherson, "and you must not worry. *Angéline* is a part of our family and I will personally ensure that she is honored. But as far as *Raymond* is concerned, you must forget him. He will be dealt with. You have my word."

"I wasn't raised to run."

"Nevertheless, you must do as I say. Our city has never been kind to strangers. Now please, go.

There is a ferry across to *Algiers*. You can pick up the road to Texas there…"

Embarrassed, Reba interrupted McPherson's narration about New Orleans. "I'm sorry, Jess, it weren't none 'o my business."

"Don't matter. You were right: I needed to talk it out." "But this man *Baptiste*, he deserved to die." McPherson grimly nodded. "He did."

"But…"

"René d'Iberville was a real strange one. I had no intention of leaving New Orleans, but with him standing there with a gun on me, I didn't have a lot of choice in the matter. Reason said to quit arguing and take the ferry. I was two days out of New Orleans, on the edge of a swamp just south of some little town called Thibodaux…

McPherson rode hard along a trail that skirted the swamp, oblivious to his surroundings. Although the sun had been up for more than an hour, the thick mists common to the bayou in early morning were yet to be burned off. His intention was to put as much distance between himself and New Orleans as possible in an attempt to forget what had happened, but he knew there was one more scene to be played when he rounded a stand of trees and discovered d'Iberville patiently waiting for him.

D'Iberville didn't say a word as he mounted his horse and rode alongside McPherson. Within fifteen minutes, they had ridden into the middle of the swamp; and McPherson finally understood why d'Iberville was there. *Raymond Baptiste* was sitting under a tree with a rope around his neck. A string of curses poured out of his mouth when he spied McPherson and d'Iberville riding up, but the horse he was mounted on remained in place. D'Iberville, yet to say a word to McPherson, rode up beside the man and laid the back of his hand across *Baptiste's* mouth, drawing blood.

"*M'sieur Baptiste*, your mouth is that of a sewer, but if you choose to continue with your offensive speech, I will be forced to deal with you before you are judged."

"Judged? For what?"

"Why, for murder of course."

"If you're talking about that…" *Baptiste* caught another hand across his face, causing the blood to flow freely.

"I would not suggest using that word, *Baptiste*. As you have seen, *M'sieur McPherson* takes great exception to it. And so do I." Baptiste fell silent. "*Bien.* You are learning. *M'sieur.* Permit me to tell you of this…this sterling example of *New Orléans* manhood. He is the result of untold years of careless breeding; and exhibits most of the traits despised by civilized man. He is overflowing with braggadocio, but has not the stones to back his boasting. He is a most base coward, yet he considers himself superior to those less fortunate. He is a thief and a murderer many times over." D'Iberville studied McPherson's reaction.

"You're thinking I should have let you rid *New Orléans* of him," he continued, "and perhaps I should have. But you would have been hounded by his friends and eventually killed. So I have now corrected that. You are no longer in *New Orléans*, and I have brought you *Raymond Baptiste*. You may exact your revenge without fear of retribution."

McPherson stoically accepted the information, realizing that d'Iberville had indirectly saved his life by chasing him out of the city. But he also realized that as much as he wanted the man to pay for killing Angéline, it would not be by his hand that day.

"I don't want to seem ungrateful, Mister, and I thank you for your efforts, but all I can see is that kill- ing him would make me no different than he is."

D'Iberville nodded. "*Angéline* chose well. But there's one other thing you should consider. If you do not kill him now, he will follow you until one of you is dead."

"I guess I'll just have to take my chances."

"*M'sieur McPherson*," he said, extending his hand, "we are very different, you and I. But I would be honored if you would permit me to call you friend."

McPherson grinned and returned the salutation. "My pleasure."
"Where do you go from here?"

"That way," he answered, pointing west. "If I had done that in the beginning, Angeline would still be alive."

"That may be true. But you would not have known her." "What about him?" he asked, motioning toward *Baptiste*. "I will try to reason with him. Perhaps he will listen."

"Goodbye, Mister d'Iberville." McPherson took a last look at Baptiste before wheeling his horse toward Texas.

D'Iberville watched as McPherson disappeared between the cypress that dominated that portion of the swamp. "*Adieu, M'sieur*," he said softly, turning his attention to *Baptiste*. "You are most fortunate, *M'sieur Baptiste,* to have a horse that is not excitable. But my question to you is whether you are a reason- able man?"

"He is a dead man, *René*. And if you are not careful, you will join him."

"Ahhh, *Raymond*," d'Iberville sighed, "you do not learn from your mistakes. I suggest you reconsider your situation. In case you 'ave forgotten, you are in a most awkward position."

"I 'ave had enough of these threats, *René*. Cut me loose."

"I am afraid that is the one option not available. *M'sieur Raymond Baptiste*, you have been judged and found guilty of murder. 'Ave you any last words?"

"*Tu peux te le foutre au cul, René*," Baptiste spat out. "That is what I thought you would say."

D'Iberville drew his pistol and shot *Baptiste* through the heart, the horse bolting before the first echoes returned. Moments later, McPherson reappeared, pulling up when he saw the dead weight of *Bap- tiste* at the end of the rope. D'Iberville rode toward McPherson, reining up beside him.

"*M'sieur McPherson*, what a pleasant surprise. I did not expect to see you again." "I heard the shot."

"Yes, a most unfortunate circumstance. He chose to be imprac-tical." "Will his death make trouble for you in New Orleans?"

"For a time. But like others of his type, he will be forgotten in a few weeks." "Then you can't go home."

"That is so," he agreed. Turning for a final glance at *Baptiste*, d'Iberville grinned. "Would you be adverse to a traveling compan-ion? I 'ave not seen Corpus Christi for some time, and there is much I would like to tell you about *Angéline*..."

TEN

The air was clear and cold as the buckskin picked its way up the mountain trail, a pair of pack horses following close behind. McPherson had expected to face colder weather than he had experienced across the southwest, but he wasn't prepared for such iciness so early in September. Leaves were well into the fall change, signaling the onset of winter, and he had yet to establish a camp where he could sit out the winter and trap for pelts to replenish his dwindling money supply. He had been told he would be wasting his time, that the region was trapped out, but he had stubbornly insisted that he intended to try.

Convinced that he was serious, an aging trapper had told him of a valley that because of rumors and superstition, hadn't been trapped in years. But since he wasn't one to believe in superstition and had been taught to ignore rumors, McPherson figured the valley sounded like as good a place as any to try his luck. In fact, it was his decision to go to that particular valley that convinced the trader at Casper to give him the supplies he needed. 'Bring back enough pelts to justify the outlay,' the trader had said, 'and I'll give you top dollar for your efforts.'

Since he was a novice at trapping, McPherson was convinced they were laughing at him. He knew the odds were considerable against his surviving the winter at all. But he took the friendly banter of the few old mountain men he met at the trading post as a dare, because if the old trapper was telling the truth, the valley would produce more than enough skins to pay for another year or two of wandering.

Two weeks out of Casper, McPherson was deep into the mountains of the Wind River range and within reach of the valley, which was situated just the other side of the next ridge if he had reckoned cor- rectly. He figured he had at most another two to three weeks to locate the old trapper's cabin at the head of the valley—if it was still there—and get settled in before the snows hit. He prodded the grey to pick up the pace: with the chill in the air, he knew time was of the essence.

Topping the ridge, McPherson surveyed the trail leading toward the mysterious valley, following it downward until it disappeared into a thick stand of fir and spruce two thirds of the way down the mountainside. The valley itself was quite long, seeming to reach for miles, at last narrowing to a point in the hazy distance. He searched for the cabin that was supposed to be below, but didn't really expect to see it amidst the dense forest blanketing the valley floor.

Figuring he had another three hours of daylight, he decided to try and make the valley before camp- ing for the night. Nudging the buckskin forward, McPherson began working his way through boulders and scrub pines bearing the impact of uncounted winters. The trail led quickly into a darkened forest with trees reaching four and five feet across and towering a hundred feet or better above the valley floor, creating a cathedral-like effect as McPherson wandered in and out of the sporadic patches of sunlight that made it through the thick branches above. The trail was wider than McPherson would have expected, but the profusion of tracks indicated that it was well traveled, and he wasn't too surprised when he came upon a small lake that he hadn't seen when he first looked the valley over.

After a quick inspection of a number of the more open spots, he decided it would be safer to pitch camp beside a small stream that fed the lake a few hundred yards away . He had found panther tracks beside the lake, and worse, tracks that looked an awful lot like bear. At this juncture, he didn't want con- frontations, even if the bears were most likely to run if given the chance. He could ill afford to lose the pack horses.

As he built a fire, he recalled with some amusement the first time he had encountered a bear. He had taken sister Maggie berry picking up a hollow that was not too far from home. There were a good half dozen clumps of blackberry bushes in the hollow and filling a gallon bucket or two was easy. Working their way around a third of the bushes, they had already picked enough to fill one bucket as well as making a good start on filling their bellies. They were working on the second when a small black bear came from the other direction, just as intent on filling its own belly.

McPherson smiled at the image because that bear was easily as surprised as they were. He threw the bucket he was carrying at the bear and grabbed Maggie to run, when he noticed that the bear was just as anxious to leave as he was. Tucking Maggie under his arm, he picked up the other pail, and headed for the house as quickly as possible, Maggie giggling all the way from the bouncing. Once back at the house, he yelled for Aaron and grabbed a rifle, beating a path back to the hollow, Aaron right on his heels. There was no sign of the bear, but the berries that were spilt when he threw the bucket were gone, and for a long time after that, he wasn't allowed to take Maggie far from the cabin unless one of his older brothers was with him. But that was a lifetime ago, and seemed even longer, because as much as he would have liked to see Maggie at that moment, thinking about her brought on a melancholy that he preferred to avoid. He had a long winter ahead of him and thinking about his family and about Tennessee would only make it worse.

The fire going, he checked the horses before returning to put on a pot of coffee. The night chill was beginning to settle around him and he needed to warm up the inside as well as the surrounding air. But other than fixing coffee, he had no great desire to cook, choosing instead to chew on some of the beef jerky he had gotten at the trading post. He was well into a second cup when he was startled by a voice coming out of the darkness from behind him.

"What're yah doin' in muh valley, boy?" To say that the disembodied voice coming out of the dark- ness unnerved McPherson was putting it mildly. His good fortune was in not reacting any quicker than he did, because the second time it spoke was in time to freeze his hand in mid-draw.

"Don't touch the iron, boy. You be dead afore yah clear leather." McPherson's left hand moved away from the holster. "At's good. Now just you step away from thet rifle and don't be turnin' round."

McPherson could hear movement, but all he could think was that he had gotten careless and would probably die as a result. As soon as he realized the movement was directly behind him, he felt the barrel of a gun poking him in the back and his revolver being pulled from the holster.

"Help yourself," he quipped.

"Intend to," the voice answered. "Any coffee left in thet pot?"

"Like I said, help yourself."

"Meebe yah could pour me up a cup?" The owner of the voice moved around to face McPherson, the rifle remaining steady.

Keeping his hands in plain view, McPherson looked the intruder over in the light of the fire. The man, standing a head or better shorter than McPherson, was clad totally in buckskin and sported matted shoulder length hair and a bushy, grizzled beard that hadn't seen a trimming in years. But even in the dim- ness of the firelight, McPherson could see that the man's eyes were clear and hard. He took comfort in the man's hesitation.

"You gonna shoot me, mister?" "Ain't decided."

McPherson nodded. "Then you best have that coffee whilst you make up your mind." McPherson pulled a second tin from his gear and filled it with the steaming black liquid, holding it out to the older man.

"Jest sit it on the ground," waving the barrel of the rifle to emphasize the point. McPherson obliged him and stepped back.

"Think you could point that some other direction?" McPherson asked.

"Meebe." He picked up the cup and tasted the coffee, before tilting the cup back and emptying it. "Purty good for a shavetail."

"Pardon?"

"Hell, boy, you ain't no trapper. I coulda kilt yah any time since you started down the hill." "Why didn't you?"

"Wern't no reason to. Yah wern't lookin' fer me. Hell, you din't even know I wuz here." He stared at Jesse with some consternation. "Who sent you here, boy? Yah din't find this valley by yerself."

By the time McPherson had answered the question, the old man was cackling to himself. "Somethin' funny?"

"Yah could say thet, boy. I'm the one thet started them stories.

"...They tell yah `bout the trappers wuz found tied to trees'n missin' their heads? Or the injun spirits thet haunts the valley?" The old man's eyes were twinkling as he embellished on stories McPherson had heard in Casper. "How `bout the one `bout the giant grizzly what kills horses with one swipe?"

"Well I'll be a..." The old man's laughter was infectious. McPherson chuckled, and then broke up with the first belly laugh he had enjoyed in what seemed to be years. "But why?" he asked, before realizing that the stories made all the sense in the world.

"I ain't much for people, boy, `ceptin' when I choose to be." He waved his hands around, gesturing into the darkness. "This valley been my home for nigh on to fifteen years. And `cept fer the pelt hunters that wander in here `bout this time ever year, I don't see nobody."

"Not surprising. Pointing guns at folks ain't no way to endear them."

"They ain't comin' up here to be friends, boy. This valley's the onliest one left what ain't been trapped out."

"That explains why they were just sittin' around."

"Meebe. But I'm bettin' some of `em left right behind yah. They be tryin' to find out if'n I'm still here without gittin' anybody else kilt."

The old man raised the rifle that had laid across his knees, again pointing it in the general direction of McPherson. Jess stiffened, waiting for the bullet that would end his discovery of the west. Swinging the rifle to one side, the old man snapped off three quick shots, followed by a single round from McPherson's revolver into the ground.

"Listen!" the old man hissed under his breath. McPherson stared in puzzlement as the gunshots con- tinued to echo up and down the valley, finally understanding as the sounds of hooves rattled on the rocks above. "You be dead now," he said with some satisfaction.

"Nervous bunch," McPherson observed.

"Got reason to be," he nodded in agreement. "Afore last year, threats wuz enough to chase `em off, but I'm gittin' old'n they know it. Buried three of `em afore they got the message thet they wern't welcome."

"I s'pose that applies to me too?"

"Meebe." The old man extended McPherson's revolver to him butt first.

"Maybe? Maybe?" McPherson laughed in disbelief. "I'm sittin' here with two pack horses, one which ain't even mine, both of `em loaded down with supplies I'm supposed to pay for next spring. And all you can say is maybe."

"Yah don't owe them thevin' buffers nothin'." "Pardon me? Course I do."

"You not listenin', boy. They sent yah up here to git kilt." "Don't matter. I'm still obliged."

A grin spread across the old man's face. "You know somethin', boy? One `o these days, thet stubborn streak gonna git yah in a pile `o trouble."

"It already has," McPherson admitted sheepishly.

ELEVEN

Anton Schlesinger had lived in the shadows of the Tetons for more than fifteen years, defending the secluded valley he called home from any and all intruders. He had emigrated from Ohio thirty-five years before, lured by tales of untold riches to be made in the West. But he quickly discovered, as had many oth- ers before him, that becoming rich was a dream to be chased but not attained, that the days when pelts were there for the taking were past. For twenty years, he had wandered from the Powder River basin, to the Yel- lowstone, and over into the Oregon Territory, scratching out a meager survival, trapping in areas no one else bothered with. Early on, he had taken part in attempts to revive the Green River Rendezvous, an annual spring gathering of trappers and Indians, but the attempts were failures, and his wanderings became a way of life.

Over that twenty years, he made a better than passing acquaintance with many of the men that roamed those rugged mountains north and south of the Oregon Trail; and at one time or another, he broke bread with the likes of Jim Bridger and Bill Sublette. But Schlesinger's continual isolation made him uneasy around others, especially around men who sought the limelight. As the years passed, his contact with the outside world diminished, and when the gatherings happened, he generally chose to go even deeper into the mountains. It was on one of those attempts to get away that he discovered the valley. Almost twenty miles long, the valley was made to order for Schlesinger. It was isolated from the rest of the area, surrounded by steep ridges thick with stands of fir and spruce. With only one trail leading in, the val- ley was easy to protect—and protect it he did.

Strangers of one sort or another came across the ridge each fall with maddening regularity: Trappers. Prospectors. Adventurers looking to take what Schlesinger considered to be his. In the beginning, they came in alone, but later on they traveled in the company of others. He found it easy to scare off the loners with threats, seldom having to resort to anything more. But that all changed as he became older. They didn't scare so easy, and each incursion became bolder, until one day, a bunch tried a new tactic in an attempt to flank him…

Schlesinger saw the three riders within minutes after they crested the ridge, pack horses in tow. They looked no different from any that had come in previous years, except that one of them was a woman. When they hit the tree line two hours later, he was waiting for them. Stepping into the middle of the trail, he cocked the rifle and aimed it at the first of the two men.

"At's fer enough." The riders reined their horses to a halt. "Turn around'n git outta here. You be tres- passin'."

"You ain't being' real neighborly, old man." Schlesinger stared at the one who had spoken up. What he saw was a good example of what many of the mountain men had become, what he referred to with dis- dain as a buffer—a hunter of buffalo.

"You ain't my neighbor. Now turn around."

"Hold on, old man. We come up here to make you a deal." For the first time, Schlesinger paid atten- tion to the second of the two men.

"Only deal I'm interested in is seein' you ride back up thet hill."

"The least you could do is hear whut we got to say," the second man continued, gesturing toward the third member of the party. "We brung you this woman."

Schlesinger stared at the woman, and what he saw was disturbing. Her hands were bound to the pom- mel, and even though she was dressed like an Indian, the dirt on her face couldn't conceal the fact that she was white. But reading her face was even more disturbing; what passed as emotion flickered ever so quickly across her face as the second man explained.

"We took her off some Crow. Figured since you wuz alone…"

Schlesinger continued to stare, trying to gauge her thoughts. Her anger was evident; but just as strong was the fear. The movement to his left told him why. He had been so intent on following their prog- ress down the trail that he failed to see a third man cross the ridge. Diving toward the ground, he snapped off a shot toward the first man, knocking him out of the saddle. Rolling upright, he levered another round and shot the trailer he missed seeing earlier. Swinging the rifle around, he once again brought it to bear on the remaining hunter.

"Now, mister, s`pose you explain to me how you come to be here. And untie thet woman's hands." "She'll run away."

"Thet be her choice," he exclaimed, firing a shot over the buffer's head. "Do it!"

The buffalo hunter pulled a knife out of his boot, leaned across to the woman, and sliced through the ropes binding her. As soon as her hands were free and the circulation had returned, she swung a leg over the saddle and dropped to the ground at a dead run. Except that she didn't flee. Instead, she ran to one of the men Schlesinger had shot and grabbed a half-drawn pistol, catching it in his belt in her eagerness, yanking it a second time before it came free. Thumbing back the hammer, she fired, killing the last of her captors. Spinning, she then aimed it at Schlesinger. He lowered his rifle and turned his back on her, checking each of the men to ensure that they were dead. Then leaning the rifle against a tree, he hoisted the first of the bodies across a saddle and tied him on while she watched intently.

"You speak American?" he asked. She nodded. "Then put down thet gun. I ain't agonna hurt ya."

Closed-mouthed and still gripping the pistol, she continued to watch as the old man finished tying the last two bodies across a saddle and mounted a horse he had tied out of sight back in the trees.

"Comin'?" he asked. "Got to bury this bunch."

After a moment's hesitation, the woman chased down the pack horses and followed along to a remote area of the valley, where the old man unceremoniously dumped the bodies into a shallow ravine. Silently, she helped cave in the banks that would become their grave. Once that was accomplished, she picked up the pack horse lead and waited while he unsaddled the horses and set them free to forage up the valley, tossing the saddles and bridles into the ravine atop the grave.

Schlesinger stowed the Henry rifles the buffers carried on one of the pack horses and reached to take the lead rope from her, but was surprised when she refused to hand it over. Shrugging, he picked up his own rifle and the reins of the remaining horse and headed back toward the trail, grunting in satisfaction at the sounds behind him that indicated that she was following, pack animals in tow. An hour later, they were at his cabin. Tying the horse's reins to the gate of the small corral, he unsaddled it, set the saddle across a corral railing, and turned the horse inside. Retrieving the Henrys, he went into the cabin without speaking to her.

•   •   •

He wasn't aware of the change, but the anger Schlesinger had seen on the woman's face was gone, replaced with a dread of what lay ahead. Since the day a Crow hunting party had chanced upon her family's farm, she had undergone agonizing torment. When the Indians first appeared, she was walking with her husband alongside the garden she had so proudly nurtured. Momentarily frozen in disbelief, she became separated from him when he ran toward the farmhouse, trying to reach the children. But her bewilderment turned to horror when what started as a raid to steal horses turned into bloodlust. She saw her husband fall, riddled by a dozen shots. Her own attempts to reach the farmhouse were frustrated as she was buffeted between the ponies, panic setting in as smoke and then flames exploded from beneath the eaves of the house. When at last she broke free, she knew she was too late: the house was engulfed in flames, and her children were dead.

The days and nights following the attack became a living nightmare for her as she was passed from brave to brave, her mind unable to deal rationally with the abuse she was forced to endure. But the outrages she suffered on the trail were only the beginning of the indignities she was to face. By the time they arrived at the village encampment, her body was a mass of cuts and bruises, the remnants of her clothing in tatters and incapable of providing the barest of protection. Her entrance into the village was greeted with jeers and ridicule from the women.

Yanked from the horse, she tried to cover herself with the rags that had once been a dress, only to have them torn away, leaving her naked, cowering and surrounded by angry, taunting women. They mocked and kicked at her, pulling her hair constantly as they shoved her toward the center of the village. Her hands bound, she was tethered with a long rope to a wooden stake and subjected to continuing abuse by the women and children, until at last she lapsed into unconsciousness.

Her world became a blur of indignity piled upon indignity until she was numb with pain and hunger. The hair pulling was constant, as was the kicking and spitting. On more than one occasion, she woke to streams of urine splashing on her nakedness. But she remembered with satisfaction that when at last she started fighting back, when her defiance finally overrode her humiliation and fear, the taunting slowed, and finally stopped altogether. She was released from her tether and led to a stream that ran past the village and encouraged to bathe. Once she did, she was given clothing and moccasins made of buckskin, and the phys- ical healing began.

The memories of her life with the Crow now raced through her mind as she unpacked the horses. She had no illusions about the time she spent as a captive: she had been a slave, plain and simple. She was given the dirtiest menial chores and pushed to exhaustion. If she refused to obey, she was beaten, but only rarely did the brutality approach the levels she experienced immediately following the deaths of her hus- band and children. In return, she was clothed and fed, and with limitations, integrated into village life.

In the early days following her capture, she had desperately wanted to be found, but as the days turned into weeks, and the weeks into months, the need to be found evolved into a fear that she would be. She saw few whites except on those rare occasions when the horse soldiers made contact with the tribe, and then she was kept out of sight. And as she adapted to the ways of the Crow, she became a part of them, and the painful memories that had helped her keep her sanity faded slowly away.

The appearance of the buffalo hunters changed all that. She remembered their passing through the village the previous summer, and since the Crow were considerably more casual about her by that time, the hunters had noticed her presence and attempted to trade for her. A year later, they rode into the village, their pack horses laden with goods. Passing around jugs of whiskey, they convinced the tribe's elders they were prepared to trade the following day, but while the village slept, two of them snuck into the tepee where she was asleep and carried her off. She shuddered as she remembered the events of that night and the following day, remembered her fear of the white men, remembered that once again her life became a living hell.

Compared to white society, the Crow behavior would have been considered cruel, but it was the hunters who were the real savages. She realized quickly that they were ruthless, and sadistic—when the Crow warriors caught up with them the next day, they were shot down in cold blood and then scalped. She survived their nightly assaults, as well as the other humiliations they heaped upon her, but the disgrace she had lived with, disgrace she thought she had disposed of, returned with a passion. Except that it was accompanied with anger. She fought them and was beaten for her efforts. She tried running away, and was beaten again. The third time she ran, they added a new element to the beatings, taking turns sodomizing her until she was bleeding, then leaving her tied up to prevent her running again.

The next morning, she woke to the three men bickering over what to do with her, at last deciding to use her as bait. They were talking about a trapper that lived in a valley in the Wind River range, except that he had quit trapping and never came out, avoiding any contact with the outside world. Their plan was to offer her up as an enticement to get into the valley, and then kill the old man at first opportunity. She laughed contemptuously. They obviously hadn't taken into account the possibility the old man might not take kindly to their generous offer. So now the three were dead, and once again she was at the mercy of another.

TWELVE

Schlesinger periodically glanced out the one window of the cabin, watching the woman as she unpacked each of the horses and turned them into the corral. The thought wasn't much to his liking, but he was going to be faced with making a decision or two about her, beginning with how far she could be trusted. Her skin might be white, but living with Indians for any length of time tended to alter a person's perspectives. And there was the matter of the buffers. Whatever it was they did to her had turned her into a very dangerous creature; and he could well be faced with having to kill her out of self preservation. But not tonight. Tonight she would get food in her belly, and a night's sleep. Tomorrow would be soon enough to look ahead.

The horses unloaded, the woman laboriously moved the supplies to the overhang located at one end of the cabin. Anything that might attract animals she carted inside. Eventually, she was forced to stop her labors—there was nothing more to carry. Schlesinger gestured toward the table, and after she sat down, handed her a spoon and a bowl he had filled with bits of meat that had been simmering in a stewpot over the fireplace. She didn't bother with the spoon, bolting down the meat chunks as fast as she could swallow them. She quickly emptied the bowl, extending it to be refilled, which he did. Once again, she wolfed down the food, not slowing until the bowl was empty. Only then, after licking the juice from her fingers and wiping them on her clothing, did she look around at the inside of the cabin, at last coming to rest on Schlesinger.

"You kin sleep up thar," he said pointing to a small loft. "They's a blanket'er two," he added as an afterthought.

She glanced at the loft, then back at Schlesinger, the look of a cornered animal growing in her eyes. She begin taking off the buckskin dress she wore, for a moment catching Schlesinger unawares. It was only when she had the dress half off that he came to the realization she expected him to bed her. He could also see the small masses of scar tissue, the results of numerous beatings.

"Keep yer clothes on, woman, gits cold at night," adding before he went outside, "got chores to do." For the next few days, Schlesinger wandered the valley as he was wont to do, the woman sometimes accompanying him. More often than not, however, she remained at the cabin and busied herself with per- ceived chores. On the days she went along, he talked to her, told her of the valley and its inhabitants, allow- ing her the freedom of feeling alive. Each successive day, she acted more and more like a woman and less like a caged animal, a development that piqued Schlesinger's curiosity. He had spent little time with women since coming west, and had quite literally not seen one for better than five years; but now that a woman had shown up on his doorstep, he found himself wanting to know who she was, where she came from. He kept pushing to find out some- thing, anything that might tell him something about her, but the one thing that remained constant was her continued silence, to the point that Schlesinger wondered if she could speak at all.

Finally, his patience strained by her silence, his frustrations boiled over and he stomped out of the cabin in anger. It was one of the times she chose to tag along. He headed straight up the valley, following a trail so faint that she would have lost her way had she not kept him in sight. An hour later, she crossed a small creek, the trail suddenly widening as it circled beneath an outcropping of rock. Schlesinger was wait- ing for her.

"Open yer mouth." Startled, she jumped back. "I said open yer mouth." Staring at Schlesinger, she slowly obeyed, again jumping back when he peered into her open mouth. "Well ya still got yer tongue. Think meebe it be time ya used it. Cain't git ya home if'n you don't tell me whar it is."

Her hand flew to her mouth as she backed away, turning in panic to run back down the trail. Schlesinger fired the rifle he was carrying into the air, scaring her even more. She lost her balance, tripping on a tree root, sprawling into the creek, her eyes crazed, fearful. As Schlesinger reached out his hand to help her stand, she recoiled, settling further into the water. He sat down at the water's edge, his apparent anger disappearing as quickly as it had flared up. He watched as the water soaked into the buckskin dress, slowly turning it black right to her shoulders.

"Woman, I told ya afore I ain't agonna hurt ya. But if'n ya don't talk…"

Her mouth worked silently, forming the words over and over until they came out in a shout. "I ain't leavin'." He nodded, acknowledging her declaration. She repeated the avowal, her voice almost in a growl. "I ain't leavin'."

The hand offered a second time, she allowed Schlesinger to pull her to her feet, supporting her as she waded out of the creek, the water falling like rain around her feet. She reluctantly released his hand, and then much to his chagrin, wrapped her arms around him in a fierce embrace. But just as abruptly, she stepped back in obvious embarrassment.

"Best ya git thet wet hide off," he said before turning on his heels and heading down the trail. "Wind'll dry ya."

She stared at his back as he walked away, suddenly shivering from the wind-chilled wetness against her skin, despite the heat of the day. Stripping the dress off, she ran after him in an attempt to catch up. It was a strange sight, the buckskin-clad mountain man, striding vigorously in and out of the trees and across the occasional meadow, contrasting with the smaller woman, following behind at a near run, naked except for moccasins and carrying a sodden wad of leather. Schlesinger set a steady pace, but made sure he was never out of her sight. When she reached the edge of the clearing about the cabin, she hesitated. She was dry, but the wet mass of buckskin she was carrying had not dried in the least. Undecided as to what to do, she glanced toward the cabin. Schlesinger was waiting beside the cabin with a quilt.

"Kin ya sew?" he asked, handing her the quilt.

"Uh huh. I used to make…" Tears welled in her eyes, in her heart a stabbing pain as memories, visions of her family flashed repeatedly in her head. "Don't matter," she whispered.

"Where be yer family?" "Dead. Injuns kilt `em." "Crow ain't knowed fer thet."

"They was tryin' to steal our horses," she explained. "My man thought they was after the boys…" "How long wuz you with the Crow?"

She changed the subject in an attempt to avoid the question. "Is they any soap around here?"

"They's a bar or two `o lye soap." "It'll do. I ain't been clean in so long."

While she spread the dress across one of the porch railings, Schlesinger retrieved the soap. Taking it, she pulled the quilt about her shoulders and walked down to a small back eddy in the creek below the cabin. Tossing the quilt aside, she waded in and began scrubbing away the dirt, guilt, and self pity that had accumulated over the previous four years. At last feeling clean, she gathered the quilt around her, picked up the soap, and walked back to the cabin. Schlesinger had waited patiently on the porch while she took her bath. Now, as she came back from the creek, he could see the change that had begun a couple of hours back.

"I asked you a question. How long wuz you…"

"Four winters," she answered. "And afore you start in agin about me goin' back, I'm here to tell you to fergit it. I ain't goin' back. I ain't fittin' to live with civilized folks. Them Injuns and the buff'lo hunters made sure `o that. And if'n you don't want me around, best you take me out to thet ravine and shoot me too, cause I ain't aleavin'."

Schlesinger reached behind his back and picked up a roll of deerskin. "Then meebe you oughta make yerself a new dress."

She tossed the cake of soap at him. "And maybe you oughta go wash." "And why might'n I want to do thet?"

"Cause you stink worsen I did."

Schlesinger leaned back against one of the supports holding up the roof over the porch and contem- plated the woman's suggestion. For all the years that he had spent in the valley, not once had he considered the possibility that he might one day be lonely, or be in need of another person, but the moment she threw the soap at him, he knew he would take the bath. Whatever the reason that had brought her to the valley, he was perfectly content that she should remain—an amazing turn of events, considering that when she first arrived, he was prepared to take her out first chance. His valley was no place for weaklings, and he had no desire to tend some crazy female. But for the moment, the woman had won an undeclared battle of will. She was strong-minded, and he suspected that with or without him, she was more than able to survive.

THIRTEEN

"…I'm dyin', boy. Somethin' eatin' away inside. Be surprised if'n I last the winter."

McPherson was startled by the old man's openness, but after spending better than a month in the val- ley, he had gotten used to expecting anything. "Why you tellin' me?"

"The woman, she's been here fer better'n three years," Schlesinger answered, "but she still be young.

Need ya to take her outta here, meebe out to Oregon."

"First time I heard tell she might want to go out to Oregon." "Ain't told her yet."

McPherson laughed. "She don't strike me as a woman that can be told anything."

"Huh! I learnt right off they ain't but two ways `o dealin' with her, and they both be her'n. But she'll go. She ain't near as stubborn as she lets on."

McPherson accepted Schlesinger's measure of the woman, and said so. A judge of women he wasn't. But he qualified the arrange-ment on the condition that the old man had indeed passed on by the time he was ready to leave in the spring. The two men had been walking up the valley for more than an hour, often cutting a new trail through knee-high snow drifts, when McPherson spied the top of a sheer wall of rock in the distance through the denuded trees.

Over the next three hours, he saw the wall grow in size as they neared it, at last standing at it's base, a hundred feet below the rim he had originally seen. Schlesinger pointed toward a faint path that wandered along the base of the rock, leading to a wide ledge crusted with ice that climbed along the rock's face. Twenty minutes later, they were standing outside a small cave entrance. The old man crawled through, and although McPherson had no desire to follow him, he finally inched his way through the opening. Inside, he discovered that Schlesinger had put fire to a lantern, and much to his amazement, found that he could stand easily.

"I ain't much for caves, Anton."

"Won't be here long," he replied, ignoring McPherson's objections, leading him deeper into the cave. "Found this cave a few years ago," the old man offered. "The woman ain't even been up here."

"Why not?"

"She been through hell, boy. Figured she din't need to know 'bout this." "I coulda lived without it myself."

"Meebe. But since I'm s'posed to akilt ya, I figure the least I could do is stake ya." "You're talkin' in circles, Anton."

"Look up thar, boy." Schlesinger raised the lantern, pointing to a spot head high on the cavern's wall. Unaccustomed to such a low level of light, McPherson didn't immediately see the narrow band reflecting the lantern's yellow light. "Thet's gold, boy. Mor'n enough fer you and the woman."

McPherson's jaw dropped as the realization of what he was staring at sunk in. He remembered clearly the tales of the travelers passing by the farm, tales of frenzy in the goldfields of California, stories that were repetitive and increasingly elaborate with each telling. But never had he imagined that he would see such wealth himself, especially not in the Wyoming territory.

"...'S the matter, boy? Cat got yer tongue?"

"Wha...?" The old man's voice penetrated McPherson's reverie of untold riches. "It be thar fer the takin', boy."

"Then why didn't you?"

"They's more to life than money, boy. Sides. If'n them fools thet kept comin' up here lernt bout the gold, they'd atore up the valley alookin' fer it."

"I s'pose I should thank you."

"Ain't lookin' fer thanks. Jest take care 'o the woman."

A determined smile on his face, McPherson nodded in agreement. "Can we git outta here now?" "Shore. But you best be aware 'o one other thing." Schlesinger lead him another twenty feet into the back of the cave. Holding the lantern over a pit situated there, he pointed down into it. McPherson could see something moving in the dim light. "Them's rattlers. They won't bother you none whilst it's cold, but come spring, they be all over this cave."

• • •

Winter settled into western Wyoming with a vengeance. Storm after storm boiled out of the moun- tains, dumping exceptional amounts of snow into the valley and creating near insurmountable problems. The winter was turning into a never-ending routine of doing what was necessary to survive. Feeding the animals was becoming difficult, and little of his East Tennessee upbringing was of any help. On top of that, Schlesinger was bedridden full time, his health deteriorating on a daily basis. McPherson had taken on all the outside chores, while the woman tended to the old man and made sure they ate regular, but even that got to be a problem. Game was plentiful, getting to it was another matter entirely. Nevertheless, the animals got fed, and the three continued to eat reasonably well, and in McPherson's mind, the only thing really wrong in the valley was the impending death of the old man.

In truth, he would have preferred to speculate on other things, such as seeing the Pacific Ocean come spring, but given the circumstances, entertaining such thoughts seemed inappropriate. Anton was dying and McPherson was faced on a daily basis with the poignant reminder that he was a long way from family and home. McPherson saw far too much of his own father in Schlesinger, and all too often, he was reminded of his father's parting words. At that moment, however, in the midst of a winter of epic propor- tions, a Wyoming cabin was home, and the old man and the woman were the only family he had. Dwelling on other people in distant places—even family— served no real purpose.

It was an odd sort of relationship he had wandered into in the valley, a relationship he had yet to decipher. In the beginning, he had assumed that Anton and Molly lived together out of a desire to be with one another, but after the first few days, he concluded that because of their constant and not-so-gentle bick- ering, the relation-ship was closer to that of a brother and sister. Her chiding had grown increasingly gentle as Anton's health deteriorated. Not that the dis-cussions had stopped or become less spirited; they were just delivered with a softer tongue and less bite. Such was the case one evening just past the new year. Leaning against the wall in a straight-back chair, McPherson listened in amusement to the conversation between Anton and the woman. They had been arguing for the better part of an hour, and it was obvious the conver- sation was going nowhere.

"Woman," said the old man with a certain amount of aggrava-tion, "for once, hit's time you started lis- tenin' to me. Cain't you git it through yore head thet I'm adyin'. Come spring, Jess here is leavin'n ya cain't stay here by yerself."

"An I told you afore, Mista Schlesinger, thet I ain't ever aleavin' this valley. If'n you want to die, then jest go ahead and die. But don't expect me to be apackin' my bags and goin' off with this boy after you be gone."

"Woman, you are the most impossible person I have ever come to know. I seen mules thet cooperate better'n you. Once them peo-ple find out I'm dead, they'll come in here'n take what they want." Schlesinger's efforts to convince her became strained, and the spo-radic coughing that had increasingly punctuated his breathing took on new life. Once able to breath normally, he added a more sobering thought. "Ain't gonna be nothing left here fer you 'cept pain. Woman cain't live out here alone."

"Anton's likely right," McPherson agreed. "It'd be wrong for me to leave you here. But I hear tell it's a purty good life in Oregon."

"Humph. You don't listen any more than this old man do. I ain't leavin'."

Schlesinger rolled over and faced the wall, mumbling more to himself than to the woman. "Why'n hell I ever let you stay in the first place is beyond me. Time ya started actin' like a woman thet's got some- thin' ta live fer."

McPherson sat quietly, watching as the old man drifted into a rough sleep, his breathing harsh, and labored. "He reminds me of my father," he observed, gesturing toward the restless form. "He means well."

"Thet be true," she agreed, "but meanin' well ain't understandin'."

"Truth be known, I don't understand either. Anton said somethin' about Indians…" "Wern't Injuns," she interrupted, spitting out, "Wus buffers."

• • •

Sitting on the front porch, Anton Schlesinger stretched out his legs, taking an obvious pleasure in soaking up the warming rays of the bright sunlight. The ravages of winter had taken a short break in the valley, and the respite was just the elixir he needed. Thanks to the warm winds that always seemed to show up when they're least expected, temperatures had been on the rise for better than a week, melting away the majority of the snowdrifts piled against the cabin. Blades of grass were even beginning to peek through here and there. The change in the weather had perked the old man up considerably, and his transformation was infectious: the depressive atmosphere that had been building in the cabin since he had become bedrid- den had lifted. Instead of the constant carping that went on between him and Molly, their language had taken on a lightweight bantering; and even though she railed against his going outside, she didn't really mean it.

McPherson was more than aware of the change in mood, and had left the cabin much earlier in the day, determined, he said, to find fresh game to celebrate Schlesinger's apparent recovery. When he returned late in the morning with a mule deer stretched across his horse, he approached the cabin from the corral side and was greeted by Molly with the news that 'thet cantankerous old man' was being pig-headed as usual and—against her better judgment—had insisted on sitting on the porch. Dismounting, he tied the hind legs and hoisted the deer up to facilitate skinning the animal. Molly watched him for a few minutes, all the time continuing her tirade until out of sheer frustration, she commandeered the knife and sent McPherson packing.

"I don't know who taught ya to skin a deer, Jess, but they oughta be ashamed. How you ever 'spect to survive out here is beyond me." It was all McPherson could do to keep from laughing. "Why don't you go talk to thet ol' coot. Maybe he'll listen to you. Lord knows he don't pay me no mind."

McPherson unsaddled the buckskin and turned him into the corral, and after setting his saddle in the lean-to behind the cabin, joined Schlesinger on the porch. "That is one upset woman, Anton," he said with a laugh.

"Humph," the old man grunted in reply. "She ain't near as mad as she puttin' on. Figure you could cook us up a cup of coffee?"

"Be my pleasure," Jess answered, rising to go into the cabin.

By the time he returned with the hot brew, Molly had skinned and butchered the deer, and was sitting on the edge of the porch, fussing at Schlesinger. Turning her attention to McPherson, she berated him for catering to the old man's foolishness. McPherson shook his head in amusement as he handed Anton the cup, but instead of replying, he handed her the second cup he was carrying and retreated inside for another. Retrieving a bar of soap, she announced to the both of them that she was going down to the creek and take a bath, adding that it was a chore that McPherson could well consider doing too.

McPherson settled down beside Schlesinger, taken aback by her openness as she wandered down the beaten path that led to the creek and stripped off her dress before wading into the fast-flowing water. Much as he tried not to look, he stared through the scant foliage at her nakedness, disturbed by the urgings well- ing up inside. Schlesinger studied the expressions on McPherson's face as he looked toward the creek.

"She be a good woman, boy," he offered.

"How can she do that?" McPherson asked, flustered.

"Do what, Jess?" he asked, sagaciously. "We ain't 'zackly in the midst of folks, an' she likes to be clean." The old man sipped on his coffee, debating on how to broach something he had been thinking on for the past few weeks. His time was short, about that he had little doubt. He knew that Molly was a strong woman—stronger than most—she would resist leaving, even after his death.

"You goin' back to Tennessee, Jess?"

"I suppose so, when I get my fill of wandering. Why?"

"Oh, been thinkin' 'bout you stayin' round here, meebe marryin' up with Molly once I'm gone." The silence radiating from McPherson was deafening, as his mind flashed once again on the image of Angéline Dubois, lying crumpled at his feet, dead from the knife meant for him. Not realizing that McPherson was no longer listening to him, the old man pressed the issue. "Women like her're rare in these parts."

McPherson continued to stare through the trees, catching the occasional glimpse of Molly as she casually brushed the water from her skin before starting back up the path. But the mists of New Orleans were now swirling in his head, appearing in rapid succession, each layered atop the previous one, dissolv- ing over and over into the moment of Angéline's death. Consumed by his memories, he was oblivious to her carefree air, unaware that she had momentarily set aside the realities that had taken her into a hell not of her choosing.

"…Mista McPherson."

Startled by the unexpected intrusion, McPherson recoiled, distress written graphically across his face. He had failed to see the healthy, mature woman Schlesinger was talking about approach the cabin, was ignorant to the fact that she hadn't bothered to dress. But his face turned beet red as the realization struck home that Molly was standing in front of him, naked as the day she was born.

"I asked you, Mista McPherson, to fetch me water so as I kin help this ol' coot bathe." McPherson jumped out of the chair like a shot, glad for an excuse to get away from her. He retrieved the two galva- nized buckets from inside and headed for the creek. By the time he had returned, she had dressed and was helping Schlesinger inside. "Two more buckets should do, Mista McPherson." Nodding, he made a second trip to the stream, and for his efforts, received thanks, along with orders to git himself down to the creek and wash. He didn't bother to argue.

They ate well that evening—Molly baked fresh bread to go with the deer roast, baked potatoes and fiddlehead greens that had poked up near the cabin in the mid-winter warmth—and for the first time since McPherson had arrived, the constant sniping between Schlesinger and Molly was absent, replaced with laughter more common between old friends. After a final cup of coffee, they went to sleep, ready to face whatever the next day might bring.

But the joviality of the previous day was to disappear as McPherson was wakened in the pre-dawn by the low moan of a woman in mourning. Molly had risen earlier to build a fire to take the chill out of the air, only to discover afterwards that the old man had taken his last breath sometime during the night. At first, she had refused to believe that he had actually died, but once the truth set in, her grief poured out: grief over losing her children, grief over the loss of her husband, and most of all, grief over the quiet hermit that had taken her in—with few questions, and fewer conditions.

McPherson dressed quietly, and after a futile attempt at consoling her, checked the fire, and started a pot of coffee. Once the coffee was ready, he tried again—unsuccessfully—to break through her veil of anguish. Kneeling beside the old man's bed, she lay across his body, semi-hysterical, refusing to loosen her grip. McPherson finally grasped her shoulders, gently but firmly, forcing her to sit at the table. After pour- ing coffee for the both of them, he laced it liberally with whiskey that Schlesinger had taken off one of his annual visitors and kept around for what he called medicinal purposes. She at first ignored McPherson and the coffee, her eyes fixed on Schlesinger's body, but eventually gave in to his continuing persistence, gulp- ing the mixture down and choking in the process.

Nevertheless, McPherson was at a loss. More than once, he tried to talk to her, and each time he tried, he tripped over his tongue in hesitation. He was puzzled as to what he could say that wouldn't sound condescending or trite, or that wouldn't serve to make things worse. That he had experienced the loss of his mother and a sister years before made little difference; he was no expert at dealing with the death of family. Back then, death had seemed unreal to him, and only later on, in New Orleans, had he even begun to understood the meaning of such a loss. At length, he crossed the room and pulled a blanket over the inert form before trying another time to speak to her.

"Look, Molly, I know if you had your druthers, you'd prefer to be left alone, and I'll do just that, but before I do, did he say anythin' about after…you know, about where he wanted to be buried?"

"He don't," she answered between the deep sobs that punctuated her speech as they continued to peri- odically course through her. "Said he wanted to be carried on the wind."

FOURTEEN

"He said he din't want to be put in the ground," Molly explained, acting as if she were betraying a confidence.

"Then how…?"

"Pratin's of a foolish ol' man, if'n ya ask me," she said with disgust. "Molly, what *are* you talking about?" McPherson asked impatiently.

"Stayed with some Injuns back when he wus trappin'. Figgered the way they honored their dead made sense," she replied. "We're s'posed to pile a buncha wood up and put him on top, and set it afire."

"Burn his body? But why?" he asked.

She stared at the covered remains of the old man. "Said he wus filled with evil. Thet the fire would kill whatever it wus."

McPherson sat back in his chair, pondering for a moment the concept. "Can't rightly say as how I've heard of the like. But maybe he's right."

"It ain't Christian," she muttered.

"Preacher Saulee would probably agree with you," McPherson mused. "Who?"

"Preacher Saulee. He used to come by the farm Sunday afternoons to argue with Pa and get a free meal if'n he was lucky enough to hit there at dinnertime."

"Thet's blasphemous, talkin' like thet."

"I s'pose to some folks it would be, but it's also true." McPherson retrieved the coffee pot and refilled both cups. "It's up to you, Molly. But whatever we do, it's got to be today. Another day or two of these tem- peratures…"

Molly refused the coffee and stomped out of the cabin, leaving McPherson shaking his head and wondering what he said to make her react in such a fashion. He was right about dealing with the old man's body; they didn't have the luxury of an undertaker. So that left his comments about Preacher Saulee to account for her touch-iness. He knew some folks got real defensive about religion, even when their reason- ing wouldn't hold water, but sometimes there was no accounting. Picking up his cup, McPherson stepped out on the porch to sit in the sun and await Molly's decision.

•　•　•

Given the situation, the preparations for Schlesinger's cremation went smoothly. McPherson rode off, axe in hand, to a small knoll an hour's ride from the cabin, a place specifically chosen by the old man for his last rites. Not surprisingly, most of the work was already done. Schlesinger had been preparing for his death for better than a year, and by early afternoon, the pyre was completed and McPherson was ready to return and collect Schlesinger's remains.

In the meantime, Molly pushed herself to do what she felt had to be done before McPherson returned. She readied the old man for his final sendoff, dressing him in new buckskins and wrapping him securely in a large buffalo robe. That accomplished, she went out to the corral and rigged one of the horses with a travois Schlesinger had fashioned a few years back. After tying the horse in front of the cabin, she walked down to the creek to bathe before donning a new dress she had been working on since the first snows had come. At last satisfied that everything was ready, she sat down next to the old man's body for the last moments she would spend with him alone.

As McPherson neared the cabin, he noted the horse and travois tied next to the porch. Dismounting at the corral, he saddled a horse for Molly before going inside. "You ready?" he asked softly. She nodded woodenly, her eyes reddened from the constant crying. McPherson carried the body outside, surprised at its lightness, and strapped it onto the travois. "Anton would have liked the dress."

Shunning the saddled horse, she untied the lead of the other and started out on foot. Realizing the futility of arguing with her, McPherson mounted the grey and fell in behind the travois; but as the small procession moved toward the knoll, they failed to notice the subtle change in the air. Molly, caught up in her grief, walked with an unwavering steadfastness, determined that the old man's sendoff would be proper and fitting. McPherson, for his part, was simply inexperienced with the unpredictability of weather in the west. But the change was there, and though he didn't know why, he frequently looked toward the sky, expecting to see something other than blue. At the knoll, McPherson dismounted and began to untie the strapping on the travois. Molly's reaction was instantaneous.

"Git away, Jesse. I'll do it."

McPherson backed off from the travois while she worked the leather thongs loose, reaching out to support her as she fell trying to pick up the inert form. But he pulled back, and made no further effort to help. He felt she would see any move on his part as interference, and that he wanted to avoid. Instead, he turned his attention to the sky, and tried to ignore her struggles. The change in the air was becoming more dramatic—in an odd sort of way he was reminded of the smell in the air before a storm hit East Tennessee in the spring—but here, in Wyoming in the middle of winter, the smell was different, and the uncertainty of it was making him edgy. The edginess was short-lived, however, and ignoring her cries to leave her alone, he stepped forward and picked up the body, placing it atop the pyre.

"There's a storm comin'." Molly was ignorant of McPherson's warning. Her eyes were glassy, her anguish seemingly impenetrable; her attention was focused entirely on the pyre. "You hear me, Molly? There's a storm blowin' up and we're a far piece from the cabin."

Molly continued to inspect the pyre, unmindful that McPherson was speaking to her. He picked up the container of coal oil he had brought from the cabin and poured it around the base of the pyre.

"If'n we're gonna do this, we can't wait any longer." he said softly as he offered her the matches, physically placing them in her hand.

She made no move to light the pyre; instead, she inspected the small fire sticks in child-like wonder- ment. McPherson took her by the elbow and guided her to one end of the pyre, but she ignored it. Instead, her gaze turned upward, toward the first traces of clouds moving across the sky, the beginnings of wind moving through the treetops.

"Strike the match, Molly."

"He loved this valley," she whispered. "Din't want outsiders comin' in here, spoilin' it."

"I know."

McPherson took the matches from her and lit the oil-soaked wood at various points. Molly stood her ground, engrossed in the flames as they began to spread slowly throughout the wood, at last engulfing the body of Schlesinger. Had McPherson not pulled her away, she might well have been drawn in, much as a moth is lured by a candle. As the fire intensified and became an inferno, they were driven further back by the heat. Sparks billowed upward, swirling in a funnel of smoke, and once picked up by the small gusts of wind, fanned out across the valley.

McPherson and Molly stood by the horses, each immersed in their own thoughts as they said their goodbyes. And although neither of them could put their thoughts into words, they both felt the cremation was at best inappropriate. Whatever the old man's reasons had been for taking them in, he had enriched their lives beyond their comprehension. Nevertheless, within the passing of an hour, the remains of Anton Schlesinger were consigned to the wind, and the old man had gotten his final wish.

• • •

The weather took a turn for the worse, and winter returned to the valley with a vengeance. They had all been lulled into complacence by the warm temperatures and melting snow, and had McPherson not paid some attention to his edginess, he and Molly might not have survived. They were so caught up in their emotions that they gave little heed to the clouds moving rapidly across the horizon, and even less to the falling temperature. But a violent burst of smoke and fiery sparks carried skyward by a sudden gust of wind startled the horses, and snapped McPherson out of his reflections. Glancing upward, he was stunned to see how swiftly the clouds had moved in. But it wasn't until he saw Molly shivering despite the heat still radiating from the funeral pyre that he fully realized that the storm had arrived and that they were in danger of being caught in the open.

"Come on, Molly," he said as he removed the travois from the horse. "We gotta get back." "What're you doin'?"

"Makin' it a little easier for the horse and you," he explained. "If'n we don't hurry up, we're gonna be in a pile of trouble."

"I ain't ready to leave."

"Maybe not, but you ain't got a lot of choice. Anton asked me to look after you and for the moment, that's what I intend to do."

"I kin take care 'o myself, Mista McPherson, 'n I ain't leaving' til I'm good'n ready." She walked away from McPherson and the horses toward the glowing embers of the pyre. McPherson shook his head and sighed loudly. He mounted the buckskin and rode alongside her.

"You sure you won't change your mind?"

Molly ignored him and continued walking toward the pyre. Rebuffed, McPherson's transformation was swift. Urging the horse forward, he again came up beside her, except that he no longer bothered trying to reason with her. Instead, he leaned over, and wrapping his arm around her waist, picked her up as if she were a sack of flour and laid her across the saddle. But he wasn't prepared for her resistance. She screamed, and continued to scream, first from fear, and then from hate, castigating McPherson in terms he had never heard before. They were a half hour from the cabin when the snow hit, and within minutes the visibility deteriorated to a few feet. But the adrenalin that fueled Molly's rage showed no signs of abating. When McPherson reined to a stop and dismounted to allow her to sit up, she slid off the horse and attacked him with increased fury, pummeling him with every ounce of anger she could muster.

"Enough!" he roared, grabbing her small fists. "Stop it, I said!" He had never seen such wildness in a person's eyes. She tried to pull away, but he refused to release her.

Her breathing labored, she whispered, "I'll kill you."

"If'n we don't get back to the cabin soon, you won't have to," he quipped. The snow was now becom- ing heavier, falling in large clusters, coating everything with a thick blanket of white. "We ain't dressed for this, Molly. You that eager to join Anton?"

He looked into her eyes, and thought he saw the wildness going away, believing that he could feel her relax. But he was mistaken. When he released her hands, she went straight for the horse and pulled his carbine, levered a shell into the breech and pointed it at his chest. They stood like that, facing each other for what seemed to McPherson an eternity, before he saw her knuckles whiten. She squeezed the trigger, snapping the rifle up and away the instant before it exploded, sending the bullet whistling past McPher- son's ear. As the shot became a muffled echo, lost in the trees and falling snow, the adrenalin that had fed her determination throughout the day faded away and the rifle became a dead weight in her hands, too heavy to continue pointing at him.

"I'm cold, Mista McPherson, take me home… Please."

FIFTEEN

The storm was into its third day, with no visible sign of blowing itself out any time in the foreseeable future. The depression that had lifted with Schlesinger's short-lived recovery had reappeared with his death, and it was deepening daily. The woman he had promised to take care of had come down with pneu- monia and McPherson wasn't too convinced she was going to pull out of it. He was sitting at the table as he had been for the better part of three days, watching her sleeping form as he tried to make sense out of the events of the past week, wondering what else could possibly go wrong.

They had been fortunate when the storm hit that they were but a short distance from the cabin. Even so, the distance was sufficient to make their survival questionable. Had the temperature dropped any quicker, the situation might well have become disastrous. The storm had intensified quickly, caking their clothes with snow, and just as quickly, soaking them to the skin. In McPherson's case, the buckskins he had taken to wearing since arriving in the valley had retained some of his body heat. But Molly wasn't so lucky. The thin cotton dress she had so painstakingly worked on and then worn to say goodbye to Schlesinger almost became her shroud. Made from a bolt of cloth the old man had squirreled away some time in the past, the dress was her only protection from the wintry blasts that had descended on them. But instead of protecting her, the dress had turned icy from the rapidly falling temperatures, and by the time they reached the cabin, she was numb from the cold, and was wandering in and out of consciousness.

McPherson dismounted and gathered her in his arms, almost slipping on the snow-covered porch as he carried her into the cabin. Laying her on Schlesinger's bed, he decided that there was enough leftover warmth in the cabin that a fire could wait, that getting her out of the wet clothes was more important; but when he attempted to remove the sodden dress, his numbed fingers couldn't work the fasteners. In a fit of frustration, he ripped the dress down the front and worked her arms from the sleeves. Tossing it aside, he wrapped her naked body in blankets until she looked like a cocoon, with only her face still uncovered. Only then did he realize that his own clothes were just as wet, and remember that his horse was still sad- dled. Deciding his own clothes would have to wait, he set about building a fire, while constantly checking the woman. But once the warmth began to radiate throughout the cabin, he loosened the blankets and was pleased to discover that her skin temperature felt more normal.

Outside the cabin, the visibility had dropped even further. Under normal circumstances, the trees surrounding the cabin served as a windbreak, allowing a person to work even when it was storm- ing, but this time was different. The trees were funneling the wind into a swirling wall of white, preventing McPherson from seeing much beyond the edge of the porch. It took him more than a few minutes to dis- cover that the buckskin had moved to the lee of the cabin in a vain attempt to escape the wind. Edging back around the porch, McPherson blindly led the horse toward the corral, missing the gate by a good ten yards in the driving snow, but once inside the corral, he stripped off the saddle and blanket and watched as the horse crowded in with the other animals that were huddled beneath the overhang. Hanging the saddle across the top corral railing, McPherson crawled between two of the lower rails next to the shed intending to retrieve a portion of meat that Molly had hung there for curing. But once inside the shed, he began to question himself.

The respite from the wind gave McPherson the momentary illu- sion that he was getting warmer and the urge to stop, to just sit down and wait out the storm was almost overpowering. Snow was common at the Gap, as was cold weather, but McPherson had never experi- enced anything like this. A few minutes of sitting in the darkened shed and remembering his responsibilities, however, convinced him to shake off the lethargy and struggle back to the cabin. He checked

Molly as soon as he was in the door; she was sleeping soundly and her breathing was more regular than when he had carried her in.

After changing into dry clothes, he diced the deer meat into a pot and filled it with water before set- ting it on the stove. He figured it wouldn't hurt to warm up her insides as well, and a hot broth was as good a way as any. When the water had turned into a broth, McPherson filled a cup with the liquid and sitting on the edge of the bed, gently shook Molly. She woke with a start, groggy and unaware of where she was. He helped her sit up, and put the cup to her lips, but when she refused the broth, he practically forced it down her. When the cup was empty, he refilled it and went through the whole routine again, only then allowing her to go back to sleep.

Exhausted, McPherson settled down at the table with a cup of the broth. The day had been long, a day filled with all manner of emotion, a day when he said goodbye to a friend. It was the first time since early morning that he was able to dwell at length on the abbreviated relationship he had shared with Schlesinger. The old man had shown him a different perspective to living, a perspective that his father had often expressed, a perspective that his own eagerness had often overshadowed. Schlesinger believed that the land was more precious than life, that he was nothing more than a caretaker entrusted with the well- being of his valley, and he had dedicated the final years of his life to that end. But while his dedication to the valley's preservation spared little room for outsiders, he was not uncaring. He had proven that point with the woman, and later on with McPherson. But more than anything else, the old man had made him realize that what he had walked away from in Tennessee was important. And the memories of Schlesinger would always be with him—if and when he got back home.

Molly slept straight through the night, rousing McPherson just before dawn with a fit of harsh, rasp- ing coughs. McPherson came awake slowly—he had fallen asleep at the table, his head cradled in his arms—taking a moment to get his bearings, but a second round of coughing was enough to bring him full awake. In the flickering light of the lamp, he could see that she had kicked off most of the blankets, expos- ing her nakedness to the increasingly chilly air. He stretched to rid himself of the stiffness from falling asleep sitting up, and pulled the blankets back over the still sleeping Molly, jerking his hand back as he brushed skin burning up with fever. He reached out again, gently touching her face and forehead with the back of his hand. Her eyes fluttered open as she flinched from the coolness of his touch.

"I'm feelin' a mite feverish, Mista McPherson," she whispered weakly.

"You're burnin' up, Molly." She was racked with still another fit of coughing. "And I ain't much for doctoring."

"You ain't got much choice..." She drifted back into unconsciousness. "I s'pose you're right," he muttered to himself. "Just not too sure how."

McPherson got very little sleep over the next three days as Molly's fever raged and she hovered near death. He tried different things in a vain attempt to cool her off, cold baths, the occasional cup of broth, finally a poultice, but to his thinking, his efforts seemed to be having little or no effect. But despite his pes- simism, her fever broke about the same time the storm did.

"Mista McPherson!" Molly whispered loudly. "What is thet awful smell?" Relieved, McPherson broke out in a grin. "How you feelin'?" "Terrible...`n ya din't answer mah question."

"I made a poultice...kinda like the ones my ma used to rub on me when I was sick." The few times that happened were as plain as yesterday. His mother had made a poultice of lard and coal oil and covered his chest and back with it. "It's a mixture of coal oil `n bear grease."

"Mista McPherson, thet grease wus rancid a year ago..."

"It still is. But you was bad sick and I couldn't come up with anythin' else in a hurry."

She lifted the blanket and was hit by a foul stench. "Just how much of thet stuff did ya put on me, Mista McPherson?"

McPherson reddened. "Five or six times."

"Five or six times," she repeated. "I kin believe it. Feels like I'm swimmin' in grease. Would you heat up some water? I got to wash this off'n me."

"But you're still sick."

"Mista McPherson, if'n I ain't died yet, I ain't agoin' to. Now please heat up thet water. An Mista McPherson? Thank you."

• • •

Molly recovered from her bout with pneumonia quickly, allowing McPherson to begin dealing with preparations to leave the valley. The weather had finally begun cooperating and he wanted to be on the move as soon as the snows were clear enough to get through the mountain passes to the west. The first step was to dig out more of the gold that Schlesinger had so generously offered, a proposition that seemed easy enough on the surface, but one that would prove difficult to overcome. The idea that he could ride around the countryside at his leisure, with little or no need to work in order to feed himself had proved tempting. The enthusiasm that idea generated, however, was tempered by the fact that he would have to spend more time inside the cave, a thought that immediately set him on edge.

McPherson was afraid of caves, afraid of being anywhere that was closed in, had been since the time he had crawled into a hole in the side of a riverbank when he was younger. The fear was the result of his own stupidity, but the memory was all too fresh in his mind. On one of the many fishing expeditions that he and Aaron had shared, his brother had shown him the entrance to a cave that was hidden by the river bank. They had guessed at what might be living in the cave and talked about maybe one day crawling in there and finding out for themselves. But it ended up being nothing more than talk—for his brother. One very hot afternoon, Jesse had ended up at that particular spot all by himself, and since the fish were taking the day off, he decided to explore the hole by himself.

Under different circumstances, Jesse might have thought things through before crawling into the hole; the river bank was red clay, and clay is as slick as grease when it's wet. But the entrance to the cave was high enough above the water that the sun had baked it dry. However, inside the cave entrance, the air was damp, and the clay took on a clammy feel. Just beyond the sunlight, the floor dropped away at an angle, and had Jesse paused to let his eyes adjust to the darkness, he would have seen it. But his eagerness to explore carried him to the edge, and before he could catch himself, he slid head-first into a shallow pool of water at the bottom. His initial reaction was panic—he was sure he would drown the moment after he hit the water—but once he overcame his initial fright, he realized the water wasn't deep, that he could easily stand. Looking back up the slope, he could see a portion of the cave entrance a few feet away, but it might as well have been a few miles: the slick clay prevented him from climbing out. And as the realization set in that he might not be able to get out, an uneasy dread set in. He wasn't expected back to the house before supper, and no one knew he was there.

As the afternoon passed and the light began to dim, his uneasiness increased, and once darkness set- tled in, the panic he experienced when he first entered the cave returned full-blown: he was trapped and would not be found; each sound magnified, imagined to be an animal ready to make him its next meal. Aaron found him, but not before he had experienced a night of utter terror. Once he was out of the hole, he had made the vow never to get into such a situation again. Yet here he was, faced with having to go into another cave. He should have told the old man, admitted to him that caves scared him, but the embarrass- ment was too much. So he kept the truth to himself, figuring he would overcome the fear when the time came. Nevertheless, once he arrived at the cave entrance, he knew that the terror was just as strong as it had been that very long night on Powell's River, and after a half dozen aborted attempts at crawling through the cave mouth, he gave up and returned to the cabin.

For two days he brooded over his failure to conquer his fears, refusing to answer Molly's questions, even those that had nothing to do with the cave. She pushed and prodded him, trying to break through his silence, until McPherson exploded in anger.

"Enough!" he roared.

Molly recoiled at the unexpected outburst; a mixture of shock and fear on her face. In the months McPherson had stayed at the cabin, he had not once raised his voice except for the time just after Anton's cremation.

"Seems to me, *Mista McPherson*, thet you have fergot how to act like a human bein'."

McPherson stormed out of the cabin, making a beeline toward the creek below. Molly gave him a couple of minutes before following along. He was sitting at the edge of the small pool Schlesinger had dammed up for her baths, throwing rocks into the water. She sat down beside him, this time wisely holding her tongue, watching as his rage slowly disappeared.

"Sorry, Molly, that was uncalled for."

"No, Mista McPherson, it's me thet should be sayin' sorry. Thet was unkind of me to say thet, after what you did for me."

"So we'll both be sorry."

They sat there a while longer, the warm sun of late afternoon beating down on their backs. "Kin you swim, Jess?"

"Some. My brother taught me how." "Water's deep enough in the middle." "Never been swimming with a female…" "First time fer everythin'," she laughed.

Jumping to her feet, she stripped off the dress she was wearing and waded into the water, diving into a deeper part of the pool to get past the shock of the cold. McPherson watched sheepishly as she gathered her feet beneath her and stood up, water cascading from her skin, quickly slowing to rivulets which out- lined the curves and crevices of her body. Wading back toward the low bank, she stood in front of him, hands on hips.

"You jest gonna sit there, Mista McPherson, or you comin' in?"

The thoughts racing through his head were muddled, confused. His experiences with women were truly limited. He was uncertain, not only about his own feelings, but as to how to react to Molly's mischie- vous antics.

"I don't…" Molly stooped, cupped her hand, and filled it with water, throwing it toward McPherson in the same motion. "Damn."

"Come on, Jesse, you won't melt."

She cupped both hands and tossed more water at him, laughing at McPherson's feeble attempts to avoid getting wet, again standing with hands on hips, naked and taunting. Bemused, Jesse stared at her, no longer seeing the woman that he had nursed back to health,

Angéline suddenly far from his mind. Molly tensed when he started pulling his boots off, the impish behavior still in her manner, but ready to take flight. Never taking his eyes off her, McPherson continued to undress, tossing his clothes aside as he took them off, until he stood on the creek bank, ready to join the battle.

Molly knew that the teasing was finished, that it was time to set aside the past, to forget the indigni- ties she had suffered. She had deliberately enticed this man-boy, and not for the first time, but this time he had reacted. She watched his eyes, wondering what he would do next, moving when he did to stay just out of reach, diving away when he finally lunged. She was back in the deep water by the time he recovered from the shock of the cold water, but once he joined her, she realized that the pool was too small, that she couldn't avoid him for long…that she didn't want to. Letting her feet settle to the bottom to ensure she had footing, she waited for him swim the short distance between them.

"Give me your hand," he said reaching out to her. "Take it if you want it."

He moved closer, grasping her hand and pulling her roughly toward him. Molly put up no resistance, instead wrapping her legs around his waist and grabbing handfuls of his hair to pull his lips to hers.

"This water is cold," he muttered. "Then let's git out of it," she responded.

They swam together over the short distance until the water became too shallow, where she allowed him to pick her up and carry her to the bank. He lay her down, kneeling at her feet.

"Make love to me, Jesse McPherson," she whispered, "make me forget…"

SIXTEEN

The sun's reflection was a streak of fire burning across the water as it touched, then sank below the lip of the horizon. McPherson had settled in for the night a half mile below a waterfall he discovered strictly by chance, surrounded for the most part by a forest of majestic redwoods, but with a clear view of the setting sun. He had paid little attention to the muffled roar echoing through the trees as he rode south, but as the noise increased in volume, so did his curiosity. He was reasonably confident the sound was com- ing from a source other than the ocean—unlike the ebb and flow sound of waves crashing against rocks, this noise was constant—but faced with finding a location to make camp before the light disappeared, he knew his curiosity might have to wait. This forest was no place to be wandering in the dark.

Picking up the pace slightly, he noticed that the trail seemed to climb, although the gradual rise placed little strain on the horses. As well, the roar continued to increase in volume. The climb ended sud- denly, as the trail took a downward turn to the right, crossing a shallow, fast-moving stream some fifteen feet across. McPherson was pleasantly surprised: the roar was no longer muffled, and he could once again see the sky. Stopping in the middle of the stream, McPherson allowed the horses to drink their fill while he basked in the warmth of the sun and took in the view. Downstream was a sight that would stay with McPherson for many years. The stream narrowed, the flow increasing rapidly, disappearing into a glisten- ing spray of a million rainbows. And beyond the mist was the ocean, the sun a golden circle suspended above the horizon.

Nudging the grey forward, McPherson turned onto a secondary path that ran more or less alongside the south side of the river, then veered around the outcropping forming the fall's escarpment. At the base of the falls, the roar was deafening, forcing him further downstream to within a hundred yards of the ocean where he discovered a small pool with an open grassy bank where the horses could graze. Hobbling the horses, he walked the remainder of the way to the beach to gather driftwood to keep a fire going for the night. By the time he had made a second trip he had worked up a sweat; and after spending so much time in the clammy coolness of the forest, he was ready for a much needed bath.

Stripping down, he waded into the icy water, and almost jumped out of his skin when some very large fish began nibbling at his extremities. Needless to say, he left the water much quicker than he had entered it. Once over his panic—Aaron would have found it amusing—and feeling clean for the first time in days, he set about building a fire and putting a pot of water on for coffee before digging a line out of the pack and setting off to catch supper. But it was not meant to be: the fish that were so prevalent when he was in the water had disappeared. Resigned to another night of hardtack, he quietly vowed that come morning, he would return the favor and dine on fish.

As the last traces of color disappeared from the sky, the reflections from the fire lent a friendliness to the nearby trees, while darkness took hold in the surrounding forest, softening even more the continual noise from the falls upstream and the occasional crash of a wave on the shore. McPherson leaned back on his saddle, sipping on the last of the coffee, sleep far from his mind. Instead, his thoughts drifted back to a Wyoming valley, to a man named Anton Schlesinger and to the woman he knew only as Molly: he had never learned the rest of her name.

Four months had passed since the old man had died; four months of bidding goodbyes to Molly and to a way of life that had seemingly become impossible; four months of sharing snow-capped mountains, streams swollen with the spring runoff and a trail crowded with the constant flow of people bound for Ore- gon and points north. It had been a relief when he had finally turned south along the trail that paralleled the coastal escarpment and had found himself to be for the most part alone.

He was told in Portland that the trail ran all the way to San Francisco, but was seldom traveled because of the dense timber, and after the first couple of days, he understood why. The coast was blanketed by massive trees that dwarfed anything his imagination could create. The occasional glimpse of the spar- kling waters of the Pacific would appear, last for a short while, and the bright intensity of the sun would be gone, replaced by an eerie glow created by vain attempts of sunlight to filter through the umbrella far above the forest floor and the cool dampness of rotting vegetation.

Smiling, his thoughts again focused on the Wyoming valley. He had thought the trees there were big, but they were like matchsticks compared to these red-barked giants. And their size seemed to increase the further south he rode. Anton would have marveled at them as would have Molly. Knowing the old man had been a pleasure, and being around him was a lot like being at home. More than once he was reminded of his father, especially when Schlesinger was talking about the land and a man's need to put down roots and stay put in one place. And there was the matter of the woman. After spending the better half of a year in the valley with her and the old man, often cloistered in the small cabin due to weather, he still had difficulty understanding how her mind worked.

Molly wasn't a large person, but her bark made you wonder just how bad her bite really was if she got mad. He felt a deep sense of sadness that he hadn't been able to honor the promise he had made to Anton; but she had made her intention to remain where she was crystal clear: short of dragging her kicking and screaming out of the valley, she wasn't going anywhere. Admittedly, her revelation about the buffalo hunters, scanty though it was, had fueled his curiosity. He remembered with clarity that he had literally flinched from the intense hatred of her words, but he quickly discovered that she wasn't going to elaborate, and no amount of cajoling would pry any more details out of her.

Anton had been right in his judgment about her. She was as stubborn as a Missouri mule, and as sin- gle-minded as a person could get. Although they both knew the old man's death was inevitable, McPherson discovered that when it finally occurred, he wasn't fully prepared for the burden of dealing with Schlesinger's death. But with Molly, there was no question as to what would take place: even if she dis- agreed with Schlesinger's wishes, she fully intended that they would be fulfilled. Yet in other ways, she turned out to be one of those unexpected surprises: after being caught in the storm and coming so close to death herself, she opened up in ways far beyond anything he could have foreseen, or expected.

•   •   •

The dense fog that had boiled in off the Pacific while McPherson slept was beginning to lift. Yester- day's spectacular view had disappeared sometime during the night, obscured by a heavy mantle of grey that cloaked the surrounding trees. A grey blanket was now floating some twenty feet above the ground, seemingly supported by massive tree stumps. He could see the waves breaking along the shoreline with ease, but even so, beyond the gently breaking waves the ocean and fog blended into a uniform greyness.

McPherson hunched over a steaming cup of coffee, his first of the morning, trying to shake loose the cobwebs of the night. The clammy chill of the mist and the fact that he could see no more than a few feet brought sharply back to mind his recollections before drifting off to sleep…and the dreams that followed. It wasn't difficult for him to imagine that he was once again in the midst of a winter storm. For what it was worth, McPherson figured Schlesinger would have been satisfied with his cremation, but he would have frowned on the aftermath, beginning with he and the woman being totally unprepared for the sudden change in the weather. McPherson realized in retrospect that they had been extremely lucky.

McPherson roused himself long enough to stoke up the fire. A large cast-iron frying pan containing a freshly caught trout nested in the fire—his vow of the previous night had paid off in short order. The smell of the frying fish was an odd blend with the dampness of the redwoods, reminding him of a small pool near the upper end of the old man's hidden valley. He had ridden up there with the old man on one of their many excursions before Schlesinger was taken so ill. They had spent the day fishing for trout and talking about him staying in the valley. Schlesinger had made a strong case, and he had been sorely tempted—the valley was as pretty a place as he had seen since leaving Tennessee—but settling down with Molly was just not meant to be.

On the spur of the moment, no doubt aided by the first hints of sunshine breaking through the fog hanging over the water, he decided to stay for at least another night. It would give him the chance to explore the coastline a little more closely, and give the horses a chance to fill their bellies with the plentiful grass alongside the creek before moving south. The decision made, he had a final cup of coffee before scrubbing down the skillet and dumping the remnants of the coffee pot over the fire. After making sure the pack horse was hobbled to prevent him from wandering off, McPherson saddled the buckskin and rode off along the beach.

When he returned three hours later, he could hear voices coming from the campsite. He dismounted and gun in hand, worked his way toward the voices. Two men were bent over his pack, going through it with abandon, seemingly unconcerned that the owner of the gear might return. When he was within a few yards, he cocked the pistol and announced his presence.

"Something I can help you with, gentlemen?"

The two men stood erect, one acknowledging McPherson's colt by slowly raising his hands. The other started to follow suit, but suddenly went for the single-shot Navy revolver jammed into the waistband of his pants. McPherson fired twice before the pistol cleared his belt. The first shot would have been enough.

"Don't shoot, mister," the second man cried out. "Why shouldn't I? You're a thief."

"Din't mean no harm."

"Oh? How you figure? Unbuckle the gun belt." McPherson cocked the Peacemaker as his captive started to reach with his right hand. "Left hand, nice and easy." The man complied, dropping the belt and pistol to the ground. "Now step away." Keeping his Colt trained on the would-be robber, McPherson tossed the belt and gun into the deepest part of the creek. Moments later the dead man's gun had joined the first.

"Gonna ask you once. How'd you come to be here?"

"Follered ya from Crescent City. Saw ya flashing gold when ya bought the supplies." "Why'd you wait so long?"

"Din't want to tangle with you—we could see you wus a gunfighter—just wanted yer gold." "Appears you missed on both accounts." McPherson gestured toward the dead man. "There's a shovel in my pack. Best you start digging." "What're you gonna do?"

"Depends on how fast you get him buried."

Dusk was settling in as the would-be thief tossed the final shovelfuls of dirt onto the makeshift grave of his less fortunate companion. "Alright, mister, he's buried. Now what?" The question was tinged with surliness brought on by the hours of digging and filling in the grave.

"We're gonna pick us out a tree and tie you to it so you'll be here come morning. Then I'm going to have myself some supper."

Once McPherson was satisfied that his reluctant guest was staying put, he busied himself with filling his stomach, a task made unpalatable by the constant reminder that this pleasant little hollow had been des- ecrated by two incompetent highwaymen bent on robbing him of the gold Anton had made available. And as the evening wore on, his irritation grew. McPherson at last reacted to the man's constant chattering.

"Come again?"

"Whut I said wus, it ain't right, keepin' a man trussed up like this."

"Could be you're right," McPherson replied, staring hard at the man. He got to his feet and drew his pistol, the snap of the Peacemaker being cocked echoing loudly in the nearby trees.

"You wouldn't shoot me like this?" he cried. "Why not? Make things easier for me." "That'd be murder."

"True enough," McPherson agreed, a coldness creeping into his voice, "but the way I look at things, I might be doing us both a favor. I can't just turn you loose…"

Alarmed, the robber interrupted in a vain attempt to reason. "Look, mister. This was my pardner's idea an you already kilt him. You turn me loose, you never gonna see me agin."

"Like to believe you, but if I let you go, I figure I'll be having to watch my back every minute. And I ain't partial to taking you with me, cause every living soul in Eureka would know about the gold I'm carry- ing soon as I turn you over to the law."

"Then shoot me, you sonavabitch, and be damned." McPherson pulled the trigger, the bullet slam- ming into the tree scant inches above the man's head. A second shot followed quickly on the heels of the first.

"Best you understand something, friend. The only reason you ain't already dead is that I'm no killer.

But insulting my family will get you a lot more than dead. You get my drift?" McPherson got a nod for a reply. "Now do yourself a favor and keep your mouth closed and you might make it through the night."

The remainder of the evening passed with no additional bait- ing, a circumstance McPherson grate- fully accepted. He had no real desire to back up his threat, and the stranger had seen fit not to test him. Up at first light, McPherson broke camp quickly, pausing only for coffee. The stranger watched in silence as he loaded the packhorse and saddled the buckskin. Once the horses were ready, McPherson turned his attention back to his captive.

"Where's your horses?"

"We left them up next to the falls."

"Fine." Pulling a knife, McPherson cut the rope. "Take off your boots, and hand them over." The stranger obeyed. "There's a cup of coffee over there."

"I cain't walk."

"Then best you crawl." McPherson mounted up while the stranger crawled over to the coffee and drank it down, choking in the process.

"What'er you gonna do?"

"First I'm goin' to give you some advice. What you did was wrong and by all rights, I should have shot you. I'll be mentioning this to the law in Eureka, so I suggest you go back to Crescent City and forget I ever existed. Cause If'n I every see you again, I'll kill you dead."

With that declaration, McPherson started back up the trail. The horses were where the stranger said. Dismounting, he searched the saddlebags for weapons, and finding none, cut the cinch straps and removed the saddles, tossing them and the boots into the water: if the man could ride bareback, he still had a horse.

•   •   •

The light was fading, the last rays of sun casting a deep reddish glow on the tree tops of the clearing. McPherson was lost in thought when the shots erupted from an outcropping overlooking the trail; he felt the searing burn of a bullet before he heard the gunfire. Panicked by the sudden noise, the buckskin bolted, catching McPherson off balance and throwing him. Momentarily stunned when his head hit the ground, McPherson fought off the dizziness as three men rode from behind the rocks, laughing derisively at the ease of their ambush. But any intimation of unconsciousness disappeared when McPherson recognized the man he had left behind two days past.

McPherson took stock of his predicament as best he could without arousing the suspicions of the drygulchers; he had been shot through his right side, the bullet glancing off a rib. Thinking him mortally wounded, they had paid him little attention: they were more interested in searching the pack horse and hightailing it before someone who heard the shots decided to investigate. McPherson had a second thing going for him: unlike the skittish buckskin, the pack horse was content to graze at the edge of the clearing, standing placidly while the three men stripped him of his load. They found the gold with little effort, but the discovery set off a heated exchange between them, followed quickly by drawn guns and death. McPherson took advantage of the distraction to struggle to his feet. Drawing his colt, he edged into the open clearing expecting to deal with all three, but the count was down to one. He was faced with taking the life he had spared the previous day.

"Drop it!" McPherson roared. The remaining drygulcher was standing over his two confederates.

McPherson could see that they had both been shot in the back. "Now!" "I think not," he growled, spinning on his heel and firing wildly.

McPherson returned fire and hit the stranger twice, finishing what he had started at the falls. Once his heart slowed, he noticed that the stranger's reckless shot had grazed him high on his right shoulder. A weakness settled over him, but he knew if he stopped, he would eventually die. The clatter of hooves rat- tling off rock jarred him back to life. He thumbed back the hammer of his Peacemaker as a half dozen horsemen entered the clearing with guns drawn. The lead rider was trailing the reins of the buckskin, and had a star pinned over his heart.

"Glad to see you, sheriff, got a small problem here…" McPherson said as unconsciousness took over.

SEVENTEEN

Sheriff Wilf Parker was enjoying a leisurely supper with his favorite lady, Miss Belle O'Connor, when they heard the burst of gunfire. They were reminiscing as they often did about the old days, when she was known as the Duchess of Barbary Coast and he was a wild-eyed hell-raiser from Texas come to Cali- fornia back in '51 looking for a pot of gold. He often teased her as to why he had never found the gold, facetiously blaming his misfortune on wandering into her establishment instead of heading out to the gold fields. She took his teasing in stride, knowing it was his way of explaining their thirty year entanglement. But the truth read slightly different, as she ever so often pointed out.

Parker had stumbled into the bordello late one evening, so drunk he could hardly stand. And while he was obviously more dangerous to himself than anyone else, none of the girls would have anything to do with him. Rather than allow the calm to be disrupted more than it already was, Belle took matters in hand and led him upstairs where he promptly fell asleep, even before she could get his boots off. When he woke the next morning, she was faced with a cowboy so remorseful, she had laughed at the sight, which made him all the more contrite.

Whether out of embarrassment or a lack of nerve, it took him a week to return to the house. But the change in him was nearly unbelievable. He was stone sober and carrying a handful of wildflowers which he presented to Belle with a flourish; and considering the fact she thought she had seen all kinds, Wilf Parker got to her. She saw him as one of the most brazenly presumptuous men she had ever known, and within a short time, had given over her heart. They carried on for better than a year, living as if each day would be their last, and were seldom seen in public without one another. But the idyllic existence they shared came to an end as suddenly as it had begun.

A local politician had decided that he would spend the night in Belle O'Connor's establishment—not that unusual an occurrence in San Francisco—but made the mistake in presuming that Belle would make herself available. Parker took exception, and when the man refused to take no for an answer, lost his tem- per and pistol-whipped the man until his face was a bloody pulp. Needless to say, his actions put him into an untenable position: he had the choice of leaving San Francisco, or taking on the bulk of the local law enforcement. As well, he had endangered Belle, and after a short and animated discussion, it was decided that she would sell her house and go with him. After some quick negotiations, payment was agreed upon and they fled the city just ahead of the law. Fortunately for everyone con-cerned, their pursuers gave up the chase as soon as they had cleared San Francisco County, but it wasn't until they reached Eureka some three hundred miles to the north that they stopped running.

As a rule, Sheriff Parker paid little attention to the sound of gunfire. Men shooting off pistols in a show of drunken exuberance was commonplace, and as long as the gunplay took place outside the town limits, he generally chose to ignore it. But as the echoes from the gunfire continued to reverberate through the trees, a riderless horse appeared on the North trail into town that passed in front of Belle's home.

"S'pose I best take a look, Belle. Thet buckskin ain't from around here." "See ya later?" she asked.

"Mor'n likely," he answered, buckling on his six-shooter.

Within a few minutes, Parker had located a half dozen men and headed up the North trail. There was no sense of urgency in any of them—they were merely accompanying the sheriff at his request—but a sec- ond round of firing spurred them into action. Guns drawn, they topped the rise where the trail entered the clearing to find three men on the ground, all apparently dead, and a fourth fully prepared to shoot at the first sign of a threat. But when he saw the sheriff's badge, he relaxed, muttered something, and collapsed. Parker gestured toward the three men lying on the ground before dismounting to check McPherson.

"These two are from Eureka, Sheriff. They both been backshot."

"This'uns dead too. Thet boy hit him good."

"Wilf?" Parker looked up. "You best take a look here."

"Just a second, Charley. Sam, you'n Jeff load this boy onto the grey and take him down to Belle's. And ya best do it quick. He gonna run outta blood if'n these holes ain't plugged purty soon. And tell the undertaker we got some business for him." The sheriff wandered over to where the McPherson's pack horse had continued to graze. "What you got, Charley?"

"See fer yerself."

"My God," Parker exclaimed, fighting a tightness in his chest.

The sheriff thought back to a conversation he had overheard the previous night: someone was riding in carrying a lot of gold. He had ignored the talk—discussions about the yellow metal were never-end- ing—he had listened to such talk for thirty years, to the point he sometimes wondered why he had left Texas. Nevertheless, thirty years had passed and he still dreamed about finding a mother lode, foolishness without a doubt, but the dreaming had never quit. And now he was staring at more gold than he had ever seen in one place.

"No wonder they was shootin' it up," Parker speculated. "They's enough metal here to start a bank." "Ya figure it belongs to the boy?"

"Prob'ly," Parker ventured, "his Peacemaker's only been fired twice. I'm guessin' thet most of the shootin' come from them three. They bushwhacked the boy and left him fer dead, and I imagine when they found the gold and argued about it. This'un," indicating the man from the falls, "backshot them two. He jest fergot to make sure the boy was in the same condition."

"Best we load this up."

"Me'n the others'll do thet. Ya ride back in and find Abner. Tell him to meet us at the bank so as we kin put the gold where it'll be safe, at least 'til I kin talk to the boy."

• • •

The reappearance of the buckskin at her front door, this time with a man draped across the saddle, came as no big surprise to Belle O'Connor. She was accustomed to looking after men: had been doing that very thing for most of her adult life. From her perspective, tending after a man who was injured—be it from getting in the way of a falling tree or being on the wrong end of a gun barrel—was little different from catering to a man's more prurient interests. In San Francisco, running a bordello had seemed the natural thing to do. The city was a boom town, had been since the discovery of gold at Sutter's mill, and the ratio of men to women meant that a good whorehouse was as much or more a bonanza than was the gold fields.

Eureka was another matter entirely. At the time of their arrival, the town was little more than an overgrown camp roughed out on the edge of the Pacific Ocean. She quickly discovered she was one of a dozen or so women that had made their way there, the remainder of the population consisting entirely of men hardened by the rigors of surviving long winters on traplines, or the endless days and nights of frustra- tion in the gold fields.

In itself, being one of a distinct minority wasn't a problem if she discounted the effect it had on Wilf Parker; but he was a circum- stance she couldn't set aside. As many times as she had admonished her girls for getting involved with the customers, she had eventually ignored her own advice. So rather than having to deal with an even- tual repeat of the incident in San Francisco, she took to mothering these roughshod men instead. She was convinced early on that most men were nothing more than overgrown children, and since real chil- dren were not a part of her life, she ended up offering them home- cooked meals and tending to their hurts. And while she would never openly admit to such a suggestion, her decision was deliberate.

As the years passed and Eureka's population grew, the settle- ment became a thriving community. She and Wilf Parker settled into a relationship that took on all the characteristics and convenience of a long- term marriage, except that they never got married. She thought about what it would be like to be consid- ered an honest woman, especially in the years just after they came north. They had even talked about tying the knot a time or two, but Wilf always reasoned that their getting hitched wouldn't make her any the more decent. She knew he was right, but she still periodically dwelled on the possibility.

Nonetheless, the years in Eureka had treated them well. Wilf had been elected sheriff by acclamation some fifteen years back and except for busting up the occasional drunken brawl when loggers and miners got together on Saturday nights, had spent most of his time settling disputes over bad whiskey and getting between itinerant gamblers when the cards turned bad. Belle's occasional home cooking became a cafe of sorts and eventually turned into a successful restaurant that was busy most of the time.

But Belle O'Connor had proved more than once that her skills went beyond cooking—she had func- tioned as Eureka's lone doctor in the early days of the settlement. That she was good at it was another mat- ter entirely. The tendering of medicine—even on the frontier—was considered to be a male bastion. That a goodly number of the citizens of Eureka were alive because of her skills was unimportant. Belle O'Connor was a woman, and while it was accepted that women could do a lot of things, doctoring wasn't one of them. Fortunately for McPherson, no one had bothered to explain that premise.

After getting the two men to carry him to the upstairs room, Belle shooed them out and set about undressing him and cleaning the wounds. His shoulder wound was little more than a scratch, but the hole in his side proved to be more serious. The bleeding had stopped, but the bullet had created havoc on its way out. She stitched him up as best she could and began the long process of nursing him through the fever she knew was bound to come. And come it did. For the better part of a week, McPherson wandered in and out of delirium, and each time he regained consciousness, she spooned broth into him.

At its peak, McPherson was incoherently rambling from New Orleans to Tennessee to Wyoming to a dozen places in between. Belle paid little attention to his mutterings in the beginning, but as the fever ran its course and his ramblings became less disjointed, her ears perked up. Bemused by some of the things he was saying, she had laughingly passed on a few of the more colorful remarks to the sheriff when he looked in—which was often. But any mutterings McPherson made about gold she kept to herself. She knew that even after thirty years, Wilf Parker would pack his bags in a minute if he thought he had the inside track on a find. Better the boy be protected awhile than be subjected to a grilling as soon as he was conscious.

EIGHTEEN

McPherson woke to bright sunlight and the smell of coffee and biscuits. His first thought was that he had had a bad dream and was lying in bed at home in Tennessee. When he tried to sit up, however, a sharp stabbing pain took his breath away, forcing him to lie back, reminding him that he had been shot. Wonder- ing where he was, he looked around the room for answers and found none. Sparsely furnished, the room contained the bed and a bureau. A small desk and a chair stood beside the bed. On the desk was an oil lamp and a Bible. Hanging on the wall was an embroidered sampler with a simple prayer meticulously stitched into the design. A single window looked out on tall trees and distant water. On the far side of the room opposite the window, a break in the floor suggested stairs. Outside the window, McPherson could see buildings scattered randomly amongst the trees, but other than concluding that he was in an upstairs room, he was no further ahead.

He tried to backtrack to when he was shot. Instead of paying attention to his surroundings, he had been dwelling on that afternoon when he and Molly had first made love on the creek bank. His recollec- tions were hazy, but he remembered having just entered a clearing when the shots rang out and he was thrown by the buckskin. From that point, things became even more unclear. He thought there was a gun- fight and he had killed a man; a sheriff showed up…and then he woke up in this room. He tried again to sit up, gritting his teeth against the pain, finally succeeding despite the waves of nausea that sent his head spinning. Once the room had stopped moving, he reached out for the chair and dragged it across the wooden floor, intending to use it as a support to stand, but he never got that far.

"So yer awake, are ya?" McPherson jerked his head around as a woman's voice spoke sharply behind him. The nausea returned full force. "Best you lay back down, young`un." Gentle hands forced him down on the bed. "An cover yerself up."

Realizing he was naked, he pulled the quilt up to his shoulders, his face turning beet red. "Where am I?"

"You be in my home. The sheriff asked me to care fer ya `til you be on yer feet agin." "How long…?"

"Two weeks. Weren't too sure you'd make it fer awhile cause ya lost a fair amount of blood." The woman sat down beside the bed. "Sheriff'll be wantin' to talk to ya. He be real curious `bout all thet gold." McPherson took a moment to digest the information. "I suppose I owe you my life."

"We'll talk `bout thet."

Surprised at her answer, McPherson took a long look at the woman sitting beside him. At first glance, she didn't appear to be anything out of the ordinary: middle-aged, greying hair pulled back in a bun, a soft face that still retained the beauty of a younger woman. She was dressed in a simple cotton dress and except for a narrow copper bracelet, wore no other jewelry. But it was her eyes that caught his attention: the hazy blue color was like looking at a late afternoon sky.

"How're ya feelin'?" "I'm hungry."

"Good," she nodded. "I'll let the sheriff know yer alive."

After the woman had disappeared down the stairs, McPherson tried sitting up again, this time work- ing slowly to prevent the dizziness from hitting him, until he was leaning back against the brass framework at the head of the bed. Hearing the woman coming back up the stairs, he pulled the quilt around his shoul- ders. She was carrying a tray filled with a plate filled with eggs, grits and buttered biscuits, and a cup of steaming coffee. She laughed when she saw how he was sitting in the bed.

"You plannin' on eatin' this under the covers?" "But I'm naked," he exclaimed, reminding her.

"You surely are an' you be a good lookin' man, but ya cain't be eatin' with thet quilt wrapped around ya like some Egyptian mummy." McPherson let the quilt drop to his waist, allowing her to put the tray on his lap. "Hell's bells, boy. If'n I was a younger woman, I'd fer sure be achasin' ya, but them days be past. Now you be eatin' slow. I don't want to be cleanin' this up cause ya couldn't keep it down."

While the woman sat and watched, McPherson forgot his manners and her admonition and dove into the food, wolfing it down as quickly as he could get it to his mouth. He attempted to drink the coffee the same way but after scalding the roof of his mouth, decided he might be better off sipping it until it cooled off.

"Thank you."

"Yer welcome."

"Two weeks?" She nodded. "Who undressed me?"

"I did, if'n it matters." McPherson reddened again. The woman smiled at his discomfort. "Ain't the first time I undressed a man—the circumstances was just different."

"Yes ma'am."

"Now s'pose you tell me who ya are. Don't like strangers in my home." "Jesse McPherson…" adding as an afterthought, "from Tennessee"

"Well. Good afternoon, Jesse McPherson from Tennessee. Welcome to Eureka. Folks here 'bouts call me Belle."

"Pleased to meet you."

"Tell me, Mister Jesse McPherson, what brings you to California? Thet gold ain't from around here." "Curiosity, mostly."

"Well thet curiosity 'bout got you kilt."

"It wasn't my curiosity—I just got careless."

"It be much the same thing," she retorted. Hearing footsteps on the stairs, she announced, "Sheriff's here. You ain't asked, but fer my opinion, you oughta go on back to Tennessee."

"Afternoon, Belle. How be yer patient?"

"Wilf," she answered, acknowledging his greeting. "I figure he'll live. He got a logger's appetite." "You mind us talkin' fer a bit?"

"I'll go refill his coffee. You want a cup?"

"Thet'll be fine, Belle." The sheriff pulled up the chair and sat facing the back. "Quite the mess you got yerself into, Mister McPherson. Yer lucky to be alive."

"So Belle tells me, Sheriff."

"Mind tellin' me how ya happened to get into thet shoot-up?"

"Weren't of my choosing, sheriff…" McPherson recited the events leading up to the shootout in the clearing, beginning with finding the two men going through his pack at the falls.

"I 'spect yer tellin' the truth. Them boys thet wus backshot been lookin' fer a place to die fer years.

I'll check with Crescent City on the other one. Shouldn't take mor'n a day'er two."

Belle reappeared with the coffee. "It's Wilf Parker ya owe yer life to, Jess. Hadn't been fer him deci- din' to check out them first shots we heard, you'd a bled to death afore anybody found ya."

"Then you also have my thanks, Sheriff… What happened to my horses?"

"I put them in a livery 'til we knew you wus gonna live… And afore you ask, I stuck the gold in the bank. Real dumb to be carrying thet much metal."

"Hadn't stopped long enough to think about it."

"Well, best ya start. Word got around right quick after we brought you in, an I expect most of Eureka knows about it by now… And a lot of them are gonna be right eager to find out where thet gold come from."

"What do you suggest?" "Depends on where yer headin'." "I'm not welcome here?"

"Yer carryin' a pack of trouble, Mister McPherson, and I ain't wantin' any. They's more here jest like the ones thet met you outside of town. Just a matter of time afore one of 'em takes another try at ya."

"All right, Sheriff. I'll move on soon as I can travel."

"Best fer all concerned," the sheriff agreed. "By the way, if'n it was me, I'd be gettin' a cashier's note from Wells Fargo for most of thet gold and be cashin' it when I was needin' it."

"I'll keep that in mind."

Satisfied he had convinced McPherson to leave, the sheriff emptied his coffee cup and set it on the table beside the bed. He was thankful that he hadn't been forced to confront this grown up boy.

In spite of the gold he was carrying, it was clear he was no miner and facing up to a fast draw artist was not something Wilf Parker relished at this stage in life. The manner in which McPherson wore the Peacemaker signified one thing: he was a gunfighter, and that spelled trouble.

"Ya picked the wrong profession, Belle, ya shoulda took up doctorin'." "They was a time you wouldn't a said thet, Wilf."

"Din't mean it thet way, but I expect yer right," Parker replied. Turning to McPherson, "Any idea where you be goin' from here?"

McPherson shrugged. "South, I imagine."

"Well, when yer up and about, come by my office. I should have thet answer back from Crescent City and you kin pick up yer guns. Be seein' ya, Belle."

"I'll go down with ya, Wilf."

McPherson was left alone to mull over the sheriff's visit. He caught snatches of conversation from downstairs—the gist of which concerned him—but he couldn't make out enough for it to make any sense. One thing was certain: his presence in this house and in Eureka was for some reason an intrusion. The sher- iff's apparent uneasiness suggested a lot more than he was letting on.

•   •   •

The afternoon moved slowly as McPherson mulled over the sheriff's visit. His introduction to Wilf Parker and their subsequent conversation left him with a lot of unanswered questions—beginning with the sheriff's apparent uneasiness and the distinct suspicion that he was somehow interfering. His thoughts were interrupted by the reappearance of Belle carrying a tray filled with fresh bandages and various metal uten- sils.

"On yer belly," she requested, setting the tray down on the table. "Time to git them stitches out." "Stitches?"

"Yep. Thet bullet ya took in the side come out funny. Wonder is it din't do worse damage." "How soon can I leave?"

"Don't be in too much of a hurry. You be healin' purty good, but ya could still break it open agin." "How long?"

"Week at least, better two." He felt her snipping the thread. "This'll hurt some." McPherson lay qui- etly while she pulled the sutures free and cleaned the wound.

"I'm thinking you'd be happier if'n I was gone in a week."

Belle stared at the wound for a moment before applying a new dressing. "An you'd be right thinkin' thet, Mister McPherson, so best ya keep them thoughts to yerself. Turn over."

McPherson rolled over gingerly, allowing Belle to pull a smaller bandage loose. She worked quickly to clean the raw tissue and cover it with a clean bandage.

"Why?" he asked suddenly. "Why what?"

"Why you so edgy about me bein' here?"

"You be healin' well, Mister McPherson," she replied, avoiding his question. "Well enough to leave in a week?" His question was more of a statement. "Yes," Belle let out a long sigh. "Well enough to leave in a week."

"Then it's settled," he declared with finality. The tension in Belle noticeably eased. "Now suppose you let me in on what's bothering you."

Belle busied herself for long minutes, fussing with cleaning up the soiled bandages, carrying the tray back downstairs. She returned a few minutes later with two cups steaming with hot coffee and sat down beside the bed. Taking a deep breath, she finally answered McPherson with three short words.

"It's the gold."

"What about the gold?"

"It's what some folks call a long story," she answered hesitantly. "Thirty year ago…"

Belle's narrative enthralled and often saddened McPherson as he saw parallels with his own life. Beginning with the early days on the Barbary coast when she first worked in and then ran a bordello, Belle recounted the coming of Wilf Parker and how she had fallen for him against her better judgment, laughing as she shared fond memories of those heady times. She described Parker's eventual confrontation with a San Francisco politico and the aftermath of their sudden flight from the city. But the bulk of her reminisc- ing dealt with their arrival in Eureka and the life they had enjoyed over the years.

At the same time, Belle tried to explain about the fever that was still prevalent in California, an obsession for the yellow metal that transcended the realm of common sense, frequently dominating every phase of a man's existence. McPherson leaned back against the headboard, his understanding becoming clearer, realizing that her biggest fear was losing Parker to some illusory gold field.

"Molly wouldn't take kindly to someone showin' up unexpected," he mused.

"Sorry. I din't…"

"Just thinkin' out loud," McPherson explained. "Who is she?"

"Molly?" McPherson smiled. "You might say she's the gold's protector; which is why I won't be passing on the location."

The tension etched in Belle's face melted away. "Time I fixed supper," she announced, adding almost as a warning, "Wilf'll probably be joinin' us."

"You figure I could put him off 'til tomorrow? Don't think I'm up to fighting off a bunch of ques- tions."

Their unspoken conspiracy agreed upon, Belle gathered up the empty cups and disappeared down the stairs. McPherson stared out the window at the setting sun, watching the shadows deepen amid the build- ings and trees. No, he thought, Molly wouldn't take kindly to outsiders. The last few days he spent with her were testament to that…

NINETEEN

Except for the glow of a lantern through the lone window of the cabin, darkness in the valley was complete. Inside the cabin, McPherson was stretched out in the loft, anticipating the whisper of Molly's bare feet on the ladder. Each evening for the better part of three weeks, they had repeated a ritual that was as old as time, seldom deviating from an established routine. While she fixed supper, he tended to the ani- mals. At length, they would wander down to the creek together to bathe. He would eventually come back to the cabin alone and climb into bed; she would follow a few minutes later. Lying in the near darkness, he would listen as she rustled around the cabin, every sound she made amplified in the loft. Eventually she would turn the lamp out and the sounds would momentarily disappear before she climbed the ladder and crawled into his arms. But just as the relationship between them had gone through a radical change three weeks previous, it was about to undergo another.

In retrospect, it was a foregone conclusion that given enough time, they would eventually share a bed. Their lovemaking was nothing more or less than the next phase in a sequence that began with the onset of the mid-winter thaw: Molly openly parading her nudity; Schlesinger's illness and subsequent death; McPherson nursing Molly back to health. Each of the circumstances contributed to an intimacy that grew between them, culminating one sunny afternoon on a creek bank. But by nightfall, the certainty of their act had unsettled them both, to the point that they sat in the cabin unable to talk to one another, a cur- tain of embarrassed silence separating them as effectively as a stone wall.

McPherson was mystified. He sensed that the circumstance of the afternoon had filled a void for both of them, that there was nothing wrong with what they did. He knew little of her past other than what the old man had seen fit to pass on—she was able to shut out the memories most of the time, but they peri- odically surfaced like a bad dream, twisting her insides into knots that took days and weeks to dissipate. But he recognized that when she finally abandoned her pretense, openly seeking a physical release, she was at the end of a self-imposed imprisonment.

His own needs were much easier to understand. The old man had recognized them for what they were soon after he had arrived in the valley, had made suggestions that McPherson had outright rejected. Angéline might be nothing more than a memory to anyone else, but he had refused to let her go. Now he was faced with looking at his own motives and coming to terms with a different reality in the form of Molly.

McPherson was out of bed at first light. He had spent a restless night, wandering in and out of sleep, much as he had when Molly was so ill. He wanted to reach out to her, to regain the moment they had shared, but their lovemaking had confused things, and forever changed the way they would look at one another. He reacted to every sound during the night, envisioning, wanting her to climb the ladder and take away the doubt of their intimacy.

But Jesse McPherson wasn't the only one who had a long night. Molly was up even before he was, had rekindled the stove, put on a pot of coffee, and disappeared outside. After pulling on his boots, he filled a cup and went out on the porch. Molly was saddling a mottled horse the old man had traded for with a member of the Nez Percé tribe. He noticed his own horse was already saddled. Seeing him on the porch, she finished up and wandered back from the corral.

"Couldn't sleep," she offered.

"I know the feelin'. We goin' someplace?" he asked.

"Thought we could ride up the valley. Maybe see about thet cave." "What about the cave?"

"It's what's botherin' you, ain't it?"

"Anton said you knew nothin' about it," he answered in a half-hearted denial.

She laughed. "Thet old bastard couldn'ta kept a secret if'n his life depended on it. Sides, I walked all over this valley'n I been there at least a half dozen times."

"But..."

"Mista McPherson... In another week or two, them snakes gonna be all over the place. If'n yer gonna git any of thet gold afore you leave, then you best be agittin' it." McPherson's jaw tightened. He stomped back into the cabin, Molly following closely on his heels. "Thet's the second time you walked away from me, Mista McPherson. Why is thet?"

He fought back the urge to lash out again. "I... I can't go back inside the cave."

"Why not?" There was now an edge in her voice, which only served to inflame McPherson's already aggravated perspective: admitting defeat was almost as bad as his failure to overcome the fear itself. "Mista McPherson..." she started, but her flippant tone disappeared when she saw the pain in his eyes. "Ain't nothin' thet bad, Jesse."

"Depends on who's doin' the figurin'."

"I s'pose, but it don't change anythin' either." Molly dropped the subject, busying herself with fixing breakfast. But once they had finished eating, she again suggested going up the valley.

"I ain't goin' to the cave."

"So you said. Thet mean you ain't comin' with me?" "Didn't say that," he growled.

The sun was an hour above the eastern ridge when they finally mounted up, Molly taking the lead, McPherson content to follow along as she turned onto the trail leading north. The valley was alive with singing birds and new growth on the small groves of aspens that were interspersed among the tall fir. He wasn't too surprised that she rode straight to the small knoll where they had said goodbye to the old man, although he had fully expected that she would head for the cave. Other than a remnant or two of charred wood, little remained to remind them of the cremation. The scorched earth was covered with blades of new grass and by fall, all traces of the fire would be gone.

"Hadn't been fer him, I'd been food fer the coyotes," she remarked. "Jesse, how come you never asked about me?"

"Wasn't any of my business"

"All the same, wasn't you the least bit curious?"

"Be lying if I said different," McPherson admitted, "but it wasn't for me to be asking." "He never asked either, but he never looked down his nose after I told him."

"He wasn't one to be judging."

"Oh, he judged alright. Made up his mind real quick, and whatever he decided about somebody, he stayed with. Thet's why he let me live here—and why he let you stay. He trusted you."

"He say that?"

"Not in so many words, but it's true. You think he woulda asked you to take care of me if'n he din't?" "I suppose not."

"It makes all the sense in the world, Jesse McPherson. He looked at you and seen himself. He seen the man he was when he come out here fifty year ago. Thet's why he told you 'bout the cave. He din't want you to spend yer life chasin' dreams like he did." When McPherson tried to protest, she shook her head and rode off, yelling back across her shoulder, "Arguin' won't change the truth, Jess McPherson."

McPherson swallowed as he watched her disappear into the trees. She had trapped him into returning to the cave whether he was ready to or not. Faced with honoring the old man's request to look after her, he had little choice but to follow along. By the time he reined up at the base of the rock face, she had dis- mounted and was already climbing up the ledge to the cave's entrance. He watched her pause to pick up a handful of loose gravel and toss it through the opening before crawling inside. Moments later, he heard her scream his name and hit the ground running.

"Molly?" he yelled. When she didn't answer, he forgot about his fear and literally flew up the path. Twice he slipped on the gravel, the second time almost losing his balance completely. At the cave entrance, he scooted through, gun drawn. Blinded by the dark, he called out. "Molly? Where are you?"

"I'm right beside you."

McPherson jumped, his paranoia returning full bore. He swung toward her voice, cocking the pistol as he turned, hesitating to pull the trigger only because he couldn't see. Molly struck a match and lit the lantern, almost dropping it when she saw the gun pointed at her. She stared at him wide-eyed, not daring to breath, aware that she had almost died.

"My god, woman, I almost shot you."

Letting her breath out, she whispered, "I'm right pleased you din't." "You alright?"

"I'm just fine…now," she replied, her voice returning. "I heard you scream."

"An you come to save me like I figured." McPherson slumped against the cave wall.

"You did this just to get me in here?" She nodded, reluctantly admitting her misjudgment as to how he would react. "Anton was right, you *do* need somebody to look after you. That crazy stunt about got you killed."

"Guess yer right," she admitted, "but look on the bright side. It worked." "And now I'm gonna leave."

"Why? You ain't no worse off, are ya?"

For one brief moment, McPherson allowed that if he ever met a woman who suffered him to make a decision without first arguing about it, he'd marry her. But in this instance, he conceded that Molly was right: if he was ever going to dig out the gold, there was no time like the present.

"I'll live," he answered tight-lipped. "Let's be gettin' on with it."

The remainder of the day went smoother than McPherson could have expected or hoped for. With Molly's help and encouragement, they dug out more than a pound of the metal before the walls begin to close in on him. She kept his mind occupied by talking a blue streak about her childhood and her hopes and aspirations when she first got married. And as much as he hadn't wanted to talk about himself, he had finally opened up about that terrible night he had spent underground alone. By late afternoon they were back at the cabin, caked with dirt and smelling of horses and dried sweat, and laughing with the light-heart- edness of children. They unsaddled the horses and turned them into the corral and while McPherson gave them a treat, Molly disappeared into the cabin. As McPherson walked across the yard, she reappeared car- rying towels and soap.

"C'mon, Jess, you smell as bad as I do."

Grinning, he trailed along behind down to the creek and watched her as she stripped to her skin before following suit. After a few minutes of gentle horseplay, they soaped each other from head to foot, then went swimming to rinse the soap off. The light-heartedness was still present, but faded slowly as the tension of their nudity and closeness took hold. Climbing out of the stream, they dried off, picked up their clothes and walked back to the cabin, tossing the dirt-encrusted clothes into a pile on the porch. McPherson gathered her up, intending to carry her through the door, but discovered rather quickly that Molly had other ideas. Putting her back on her feet, he sheepishly followed her through the door. Suddenly embarrassed by their nakedness and unsure as to what had happened, he climbed up to the loft to get a pair of denims while she slipped on a cotton shift.

When at last she busied herself with supper, he climbed back down the ladder and fired the lamp, using the distant howl of a wolf as an excuse to check on the horses. When he finally came back inside, they ate in silence, searching for a word or words that would extricate them from their discomfort. But each time Molly tried to explain her reaction, she looked at McPherson and saw misunderstanding, and the words would catch in her throat. Jesse found conversation just as difficult, and after stumbling over his tongue a half dozen times, mumbled a goodnight and retreated to the safety of the loft. The ritual started that night.

TWENTY

McPherson was troubled. He conceded that understanding women was not his strong suit, a good thing considering that Molly had confused him totally. Not since Angéline had he been with a woman in that way, but at the slightest suggestion that he and Molly might again make love, she had come close to panic. Strangely enough, there hadn't really been that much of a suggestion—all he did was pick her up on the porch—but his actions were sufficient to turn her body into knots.

Time crawled as he tossed and turned, trying without success to sleep. He was conscious of every sound as Molly readied herself for bed, but as much as he tried to ignore the sounds, his efforts only seemed to heighten their intensity. But as the last vestiges of light disappeared when she turned down the lamp, so momentarily did the sounds. When they reappeared, they were more like a whisper, coming from directly below him. Only when she touched his bare arm did he realize she had climbed the stairs and was now beside him.

"You scared me when you picked me up… Made me remember somethin' I wanted to fergit." "Didn't mean to…"

"Shhhh…" Molly reached out in the dark and pressed his lips. "You din't know. Is there room under yer blanket fer me, Mista McPherson?"

Jesse lifted the blanket enough for her to slide into his bed, only a little surprised that the cotton shift she had been wearing was gone.

"Your skin is cold."

"Then best you warm me up, Jesse McPherson."

McPherson awoke the next morning alone. Molly had fallen asleep in his arms, but unbeknownst to him, sometime during the night she had returned to her own bed and the pattern was set. Twice more they returned to the cave: the first trip they brought back another pound or so of gold; the second trip became an encounter with a nest of rattlers on the rampage. During the day, nothing was said about their lovemaking, but come the night, they would go through the same routine: eating and bathing together, then searching out their physical limits until exhaustion set in; and each night she would fall asleep in his arms, and each morning he would wake up alone.

But just as their sharing a bed was certain, it was inevitable that a parting of the ways would become a reality. Molly began speaking of the time when he would leave, at first casually dropping hints into their daily conversations, then mentioning it more and more frequently until his impending departure was the primary topic of conversation. And while McPherson was hedging on when he would leave, had even con- sidered the possibility that he wouldn't leave at all, Molly had for all intents and purposes packed his bags. Yet each night, she would climb the ladder to the loft.

• • •

His final night in the valley started out much as the others had over the past few weeks. He and Molly had gone down to the stream together to bathe, but on this occasion, the bath took a little longer, the horseplay a little more sedate. At length, they waded to the bank, roughly toweling the water from each other. Instead of waiting for him to return to the cabin alone, Molly walked slowly up the hill beside him, now and then letting her hand brush against his. Inside the cabin, she stood on her tiptoes and cupping his face in her hands, kissed him softly again and again. Jesse pulled her tight against him and returned the kisses, marveling that her nipples felt like the heat of sun through a piece of glass. For a brief moment, he stopped breathing, reluctantly easing his embrace as he felt the muscles in her back tense up. He was sur- prised and delighted when Molly didn't pull away.

"Go on up to bed, Jess," she urged. "I'll be there in a few minutes."

His breathing slowly returning to normal, Jesse climbed the ladder and stretched out on bed. Savor- ing the sensation, McPherson thought little of the deviation from their nightly routine of the past weeks. He was content to listen as Molly scurried about before dousing the lamp and joining him. He could never fig- ure out what it was she did each night before climbing the ladder, but he refrained from peeking rather than invade what little privacy she had. As the lamp's glow disappeared, his anticipation was underscored by the sound of her foot on the bottom rung of the ladder.

A subdued glow reappeared as she set the lamp to one side in the loft, well away from his bed. As she stepped onto the loft's floor, the light from the lamp accented the outline of her body beneath her thin cotton gown. Moving with the speed of molasses, Molly tantalizingly hiked the gown's hem to mid-thigh before kneeling beside him, the soft glow behind her creating a fiery halo in her hair. The effect on McPherson was mesmerizing. Leaning forward, she ran her fingers across his chest and stomach in a gen- tle caress, tracing the thin line of downy hair that ran from his chest to the thatch below. Bending over him, her lips traveled a similar path to that of her fin- gers moments before.

Raising up on her knees, she pulled the shift over her head. The fiery halo in her hair now spread around her body as the lamp's glow reflected off the damp sheen of her skin. Cupping her breasts, he rolled her nipples between his fingers until a moan escaped from deep within her, sliding one hand down across her belly through the bushy triangle to the open crease between her legs, eliciting from her a sudden effort to breathe.

"Damn, Jess…"

Molly's emotions were bordering on madness. Things were not progressing as she had planned. Come morning, she would send this man away, yet her hunger for his love was peaking in a way she had never experienced, never anticipated. She was fluctuating between laughter and tears as wave upon inde- finable wave washed over her, wondering how much more she could stand before she exploded. Collaps- ing beside him, she smothering his face with kisses, aston- ished that she was affected so.

Molly watched with curiosity as Jesse knelt at her feet, sensed his hands as he caressed her thighs with a feathery touch. What little composure she had left disappeared along with her self-control as the indefinable waves of lightheadedness returned, drowning her with the magnitude of her feelings.

She cherished the moment, thinking that nothing was more important, that she could die tomorrow and it wouldn't matter, but the notion disappeared along with the heat of euphoria. Jesse McPherson stay- ing in the valley could not, must not be. At length, Molly pulled a quilt over them to fight off the chill in the air. He would be leaving tomorrow, but she intended to be with him until he left.

"Jess?" she whispered, snuggling closer to him, "I wish… I wish things could been different." "From what?"

"From" She avoided answering him, choosing instead to bury her head in the hollow of his shoulder. "I'll tell you later…"

Except that she never did. The last night he spent in the valley was very clear to McPherson, or at least as clear as it could be given that Molly never explained what she meant about things being differ- ent. They repeated their lovemaking, though not to the same extent, and she slept beside him for the remainder of the night, a small detail he sincerely regretted experiencing but the once.

McPherson's gaze out the window had become a hardened stare. The sun was a distorted ball in the distance, a dull red reflection in the late afternoon haze. Any other time, the view would have enthralled him, but having once more dragged out the details of his departure from the valley, his mood had turned sour. He had decided that the old man was right, that he could do a lot worse, but instead of talking about the possibility with Molly, he just assumed she felt the same way. At the time, he heard a thinly veiled plea that he leave, and if he had listened, he would have realized it. In retrospect, how- ever, he could very plainly see in his mind's eye that she had planned his leaving, beginning with the ride to the cave, and as far as he was concerned, it finally made perfect sense.

"You look real serious, Mister McPherson." Belle's reappearance startled McPherson, so deep was he in his reminiscing.

"Just rememberin'."

"Molly?" McPherson nodded.

"Then maybe ya shouldn't a left her behind."

"'Shouldn't of' is gittin' to be the story of my life," McPherson replied bitterly. "I shouldn't of left Tennessee; shouldn't of fallen in love with a whore in New Orleans; shouldn't of left the valley…"

"You missed one, Mister McPherson. Ya shouldn't of been carryin' all thet gold around neither." "Like I said."

"Now s'pose you come downstairs and sit down to supper like normal folks. Wilf ain't gonna be around tonight."

Moving very gingerly, McPherson retrieved pants and a shirt from the cupboard. Sitting on the edge of the bed, he struggled with the pants, biting his lip to fight off the pain. He found putting on the shirt even more difficult. He couldn't remember ever having so much trouble getting dressed, but in time, he was able to inch down the stairs and join Belle at the table.

"You gonna make it?"

"I'll live, but if I got a choice next time about gittin' shot, I think I'll pass."

"Don't doubt it. But you keep movin' around and most of that soreness'll go away in a day'er two.

Now sit yerself down, food's gittin' cold."

"How come the sheriff never married you, Belle?" "Don't figure he thought it was necessary."

"You ever tell him you wanted to get hitched?"

"A time or two, but he's always known thet marryin' me wasn't necessary: I was always gonna be there. Don't matter," she added, "I love him anyhow."

"He know how special you are?"

She smiled. "He knows. The old fool's jest too pig-headed to admit it." She got up to pour them a fresh cup of coffee. "Seems to me ya got some of thet same kinda stubbornness."

"Don't know what you mean."

"Then why'd ya leave yer Molly behind?"

"Didn't have a whole lotta choice. She was holdin' a scattergun on me." "What in God's name did ya do to her?" she asked incredulously. "Been askin' myself the same question."

"You come up with an answer?"

"None that I cared for. Seems to me like falling for a woman is bad luck." "Humph. Thet street got two sides to it, Mister McPherson. Did you love her?" "I don't know."

"And what about this Angéline? Did you love her?"

Unconsciously, McPherson closed his eyes to shut out the image of Angéline lying in a pool of blood.

"I only knew her for three days."

"Didn't ask you how long you knew her." McPherson looked away, but before he did, Belle saw the truth written across his face. "Then why didn't you marry her?"

"She's dead. Took a knife that was meant for me."

"No *whore* would have done that, Mister McPherson," she observed caustically. "Wasn't intendin' to suggest anything."

"Bite yer tongue," she snapped. "I know ya called her a whore cause you be mad about somethin', but thet's a word I never cottoned to, even when I was plyin' my trade. So you rode all the way up to Wyoming to git away from the memory, ceptin' it didn't work. And now you be sittin' here tryin' to understand another woman when you never figured out the first one. Boy, if'n you don't take all."

Flustered by her tongue-lashing, McPherson paid close attention to the remaining food on his plate, wishing she'd drop the subject. But although her words were more gentle, Belle wasn't quite ready to let it go.

"Mister McPherson, you cain't be goin' through yer every day dwellin' on lost loves."

"Belle, I don't know how I'll ever be able to repay your hospitality," he began, choosing his words carefully, "but I can't see that discussing private matters is gonna make it any the more easy." McPherson felt trapped between a desire to keep his misery private, and showing the proper respect.

"Mister McPherson, the day you ride outta here and take the secret of thet gold with you, any debt you might'n be owin' to me will be paid in full. As far as yer privacy is concerned, I was only tryin' to help. Bein' nosy and buttin' in where I ain't welcome ain't my way."

Chagrined, Jesse tried to make amends. "I apologize for my shortcomings, Belle. I was taught better than that. It's just that sometimes the whole thing eats away at me, and…"

"And you think thet somehow, it's all yer fault," she added, finishing his thought.

"Wasn't her idea to leave. I talked her into it. She'd still be alive if I hadn't tried to take her away." "You don't know thet. Besides, I seriously doubt you coulda talked her into leavin' if'n she hadn't wanted to go."

"I wish…"

"Ah, Jesse, you sure are somethin'. Women who… *Decent* folk figure thet any woman who ends up workin' in sportin' houses ain't fit to walk down the same side of the street. Don't especially matter thet given a choice, many of 'em would just as soon be married and raisin' youngun's; they still be considered the scum of the earth. It ain't right, but them folks don't tend to let a little thing like right guide their opin- ions. 'Once a whore, always a whore' they say. It's no wonder I hate thet word. Ya git stared at and pointed out and just generally shunned by the so-called good men and women of the community, and at night, them same men would visit us to git what they couldn't git at home.

"What I be gittin' at is thet ya learn to never let things git personal 'twixt you and the customers, thet if you do, you'll just end up gittin' hurt. Then along comes somebody a little different, and ya git involved in spite of yerself. But when a woman's bedded fifty or a hunnerd different men, it be difficult to convince one of 'em thet he be special, even when he wants to be convinced."

"I gather you never convinced the sheriff?"

Belle grimaced self-consciously. "Some of us just never take our own advice." "And you're putting me in the same category as him?"

"No, Mister McPherson, you put yerself there. But you be young enough to learn from it." "Which brings us back to Molly…"

TWENTY ONE

McPherson recovered from his wounds quickly, and true to Belle's word, the sheriff's interest in the gold was more than passing. McPherson tried to skirt the issue, but Sheriff Parker became more and more blatant with his questions, finally coming right out and asking for the location of the lode.

"Sheriff, I'm afraid that's one answer you're gonna have to live without."

"Mind tellin' me why?" he asked, his irritation showing. "It ain't like it be all yourn. You as much as said there ain't been no claim filed."

"You're right," McPherson conceded, "but there's a reason."

"Thet ain't good enough, Mister McPherson. I brought you in, protected yer belongin's. Belle nursed ya back to health. The least ya could do is share some of yer fortune with the both of us."

"Fully intend to, Sheriff," McPherson replied coolly. "I was raised to show gratitude where it's due. But at the risk of offending you, my gratefulness doesn't extent as far as you might like. If I tell you, then I might as well tell the whole town."

"Belle deserves better from you."

"Can't argue. We already talked about it. But you ain't asking for Belle's sake." "You be a greedy man, McPherson."

Jesse bridled at his accusation. "Sheriff, I'm gonna forget you said that. I appreciate what you've done for me, but you're pushing hard. I told you there was a reason, and there is. Suppose you answer me a question: you a good shot?"

"Good enough. Why?"

"Can you hit a man at three hundred yards?"

"What's thet got to do with anythin'?" the sheriff asked angrily.

"Where the gold is, there's a woman, lives there all by herself. She ain't partial to strangers paying a visit when they ain't invited."

"So?"

"Well, Sheriff, there's only one way in there, and since she's a dead shot from that distance, the only way you could get at the gold would be to kill her—that's assuming she missed you. And to be honest, I'd take real exception if you or anyone else did that. Now if you'll excuse me, time I be getting my things together. I'll be pulling out in the morning."

McPherson left the sheriff's office with Parker sitting behind his desk, his chin sitting on his chest. He hadn't intended to talk to the lawman that way and certainly had not intended to threaten him, but he felt it necessary to get the word around that he wasn't in a generous mood, that the gold he had been carrying was a dead issue. Stopping off at the bank, he cashed in most of the gold and arranged for the transfer of half the money to a bank in Denver, stuffing the remainder of the gold and cash into the saddlebags he was carrying.

Tossing the bags across one shoulder, he bid the banker goodbye and headed for the general store to replenish the supplies lost when he was ambushed, arranging to pick up the supplies in an hour or so. From there, he walked over to the stable where the buckskin and packhorse had gotten fat from weeks of idleness and paid for their upkeep. Returning to the general store, he tied the horses up and went into the small saloon next door.

It was the same story there as it had been at the sheriff's office—questions about the gold and its ori- gin—and his solution was the same: a hint of intimidation and open threats if he was pushed too far. Fin- ishing off a second shot of whiskey, he tossed a dollar on the bar and walked through the batwings connecting the saloon and the store to collect his supplies, adding a third box of ammunition to his list at the last minute. If he was going to have to fight off anyone when he rode out, they would pay a steep price. Belle was sitting on the front porch as he rode up, taking in the afternoon sun and seemingly at peace with the world. Dismounting, he tied both horses to the hitching post, pulled the saddlebags off the grey's rump and joined Belle on the porch.

"It be a fine day, Mister McPherson."

"Yes, ma`am," he agreed, setting the bags beside the chair. "Wilf came by awhile ago. He's not be too happy with you."

"He's got company. Must be a half dozen of Eureka's citizens down at the saloon that ain't too pleased with me either."

"I owe you my thanks."

"You don't owe me anything, Belle. I'm just sorry he wouldn't back off."

"Not too surprisin'," she acknowledged. "But I don't think he ever learned how."

"Probably not, but he was right about one thing. You're deserving of more than just my gratitude." McPherson opened one of the bags and pulled out a small leather pouch and handed it to her.

"What's this?"

"It's a nugget—the banker said larger than most."

"I don't want this," she protested, trying to give it back.

McPherson threw back his head in laughter. "That probably makes you the only one in town that don't. Please… Keep it."

"When you leavin'?"

"I figured I would pull out around daylight." "Any idea where yer headin'?"

"No more than usual."

"Cain't say I'm surprised. I'm still thinkin' you oughta go on back to Tennessee." "Seems like everybody I meet says that."

"You got some reason fer not listenin' to good advice?"

"Ain't much of a reason, but my daddy said I got the wanderlust."

"I expect a better answer than thet, Mister McPherson," she admonished. "Most of the men in Cali- fornia kin make thet claim."

"Oh, I expect if enough people tell me I don't belong, I'll eventually start paying attention. I plan on going back home one of these days, but not just yet."

Much as McPherson's father had discovered early on, Belle realized the futility of arguing with him, abruptly changing the direction of her barb. "Well I hope you'll have the good sense to stay outta the way of any more bullets. I din't nurse ya back to health just to see ya kilt somewhere else."

McPherson nodded solemnly. "I know it seems like it takes a long time to get through, Belle, but maybe this time the lesson will stick. See, when I first got to Texas a little over a year ago, I got into a scrape with this cowboy. I had never even drawn my gun other than to shoot at rocks and empty bottles, and I for sure had never shot anybody; but he was drunk and he forced my hand, if you want to call it that. Truth is, if he'd been sober, he woulda killed me plain and simple. I was luckier that time, a minor point the town sheriff was quick to mention. He thought I should turn tail and go home too."

"You shoulda paid him heed."

"I did. Listened to him and Anton and Molly and Angéline—they were all sure of what was best for me—and from their way of seeing things, I suppose they were right." McPherson's mouth tightened in a scowl. "But I keep thinking there's something I gotta do before I quit wandering."

"That kinda thinkin' kin git ya into a lot of trouble." "I hope not. About had my fill."

"I am afraid, Jesse McPherson, thet yer gonna find trouble every time ya turn a rock over. And one day, thet trouble's gonna be mor'n you kin handle. Go home. You already got more than most. Go back to Tennessee and be satisfied thet you survived."

"I'll at least give it some thought."

"Guess thet'll have to do. Now go on and pack while I fix us some supper."

● ● ●

McPherson was up an hour before dawn, figuring that since he couldn't sleep any longer, he might as well get the pack horse settled down before hitting the trail. He had spent a restless night, the adrenalin pumping as he thought about what might lay ahead. Over a supper of ham and red-eye gravy and hot bis- cuits, he and Belle had talked at length about San Francisco, and she had convinced him that he would do well to avoid the city altogether. Sheriff Parker had dropped by during the evening, but surprisingly, it was only to say goodbye. McPherson had expected that he was there to make one final stab at getting the loca- tion of the valley but to McPherson's delight, the subject never came up.

What didn't surprise him was the smell of fresh coffee brewing downstairs. He had come to believe that the woman never slept. He dressed quickly and buckled on the Peacemaker for the first time since the ambush, consciously drawing the weapon and checking the load. Taking one last look around, he reached into the saddlebags and took out a second pouch resembling the one he had given Belle the previous night, laying it on the table next to the bed. He knew Belle would never take it willingly, but he figured that once he was gone, she would have little choice. Draping the saddlebags across his shoulder, he picked up his rifle and went down the stairs a final time.

"Good mornin', Miz O'Connor."

"And a fine good mornin' back to ya, Mister McPherson. Would ya be likin' to fill yer belly afore ya ride outta Eureka?"

"Wouldn't take much to twist my arm, Belle, seeing as how I been smelling the food for half an hour."

"Fine. You git washed up and I'll set the table."

McPherson leaned the rifle against the wall next to the front door and set the saddlebags next to it, and after washing his hands, set down to breakfast. When he had finished eating, he refilled his cup and pushed away from the table.

"I'm gonna miss your cookin', Belle."

"An well you should," she teased before turning serious. "Jesse, you figure you might be in the Ari- zona Territory sometime?"

"Could be. Heard about a canyon down on the Colorado. Thought I might take a look at it. Why?" "An old friend, man by the name of John Carr is supposed to be in Tombstone. You make it down there, you look him up and tell him I said you was to introduce yerself." "Any particular reason?"

"None thet I kin think of at the moment, but it's always good to know somebody wherever you are." "I'll make a point of it."

"And if'n yer back this way, don't be a stranger."

"Ain't likely I'd miss a chance to feast on your cooking. Belle…" She looked at him expectantly, but the shyness she had occasionally noticed took charge. "Best I get going."

"You go ahead and saddle up. I'll be out in a minute or two." McPherson nodded, almost turning over his chair in the haste to get outside.

The buckskin fidgeted nervously as McPherson saddled him, playfully nipping at his shoulder. The horse had stood quietly as McPherson finished stowing the last of his gear on the packhorse, but once he tossed the saddle blanket across the grey's back, the horse's feet shuffled in a dance, seemingly aware that they were about to return to the trail. Once the cinch was tightened, McPherson tied the saddlebags behind the saddle and shoved his rifle into the boot. Looking to the east, he could see the first traces of daylight across the sky. It was time to leave.

After McPherson had gone outside, Belle continued sipping on her coffee, curious as to what was on his mind, wondering why he decided not to tell her. It couldn't be Molly, they had talked that out a week ago. Setting the cup down, she climbed the stairs to make sure he hadn't forgotten something, but the only thing she noticed was that he had attempted to make the bed…and had left a leather pouch on the table. She sat on the edge on the bed before picking it up, quickly realizing it was even heavier than the previous one. A smile crept across her face. Of the many men she had doctored, few had gone past saying thanks, and none had seen fit to pay her for her services, or even offer to. She put the pouch back on the table and went downstairs and pulled on a wool shawl to ward off the morning chill before going out to the porch. McPherson had just finished saddling the grey and was looking to the east.

The change in his face startled her. Gone was any trace of indecision, or the boyishness that gave his shyness credence. In its place, she saw a strength—and determination—that was not evident the first time they had talked. She was fascinated by the realization that she had misjudged him, by the knowledge that Jesse McPherson was a survivor. Pulling the shawl a little tighter around her shoulders, she stepped off the porch.

"Time to say goodbye, Miz O'Connor." "So it would seem, Mister McPherson."

"I left something for you on the table upstairs." "I thank you, but it wasn't necessary."

"It's little enough for all you've done, Belle. I will be forever grateful." "It was my pleasure, Jesse."

The small talk seemed strained as they avoided saying the one thing remaining to be said. Belle sud- denly stepped forward and wrapped her arms around McPherson's waist. Taken aback, McPherson hesi- tated for a moment before returning the embrace, holding her a little tighter as she laid her head in the hollow of his shoulder. The minutes passed as they stood unmoving, the silence broken only after she had reached up and kissed him gently on his cheek before stepping back.

"Wish you'd come along years back, Jesse McPherson. I'd afought to make you mine. Now git outta here afore I start cryin' and embarrass the both of us."

McPherson grinned, understanding, as she stepped back onto the porch. Walking around the grey's rump, he pulled the reins from the hitching post and stepped into the saddle. Gathering in the pack-horse's lead, he nodded his head in a silent goodbye before wheeling around and turning the horse south.

BOOK 3:

We are as one;
Living within frameworks
Sculptured by the winds of time, and
Tempered by self-imposed moralities.

I feel the caress of your mind;
Massaging emotions run rampant
With hearts desires.

I reach out to touch
The elusive butterfly;
Seeing the dreams of ages,
An evolving metamorphosis
In a static world.

Twenty Two

The ridges and valleys surrounding the Picquett farm stood in silent witness as Jesse McPherson and the widow Hatty Picquett plunged headlong into an affair of the heart. Each day and night was filled with the unexpected, the unforseen; the physical attraction intoxicating in its spontaneity.

His relationships with Angéline, Molly, and Belle O'Conner; the aftermath of New Orleans and then Wyoming; the seven years of wandering; all had contributed to the creation within McPherson of an ability to remain calm and detached. He had learned in his years in the West to evaluate situations for what they were, to quickly recognize the underlying motives of the people involved; and on numerous occasions, the ability had served him well—that is, until he came face to face with Hatty Picquett.

She personified many of the particulars that characterized the women who had played a part in his growing up: strength of purpose, courage, a freedom of spirit. Her self-assurance gave new meaning to his concept of being alive. She probed the depths of his emotions, flouting customs she was raised with, yet their tryst was very much affected by the times in which they lived. Caught up in the dizzying atmosphere of love, they tossed caution to the wind, unconsciously avoiding the consequences of their passion...

As the early hint of sunshine began to peek over the ridge east of the farm, Hatty busied herself by starting a pot of coffee and making breakfast to share with the man she had invited into her bed. Since ris- ing an hour or so before, she periodically looked in on him, taking pleasure in seeing him asleep in her bed, yet each time wanting him to be up and around. It was the first time since his arrival that he had relaxed enough to let go completely, and had slept through the better part of the night. It was also the first morning that she could reflect on what had transpired over the previous month, to consider the implications of his presence—his appearance at the farm had caused her life to take a most unexpected turn.

She had resigned herself to being Mister Picquett's wife whenever he saw fit to stop in, but she had long past grown weary of making excuses for her errant husband. She tired of hearing the loudly whispered asides of women she passed on the street when she went into town for supplies, tired of the insinuations made toward her when she was seen talking with the menfolk, and most of all, tired of the blatant accusa- tions that followed in her wake. As a consequence, she stopped going into town except when absolutely necessary. Then one day out of the blue, a stranger rode into her life, a stranger who seemed to fit into every dream she could remember. Jesse McPherson was a person who respected her and gave freely of his love, a contrast to the painful lessons she had endured in her marriage.

Pouring herself a cup of steaming coffee, she sat down at the table and looked around at the contents of the cabin she had quite literally grown up with. Only seventeen when she first arrived, she had painstak- ingly transformed it over the seven years since into her preserve, and though trappings suggesting a man's presence were in evidence, the few decorations that existed in the cabin embodied her own tastes—not that her decorating was an ongoing problem with Mister Picquett; he seldom paid attention to anything she did. And on the rare occasion when he had, it was mostly to criticize.

When originally built, the cabin was little more than a single room, incorporating the basic necessi- ties required for living: a table and chairs, a bed, and a fireplace for cooking. The one and only door was approximately centered with a single window the only other opening in the four walls. The large stone fire- place occupied one corner of the cabin, providing warmth as well as serving as a stove. The other two thirds of the cabin comprised the living area: simply furnished with a rough-hewn oblong plank table and four chairs. Her bed was nothing more than a straw mattress located in a loft above the fireplace.

But since those early days, Hatty had changed things considerably. She added a large alcove at the rear of the cabin and furnished it with a large brass bed and a chest of drawers. She hired a carpenter from town to cut a hole in the wall beneath the loft for a second window, supplying his family with vegetables and eggs for an entire summer to pay for his work. She acquired a cookstove and turned the opposite end of the cabin into a kitchen. The loft itself was transformed into a place where she painstakingly stitched quilts that she either used as blankets or traded in town for the staples she needed. The table was now more cen- trally located, enabling her to build shelves beneath the loft and fill them with her beloved books. She found a stuffed chair that was comfortable and placed it near the fireplace. Daguerreotypes hung above the fireplace and a pair of samplers were positioned on either side of the front window.

Her eyes at last came to rest on the wooden pegs driven into one of the logs beside the door, focusing on the worn leather holster and the pistol it contained. McPherson had hung it there the day he arrived and had not touched it since. The curious thought struck her that it was probably the gun that had killed her husband. Hatty glanced toward the stirrings at the back of the cabin, unconscious of the subtle change in her breathing. She wondered for a brief moment if McPherson would be prepared to let the gun hang there forever and forget about moving on. He hadn't talked about it, but she was honest enough with herself to recognize that wandering was in his blood, and expecting him to take root for any length of time was maybe expecting too much.

Setting the cup down, she walked back to the alcove in time to see McPherson open his eyes for the first time that morning. Leaning over, she touched his lips with her own, standing quickly as he reached for her.

"'Bout time you was awake," she teased. "Sun's been up for better than an hour."

"Not my fault. Bed's too comfortable."

"Should I take that as a compliment, Mister McPherson?"

"Meant you should. Been a long time since I slept in."

"Well now that you're awake, you plan on staying there all day?" Hatty's teasing took on a challeng- ing tone.

"Interesting thought," he answered, again reaching out for her. "Any reason why I shouldn't?" Hatty sat on the edge of the bed. "We got things to do today."

"And what might that be?" he asked, tracing the outline of her face.

She returned the caress, running her fingertips through the sparse hair on his chest. "Time I went into town. Thought you might come along with me."

"You think that's a good idea? It'll set tongues wagging for sure." "I thought about that. Guess they'll just have to wag."

"Even so…"

"Will you hush up. I been puttin' up with backbitin' since I first set up housekeeping with Mister Pic- quett. Ain't nothin' they can say or do now thet's gonna make things any worse."

McPherson bit off further arguments. If he had learned nothing else, arguing with a woman that had already made up her mind was a waste of time and effort. But the foreboding he felt coming down from the Gap returned, a little stronger, the danger to her a little more real. Half sitting up in bed, he pulled her close enough to plant a kiss in the middle of her forehead.

"Up," he commanded, tossing back the quilt as she got to her feet. But rather than step back, she stared brazenly at his nakedness, embracing him with a sudden intensity.

"Let 'em talk, Jesse. They can't take this feeling from me."

No, he thought, stroking her hair, *they can't take the feeling, but they can sure as hell make a person regret it…*

Against his better judgment, McPherson accompanied Hatty for the five mile ride into Clinton. He felt ill at ease—more than once before they left, he had considered strapping on the Peacemaker— but com- mon sense said it would not be the most intelligent thing he could do. After all, East Tennessee was not the wild west and McPherson saw no reason to go out of his way and give people an excuse to talk. Although it was a good two hours before noon when they reached the Clinton ferry, traffic was light and their wait was short. Located just below the railroad bridge, the ferry crossed the Clinch where the Knoxville turn- pike ended. Once on the Clinton side, McPherson wheeled the wagon to an open lot just below the court- house and tied feedbags on the animals to keep them occupied while they shopped.

Offering his hand, he assisted Hatty to the ground, smiling in spite of his uneasiness. Although she would have denied it, the trip into town provided Hatty with an opportunity to openly flaunt convention, to don her Sunday best and show disapproving townsfolk that their opinions meant little or nothing to her. It was not how he would have gone about things, but given the circumstances, he understood. After a short stroll toward the river along the south side of Broad Street, Hatty steered him into the general store and proceeded to fill the counter with staples as varied as salt and a half bolt of cloth, accumulating enough goods to convince him she had no intention of returning anytime soon. When she had finished, she loaded up his arms and led him back to the wagon. McPherson wasn't too surprised, as they packed the goods into the wagon, to see a man wearing a badge approach them.

"Mornin', Miz Picquett."

"Why, good morning, Sheriff Rainey."

"And how might you be this fine day, Miz Picquett? We ain't seen much of you in a while." McPher- son couldn't put his finger on it, but something about the sheriff's voice grated on his sensibilities.

"Well, you understand how things are, Sheriff," Hatty countered. " I ain't exactly been made to feel welcome around here."

"Uh-huh, I surely do understand," Rainey allowed, eyeing McPherson. "Folks here'bouts never was too partial to strangers."

"I been here going on eight years, Sheriff. Ain't like I'm a stranger anymore."

"Yes ma'am, I do recall when yer husband first brought you here. Real tragedy, him gittin' killed."

" How did..." she started to ask, biting off the question as she answered herself. Unable to ignore the sheriff's interest in McPherson any longer, she introduced him. "This is Jess McPherson…a friend of the family."

"Mista McPherson," he acknowledged, nodding his head. "Yer not from around here." He made the comment in a matter-of-fact manner.

"No sir. I'm from up Cumberland Gap way."

"All due respect, Mista McPherson, but you don't look like anybody that might be from the Gap neither."

"That so? I wasn't aware folks up that way looked different." McPherson noticed Rainey's eyebrows arch in indignation. "Sheriff, my family's been there on that piece of land for better than fifty years." "Uh-huh. Well, how long you figure you'll be visitin' round here?"

"Don't rightly know, Sheriff, but pretty as this part of Tennessee is, I might even decide to settle down here."

"Do tell. Well afore you git too comfortable, I s'pect you should know thet folks round here don't cot- ton to gunfighters any more than they do strangers." Touching the brim of his hat, he bid them good day.

He stared silently at Rainey's back as he walked away from them, reading a good deal more into the sheriff's remarks than was actually said. Wonder who you been talking to," McPherson muttered to him- self.

For a moment, he wondered about the nagging apprehension he sensed. One thing was clear: he would have to be on guard to a far greater extent than he had previously considered.

"Jess… Jesse?" McPherson continued staring at Rainey, only dimly aware that Hatty was speaking to him. "Mister McPherson!"

"Sorry, Hatty, I was somewhere else. What'd you say?" "What was that all about? You're no gunfighter."

"There's some that would disagree about that, Hatty. Just because I ain't wearing the gun…" "They can disagree all they want," she stated emphatically. "You're no gunfighter."

"Maybe not here," he mused. "But out there…" McPherson gestured westward. "You trying to scare me, Jess?"

"Nope. It's just that gunfights do happen once in a while—wasn't something I looked for, but they found me out often enough."

"Well, Mister McPherson, you're safe here. We're practically civilized."

"That's what concerns me." Hatty looked at him quizzically. "That sheriff. Either he's a real good guesser, or he knows more than he's letting on. How'd he know your husband was killed?"

"Can't say. The only time Rainey ever saw fit to talk to me before was to tell me that Mister Picquett had gotten into trouble again. But since I sent word to the Picquetts up in Virginia, I s'pose it's possible he found out somehow."

"Did you mention my name?"

"No, saw no reason to. Just said he was kilt in a gunfight."

"Let's finish up whatever it was you wanted to do and head back to the farm. Suddenly I'm feeling mighty naked."

• • •

"I met this old sheriff in Texas, six, seven years back. Told me to either learn to shoot properly or put my gun away and go back to Tennessee…"

Hatty unwrapped herself from McPherson's arms and rolled onto her stomach, perching on her elbows so her face was above his. "What ever in the world are you talkin' about?"

"Good advice I chose to ignore."

"Told you to stay away from fallen women, I bet," she mumbled between kisses.

"I never should have come back here," McPherson resolved. "I've just made your life more difficult." "If this is a difficult life," she sighed as she straddled him, "I wish it had started a lot sooner." "Damn it, Hatty, I got this suspicion you're in some kinda danger and for the life of me, I can't see past the fact that I'm part of it."

"You talking about the sheriff again?" "He can cause you a lot of trouble."

"He can try. 'Sides, I got you to protect me." She trailed her fingertips in circles through his chest hair, softly taunting him. "You will protect me, won't you?"

"I been telling myself that's why I came back."

"Huh. And all this time I though it was 'cause you couldn't stay away." "You're funning me."

"Only 'cause you deserve it. You remember the first day you rode up?" "Not likely to forget it. Why?"

"Mister Picquett being gone so much, I had more'n a few men visitors thinking they could take advantage of the situation. After the first time or two of arguing with 'em, they learned right quick I would as soon shoot 'em as not."

"How come you didn't shoot at me?"

"Maybe it was cause you didn't look like you needed shooting." "I s'pose I should be thankful for small favors."

"And don't be forgetting it," she admonished as she lay her head in the crook of his shoulder. Feeling the chill on her back, Jesse pulled the quilt over the both of them.

"Jess?"

"Uh-huh."

"I'm glad you're here. I didn't really know what it's like to need someone."

TWENTY THREE

The day started hot, and quickly got hotter as the sun cleared the East ridge. In a field below the cabin, Jesse was stripped to the waist and barefoot, the third member of a team that also consisted of a horse with the innocuous name of Jake and a cantankerous ill-tempered mule named Prince. He had spent the better part of the morning riding atop a harrow, preparing the ground for a late crop of tobacco, late because of his presence for the past month. Had it been up to McPherson, he would never have chosen to plant tobacco, but since it was Hatty's farm and her choice, he felt obligated to help any way he could. Even so, his memories of working in a tobacco patch when he was a kid were as strong as ever—and just as distasteful…

Jesse's father had decided, with encouragement from Jacob, to make an attempt at growing tobacco. The war was just over, and the demand was such that if they were able to produce a high enough quality crop, it would pay handsomely. But before that could happen, they had to produce seedlings, and then transplant them into row after backbreaking row. Once that was accomplished, the plants needed constant weeding, and as they matured, suckering; and each step of the way, the plants had to be treated with the utmost delicacy—they were as fragile as glass.

The first year's crop was an unmitigated disaster. Between the heat and the unprecedented hail storms, the plants didn't have a chance. But Zeb McPherson was tenacious if nothing else, and by the third year, had harvested a large enough crop to call it a success. Jesse, however, had a slightly different interpre- tation as to the family's good fortune. It wasn't that he was opposed to work so much as he was opposed to working in the tobacco fields. Each spring, as his older brothers dropped seedlings into the newly created rows, he and sister Kathleen would have to crawl behind the horse-drawn plow and gently pull the soil around the tender shoots.

But that chore was just a preamble to the work that would come for them later—the task of suckering the plants. They would again have to crawl between the rows, pulling off the dead leaves at the base of each plant, while their brothers and father followed along behind, weeding between and around each plant. And while that in itself would not have been so bad, at the end of the day, they would be covered by the resinous tar that oozed from the plants. And there were the worms. Ugly green worms, often as big as a man's finger, grown fat from feasting on the broad leaves. For some unexplainable reason, Jesse had a deep-seated fear of the worms, and Jacob took great pleasure after pulling them off the plants, of ripping them in half and then throwing the pieces at him, a practice that continued until the day that Jesse ran screaming from the fields, breaking the broad plant leaves that hung heavy on both sides of the row. From that day forward, Jesse refused to return to the tobacco fields.

Until now, he thought. He had never been too good at plowing on the family farm, and age hadn't improved his abilities in any way. Working a pair of animals that paid attention was difficult at best, but these two were unique. The mule moved slower than a snail when plowing away from the barn. The return trip was a case of hanging on for dear life. The only saving grace was Jake. While the horse would work all day, his pace never varied. Even so, after three days of trailing the team, McPherson was beginning to won- der what he had gotten himself into. Of course, each time Hatty came down to the field with another pail of cold water, he quit wondering. She was a breath of fresh air each time she appeared, and each time he would rein up the team just to watch her walk toward him.

"Woman, you got a habit of showing up at just the right time."

"Getting thirsty, are ya?" Hatty asked laughing. She filled the ladle with water and handed it to him. "Looks about ready."

"One more pass, I figure, if'n that damn mule will cooperate. Where'd you find him, anyhow?" "Traded a pair of quilts for him a couple of years back. Why?"

"You lost out," he replied, shaking his head.

"He does seem to have a mind of his own," she offered. "That's like saying the sun'll rise tomorrow."

"Try scratching him between the ears."

"Huh! Stick of firewood might do the trick better." "That won't make him work any harder."

"No, I don't reckon it will," he agreed, adding "but it might get his attention." "You hungry?"

"Yeah, but I think I'd like to finish up here first. It's getting pretty hot, and this afternoon'll be even worse." McPherson poured half the remaining water into a second bucket and while he held one up to Jake, Hatty did the same for the mule. "Maybe after dinner we could go try out that swimming hole you told me about. Beat trying to get clean in that galvanized wash tub."

"How long?"

"Hour at most." McPherson climbed back on top of the harrow and picked up the reins. "Alright, you mangy long-eared excuse for a horse, do your damndest. Giddup…"

• • •

McPherson lay back on the soft cushion of pine needles, watching the diminishing rivulets of water follow the gentle curves of Hatty's body as they disappeared into the matting beneath them. After unhar- nessing the team and turning them loose, they decided to pack the food along to the swimming hole with the intention of eating after he had bathed and cooled off. Instead, he and Hatty had bathed together and made love, never bothering to leave the water. McPherson reached out to cup one of her breasts, tracing with a fingertip the narrow trail of a drop of water that had run down from her shoulder to hang suspended from the swollen nipple.

"Man could get to liking this…even expecting it."

"Wouldn't mind too much if'n you did, Mister McPherson. Truth is, I hope you do." "Folks hereabouts might not take too kindly to that."

"Ain't the people here'bouts that's saying it, Jess. Nothing I ever learned in all my years explains how I'm feeling about you." Seeing the sudden concern on his face, she leaned forward and kissed him ever so gently. "I'm telling you, Mister McPherson, that I love you and I want you to stay here and be with me."

"Love's a mighty strong word, Hatty."

"Ain't near strong enough in this instance." Touching his lips to silence his protests, she continued. "I was seventeen when I married Mister Picquett. But it wasn't 'til you come round that I understood why it was wrong, me marrying him. I just couldn't or didn't realize it then."

"Let's get dressed and eat." McPherson said, abruptly changing the subject. "I'm starving."

Although she didn't openly react, Hatty was shaken by the sudden change in McPherson's mood. But she was no more unnerved than was Jesse himself. Hearing Hatty's declaration of love resurrected unwanted memories of Angéline and Molly, memories of his own declarations and of the aftermaths. The short time he spent with Angéline could be explained away, or at the very least, accepted as indicative of the times. As well, the intensity of his relationship with Molly following the old man's death could also be explained away. René d'Iberville had certainly made that point a number of times during the year he had spent wandering the Arizona Territory in his company. But his involvement in their lives was a fact he couldn't—or didn't—want to ignore.

An embarrassed silence settled over the glade as Hatty covered her nakedness with denims and a shirt. McPherson looked on with regret, finally getting dressed himself while she laid out the food. But despite an avowal of severe hunger, his appetite had disappeared. As he picked at the food, he realized that unlike his affairs with Angéline and Molly, his ties to Hatty were something that couldn't be easily rational- ized. That he was torn as to what to do was another matter entirely. He was uneasy with the thought of making comparisons, but given the minor confrontation with Clinton's sheriff a few days before, he knew it was unavoidable. His problem lay in facing up to the situation because Hatty's words about loving him rang true—and they echoed his own thoughts.

• • •

The late afternoon heat settled on the troubled pair as they trudged back from the swimming hole, adding to the oppressive sense that something terrible had happened between them. But that feeling was to become secondary to the heightened uneasiness as they rounded the corner of the cabin. McPherson noticed their visitor first, and to his amazement, Hatty treated the sheriff as if he had been expected all along.

"My goodness, Sheriff, you look all hot and thirsty. Been waiting long?"

"Afternoon, Miz Picquett. Bout an hour, I reckon. And I wouldn't mind a cool drink of water if'n it wouldn't trouble you too much."

"No trouble atall, Sheriff. Jess, would you go out to the pump and fetch some fresh water?" McPher- son nodded and took the pail sitting on the edge of the porch. "What brings you all the way out here on such a hot day?"

"Oh, thought I might trade a word or two with yer friend Mista McPherson."

"Now why would you be wanting to do that? Never know'd you to take that much interest in folks." "Well now, Miz Picquett, it is my job to pay attention to the goin's on in the county."

"So it is, Sheriff," she agreed, smiling sweetly. "You figure something is going on out here?" "Well, I don't rightly know…" he hinted before she interrupted.

"So you thought you'd maybe come out here on a fishing expedition and nose around?" "Thet's not it at all, Miz Picquett," Rainey answered uncomfortably.

"Well then I guess I can't see what you're getting at."

"Been doin' some checkin' up on your *friend*. Cain't say I'm too pleased with what I found out. I don't think you know who this man is," he declared just as Jesse returned with the water.

"Then maybe you should tell her," McPherson suggested, offering the ladle to the sheriff. "Hell, I'm kinda curious myself."

"And I'm thinkin' we should talk alone, McPherson," Rainey countered, his discomfort increasing. "Why's that, Sheriff? I got nothing to hide."

"Well, now. I don't know that Miz Picquett needs to be ahearin' this."

"That so? Must be something mighty powerful for you to come out here and make insinuations with- out saying why."

"Jess is right, Sheriff. If you got something to say, then please say it."

"Just remember I tried to protect you, Miz Picquett." Now openly fidgeting, but with obvious con- tempt, Rainey finally blurted out his accusation. "This here gunfighter thet you called a friend of the family is a cold-blooded murderer."

"That's a real serious charge, Sheriff." McPherson fought to contain his anger. "Who'd I murder?" "What I hear, five or six people."

McPherson laughed in spite of himself. "Now where'd you hear that?"

"Yore reputation's followin' you like some egg-suckin' hound," the sheriff answered with a sneer. "I don't understand," she said, adrenalin flowing. "How do you know he's a murderer?"

"After I talked with you in town, I sent a message up to the Gap askin' about McPherson. His brother was more than willin' to set us straight."

"You're taking something my brother said as being gospel?" McPherson asked incredulously. "Sher- iff, you're a bigger fool that I thought."

"Don't change the fact thet you threatened him," Rainey scoffed, adding triumphantly, "and it don't change the fact thet Mista Picquett's unfortunate death was cold-blooded murder."

"Jess!" Hatty screamed. McPherson had reacted the moment the words passed the sheriff's lips, grab- bing him by the front of his shirt. "Don't do it, Jess," she pleaded. "Let him go… Please."

The moment was frozen in time as McPherson slowly relaxed his grip on the sheriff, suddenly giving him a not-so-gentle shove backwards with the flat of his hands. Hatty stepped between them, facing the sheriff.

"At this moment, Sheriff Rainey, I'm fairly ashamed to admit that I know you. That was uncalled for. Are you here to arrest him?"

"I cain't," he answered nervously, his bravado disappeared. "He ain't done nothin' wrong here." "And if'n you'd asked the right questions from them folks over in Texas, you'd know he didn't murder Mister Picquett neither. I don't know what your real reason was for coming out here, but whatever it was, I'd suggest you go on back to Clinton and forget it."

"I was only tryin' to protect you…"

"From Jesse? Hardly. There was a time, Sheriff, when I might have believed you, but those days are long past. For your information, I've invited Mister McPherson to share this farm with me, and I'm hoping he agrees. You, on the other hand, have more than worn out your welcome here. Now unless you got some- thing more to say, I'll thank you to get on your horse and don't be bothering us agin."

"Sheriff?" McPherson had followed the sheriff out to the gate. Holding on the reins to prevent him from leaving, he spoke in a very determined tone. "Since you've expressed so much concern about Miz Picquett's welfare, maybe it's best if we come to an understanding. I'm no gunfighter, and I ain't one to make threats, but I'd take it real personal if these so-called *facts* you've gone to so much trouble for were spread around the county. And Sheriff? If Hatty's name was sullied about… Well, I think you get my drift." The sheriff leaned over and yanked the reins out of McPherson's grasp. "Oh I do indeed, Mista McPherson. But you best be understandin' somethin' yerself. Decent folks got no use fer people like yer- self—don't want 'em around. They elected me to keep yer kind out. So best you remember the next time you come into Clinton, you break one law and I'll do a lot more than take it personal. Good day, *Mista* McPherson."

• • •

The chores done and supper over with, Jess and Hatty settled in on the porch to enjoy the cool of the evening. It was a vibrant time of the year, the air alive with the sporadic twinkling of fireflies and the ebb and flow of the cicada's roar. Little had been said after the sheriff left, but the burden of his visit weighed heavy on them both. They had been whipsawed between euphoria and worrisome intimidation, and in the quiet of the night, they seemed content to stay within their own thoughts. But too many things had been said or implied, and although both were hesitant to broach the subject, once it started, their conversation went late into the evening.

"When I was a youngun," McPherson reminisced, "me and my kid sister Maggie used to borrow Ma's canning jars and catch a bunch of them lightning bugs. We figured if we caught enough of them, it'd be as bright as a lantern. Seems like a long time ago."

"You really miss your family."

"Yeah, I guess I do. Sometimes I get to thinking about them—specially Aaron and Maggie—but I've mostly forgotten what it was like, being a kid. Seems like most of my growing up was done somewhere else."

"I used to miss my brothers and sisters something terrible. When I married Mister Picquett, I wanted to leave home so bad I could taste it. I just wanted to get away. I finally quit thinking about them. Only way I could handle it."

"Why'd you want to leave?"

"They was twelve of us kids. Guess I tired of sleeping with half of `em." "You keep in touch?"

"Not really. Us Morgans were never much for writing letters."

"Huh. Maggie married a Morgan, from up Kingsport way. Name's Jonathon." "My baby brother's named Jonathon," she laughed. "Wouldn't that be something." "You figure it's possible?"

"Could be. Ain't too many Morgans up that way." "I'll ask next time I go home."

"You're going back?"

"Hadn't planned on it, but anymore out of Jacob and I'm gonna have to have another talk with him." "Did you really threaten him?"

"He thought I did." McPherson explained what happened when he returned home.

"Would you have hurt him?"

"Hard to say. I might have if he'd given me the excuse. But it wouldn't of been any less than what he handed out to me a few years ago."

"How's that?"

"Jacob didn't take kindly to me being favored. So he took to hitting me ever time my daddy was looking the other way... Seemed like he took pleasure in it."

"Sounds a whole lot like Mister Picquett..." Hatty shivered in the deepening shadows. "Would you get me a wrap, Jesse? I'm suddenly feeling a chill." McPherson returned with the shawl quickly, wrapping it around her shoulders almost as a caress.

"I can't see it...you and Picquett."

"He showed up to one of the camp meetings Pa was always taking us to. Sat there the whole time just staring at me. When the meeting was over, he come up and asked my name and then disappeared. Next morning, we was gathered down on the Nolachucky to baptize the ones saved at the meetin' and there he was. When the baptizin' was over, he asked Pa for permission to come by the house and pay his respects. Pa being the good Christian man he was, invited him to Sunday dinner. Mister Picquett was the perfect gentleman, but he let on to being more than he was. He fooled most everybody, especially me. All I could see was a fancy man from Virginia with eyes for me..."

"Doesn't sound like the man I met in Texas."

"Believe me, Jess, for once, I should have listened to my Pa, 'cause he saw through him. But I was spellbound, and when he asked me to marry him, I agreed without even thinking about it. By the time I found out the truth, I was just too ashamed to admit it. Besides, a wife wasn't supposed to criticize her mate."

"You don't strike me as someone who would let what you're *supposed* to do get in the way." "Age'll do that to you, age and living alone..."

McPherson got to his feet. "I'm gonna have one more cup of coffee. You having any?" "I think not, Jess, but you go ahead."

While he was inside, Hatty gazed out into the darkness. A mist was beginning to develop over the newly plowed ground in the flat below the cabin, the air taking on a decided dampness which quickly added to the chill. The early onslaught of fireflies had diminished to a random glow in the thickening mist. The siyunds had diminished to the occasional hoot of an owl and the chirping of crickets. As he came back onto the porch, she felt his hand resting on her shoulder, felt his lips brush the top of her head.

Jess, what are you going to do?" "Do? About what?"

"Me. This farm."

"That's a loaded question, Miz Picquett." "Meant it to be."

"I'm not sure how I should be answering it."

"Mister McPherson, I didn't tell you I loved you just to be making conversation." "I know that, but my staying on could end up being a lot of trouble for you." "You're thinking about it?" she asked, unable to hide her elation.

"Since the day I first set foot here. But Rainey's going to be a problem. I've met his kind before—he figures wearing that badge's like being God, that it gives him liberty to meddle in the affairs of others."

"He's just an ol' county sheriff, Jess."

"Ol' county sheriffs got a way of creating problems where they ain't none," he said with some finality.

"It's funny, Jess. There's times it seems like I been on this farm forever and a day. When I married Mister Picquett, I thought I was going to experience most everything I had ever read about, but I found out right quick that things got a ways of being different than you'd expect."

"Expect the unexpected," he mumbled to himself. "Pardon?"

"Somethin' I heard a few years ago," he explained, repeating the comment. "Expect the unexpected." "Maybe that's how you gotta look at the sheriff."

"I would like to think you're right, but I'm afraid for you."

"Don't be." Reaching up, she grasped his hand, pressing it against her cheek. "It's enough that you care."

McPherson lay awake long after they had gone to bed. He took comfort that Hatty was sleeping soundly beside him in spite of the things said by the sheriff. Hatty was right. He did care about her—he was much more involved than he was prepared to admit, and therein lay the predicament he faced. He had vowed after his return that he wouldn't leave her side as long as his premonitions remained unfocused and unexplained. But he hadn't taken into account the possibility that he might become a liability, had never before seen himself in that light. Expect the unexpected. Weighed against the past seven years, the remark was good advice—be prepared for any eventuality. His life had revolved around one unexpected event after another, and not once had he come close to being prepared. Expect the unexpected.

McPherson drifted off to sleep, the words tumbling over and over in his head as he tried to apply them to Hatty and to himself. Expect the unexpected, he had said, the words echoing off the clap-board storefronts of dusty towns, reflecting from the walls of empty canyons. Expect the unexpected, flowing from unrecognizable faces, overlapping in and around the countless saloons and campfires, warning him of the dangers he braved. Expect the unexpected, riding on the strength of love and compassion as Angéline became Molly and then Belle, all three becoming Hatty as their faces blended into one. Expect the unex- pected…

TWENTY FOUR

The excitement of spring rushed into summer with no signs of abatement in the torrid romance of Jess McPherson and the Widow Picquett. The days were characterized by backbreaking work: caring for the delicate tobacco plants, repairing old fences and building new ones, laying in firewood for the coming winter, and breaking ground for next spring's crops. Nights—and the occasional daytime interlude—were devoted to each other. They seldom left the farm, choosing instead to deal with the occasional drummer that stopped by. They had concluded, after the sheriff had made his threats, that antagonizing him wasn't worth the effort and stayed away from Clinton. Thankfully, Sheriff Rainey had seen fit for whatever reason to return the favor and leave them alone. Unfortunately, an ever-increasing number of itinerant preachers had no such qualms.

For the twenty years following the end of the war, much of the South was inundated with these wan- dering men who had felt a call to spread the Word. No where was it more prevalent than amongst the ridges and valleys of East Tennessee. Hatty and Jesse could count on a minimum of two to three unannounced visitors a week, each one deeply concerned for their souls and fully prepared to minister to their needs and aspirations. At first, they had found the unwanted attention amusing, but their amusement was short-lived. Increasingly, their visitors went out of their way to pass judgment, openly berating them for living in a sin- ful way, and more than once driving Hatty to tears. Finally, McPherson reached the end of his patience and threw one of the self-appointed vigilantes of public morality off the farm.

Hatty was taken aback by McPherson's reaction. She had been raised to believe that treating a preacher—any preacher—with anything short of complete respect was unthinkable. For most of her broth- ers and sisters, their father's perspective was just another part of living, but from the time Hatty could first make out the words in the Bible, she accepted the Gospel as inviolate, a conviction encouraged and abetted by her father. The elder Morgan was a man that fervently believed the hand of God was involved in every aspect of life and brooked no disagreements to the contrary. With his guidance, Hatty eagerly participated in the rites of passage, accepting baptism as the final step in being cradled in the arms of the Lord.

As she grew older, however, her attitude went through a metamorphosis of sorts. Married to a mis- creant, faced with the loss of her children, Hatty was forced to deal with realities that bore little relation- ship to the values with which she had been raised. Nevertheless, the influence of her father was still significant. She tried to explain about her misgivings after the preacher had taken his leave, and for the sec- ond time since McPherson appeared at the farm, an unexpected chill settled between them.

Just as the case had been at the swimming hole when she told him of her love, McPherson chose to change the subject rather than deal head-on with the problem. After listening to her objections regarding the preacher, McPherson took her by the hand and suggested they go for a walk. An hour later, they were sitting on an outcropping of rock near the top of a ridge overlooking the Clinch River. Spread out below them was an open meadow randomly filled with wild flowers and the occasional patch of Queen Anne's Lace. To the West, puffy white clouds floated above the escarpment of Walden's Ridge.

"That's where I first crossed the Ridge," he said, pointing toward a gap in the distant summer haze. "Thought I was going to see the world... Guess in a way I did."

"You want to go back?"

"I don't know. It was different out there…not like this. I'd get up in the morning and all I could see for miles was sky. It was easy enough to ride for a week and not run into a soul, but when I did, they weren't trying to tell me what to think or how to live."

"Jesse, I wasn't telling…" she started to say, an underlying sense of panic building within.

"No, I know that. But that preacher… Him and others like him—even Sheriff Rainey—none of them can stand the thought that somebody might not take kindly to being told they're living wrong, or that they're not welcome to settle down among them." McPherson sighed deeply.

"I spent the last seven years around people that for the most part take a man at his word. They figure that it's hard enough just staying alive and unless a person gives them reason to think differently, he's accepted without question. Took me a long time to realize that my father had the same attitude. He used to put up with the same sort of foolishness. There was a preacher by the name of Saulee…"

Another scorching hot Sunday afternoon had arrived. The sky was a hazy blue, with the threat of rain hanging ominously in the air. It was one of those afternoons that the good Preacher Saulee had picked to come by and spread the gospel, and while he was at it—if he was so fortunate as to have arrived at the appointed hour—he'd be delighted to sit down to one of Kathleen's fine Sunday dinners. The preacher was one of those uneducated Southern men who had felt the call to preach the word; but as he put it, he had fought off the Lord until His will became overpowering, and he no longer had any choice.

Zeb McPherson had questioned the degree of his zeal on a number of occasions, marveling that the preacher always seemed to show up just as they were sitting down to eat, but was kind enough to never say anything to his face. He just had Kathleen set another place and welcomed him to the table. But Saulee's presence at the McPherson dinner table also meant the family would be subjected at the very least to a short sermon, and as usual, Jesse was enthralled, anticipating the exchanges that were certain to occur between the preacher and his father.

"I tell you, Brother McPherson, I spend the livelong day, a meditatin' on the will of the Lord. 'Go ye into *all* the world and preach the gospel to every creature, and Lo! I am with you even to the end.' I been preachin' the Word for nigh on to twenty and six years, laborin' in the vineyard of the Lord, and my heart ain't set on the comforts of this earth. Sweet heaven is my home, an I'm a beginnin' to git homesick."

"Well, I'm sure you'll git there, Preacher," Zeb replied dryly. "Would you be havin' another piece of chicken?"

"Thank you, Brother, don't mind if I do." He helped himself to the chicken and another helping of potatoes and gravy as well. "You know, Brother, I wonder that I ain't seen you and yorn in church. I figured we was of like mind after the last time I visited."

"What's to wonder, Preacher? Ain't changed my beliefs about church goin', and I'm surprised you'd bring it up again."

"Well, sir, it's like I told you afore. Us Baptists believe that the whole law was given to Adam, and whilst he could do as he wanted, he must not eat of the fruit of the tree of knowledge. But Satan tempted Eve and she *did* eat, and through Adam we all became sinners. Now I look around me here, and I see books other than the Bible, and I wonder about yore children. The Lord says 'Mine elect have I called', and in the words of Peter the second, we must make that callin' sure… It's only through gatherin' together and singin' the praises of the Lord that it's possible." Having heard this particular discussion before, Jesse watched the animation in his father's eyes, speculating on what his response to the preacher's accusation would be this time.

"Uh huh! Well I'm real glad that them sinners are bein' dealt with, Preacher. Wouldn't want too many of them runnin' loose round here." The preacher blanched, choking on a mouthful of chicken. "Words hard to swallow, Preacher?" Zeb asked caustically.

"Brother McPherson, makin' fun of biblical teachin' is beneath you."

"Ain't makin' fun of the Bible, Preacher. But sharin' our food ain't no invitation for you to insult my beliefs either."

"If you don't want me here…"

"Whoa up, Preacher. As long as there's food on our table, you're more than welcome to share in it with us. But I don't recollect as how the Bible mentions anything about readin' and writin' being sinful. And as far as your church is concerned, I'd just as soon my offspring wasn't around that bunch of self-righ- teous pharisees."

"My brethren're good Christians," he said indignantly.

"I ain't passin' judgment, Preacher, but if'n they are *good Christians*, they're leaving it at the door after the invitation. You fergit I deal with most of your brethren regular and that goodness you speak of ain't too apparent."

"Now who's bein' insultin'?"

"Just an observation, Preacher, just an observation." Zeb pushed back his chair. "Why don't we sit on the porch and let dinner settle awhile. Seems to me I smelled a cobbler bakin' afore you got here."

"All right, Zeb, but we got to talk about this agin." "I'd be right disappointed if'n we didn't, Preacher."

Preacher Saulee nodded. "Mighty tasty vittles, Sister Kathleen."

"Well, thank you, Preacher," she replied, accepting his praise. "Now, you go on outside and I'll bring you some cobbler in a bit. Jesse, will you help your sister clear the table?"

As the men moved onto the porch, they noticed that the threat of rain had increased dramatically. The heaviness of the air had increased; large thunderheads filled the sky to the southwest, accentuated by numerous flashes of lightning and the accompanying rumble of thunder.

"Appears as how we'll get some rain, Brother McPherson," said the preacher as he settled down in one of the half dozen straight-backed chairs that were on the porch.

"Be an hour or so if'n we do. Them storms tend to go around us more often than not."

The two men seemed content to sit and watch the building storm and avoid further conversations about religion, focusing instead on crops and the availability of a decent mule. Kathleen came out on the porch. "Aaron, go down to the spring house and get that container of cream. Would you like a glass of cold milk to wash that cobbler down, Preacher?"

"Why, yes, sister, that'd be real fine."

"And a jug of milk, Aaron," she added before returning inside.

"Miz McPherson's a fine cook, Zeb," Saulee observed. "You're a fortunate man."

"You're right, Preacher," he answered, gazing at the clouds that were moving steadily toward the farm. "Jacob. Any stock in the barn?"

"Yes sir."

"Best make sure they're loose. This one ain't goin' round."

By the time the cobbler had arrived, the sky had darkened from the impending storm, the air crack- ling from the frequent bolts of lightning. As the boiling front of the storm passed overhead, the wind increased dramatically, kicking up eddies of dust from the road, whipping through the young oaks that guarded the front of the cabin. The underside of the clouds emitted a strange greenish hue, almost bright after the blackness of the storm's edge.

The lightning was now continuous, the flashes overlapping, competing for intensity, each bolt larger and more spectacular than the last. A dust-laden smell of fresh rain permeated the air. Small pockets began to appear in the distance, slowly spreading across the entire hori…zon, forming a wall that obscured any- thing behind it. The wall moved steadily up the valley, seeming to pick up speed and strength as it neared. As the rain hit, a massive bolt of lightning struck the barn, the sound ripping through the constant roar of the thunder, turning the loft into a ball of fire. Zebadiah and Jacob took off for the barn in a dead run, com- ing close to being trampled by the crazed animals fleeing the fire. They checked quickly that the barn was empty, escaping just as the loft cascaded to the floor.

The storm blew by as quickly as it had arrived, but the dam-age was done. Within minutes, the barn was gone, the pouring rain having little effect on the flames until it was too late. Zeb and Jacob, soaked to the skin, walked slowly back to the cabin, already discussing how long it would take to rebuild the barn. As they stepped onto the porch, Preacher Saulee gave Zebadiah a smile of righteousness.

"Somethin' amusin', Preacher?"

"I was just thinkin' thet the Lord works in peculiar ways." Zeb stared at Saulee for a long minute or two before replying.

"Yer outta line, Preacher."

"Not atall, Brother McPherson. I'm jest statin' the obvious. It appears to me thet you been warned.

Surely you don't think it was anythin' but the hand of the Lord?"

Zebadiah's stare hardened into a coldness that send shivers through the preacher. "What I think, Preacher, is that it's time for you to get off my land."

• • •

Hatty had listened quietly as Jesse told the story, empathizing with him despite her upbringing, but unsure of why she did. She remembered the many times her own family was visited by wandering preach- ers, how her father had often talked into the night with them, discussing at length the Bible and its teach- ings; but that life seemed so far away as she sat beside Jesse McPherson on a hill above the Clinch River. For days, she had sensed a growing conflict, one without definition, perhaps relating to the uneasiness Jesse had seen fit to mention on one or two occasions. Of one thing she was sure— she was afraid she would lose this man that had become so much a part of her life.

"Jesse? That preacher... Saulee? He was just doing what he thought was right."

"I guess so, but his version of what was right sure did made life difficult. We heard every once in a while that he was using Pa as an example in one of his sermons."

"I must be getting slow in my old age," she exclaimed. "That's what you're afraid of, that folks around here are going to talk about us...about me."

"Woman, you seem to have some undying faith that talk can't hurt you."

"Mister Jesse McPherson," she scolded. "You're dwelling on what people are saying and thinking about it way too much. Talk can't hurt if'n you don't let it."

"I can't agree with you."

"Listen to me, Jess. About six months after I settled in with Mista Picquett, Sheriff Rainey—he was new at the job back then— Sheriff Rainey, he come by to let me know in no uncertain terms that our kind wasn't welcome in Anderson County."

"He hasn't changed a lot."

"And it's not likely he will. All I know is, he scared me silly. Mister Picquett was away and I was with child and I didn't have a clue as to what he was talking about. When my husband saw fit to come home, I told him about the visit and all he did was shrug it off. I don't know why, but that scared me even more. It wasn't until after the baby was born that I learned Mister Picquett was frequenting every road- house in the county. The doctor let it slip."

"I didn't know you had a baby," McPherson said with surprise.

"I guess I never had a reason to tell you…" She jumped to her feet, tears beginning to stream down her face. "Mister Picquett gave me a boy and a girl, but they were both taken by fever. It was a long time ago…"

Hatty started back down the path toward the farm, breaking into a run as McPherson called out to her. McPherson gave chase, catching up to her only when she lost her balance after tripping over a root hidden by the thick blanket of pine needles covering the ground.

"You okay?" he whispered, kneeling at her side. The tears now flowing unchecked, she nodded. "Let me help you."

Taking his hand, she struggled to her knees until they were face to face, suddenly throwing her arms around him, overwhelmed by the enormity of it all.

"My God, Jess," she cried, "I don't want to lose you."

"Shhhh," he murmured, stroking the back of her head. "I'm not going anywhere—if you'll be my wife."

"Do you mean it?" She leaned back far enough to gaze into his eyes, cupping his face in her hands, searching for the sincerity of what she had just heard.

"You're a very special woman, Hatty." McPherson wiped the tears that continued to break free. "I'd be a fool to walk away from you."

"If thou must love me, let it be for nought but love's sake only." Hatty smiled ever so gently at the effect of her words. "Something I once read. You don't have to marry me, Mister McPherson. Loving me's good enough."

"Miz Picquett, I wouldn't have it any other way. But there are problems, beginning with Sheriff Rainey."

"That's what I was trying to tell you. He talks a lot but that's all there is to it—talk."

"You may be right, but part of that talking was with that preacher I sent packing, and probably to oth- ers as well."

"Without a doubt he has, Jess, but I just don't care…" Once again she threw her arms around him, kissing with a renewed intensity. "Yes, Mister Jesse McPherson, I will become your wife—to have and to hold til death do us part…"

BOOK 4:

So it has come to pass,
The confrontation
With the impossible.

And the winds of change
Continue to blow across the heavens,
Enveloping all who live below...

Twenty Five

McPherson listened with fascination as Wyatt Earp read his testimony in defense of the killings. He had been attending the hearing for the better part of two weeks following his arrival in Tombstone that cold grey dawn near the end of October—just three days after the Earp brothers and Doc Holliday had con- fronted and shot Billy Clanton and the McLaury brothers in a vacant lot off Fremont street.

Tombstone was still buzzing about the shootout when he rode into town and checked into the Grand Hotel. It seemed that everyone he talked to, from the hostler over at the Dexter Livery to the desk clerk at the hotel, had an opinion about the shootout. Holliday and the Earps were either cold-blooded murderers, or duly appointed lawmen who were just doing their job. It wasn't his first experience with the vagaries of western justice—he had been forced more than once into using a gun himself—but it was the first time he had heard of lawmen having to justify their actions in court.

It was almost two months to the day since he had first set off for Tombstone, intending to stop for a while and use it as a base of operations to look around the Arizona Territory if the town seemed a reason- able place. The word around California was that Tombstone was booming and it seemed as good a place to be as any other. While he was there, he planned to seek out John Carr, assuming he was still around, and pass on Belle O'Conner's greetings. It was the least he could do to repay her doctoring after he was ambushed outside of Eureka. But quite unexpectedly, his loose-knit plans changed within hours of his arrival.

He had wandered up the street to the Alhambra Saloon on the chance he could meet Carr—the desk clerk at the Grand had suggested that Carr was known to take his nightly constitutional there. Stepping through the Alhambra's bat-wing doors, McPherson stopped short, momentarily taken aback by the opu- lence of the drinking establishment. He exchanged glances with a few of the younger men as they sized each other up, and once satisfied that he wasn't threatened, he leaned against the bar and ordered a short beer, inquiring if Carr was present.

"Don't recall seein' him this evenin', stranger. But if'n he comes in, who might you be?"

Jesse didn't get the chance to reply as a familiar voice answered for him. "You may tell John that *M'sieur Jesse McPherson* of Tennessee is inquiring."

"René," McPherson exclaimed, grinning from ear to ear. "What in blazes are you doing here?"

"I am…" indicating with a sweeping gesture, "what you call a silent partner in this establishment." "I never figured I'd see you again."

"I am like a bad penny, my friend," *René* laughed, "when you least expect it, there I am. Now tell me.
What brings you to Tombstone?"

"No particular reason other than doing a favor for a lady."

"*Mon vieux*, that can get a man in much trouble," d'Iberville observed. "I trust it is not another affair of the heart?"

"No, no, nothing like that. She doctored me a few months back after I ended up on the wrong side of a bullet."

"You were in a gunfight?" he asked with obvious concern. "Ambush. Almost bled to death. Hadn't been for Belle…" "Belle?"

"Belle O'Conner. She's why I was asking about Mr. Carr; she said she is an old friend."

"And how is Belle?" Standing just behind McPherson was a slender man, nattily dressed in a suit and string tie and walking with a knobby cane that appeared to be more for effect than anything else. "Evenin', *René*."

"*Bonsoir*, John. Permit me to introduce an old friend, *Jesse McPherson*." "How'd ya do, Mister McPherson. I understand you was askin' for me?" "Yes sir. Belle suggested I introduce myself to you if I came this way."

"And so you have. Perhaps you and *René* will join me at my table." Without waiting for a reply, Carr led the way to the rear of the saloon, gesturing at a table partially hidden by a thin latticework partition. The bartender placed an unopened bottle of whiskey in the center of the table and glasses for the three of them. Carr opened the bottle and poured drinks all around.

"Mister McPherson, it's been many a while since I last saw Belle. Has she aged well?"

"Yes sir, she has. Wasn't for her hair, I would have figured her for a much younger woman." Carr nodded. "And thet cowboy Parker, he still around?"

McPherson hesitated before answering, sensing an underlying motive to Carr's question. But rather than unknowingly volunteer some secret, he decided to keep his answers short and to the point.

"Yes sir, he's the one that found me when I was shot." "Fortunate. Did they ever get married?"

"No sir. I got the impression marriage wasn't at the top of the sheriff's list of things to do." "She deserved better."

"Maybe so, but it ain't for me to be passing judgment."

Getting to his feet, Carr abruptly bid them good evening. "You gentlemen will excuse me?"

Caught off guard, McPherson could only stare at Carr's back as he left the Alhambra as suddenly as he had appeared. "Did I say something to offend him?"

"No, my friend. He suffers from the past. You just reminded 'im of it." D'Iberville refilled their glasses before leaning back in his chair. "I see a very different person from the one I bid goodbye in Texas. You are no longer the boy."

McPherson contemplated the glass of whiskey sitting in front of him, faces from the past two years reflecting in the swirling of the amber liquid, reminding him of how much he had experienced, and how lit- tle he had learned. "Don't know that I'd go that far, René. Some folks would find it amazing that I'm still alive."

"Perhaps, but I trust my own judgments. Now. How *did* you come to be here? The last I saw of you was in Corpus Christi."

"I s'pose you could say I been riding in circles." "You are talking in circles as well, my friend."

"Not really," McPherson answered. "Spent most of the last two years just looking around, dodging bullets and crazy cowboys… Thinking about things."

"Ahhh. *Angéline*. She was not easy to forget?" d'Iberville asked encouragingly.

"No, not easy," he replied with a soft chuckle. "More like impossible. But the good side to it was that I learned not to drink some of the rotgut some people got the nerve to call whiskey."

"You are still talking in circles, Jesse."

"Yeah, I guess I am. After Corpus Christi, I wandered all over Texas." McPherson laughed. "You'd be amazed how many saloons there are called The Long Branch. Spent last winter in Wyoming, taking les- sons in growing old and trying to understand women."

"And?"

"Huh. Ain't too sure women *can* be understood."

"My young friend, you have learned much more than you can imagine. Tell me, do you have plans for the next month or so?" McPherson shook his head. "*Bon.* There is a restaurant nearby where the cook has learned to treat steak with reverence. Let us pay *Mademoiselle Cashman* a visit and sample the won- ders of Arizona beef and I will tell you of a venture I am planning…"

•   •   •

McPherson leaned back in his chair at the Russ House and tried to make sense of d'Iberville's pro- posed undertaking. He'd heard stories in his travels about landgrabs and crooked dealings and murder by the railroads in their movement west. The stories were enough to make him wary about getting involved.

"What makes you think the right-of-way is going through that particular place?" McPherson puzzled. "It is, how you say, an arrangement. I have been contracted to negotiate for the right-of-way," d'Iberville explained. "If I am successful, I will realize considerable profit." "How do *I* figure in your planning?"

"You would accompany me to Camp Verde, and should I need assistance, you would make your gun available."

"Whoa up, René," McPherson laughed. "You of all people should know I'm no gunfighter." "Of course not. But you have proven you are a survivor, and that is more important."

"My survival has been more luck than anything else."

"Then I shall trust to your luck. There are those who have very different interests from my own, men who would prefer that the track follow a different route. These men will have no qualms about eliminating their competition, which happens to be me. I require someone that I trust to stand at my back, to act as a second set of eyes. These men do not know you—they will hesitate because you are there."

"Guess I can't argue with your reasoning."

"*Bon.*" D'Iberville stared at his coffee for a moment. "There is one other matter—the Apache."

"I heard talk about them in California, but folks seemed to feel things had calmed down since the Army cornered that bunch up in the Tonto basin."

"It is an illusion, this control. The Apache is not a sheep to be herded. He is like a wild animal—he simply waits for the right moment to strike."

"Sounds like you admire them."

"Oh, I do, my friend, I do. The Apache are a brave and fearless people who have lived in this country for centuries. They have always viewed the arrival of the white man as an invasion, and they are right. It will be a sad day when they are finally beaten."

"So you don't think it's over?"

"It is inevitable the day will come—our numbers will ensure that is the case—but as long as there are men like Mangas Coloradas and Victorio to step forward, it will not be easy. We have taken their homes from them…massacred them. And still they fight. Even now, it is rumored there are raids along the bor- der."

"Then maybe this plan should be delayed…"

"*Je régrette*," d'Iberville replied with great seriousness, "this cannot be. I have committed to return here no later than July."

"Okay, René," McPherson laughed, shaking his head. "I'm your man, though I wonder what you would done if I hadn't happened to show up when I did."

"It is a moot point, my friend. You are here." "I suppose it is. When do we leave?"

"Day after tomorrow. I must make arrangements."

"Good. It'll give me a chance to catch up on my sleep in a real bed."

"You are staying at the Grand?" d'Iberville asked. McPherson nodded, giving him the room number. "Perhaps it is best you wait there. I will send a message when it is time to leave."

"I'm not interested in sitting in a room for two days," McPherson warned.

"You are right, of course. Permit me to think on it. Perhaps I can change my schedule."

With that, McPherson and *d'Iberville* parted company and McPherson returned to the Grand Hotel. Once back in the room, he stripped off his boots and shirt, splashed water into the wash basin, and rinsed off the dust. Refreshed, he stretched out on the bed and instantly regretted he hadn't asked for something at the other end of the building.

The Grand Hotel stood on the corner of Fourth and Allen. His room, located on the second floor, overlooked Allen Street. The loud music emanating from four different saloons, when added to the general street noise, created a cacophony that would have kept the dead awake. But even with the noise, he drifted off to sleep with now distant memories of Angéline DuBois dominating his thoughts.

The soft tapping on the door had little effect on McPherson, other than adding to his dreams. But as it became more insistent, he came fully awake. For a moment, he wasn't sure where he was, but the contin- ued noise billowing up from the street brought him back to reality. Even so, he couldn't imagine why any- one would be knocking on his door. No one knew he was there except for *d'Iberville* and the desk clerk. Reaching behind his head, he drew the Peacemaker and cocked it.

"Yeah?" he called out.

"*Señor McPherson?*" The woman's voice was soft but carried a heavy accent. "Who wants to know?"

"*Señor McPherson*, it is late. I do not like standing in hallways and talking to doors."

By the time she had finished the sentence, McPherson was on his feet and positioned behind the door. Pulling the hasp, he opened the door.

"Come in." The woman inched into the room, the only light a reflection from the lamps at each end of the hallway. As she cleared the door, McPherson eased it shut.

"*Señor…*"

"Right here, lady," he said behind her.

"*Caramba!*" she screamed as she jumped back. "Is this how you greet your visitors?" "Who are you? What are you doing here?"

"I am *Maria del Carman Ranz de Inez*," she answered in a haughty manner. "Beg pardon?"

"*Maria*. You may call me *Maria*."

"All right, Maria, now that I know who you are, what are you doing here?"

"Will you put that thing away," she gestured at the gun in his hand. "I promise not to hurt you." "Oh," he reacted, glancing at the pistol in his hand. In his surprise at the woman's appearance, he had forgotten about the gun. He walked across the room and reholstered the pistol. "Happy?" "I have not decided. *René* did not mention you would threaten me."

"René? What've you got to do with René?"

"He is a friend. He asked me to keep you company."

"Well, that's real nice of René, but what if I don't want company?"

"Then, *Señor McPherson*, you will miss out on the pleasures of sharing a bed with the most beautiful woman in all of Arizona."

McPherson burst out laughing. "Well, Maria, that is an argument that's hard to resist." "Then sit and feast your eyes," she brazenly instructed as she removed her wrap.

Grinning from ear to ear, McPherson fired the lamp sitting next to the bed before straddling the straight-backed chair and leaning his folded arms on the top slat.

The image she portrayed was that of a fancy dance hall girl, complete with billowing hair curled beneath a feathered hat, a gown made of glossy fabric, and black high-heeled button shoes. But as she removed the pins holding her hat and hair in place and deposited them on the bureau, he could see the beginnings of an amazing transformation. The removal of the pins allowed her hair to fall in cascading waves across her shoulders.

As she returned to the middle of the floor, she reached behind her shoulders and slowly worked her way down the hooks holding the dress closed until it was loose from neck to hips, peeled the sleeves from her arms and let the dress fall to the floor in a heap. Now all that remained was a silk camisole held in place by a pink ribbon tied just below her neck, white silk stockings and the shoes. Continuing her strip tease, Maria untied the pink ribbon and allowed the half slip to fall to the floor. She heard his sharp intake of breath as her nakedness came into view, knowing the effect she was having on McPherson.

"Well, *hombre*, what you think? Am I not the most beautiful woman in Arizona?"

The thought occurred to McPherson that he would have to have a talk with *René* about sending women to his room unannounced. The most beautiful? As *René* would probably have put it: a moot point. Standing before him was a woman who was at ease with herself and what she was. Admittedly, by the mid- night light of a lamp, she was as beautiful as she claimed to be. Dark eyes to match her raven black hair; dusky brown skin that glowed next to the white stockings; nipples almost black in the dim light, a thatch of unruly black at the apex of her legs. Spanish? Indian? Whoever her parents were, the combination worked.

"You have lost your tongue, *Señor McPherson*?"

"No… I was just thinking I should have a talk with René."

"You will have much time to talk to *René* after you leave," she teased, locking her fingers behind his head and pressing his face between her black-tipped globes. "Now, you must show me you think I am beautiful."

McPherson was slow to get to his feet, the faint odor of her perspiration clinging to his nostrils. He glanced out the window as he trimmed the lamp, and was not surprised to see d'Iberville standing on the wooden sidewalk in front of the Alhambra, the glowing tip of a cigar just visible in the darkness. A most unusual man. McPherson turned his attention to the woman.

TWENTY SIX

McPherson woke in a stupor, bathed in sweat from the heat of the late morning sun pouring in the closed window. He couldn't remember when the woman had left, only that she had. The constant din just outside his hotel room was becoming annoying, especially since it was competing with an even louder pounding at the back of his head. Crawling off the bed, he staggered across the room and poured the pitcher of tepid water over his head in a vain attempt to stop the pounding. The din outside the room was joined by a voice calling out his name.

"Go'way," McPherson mumbled as he returned to sprawl on the bed.

"*M'sieur McPherson?* It is *René*." His voice was taking on an edge of exasperation. "Open the door, *Jesse*. We must talk." "It's unlocked."

As d'Iberville entered the room, his senses were assailed by the musty odors of sex and stale whis- key. "I gather you have enjoyed the pleasures of *Maria*?" he asked as he opened the window.

"I thought so, but my head says otherwise." "You will live, my friend."

"I wonder. Time to leave?"

"No. An unexpected problem has developed. Our journey will be delayed." "How long?"

D'Iberville shrugged. "Two weeks. Perhaps a month. *Maria* can keep you company."

"Don't think I could last that long," McPherson groaned. "That woman don't know the meaning of sleep."

"She is unimportant," d'Iberville replied, dismissing McPherson's remark with a wave of the hand. "You should have sent her away if she annoyed you."

"That's easy for you to say," McPherson said, smiling. "She's got a mind of her own."

"Do as you will," d'Iberville countered brusquely, outright dismissing her. "She is of no conse- quence."

"Seems to me I missed something somewhere, René," McPherson commented. "Two days ago, we're in a big hurry and I'm s'posed to stay out of sight. Now you're telling me it don't matter one way or the other, not to mention the fact you're biting my head off. Mind telling me what's going on, or would you prefer I just disappear into the sunset?"

"I apologize, *M'sieur*." D'Iberville was contrite. "I have considerable expenses and this difficulty of the Earps has created problems."

"Now it's you that's talking in circles, René."

"You would be better off knowing as little as possible."

"Let's get one thing cleared up, René." McPherson's tone became testy. "I agreed to go along because of New Orleans, and the offer stands. But don't mistaken my willingness to help as blind allegiance. The one thing I've learned out here is to not get involved in things that don't concern me."

"A wise decision," d'Iberville agreed. "One that I should follow more often. But since I am obligated to make this journey, I would prefer that it be you that accompanies me. Please. Get dressed and join me for breakfast. I will tell you what I can."

• • •

McPherson was into a second cup and waiting patiently for d'Iberville's explanation. The food had done wonders for his head. He was even prepared to believe he would survive the carousing of the past two days. D'Iberville had spent the past hour describing how he had come to meet Maria.

"…The army discovered them with Cochise's people. Eventually, they sent *Maria* and her mother back to Mexico, but Don Inez, *Maria's* grandfather, was unsympathetic and even less understanding. In his eyes, his daughter was dead."

"His own flesh and blood?"

D'Iberville shrugged. "It was bad enough, *Carmina* being a captive of the Indians. Bearing the off- spring of an 'eathern Apache placed her beyond redemption."

"So she ended up in Tombstone?"

"Not right away. A kindly priest offered *Carmina* and the child sanctuary: a life of austerity, hard work and little else."

"Hard to imagine that woman being raised in a church."

"I suppose it depends on your perspective, but you are right. It was not a life they chose to continue." D'Iberville shook his head in amazement. "She is a strange one, *Maria*. She has the beauty and fire of her mother and the wildness of her father. I am convinced the blood of a high-born Spanish lady and an Apache warrior do not mix"

Jesse listened with amusement as d'Iberville rambled on, convinced his friend was deliberately avoiding the real subject. But d'Iberville must have read his thoughts as he abruptly changed direction.

"It is said that Tombstone is the last frontier," d'Iberville observed with sadness. "When it is finally civilized…"

"Don't seem that different from a lot of other places I've been."

"There is much bad blood here… The Clantons and McLaurys have many friends."

"Ain't been here long enough to know, René, but what little I've heard ain't good. People say they're cattle thieves."

"They have been accused of many things, my friend, as have the Earps and many others as well, but it is normal for those who live on the edge of society to be in that position."

"So what does the gunfight have to do with you? Or am I supposed to guess?"

"A few years ago, I made the acquaintance of John Clum when he was the White Mountain Agent." McPherson interrupted. "The mayor?"

"The same. After you and I parted company in Corpus Christi, I decided to pay him a visit rather than return to *New Orléans*. He 'ad settled in Tombstone and started the *Epitaph*. It was through his efforts that I gained an interest in the Alhambra."

"The *Epitaph* seems to think the Clantons and McLaurys deserved what they got."

"John has long been an admirer of the Earps." "You don't agree?"

"I try to not take sides. I have had dealings with them all." "So what's the problem?"

"The Earps have been accused of murder."

"First time I heard of a man carrying a badge being charged with murder."

"Innocence is a virtue in short supply here," he explained with a shrug. "Everyone is guilty of some- thing. There will be an official investigation."

"You're losing me, René."

"The Santa Fe Railroad crosses the Arizona Territory north of Prescott and the Verde Valley. The Southern Pacific runs across the south. The plan is to lay track along the San Pedro and Rio Verde and con- nect the two lines at Benson and Prescott. Mayor Clum and Wyatt Earp are two of the *entrepreneurs*."

"Huh?"

"They were to use their prestige to raise money for the venture." "And the gunfight is making people nervous?"

"Just so. I must now endeavor to find other backing in case the hearing goes poorly. It will require time."

"Look, René. I'm not in any rush to get back on a horse. The delay'll give me a chance to look around and sleep in a warm bed for a while. Maybe even play a few hands of cards."

"You are most understanding, Jesse. Is there anything I can do to make the wait more pleasant?" "Nothing comes to mind," McPherson acknowledged.

"I will ask *Maria* to look in on you." "Maybe she's got other things to do." "Not at all. It was her idea."

D'Iberville remained at the table long after McPherson had excused himself and wandered off toward the Dexter Livery to make long term arrangements for the buckskin. He hated lying to the boy, but circum- stances were such that a lie or two were essential if he was to deliver on his promises to Carmina. That was the problem with reality—someone, usually an unsuspecting soul, is often drawn into a fight not of his own making. He had wrestled with the situation for months, years really, and now that it was about to unfold, he was having second thoughts. But a promise is a promise, even one made in a moment of com- passion. He was attempting to create an illusion and the boy was an integral part of the mirage, but at risk, besides their lives, was the friendship that had grown between him and McPherson. Should he discover the truth of what was being asked, all d'Iberville could hope was that he would understand.

Long before he had made the acquaintance of Jesse McPherson, d'Iberville too had felt the lure of the frontier. His travels took him across the southwest and deep into Mexico; and on one of his sojourns to the south, he met Maria's mother and for six glorious months, lived with her in *Puerto Vallarta*. But a sudden outbreak of cholera in the coastal village had ended their idyllic existence. For whatever reason, he was unaffected by the epidemic; Carmina wasn't so fortunate.

He watched helplessly as the disease ravaged her once vibrant body, unable to stop her suffering, unwilling to leave her side. The day before she died, the fever seemed to break and while he felt she should be resting, she was determined to tell him of her past, of her capture by the Apache, of the warrior who took her as a wife, of the daughter she had abandoned to the church. She had extracted promises from him, one of which was that he would see to her daughter's welfare.

After her death, he followed the coast north, vowing to honor his promises, but the undertaking was complicated, and seemed impossible. For months, he wandered the northern region of Mexico, visiting the dozens of missions that had sprouted everywhere—she had been unclear as to where she left the child—but except for obscure recollections, he could find no trace of the girl. Frustrated by his lack of success, he decided to give up, believing he had given the search his best effort, but on the spur of the moment, he stopped off at the *Mission de San Francisco Xavier* in *Magdalena*. The previous time through, they knew of no child fitting the vague description, but on this occasion, a message was waiting for him to proceed to the *Mission de San Ignacio*, a few miles to the north; a child fitting his description was living there.

His first meeting with the child was one of shock. Maria del Carman Ranz de Inez, even at the age of twelve, was the spitting image of her mother: smaller, not yet a woman, but a likeness in every other respect. There was something more, however—a hint of wildness that made him wary. Nevertheless, the impression that she was unaffected by the news of her mother's death was unnerving. She would reluc- tantly walk with him, mostly at the behest of the mission padre, but when the discussions turned to her mother, the walks would end abruptly.

He remained at the mission for more than a week, but once he realized his presence meant little to the child, he made arrangements with the mission to ensure she would continue to be cared for and departed for New Orleans. And that, he believed, was the end of it— he could do no more. Still, his ties with the girl were never completely severed. While he didn't dwell on his failure to break through her resistance, the occasional short message from the mission served to keep alive the memory of her mother and of his promise. The arrival of a letter notifying him that she had left the mission for parts unknown, however, brought everything back into sharp focus—her mother, the promises, his assurance to the child that should she ever need him for anything, he would return. Most of all, he remembered the wildness in the child's eyes and her insistence that when she was old enough, she intended to find and live with her father.

The only problem with the child's plan was that her father was dead, killed by the army when she was a baby. Her mother had been very clear about his death. But when he informed Maria of that fact, it was another detail she refused to discuss. But after rereading the six month old letter, he became convinced that finding her father was exactly what she intended to do. After a few days consideration, he decided the best approach he could take was to head for Fort Apache and the San Carlos Reservation, reasoning that if she actually stuck to her vow and was able to get that far, Fort Apache is where she would eventually show up. Nevertheless, six months was a long time and the odds were strong that even if she had made it to the reservation, she would be gone once she discovered the truth. D'Iberville smiled as he got up from the table. He had been wrong on both counts.

• • •

McPherson's month of waiting turned into two and then three as d'Iberville wandered in and out of Tombstone in his quest for financing. His plans to look around, maybe even take a peek across the border had been put on hold—becoming the victim of marauding Apaches was not high on his list of preferences. Instead, he took to reading the two daily newspapers in an attempt to follow the convoluted power struggle for control of Tombstone. John Clum's *Daily Epitaph* sided with the Earps while the *Tombstone Nugget* took the position that the McLaurys and Billy Clanton were victims of cold-blooded murder. As well, with the assistance of Clum, McPherson was able to wangle a seat and became an interested spectator at the Spicer hearings on the murder charges.

But while the charges against the Earp brothers and Doc Holliday were eventually dropped, the ten- sions between the Earp faction and the Clanton/McLaury faction continued to escalate. The stage running from Tombstone and Benson was attacked in the middle of the night by unidentified men. Startled by the gunfire, the team of horses bolted, effectively thwarting the hold-up. When the coach was stopped, it was discovered that one of the lead horses had been hit by a stray bullet and had to be cut out of the traces. Mayor Clum, who happened to be one of the passengers, claimed it was an attempt on his life and chose to walk the remainder of the way to Benson. A few days later, Virgil Earp, just recovered from the wounds of the original shootout, was hit in the left arm and side by the twin blasts of a double-barreled shotgun as he left the Oriental Saloon, rendering the arm a useless appendage. Wyatt, using his status as a Deputy United States Marshal, went on a hunt in and around Tombstone in search of Virgil's assailants.

With tensions running so high, McPherson and d'Iberville had decided early on that the less conspic- uous he was the better. So after McPherson had spent the better part of November living in the

Grand Hotel, d'Iberville found him a small house near the corner of Sixth and Tough Nut to live in while he waited, an arrangement that proved to be more than convenient. His days blurred into a daily pattern of late rising and late night poker games, more often than not culminating in another session with the seemingly boundless energy of Maria.

In the meantime, Tombstone was going through another political shift. John Clum stepped down as mayor, to be replaced by John Carr, the erstwhile friend of Belle O'Conner. As well, the violence continued with threats and counterthreats, and gunfire in the streets became commonplace. Wyatt Earp and a posse of gunfighters and ranch hands ransacked Charleston, a small mining town just west of Tombstone on the San Pedro. And all the time, Ike Clanton and a third McLaury brother, Will, continued to press their claim that the Earps and Holliday should be tried for murder.

It was with a sense of relief that McPherson began packing after d'Iberville appeared late one eve- ning in February and said it was time.

TWENTY SEVEN

The ride north was uneventful. McPherson and d'Iberville followed established trails along the San Pedro River to the old site of Fort Grant at the mouth of the Arivaipa before cutting northwest and crossing the Gila at Florence. From Florence, they skirted the Superstition Mountains to follow the Rio Verde upstream. It was a decision they were to regret—the only level surface was the river itself and that was complicated by the runoff from the melting snows on top of the craggy mountains that rose on either side. McPherson found himself cursing the day he had agreed to accompany d'Iberville, and on more than one occasion, he made a point of mentioning that the time he had spent with the lovely Maria didn't begin to make up for the experience. But after a month of skirting rockfalls and crossing waist-deep streams, they rode into the lower end of the Verde Valley, and McPherson knew instantly it had all been worthwhile.

"My God, René…"

"It is beautiful, is it not?"

"It's like paradise after what we've seen lately."

"Yes," d'Iberville agreed. "One can appreciate why a man would want to stop here…and why the Apache is so unwilling to give it up."

"Hard to understand why they can't share the land."

"Not really. The Apache's concept of owning the land is much different from our own. He is a nomad; he does not recognize fences. He believes it is his right to travel where he wants, when he wants."

"What's wrong with that?"

"Nothing," d'Iberville answered as he spurred his horse forward. "Nothing at all."

The remainder of the ride into Camp Verde was made in silence, broken only by the sounds of horse hooves scraping on rocks and the occasional scream of hawks soaring high above them. For the second time since McPherson's arrival in Tombstone, d'Iberville was troubled by the conflicts created by McPher- son's innocence in the face of reality. Instinctively, McPherson seemed to feel that the Apache deserved better, but convincing him that they should be helped was another matter entirely. For the moment, it was better he continue to believe their purpose for being in the valley was to purchase a railroad right-of-way.

The buildings of Camp Verde were a collection of single story log and adobe structures, arranged within the lay of the land to gain the best advantage possible against attack from hostile Indians. Except there was no chance of attack. The Indians had been forcibly removed to the San Carlos Reservation some years before. Since that time, most of the soldiers had been transferred to other posts. The few that remained were preparing to close the fort, much to the objection of the two hundred or so whites that had settled in the valley. In their eyes, the departure of the soldiers meant they would be left defenseless; but after five years of relative peace, the army felt Camp Verde was unnecessary.

Nevertheless, the Sutler's Store was still in business and seemed to d'Iberville to be as good a place as any to start asking questions. Originally established to supply the army garrison, the general store had evolved into the center of activity in the valley. It functioned as a dispenser of information, as the town hall and as a place for the settlers to gather for protection when threatened by Indians. As such, it was the per- fect location for d'Iberville to set up shop and get the answers he needed. The excitement built as word spread that he represented the coming of the railroad. Within a week, every rancher in the valley had put in an appearance, and with one exception, were more than ready to sell the land needed for a right-of-way. The possibility that they would be able to get their cattle to market with minimal effort was an enticement they found hard to resist.

Over the following month, d'Iberville and McPherson wandered at will, taking the various ranchers up on their invitations to drop by. McPherson was delighted. The leisurely tour was reminiscent of Sunday afternoons on the family farm, sitting down to home-cooked meals and good company. Unknowingly, his presence was masking d'Iberville's real motive for being there. McPherson's involvement with the valley's citizens, however, increasingly concerned d'Iberville. The possibility of him siding with them was a prob- lem he hadn't anticipated. To counter his buoyant mood, d'Iberville decided it was time for a history lesson and another taste of reality…

The Arizona Territory was a boiling cauldron in 1881. Pressures on the region had been building for years, first from the West as pros- pectors that had failed to strike it rich in the gold fields of California appeared along the lower Colorado River, and then from the East, as immigrants poured into the New Mexico mountains in ever-in- creasing numbers, also in search of the elusive yellow mineral. Towns sprang up quickly as word spread about a strike and disappeared just as fast as the few pockets of ore that were found petered out. But the occasional discovery of small deposits wasn't enough, and many of the miners tired of the daily diet of heat and dust and lack of reward for their efforts. They began prowling the moun- tains and valleys of Arizona looking for other ways to survive, and straining the already difficult relation- ship that existed between the army and the various Indian tribes that called that part of the world home.

From the very beginning, the army warned the settlers that the region was not healthy for whites, that the region was controlled by hostile Indians who would not look kindly upon their presence. But these warnings were complicated by the fact that many in the army saw themselves as being the leading element in the settlement of the West—a point that didn't go unnoticed by the very people they were supposed to protect. The army's warnings were ignored, setting off an escalating cycle of violence that would scar the territory for years to come, and nowhere was this more evident than in the eastern and central portions of the Arizona Territory.

As had been the case over much of North America, there was never any serious attempt by the new- comers to understand the position of the people who already lived there. The Indian was seen as a nui- sance, to be contained if possible, eliminated if necessary. In a few cases, tribal leaders recognized the inescapable truth that they were outnumbered and could not win. They attempted with limited success to make whatever deal they could to allow their people to survive. Others were not so easily convinced; none less so than the Apache.

The conflict between the Apache and their neighbors was an old story. The Apache were unique in the region: a nomadic people in the midst of a number of sedentary tribes, and from a time preceding the first incursion of the Spanish explorers, the Apache had fought tooth and nail to retain what they considered to be their land, a vast region encompassing most of the Arizona and New Mexico territories as well as portions of Colorado, Texas, and Old Mexico.

By the middle of the 1700s, the Apache had become masters of guerilla warfare, combining hit-and- run tactics with an intimate knowledge of the rugged desert landscape to terrorize their enemies. But it was not until the arrival of the gold seekers and would-be homesteaders in their wake that the Apache way of life was seriously threatened. Their reaction was immediate and violent. Small bands, acting on their own initiative, launched random attacks, one day laying waste to a new homestead and leaving the occupants dead or dying; on another day, attacking a way station, a wagon train or a mining operation.

The focus of the Apache attacks—white-skinned invaders who overran land the Apache had called home for centuries—were at least as responsible as the Apache for the situation. They showed no respect for the rights of the Indian and, in fact, saw themselves as innocent victims and demanded army protection. The army, responding to the outcry, retaliated indiscriminately against the Apache, lumping the different factions into a common enemy: Apaches were Apaches, to be contained or ground into the dust.

The attitude of the army was contagious. The Apache was at the mercy of whites who lured them into the agencies with false promises and then mercilessly killed them. Mangas Coloradas was taken pris- oner under a flag of truce, then tortured and finally murdered. Cochise, after living peacefully for a number of years under the auspices of the army was falsely arrested. The Aravaipa, massacred.

Victorio, killed. Camp Grant. Skull Canyon. San Carlos. Pinole. Verde Valley.

The valley was appropriately named. Located in the northern Arizona Territory between the Mogol- lon Rim to the East and the Black Hills to the West, the valley flourished as few other locales in the region could. Fed by the *Rio Verde*, the valley was thick with syc- amore and cottonwood and tall grasses. As well, it hinted at mineral wealth just waiting to be dug from the ground. To the first whites that ventured into the valley, it seemed a Garden of Eden amidst the des- ert; and for those that eventually stayed, the river and its outgrowth became a lifeline, just as it was for the many Indian tribes that for cen- turies had called the valley home. But therein lay the problem—the Indians. They were a problem that refused to go away…

"It is referred to as Bloody Tanks. I am told they were enticed with promises of food and tobacco and then slaughtered like sheep." A soft anger underlined *d'Iberville's* explanation. "The Yavapai were too trusting…"

McPherson had been inundated with story after story of attacks against the Apache for the entire ride since leaving Camp Verde, and now as they neared Fort Whipple, he had severe doubts as to what he would see at the Indian encampment outside the fort. He had already heard more than he cared to, even agreed that the Apache had gotten a raw deal, but there were enough stories about Indian savagery from the settlers in the valley to more than make up for anything …could come up with. Moreover, he saw no con- nection to the accepted reason for his being there and d'Iberville wasn't helping—he suddenly seemed to be more interested in teaching history than establishing a right-of-way for railroad tracks. It was a puzzling change, and one that needed clarifying.

"How much longer you going to need me, René?" The question caught d'Iberville off guard. "A month, perhaps. Why do you ask?"

"Nothing specific. Guess I'm just getting the urge to move on." "You are not enjoying my company?"

"Not that…" "Then what?"

"It's… I s'pose I can't see why you're going to all this trouble just to educate me." "I am merely informing you of Arizona history," d'Iberville replied guardedly.

"Maybe so, but if'n I'm to believe any of what was said in the valley, you're only telling part of it." "The Apache were only protecting that which was theirs."

"I'll grant you that. But you told me in Tombstone that the reign of the Apache in Arizona was at an end."

"Not quite yet, my young friend. Not quite yet."

TWENTY EIGHT

The map they were using called it Promontery Peak, but it was more appropriately a butte that jutted out from the Mogollon Rim. McPherson and d'Iberville had idled away the better part of two days there, waiting McPherson assumed, for someone to appear or something to happen. D'Iberville had spent the entire two days at the edge of the butte, staring out over the panorama of the Tonto Basin to the south. Late in the evening of the second day, he got slowly to his feet, his attention concentrated on an arroyo off to the southwest.

"*M'sieur McPherson*! We are about to have visitors. It would be a most opportune time for you to show restraint should you feel threatened."

"Who are they?"

"They are of the White Mountain Apache." "Do we have business with them?"

"Not we, my friend. Me. They are here to see me." "Am I allowed to ask why?"

"*Certainement*. I have agreed in principle to make rifles and ammunition available to them." "You've lost your senses," McPherson exclaimed in amazement.

"Not at all, Jesse. I am merely offering them a more honorable way of dying. You saw the encamp- ment at Fort Whipple. They are nothing more than prisoners in their own land, condemned to live by rules they neither asked for nor understand."

"That may be so, but supplying guns to them is just gonna get a lot of innocent people killed."

"An unfortunate consequence," *d'Iberville* conceded. "But innocence is not restricted to the one side."

"With all due respect, René, maybe it's best I move on. I want no part of this."

"Regretfully, you have no choice. You are here and you must remain here until they depart." "Damn you, René," McPherson protested angrily, "it ain't my fight."

"There will be no fight here," d'Iberville patiently countered. "It is merely a place far beyond the eyes and ears of the soldiers. Tomorrow, I will conduct my business with the Apache and we will then be on our way back to Tombstone."

"No," McPherson countered. "After tomorrow, we go our separate ways…and any debt I owe you will be paid in full."

"I am sorry you feel that way; but if those are your wishes…"

"René, back in New Orleans you taught me a valuable lesson about choosing a time and place. But you didn't give me the chance to do either."

"We do not always have the luxury of choosing our moments. They come suddenly and without warning. If I had misjudged you…"

"I gave you my word. That should have been enough."

"You must understand, Jesse. Many years ago, I made commitments to a woman such as *Angéline*. Tomorrow will be the culmination of those promises. I could not take the risk that you would change your mind."

"I still might. Now suppose you tell me about those promises. And for once, don't leave anything out…"

"…I loved her, Jesse, more than I thought it possible to love anyone. When she died, a part of me died with her. She was warm and giving…and she asked little in return. For the first time in my life, I was helpless to do anything. I would gladly have exchanged places with her, but such bargains are not possi- ble." D'Iberville's eyes misted over.

"Once she knew she was dying," he continued, "she made two requests: that I look after her child, and that if possible, I try to help the Apache regain their dignity and their honor. I failed with the child, an admission I find most painful. I would not have chosen for her the path she took, but she has made her own way in spite of my interference. The irony is that once I stopped intruding in her affairs, we became friends, and I was able to talk to her of her mother, to tell her of the promises I made and the impossibilities they presented. It was she who suggested how I could best help the Apache, and tomorrow, my promise will be fulfilled."

"But selling guns…?"

"The Apache are an honorable people. They would not allow me to give them the guns without pay- ment."

•   •   •

McPherson stared out into the moon-lit night, wondering how he had come to be in the middle of Arizona, wondering if he would ever see Tennessee again. Nothing out there but desert and hostile Indians, his father had said. He had been wrong about there being nothing but desert, but the warning about hostiles was very much in his mind. Certainly, it wasn't the first time he had speculated on the possibility his time had come, but the fact that his survival was dependant on d'Iberville and his Apache friends didn't set too well.

He accepted that d'Iberville had finally told him the truth and in a strange sort of way, he wished he hadn't. Since the day they arrived at Fort Whipple, d'Iberville hadn't been too forthcoming with explana- tions as to why they were there, but in retrospect, he hadn't been too forthcoming about anything. Once they reached the fort and paid their respects to the commander, d'Iberville had left McPherson to his own devices and ridden off toward the Indian encampment, not reappearing until the next day. He made no effort to explain his disappearance, or how long they would remain in the area. For better than a week, McPherson passed the time in front of the Sutler's Store just outside the fort aimlessly whittling on a length of dead wood he had found at the side of the building, interrupting his efforts only to grab a bite to eat or to wander off to the campsite to sleep.

Initially eyed with suspicion by army personnel, he was ignored after a couple of days as the soldiers went about their business. McPherson was bemused by the activity; by all indications, they seemed to be scurrying about and accomplishing little or nothing. The soldiers were a ragtag bunch, a collection of misfits and ne'er-do-wells who had fled the misery of the Eastern cities and the oppressive aftermath of the Southern defeat. Except for regulation blue pants with a yellow stripe and yellow handkerchiefs knotted about their necks, there was little consistency to their uniforms. Hats and shirts were as varied as the wear- ers and their choice of weapons was just as inconsistent. He was struck by the thought that if this bunch was any example, it was a wonder they were able to beat the South.

At long last d'Iberville put in an appearance, and just as he had in Tombstone, announced that it was time to move out. But instead of trailing south as he had originally suggested, *René* decided at the last min- ute—or so McPherson thought—to follow the trail laid down years before by General Crooke in his fight with the Apache, a trail that traversed the central part of the territory between Fort Whipple and Fort Apache along the escarpment known as the Mogollon Rim. McPherson had questioned the change for the simple reason that the rumors they heard in Tombstone had been repeated and expanded on at Fort Whip- ple. Fears that the Apache were once again preparing to bolt the reservation persisted, as did the warnings that travel along the rim was dangerous. Even so, d'Iberville had shown little concern about the possibility they would encounter renegade Apaches, a con-fidence McPherson didn't fully share.

But getting *René* to talk about the potential danger was a waste of time. When pushed on the point, *René* had surprised him by suggesting that perhaps he should move on, and the fact was, he had already decided to head toward Colorado. D'Iberville's appar-ent change of heart, however, had piqued McPher- son's curiosity, enough to convince him to stick around and find out why *René* was being so secretive. He understood d'Iberville's problem. A man's word was the one consistency of the frontier; it was accepted at face value because survival often depended on it. Even so, supplying weapons to the Indians—any Indi- ans—was a hanging offence.

It was near dawn when he finally dropped off to sleep, but the low drone of voices off to one side was enough to snap him back to consciousness. Squatting a few feet away was a small bare-chested man dressed in buckskin pants and calf-high moccasins, his shoulder length hair contained by a wide cloth head band. Lying casually across his knees was an army issue Springfield. Without thinking, Jesse reached for the pistol laying next to his head.

"*M'sieur!*" D'Iberville's tone was enough to stay his hand. "They will regret killing you since you are my friend, but kill you they will if you touch that weapon." Seeing that McPherson intended to get up, he added a warning. "Please move slowly until they see that you pose no threat."

Peeling off the blanket still damp from morning dew, McPherson got to his feet slowly, exaggerating each movement. The squatting youth, rifle cradled in the crook of his arm, also stood up, never taking his eyes from McPherson.

"Am I allowed to make coffee?"

"Of course," d'Iberville answered matter-of-factly before rattling off a few guttural words to the youth. "The boy will follow you to the spring."

Continuing to exaggerate his movements, McPherson retrieved the coffee pot, all the while taking stock of the situation. He concluded that d'Iberville was right. Besides the boy, he counted eight others scattered around their camp, and was forced to assume there were others. It would be suicidal to try any- thing. Coffee pot in hand, he followed a worn path that circled a small rise in the terrain down to a water- filled depression fed by an underground spring, his Apache escort hard on his heels. After rinsing and fill- ing the pot with fresh water, he knelt beside the small pool and splashed water on his face to cut through the dust and remnants of sleepiness that still prevailed. All the while, the boy maintained a respectful dis- tance from McPherson while following his every movement.

Both McPherson and the boy were startled by the unexpected appearance beyond the spring of an armed Apache wearing a blue army tunic. McPherson thought for a brief moment that he was just another member of the band, but the boy reacted instantly, snapping the Springfield to his shoulder. Caught between them, McPherson froze, fully expecting to be shot in the cross-fire.

The two Indians fired simultaneously, but only one bullet found its mark—the boy was dead before he hit the ground at McPherson's feet. McPherson dove for the boy's rifle, but yanked his hand back as the dust kicked up from another round fired in his general direction. Meanwhile, the echos of the three shots disappeared in the sudden onslaught of rifle fire beyond the knoll. As the barrage became sporadic, the Indian in the blue tunic silently gestured toward the path with his rifle barrel.

Mechanically, McPherson got to his feet and picked up the coffee pot, retracing his steps to the campsite, the Apache dogging his steps. Standing next to the fire was an army officer in serious conversa- tion with d'Iberville, while all around, his troops were methodically slaughtering the Indians that had sur- vived the initial assault. McPherson stood dumbfounded, his gut in knots, as the last two found alive were summarily executed where they lay.

"You McPherson?" the Captain asked. Jesse nodded, paralyzed by what had just transpired. "You wanna tell me what yer doin' here?"

"Wha…? Who…?" McPherson stammered, all the while staring wild-eyed at the carnage. "I ask you a question, boy!"

"I'm…" McPherson looked to d'Iberville for help, his tongue still refusing to work.

"I asked the good Captain the same thing, Jesse," d'Iberville offered, "but you can see that for yourself."

"What yer seein' is the completion of an army operation. We been followin' these hostiles since they bolted the reservation at White Mountain."

"This the army way," McPherson asked, the numbness turning to anger, "shooting unarmed men?" "Ya got more sand than sense, boy," the officer answered contemptuously, "Far's I'm concerned, the only good Injun's a dead'un."

"You will notice, Jesse," d'Iberville interjected, "that Captain Reinhold has double standards. He uses the Apache to find the Apache."

"Best you give that mouth of yorn a rest, Frenchie. If it was up to me, you'd be joinin' them friends of yorn in their happy huntin' grounds. The only reason yer still alive is the Colonel wants to use you as an example.”

“Ahhh. Then there is still hope. And what about my young friend here? He had no part in this.”

“So you said. That right, Mister McPherson,” the Captain asked, “you not involved in the French- man’s gun running?”

“Tell him the truth, Jesse,” d’Iberville counselled. “It will not change my destiny, but it may well save your own life.”

“Well, Mister McPherson?”

“No, Captain, I wasn’t involved, but after seeing your methods of justice, I’m beginning to think the wrong bunch is winning.”

“Humph! Time you and others like you understand that civilization’s movin’ in and they ain’t no place fer these savages. Sergeant!” he barked.

“Yessir!”

“See to gettin’ this traitor and his friend mounted. We move out in fifteen minutes.”

D’Iberville protested. “But you said…”

“I said I’d listen,” Reinhold interrupted, “but it ain’t fer me to judge. The army’ll decide if’n he’s tellin’ the truth. Now git yer horses saddled or you’ll be walkin’.”

“Captain?” asked McPherson. “May I have a moment with *René*?” “Give them five minutes, Sergeant,” the Captain said as he walked off.

McPherson waited until they were both out of earshot before speaking. “What are we going to do, René?”

“*We* are going to do nothing. They will put me on trial at Fort Apache. You must testify against me; it is the only way you can survive.”

“But what about you?”

“I suspect they plan to lock me in Yuma Territorial and throw the key away. If I am lucky, maybe they will hang me. Yuma is not a healthy place to live out one’s life.”

“I can’t let that happen.”

“You do not have a choice in the matter, my friend.” D’Iberville laughed. “I have been a thorn in the army’s side and they are not very forgiving. But then, neither are the Apache. When they hear of this, it will start all over again." Reaching out, d'Iberville shook Jesse's hand firmly. "Have faith, my friend. Despite what I just said, I have no intention of providing entertainment for them."

As McPherson saddled the buckskin, his growing animosity was visible to one and all. At length, the Captain rode over to confront him.

"Somethin' on yer mind, boy?"

"Just thinking that this is the first time I've understood why folks back home hate that uniform." "I'm gonna give you a piece of advice, *Mister* McPherson. That's twice you've insulted the army, and twice you've insulted me. Now personally, I'm willin' to ignore it, but if I was you, I'd bite my tongue afore makin' any more comments. Sergeant! Move 'em out."

Despondency set in quickly as McPherson fell into line as the troops moved away from the campsite. His worse fears about d'Iberville's dealings had suddenly and violently come to pass. The soldier's massa- cre of the Apache band without their giving a second thought stunned him. He'd heard talk about other such occurrences, but to actually witness the murder of unarmed men by the army simply because they were Indians shook him to the core. As well, d'Iberville faced prison or a rope and unless he was able to convince the army otherwise. So did he.

Two hours north of the butte, the soldiers and their prisoners rode slowly eastward in single file, their movement raising a choking cloud of fine dust that permeated any and everything. Eyes were bloodshot, throats parched from the irritating dust, raising the level of irritation to new heights. *René* d'Iberville, in his position near the front of the procession, became the focal point of their irritation. The massacre of the Apache band had been forgotten as soon as they had ridden away—it was now a thing of the past. D'Iber- ville was the real cause of their discomfort. At the behest of the first sergeant, Captain Reinhold had called a halt to allow the troop to dismount and clear the dust from their mouths and throats. His hands still tied behind him, d'Iberville kicked free of the stirrups and swung his right leg over the pommel before sliding to the ground.

"Who told you to dismount, Frenchie?"

"Why, no one, Captain. But I am thirsty just as your men are."

"That so?" Reinhold looked around at his motley bunch. "Anyone here want to give the Frenchman a drink of water?" The only reaction to his question was a ripple of derisive laughter. "Looks like yer outta luck, Frenchie."

"Surely you don't intend to deny me food and water until we reach Fort Apache?"

"Far's I'm concerned, it'd be a waste to give you anythin', but I ain't give it a lot of thought an that's a fact."

"I'm curious, Captain, as to why you dislike me so much. I've done nothing to you."

"Understand me, Frenchie. Hadn't been fer scum like you, we'd afinished the Apache off years ago.

Now git mounted. I'm gonna take pleasure seein' you hang." "I think not, Captain."

D'Iberville took a hesitant step and then another, caught up in defying the army one last time, at last striding confidently toward the rear of the column. Reinhold watched until he had passed the last man before giving the order to shoot. A half dozen soldiers fired a volley into his back, laughing as he pitched forward into the powdery dust.

For the second time that day, McPherson's senses were assaulted by the mindless actions of the rag- tag army troop. *René* had died without a struggle, the result of a half dozen bullets in his back, his hands still bound. The senseless slaughter of the Indians was numbing, but d'Iberville's murder pushed him beyond any realm of understanding. Supplying weapons to the Apache might have been a poor decision on his part, but he didn't deserve such an end.

"You gonna shoot me in the back too, Captain?" McPherson asked, fighting to keep the bile out of his mouth.

"No, but I'm gonna give you some advice. There's a trail fifty mile east of here that leads out of the Arizona Territory. I'd suggest you take it."

"And if I don't?"

"Then you'll likely find yerself charged with the Frenchman's murder." "What about my weapons?"

"If I'm of a mind to give 'em back, they'll be waiting for you up ahead. Best you think on that. Move 'em out, Sergeant."

TWENTY NINE

An embittered and angry McPherson began digging a final resting place for d'Iberville out of the dry, hard-baked earth even as the soldiers rode out of sight. With each exertion, McPherson's anger intensified, fueled by memories of d'Iberville's intervention in New Orleans following Angéline's death. *René* had befriended him, had taken him under his wing and taught him how to survive in a world that was often vio- lent and unrelenting.

McPherson threw the small spade aside and bent to pick up the lifeless form that was once his friend, laying the d'Iberville's remains in the shallow depression with a reverence he had seldom experienced. After covering the body with a cloth from his pack, he began piling stone on top until he was satisfied the grave would not be disturbed.

"Dust to dust, my friend," McPherson muttered with a quiet intensity, and just as d'Iberville had seen to Angéline's burial, he committed *René* to his grave with a vow to follow Reinhold to the ends of the earth. *"Vengeance is mine, saith the Lord."* Well, *Not this time,* thought McPherson. *Not this time. There's a debt involved…*

After a final goodbye, McPherson mounted and turned the buckskin east along the Mogollon Rim, a cold fury prodding him onward. To the east, the trail would divide. To the northeast lay Colorado and beyond that, Wyoming. To the southwest was Fort Apache and certain trouble. Under normal circum- stances, common sense would have dictated that he take Reinhold's advice and ride north, advice he was sure René would have echoed. But the circum- stances were decidedly abnormal.

Two days later, McPherson pulled up at an obscure junction in the trail. He would probably have missed it had it not been for the fact that some thoughtful soul had stuck a broken board in the rocks point- ing away from the rim, the name Durango roughly lettered across it. But other than to give him pause, the sign was wasted on McPherson. What did catch his attention was that his rifle and pistol had been left next to the sign.

Dismounting, he clambered up the rocks to retrieve the weapons, automatically checking their loads. He was not too surprised to find they were both empty. Glancing toward the southeast, McPherson decided that Reinhold could wait. The first thing he had to do was clean the weapons: it wouldn't do for either of them to jam at the wrong moment.

At sunrise, McPherson pushed on, allowing the horse to pick his way along the boulder strewn trail, unmindful of his own words that "it was not his fight". He could see, in the distance below the rim, the cloud of dust being kicked up by Reinhold and his men. Why they hadn't shot him down as well was puz- zling: he was wit- ness to the slaughter of the small band of Apaches and the subse- quent murder of d'Iber- ville. But since he was still alive, the least he could do in return was to exact payment from the army captain for Rene's life. To do anything else would have been akin to running away from himself…

The shifting cloud of dust that marked Reinhold's position for the past week had disappeared, replaced by a static haze that hung in the air like fog on a fall morning. McPherson had paid little interest to the cloud since turning southeast, other than to ensure he didn't ride up on the troopers unexpectedly. The disappearance of the cloud, however, was reason enough to take notice. But as he drew nearer to the fort, McPherson could see the reason for the haze. There were formations marching both in and outside the fort kicking dust into the air; and with the fort sitting nestled against the side of a series of low hills, the dust had nowhere to go but up. The question that piqued his curiosity, however, was why all the activity?

Leaving the trail, McPherson concealed himself on high ground within spitting distance of the fort and kept an eye on the furor until late into the afternoon, taking note of all the comings and goings. His anger had cooled somewhat, enough to make him think ahead instead of stumbling pell mell into a hornet's nest—and a hornet's nest described Fort Apache precisely. He had already concluded that he should at least make an effort to go about things legally, to report the events as they had occurred up on the Rim and let the law handle things, but the formations and frequent patrols charging in and out of the fort unnerved him. This was not the lethargy of Fort Whipple: these people were going about their business with great serious- ness—a small detail he should have been paying more attention to.

For the second time in a week, he was taken prisoner—in his effort to make out the occasional raised voice drifting toward him, he failed to hear the Apache scouts that had come up behind him. The massacre of the White Mountain band ingrained in his memory, he got slowly to his feet, obeying their silent gesture to mount up. There was no effort to disarm him, but he took little comfort in that fact. For a brief moment, he had forgotten the lessons and let his guard down. He realized very clearly it was a mistake that could prove to be costly.

• • •

"Have a seat, McPherson, be with you in a moment."

The ride into the fort had been an education. Apparently, every Indian at the fort had been herded into a fenced compound and placed under armed guard. Why he thought he would be able to avenge *René's* senseless death was curious at best. Now, as he sat impa- tiently across from the fort commander while the Colonel fussed with papers on his desk, his problem was his own survival.

"Well, Mister McPherson. You're not much for taking advice." "Free country, Colonel," McPherson offered as explanation.

"Not out here, Sir…" the officer countered as he took a cigar from a humidor sitting on the corner of his desk. McPherson watched as the colonel took a small pair of scissors from the humidor stand and care- fully cut the tip from one end of the cigar, dampened the length of the cigar with saliva, and lit it. "Not when Geronimo's on the warpath and you're sitting up in the hills spying on my fort."

"I wasn't exactly spying, Colonel. Just being cautious."

"Cautious? About what? Fort Apache's one of the safest places in the Arizona Territory."

"I had a run-in with one of your officers. Didn't especially want to meet up with him just yet." "Captain Reinhold? Good officer. Mind you, he's a bit rough around the edges."

"He's also a murderer."

"A murderer? That's a serious charge, Mister McPherson. Just who is it that he murdered?"

Had McPherson paid attention to the patronizing tone in the colonel's question, he might have saved himself the embarrassment of plunging into the details of the massacre and subsequent death of his friend. But it wasn't until the colonel laughed that he understood he was wasting his time.

"Mister McPherson, that band of marauders you say were murdered escaped from here a few weeks ago. Their sole purpose in doing so was to make war on the white man. And that so-called friend of yours was intending to supply them with guns. Do you understand? We are at war out here, and it's one I don't intend to lose."

"You figure to kill them all?"

"I am indifferent to their fate," he answered with a shrug. "They have been given a place to live and the choice to do so. If they prefer to die instead, then I intend to accommodate them."

"Uh huh," McPherson replied caustically. "I saw an example of your methods on the way in." "Mister McPherson," he explained philosophically, "my job is to protect the settlers, not these savages. The time of the red man in Arizona is over. Not too long into the future, this territory will be judged as civilized and Arizona will become a state."

"Geronimo might have something to say about that."

"Geronimo be damned. All he can do is delay the inevitable and get a lot more people killed. But it's only a matter of time until we find him, and when we do, it will be over. We are here to stay."

"Then you intend to do nothing?"

"Nothing to be done. Captain Reinhold was following his orders." "Does that include shooting a man in the back?"

"I'm told he was trying to escape."

"How far could he have gotten, Colonel? His hands were tied behind his back."

"Mister McPherson, I am making an effort to be patient, but you are becoming trying. D'Iberville sold guns to the Indians, guns that were used to kill God-fearing men and women that came out here to make a new life. In my book, that made him the lowest scum on this earth. My officers are allowed discre- tionary judgment in the field. While I would have preferred that d'Iberville be tried and hanged, if Reinhold says that he was trying to escape, I do not intend to second guess him."

"Well, that's clear enough." McPherson got to his feet. "I guess I'll be on my way."

"Not so fast, McPherson. Just as soon you stick around for a while. I don't especially want civilians wandering around the countryside until this thing is over."

"You preventing me from leaving, Colonel?"

"No sir. I'm trying to do my job, which is to help you keep your scalp." "And if I don't want your help?"

"Your choice, Mister McPherson, your choice. Personally, I don't care if you live or die, but if I were you, I'd think about it. You were fortunate to get this far. You might not be so lucky if you leave."

"Fair enough, Colonel, I'll think about it."

• • •

The evening was late. The only men still in the small saloon run by the sutler were gathered around a table with a half-empty bottle of whiskey and an abandoned deck of greasy cards. The poker game had bro- ken up more than an hour before, but with nothing more than a campsite to return to, the men were hesitant to abandon the evening, choosing instead to exchange observations and more than a few tall tales about their experiences.

McPherson had joined the game out of boredom, a fact of life for each of them since the fort com- mander had not so subtly sug- gested that all civilians temporarily call the fort home. These men— prospec- tors all—reminded McPherson of the many travelers that had stopped by the family farm with their tales of the west, and more than once, they made him think of Anton Schlesinger. The difference, however, was that he was now older and wiser, and a little less inclined to believe everything he heard. In a sense, he was now one of them, sharing pieces of information heard along the way.

His anger had eased somewhat, not enough to make him forget what had happened on the Rim, but enough to make him wonder why he was sitting on his backside and twiddling his thumbs. He had now spent the better part of a week lazing around the fort and had yet to see Reinhold, much less confront him. But as the time passed, his thoughts dwelled less on revenge and more on other places and other times. He hadn't changed his mind. Reinhold deserved punishment, but killing him wouldn't bring *René* back. What it would do was guarantee a hangman's noose. He concluded the best decision he could make was to ride north and forget about Reinhold, perhaps drop in on Molly and see how she was faring.

Circumstances, however, often take on a life of their own and the decision to leave was made for him.

Outside the saloon, a sudden commotion disturbed the quiet conversation, but before they could react, the commotion moved inside as Captain Reinhold and a couple of other officers came through the doors, roughly slapping their tunics in an attempt to remove part of the accumulated dust. Stepping up to the bar, they splashed whiskey into glasses from the bottle set in front of them, tossed them back, and filled them again. It wasn't until the glasses had been upturned again that Reinhold noticed McPherson.

"Well, now, if'n it ain't the Injun lover," Reinhold jeered. "Thought I told you to ride north."

"It's like your Colonel said," McPherson replied, "I ain't much for taking advice."

"Seems like that's a fact. I'm surprised the Colonel let you stay around, bein' as how you hang out with gun runners and all."

"Maybe if you put in a good word for me, he'll change his mind."

"I just might, now that you mention it. Meantime, you best stay out of my way." "What's your problem, Captain? Couldn't find any Indians to kill today?"

"Why you no good…" Reinhold drew his pistol as he rushed across the room, but Reinhold's momentary burst of anger was a serious miscalculation. McPherson was waiting for him, the Peacemaker cocked and aimed, his finger on the trigger.

"Put it away, Captain. Much as I'd take pleasure in pulling this trigger, this is not a good time for either one of us to die."

Reinhold's immediate instinct had been to duck when he saw the .44 in McPherson's hand. McPher- son's reluctance to fire, however, had only served to make him look foolish.

"You won't shoot me…" he taunted. "You'd hang."

"You willing to bet your life on that, Captain?" McPherson asked in a whisper. "Drop it." "I can't do that."

"You don't have a choice."

An eternity passed as the tense standoff between McPherson and Reinhold enveloped everyone in the room, so much so that no one realized the Sutler had stepped from behind the bar with a 12 gauge shot- gun.

"Okay, Gents, time to put 'em away." Both Reinhold and McPherson ignored the Sutler, but the unmistakable sound of shotgun hammers being cocked got their attention. "Come on, Cap'n. You know the Colonel don't take kindly to shootin's in my saloon."

"Not your concern, Storekeep."

"Well, Cap'n, this here scattergun says yer wrong."

"I'm warnin' you, Storekeep. You're interferin' in Army business."

"That so? Lest I got my information wrong, Cap'n, Mister McPherson has spent the last week here at the Colonel's behest."

"The man's a troublemaker."

"Seems to me yer the one thet's startin' things, Cap'n. This man ain't even raised his voice." "Damn it…"

"Cap'n, whatever it is, yer gonna have to take it somewhere else. Now, please, put the gun away and go home."

Reinhold again started to argue, but suddenly spun on his heels and storming out the door, his com- panions close behind.

McPherson felt a sudden sense of relief, as he eased off the hammer. The spell that held them all in its grip was broken, and while he had followed Reinhold to the fort with the intention of seeking vengeance, he was once again reminded it was not his way. McPherson got to his feet and returned the Peacemaker to its holster, surprised at the weakness he felt in his legs.

"Mista McPherson!" Jesse glanced toward the bar. "I gather you ain't much fer takin' advice, but it might be best fer you to consider movin' on. What with Captain Reinhold and all, it'll be no more risky than stickin' round here."

"Shouldn't have come here in the first place," McPherson declared. "Be seeing you."

McPherson slipped outside and looked around before climbing aboard the buckskin. He was tired, but his fatigue had an edge to it that would make it difficult to sleep. As he rode toward his campsite, he concluded the Sutler was right—the best thing was to move on, and tonight was as good a time as any.

He broke camp quickly and rode slowly away from the fort, all the while expecting a bullet to come out of the darkness. But except for the occasional howl of a dog and the restless shuffle of horses, the night seemed peaceful enough. Nevertheless, he stopped periodically as he distanced himself from the fort and looked back down the moonlit trail. Although he could see little or nothing in the dim shadows, he couldn't escape the feeling that he was being followed. But it wasn't until he was high above the fort that he could hear the faint sound of hooves scraping on stone.

His fatigue became secondary as he turned the horses and spurred them into a gallop. He knew it was foolish to run the horses in the dark, but waiting for his pursuers to catch up in unfamiliar terrain made even less sense. By daybreak, McPherson was deep into the hills beneath the Mogollon Rim, and searching for a likely place to wait.

The search was short-lived. In the climb to the top of the Rim, the trail meandered through boulders piled higher than a man on horseback, the path often narrowing so much that riders had to pass through in single file. Twice and then three times, McPherson dismounted and scrambled up the rocks, finally opting for a location that gave him a clear view of the trail, but offered a semblance of protection. After hobbling the horses in a small hollow behind the rocks, he grabbed his Winchester and a box of shells from the sad- dlebags, climbed back up and settled in. He had held fire at the saloon. If Reinhold was blind to that fact, if he wasn't smart enough to leave well enough alone, then so be it. He would have to pay for his persistence.

It was mid-afternoon when he heard the clatter of horse hooves echoing off the rocks. Perched above the trail, McPherson had grown drowsy in the heat of the sun, nodding off more than once as he awaited Reinhold. He was surprised that Reinhold had taken so long to catch up—the sun was already well along its downward trek. Even so, the sudden appearance of a horse and rider in his sights startled him. Without warning, McPherson pulled the trigger, snapping the barrel aside in the last instance when he realized the rider wasn't in an army uniform. The ricocheting round stopped the rider in his tracks.

"That's far enough, Mister," McPherson called out, the echoes from the shot multiplying even as they faded into the distance.

"Thet you, McPherson?" the rider asked.

"It is," McPherson answered testily, straining to make out the identity of the rider through the heat waves coming off the rocks and sand. "Why're you trailing me?"

"Name's Guthrie. Alright if'n I ride a little closer?" McPherson couldn't put a face to the voice either, but it wasn't Reinhold. The man was bearded and dressed in clothes more common to prospectors. He was carrying a long rifle covered by a leather sheath balanced across his lap.

"I can hear you fine right where you're at, Mister," McPherson countered, levering another round into the rifle. "I'm waiting for an answer."

The rider stepped down from his horse and let the reins drop to the ground, unsheathing the Sharps as he took a few tentative steps in McPherson's direction. McPherson fired a second time, the bullet kick- ing up dust at the rider's feet. He glanced down in seeming indifference.

"Yer not very friendly toward strangers, Amigo."

"My lack of friendliness is the least of your worries, Mister. You take another step toward me and I'm gonna put a bullet where it'll hurt."

Guthrie allowed the Sharps to hang loosely in his grip as he looked around, at first focusing his atten- tion on McPherson and then on the rocks behind him. McPherson tensed, puzzled at what the man expected to see, caught between the urge to look for himself and the unwillingness to turn away from the danger below.

"Time you answered that question, Mister."

"You left a bad taste in Cap'n Reinhold's mouth. He asked me to track you down."

"Well, Mister, you have sure as hell found me. Now s'pose you ride out of here while you can."

"Uh huh. I do appreciate the offer, Amigo, I truly do. But the Cap'n figures he's got some unfinished business with you."

"That so? Where is he?" "I'm up here, McPherson."

The unexpected sound of Reinhold's voice behind him gripped McPherson with a cold dread. He was caught in a cross-fire. His back pressed hard against the rock, he cursed himself for being so dense to think this trail was the only one—while he was occupied with the stranger that had been following him, Rein- hold had circled around and was waiting.

The stranger... Where was the stranger. McPherson glanced below, but the man who had followed him from the fort had disappeared. *But where?*

"McPherson!" Reinhold bellowed. "Time to meet yer maker, McPherson."

McPherson inched his head around the rock, flinching as a bullet skated off the rock above his head. Once more, he offered a momentary target, firing two rounds from the Peacemaker and again drew Reinhold's fire. But this time, he was able to pinpoint Reinhold's position. Dropping to a crouch, he tossed his hat around the rock.

Reinhold took the bait, shooting at the hat's movement. McPherson returned fire, blasting away at Reinhold as fast as he could lever new rounds into the chamber, spraying lead all around him. In an effort to avoid the ricocheting bullets, Reinhold gave McPherson a clear shot. It slammed into him with the force of a sledge hammer, killing him long before he hit the trail below.

McPherson reloaded the carbine as fast as he could stuff the shells in and clambered down toward the trail. He still had another one to deal with, and wherever the so-called prospector had disappeared to, he had a decided advantage—he knew where McPherson was. But after the gunfire between Reinhold and himself, it was strangely quiet and unnerving.

Back on solid ground, McPherson continued to scan the rocks for any sign of the man, but came up empty—until he got to the horses. Guthrie was sitting on a small boulder, calmly smoking a *cigarillo* as if he had all the time in the world, his Sharps leaning within easy reach. McPherson leveled his carbine.

"The gunbelt, Mister… Guthrie is it?" McPherson motioned. "Nice and easy."

Guthrie reached down with his left hand and untied the thing holding the holster to his thigh, his movements calculated not to draw McPherson's fire. Unbuckling the belt, he tossed it toward McPherson.

"Yore shootin' was plain sloppy, Amigo." "I'm alive," McPherson muttered.

"Yep," he acknowledged, "saw the whole thing. Onliest problem is, the Cap'n ain't. Thet makes you a wanted man."

"I was defending myself."

"Thet's a fact," he readily agreed. "The Cap'n shot first, had you pinned down." "Then I don't see…"

"Thet's cause you ain't openin' yer eyes. All the army's gonna know is thet one athern is dead." He shrugged. "Yore misfortune."

"That's not a strong argument for letting you live."

"Shootin' a man in cold blood ain't yer way, Amigo. The fact thet I'm asittin' here talkin' to you is proof of thet." He tossed the stub of the *cigarillo* aside, took another out of his breast pocket and lit it. "Course, you could still prove me wrong, but killin' me won't change nothin'."

"It would buy me time," McPherson argued half-heartedly.

"True 'nuff, but look at it this way. Yer gone. Cap'n Reinhold's gone. The Colonel's gonna eventually put two an two together—probably already has. But thet don't matter. Three, four days, yer outta the terri- tory, and what with Geronimo on a rampage, the army gonna be too busy to worry 'bout you."

McPherson took a deep breath, recognizing that Guthrie had won his argument, the moment had passed. "You leavin' him behind?"

"No… Won't take long fer the buzzards to gather, an thet'd bring the Colonel arunnin' fer sure." "Why you doing this?"

"The Frenchman deserved better…"

• • •

Despite the probability there was no longer anyone on his trail, McPherson continued to push him- self and his animals hard, reaching the trail that lead toward Durango in less that a day. Other than back-checking his trail, there had been no lingering to enjoy the beauty of the Arizona wilderness—until he could put a lot of distance between himself and Fort Apache, he wouldn't be able to let down his guard. He was fleeing what would be seen as another murder, except that it was himself that did the shooting. It was unimportant whether Reinhold deserved his fate—killing him was a decision he would take to his grave.

THIRTY

The sun stood high above the valley as McPherson dismounted at the top of the ridge to give the buckskin and packhorse a breather before starting down the rocky path. An eagle spiraled in ever-widening circles, buoyed by the rising currents of air flowing across the valley. Pouring a portion of the water from his canteen into his upturned hat, McPherson scratched the grey's ears while he held the hat for the horse to drink. He emptied the canteen into the hat and repeated the process with the packhorse. Pulling out a pair of binoculars, he scanned the valley as if it was the proverbial valley of death. Anton Schlesinger might be dead and gone, but if Molly had taken up the old man's habit of shooting first and asking questions later, the danger he faced was clear enough. Satisfied he was seeing nothing out of the usual, he stowed the bin- oculars, remounted, and began his descent.

Once into the dense forest, the tension he felt on top of the ridge was quickly replaced with the feel- ing that he was returning home. As he worked his way along the trail, he marveled at how much smaller the trees seemed than before. Although still quite large by Tennessee standards, they were dwarfed by the giant sequoias along the Pacific coastline. McPherson smiled to himself and quickened the pace. He could hear the old man's voice as if he were beside him, going on about the woman. It would be good to see Molly again, if only to know she was alive and well.

McPherson rode into the clearing below the cabin, pausing at the edge to take stock of the situation. Although the clearing was a little more overgrown than he remembered, little else seemed to have changed since his departure. True, the corral looked a little worse for the wear, but it did show signs of repeated repair. Inside the corral, a couple of horses stood placidly on the far side, moving only when disturbed by the occasional bite from a fly.

Continuing to look around, he turned his attention toward the cabin. It was more weather-beaten, but other than that, nothing appeared any different. Even the chairs on the porch seemed to be sitting in the same position he remembered from before. Still, the quiet made him nervous, and the fact that the cabin door was standing open made him even edgier. He continued to glance around nervously as he approached the cabin, stopping just short of the porch before calling out.

"Hello the cabin," he shouted. He waited patiently before hollering again, but was met with silence.

He called out another time. "Molly? You in there, Molly?"

He was surprised that he hadn't been greeted by her, even though he was uncertain whether she was still living in the cabin. Almost two years had passed since he had left the valley at the point of a gun. He never believed that Molly would actually shoot him—they had shared too many intimacies for him to accept that—but the business end of a scattergun was nothing to argue with. Even so, returning to the val- ley might prove to be a mistake, but his curiosity was enough to take the chance.

Nevertheless, he was faced with a persistent silence. As near as he could tell, there were no signs of life except for the horses. As well, he was puzzled over the absence of the old man's Appaloosa. Dismount- ing, he led his two horses toward the corral, tying them to the top crossbar next to the gate. He levered a round into the Winchester and returned to the cabin, stepping cautiously onto the porch and to one side of the door. Expecting the worse, McPherson pushed it the rest of the way open. The cabin was empty, had likely been that way for a day or two. Inside, he continued to nose around, looking for any signs that Molly still lived there. Preoccupied, he was startled when she spoke his name.

"Hullo, Jess."

Instinctively, he brought the rifle to bear. Molly was standing in the doorway, the intensity of the sun- light streaming around her, masking her features. Behind her at the edge of the porch, he could see Schlesinger's missing Appaloosa. He could also see that she was not alone. Spread out across the front of the porch were at least a half dozen Indians, all but one mounted on the familiar mottled horses. Without giving his actions a lot of thought, he took a step toward her, but froze in his tracks when she jumped back- ward.

"What're you doin' here?" she asked nervously.

"I was travelling North," he replied, following her onto the porch. "I stopped by to see how you were doing, to see if you needed anything."

"You shouldn'ta come back. Yer not wanted here." "I'm sorry to hear that, Molly."

McPherson examined the woman standing in front of him, all the while maintaining a wariness with respect to the Indians. The lessons of Arizona were deeply ingrained—he wasn't about to give them a rea- son to mistrust him any more than they already did. Molly was the same woman he had bade goodbye, but with small variations. Dressed in buckskin, she had used beadwork selectively to decorate the clothing, something she had not done when he was previously in the valley. As well, the beads were woven into her braided hair. The most striking difference he noticed, however, was the wildness in her eyes and her appar- ent skittishness, like a deer ready to take flight.

"You shouldn'ta come back," she whispered.

"Molly, it was my intention to look in on you and then go on my way. I did not ride in here to cause problems."

Molly was unmoved as McPherson continued attempting to reason with her, to assure her he meant no harm. He had already concluded that the Indians were intent on protecting her, and was convinced that if he was unable to break through her resistance, he would be forced to take them on. And that was a fight he couldn't win. He was also convinced that his time was running short. The Indians were getting restless, reacting each time her voice intensified.

"Maybe you're right, woman, I should have ignored the fact that I saved your life; forgotten about the promise I made to the old man. And while I'm at it, I'll pretend we hated each other, forget that we made love night after night. That what you want?"

For a long minute, McPherson thought he had gone too far. Tears were beginning to stream down her face and the panic he sensed in her seemed closer to the surface. Suddenly, she turned and spoke to her escorts.

"(Please go.)"

"(He cannot be trusted.)"

"(You are mistaken. He is a respected friend. He will not harm me.)"

"(His pain will be long-lasting if you are wrong.)"

Much to McPherson's surprise, the Indians peeled off and turned toward the upper end of the valley.

Not until after they had disappeared from view did he realize he was shaking. "What did you tell them?" McPherson asked.

"It's wrong fer ya to be here now," she said, ignoring his question. "You keep saying that."

"Many things are different," she explained with a shrug. "I can see that," he replied.

"They care for me."

"As I would have, given the chance." "I was wrong to send you off."

"Do tell," he snapped. "Hell of a time to be finding that out, if you ask me." Molly flinched at the obvious bitterness in his voice.

"I ain't deservin' of thet, Jess."

"Maybe not, but it's hard to forget how you looked holding that shotgun on me." McPherson took a deep breath and let it out slowly. "Look, Molly, promises aside, I care for you a lot more than you realize, probably more than I realize, and the one thing I didn't do is ride in here to argue with you. I brought you some supplies. I figured you'd be out of things."

Her eyes brightened. "Did you bring coffee? I ain't had coffee in more'n a year."

"And a lot more. Tell you what. I'll unload this stuff and you can catch me up for the last two years." "Wouldn't know where to start."

"The Indians—who are they?" "They are of the Nez Percé."

"The people Anton traded with for that horse?"

"He din't trade fer it. They gave it to him as an honored friend. Anton was friends with them a long time afore I come here."

"What are they doing here? When I was on the Oregon Trail, I heard stories that the army had defeated the Nez Percé at some place called Snake Creek up in the Bear Paw. Folks at the trading posts said the army killed off most of the tribe and the rest were put on reservations."

"Them tales ain't all true," Molly corrected him. "Some of them got away."

"More'n you can say for a couple of tribes in Arizona." McPherson untied the ropes holdingthe load on the packhorse. "The army was pretty vicious. They blamed the Apache for brutality, but they weren't any better. Here's the coffee—enough for more than a year if you ration it. Salt, sugar… Ahhh." He handed her a large package wrapped in brown paper. "This is a bolt of cloth to replace that dress I ripped when you were sick."

"It's like Christmas, Jess," she exclaimed in delight. "You din't have to do this." "Sure I did. Couldn't very well drop in for a visit without bearing a few gifts."

"You ain't foolin' me, are you?" she asked, the mask of seriousness once again dropping into place. "You din't come back to stay?" McPherson stopped in mid-stride, caught unawares by her unexpected question. He finished unloading the packhorse, pulled the saddle off the buckskin, and turned them both into the corral. "You din't answer me, Jess."

"Tell you what, Molly. Let's carry this stuff up to the cabin and make some coffee. Then I'll answer your questions and maybe you can answer a couple of my own." With that, he loaded his arms and walked off. Molly scurried to pick up the remaining supplies and the bolt of cloth and ran after him.

"You build a fire," he directed, "and I'll fetch some water."

McPherson picked up the bucket standing near the door and started for the creek, returning a moment later to pick up the rifle. Trusting was one thing, being foolish was another. By the time he had returned, the stove was throwing off enough heat to start the coffee. He rinsed out a pot that had gathered dust for more than a year, filled it with water and dumped in the raw coffee grounds. Within minutes, the pungent aroma of hot coffee permeated the musty air of the cabin. After splashing water in a pair of cups to rid them of the accumulated dust, he filled them with coffee and settled in on the porch.

"Now, Molly, to answer your question. I came to visit and bring you supplies...no more, no less. As to how long I'll stay, I never give it much thought. Why don't you tell me. Maybe it'll make it easier on both of us."

McPherson glanced at Molly as she leaned back in her chair and sipped on the hot coffee. He waited for the forthcoming explanations, not only about her reaction to his sudden reappearance, but as to the ongoing presence of Indians in the valley. However, the explanations were anything but forthcoming—her reticence to discuss the past, especially when it concerned her, had not changed.

"Jess, I..." Shaking her head, Molly set the cup down and started toward the creek. McPherson gave her a minute and then followed along, rifle in hand. She was sitting on the edge of the creek bank with her feet dangling in the water. McPherson pulled off his boots and joined her.

"Funny thing about memories, Molly. Some of them are important enough that they just never go away. Like when I stormed out of the cabin cause I didn't want to admit being afraid of caves. I come down here and sat on the bank and stared at the water. But you wouldn't let it lie—you pushed me 'til I admitted what was bothering me. Now the shoe's on the other foot. It's you that's afraid—saw it the moment we started talking—but I don't know what you're afraid of."

"You... I'm afraid of you." "Me? But why?"

"I don't know..."

"Molly, what happened here since I left? Why are the Indians here?"

Molly scooted off the bank into the creek, peeled off the dress and tossed it on the bank before diving into the deeper part of the pool. She swam alone, absorbed in the exertion, oblivious to the fact that McPherson was sitting on the bank remembering the daily baths they shared. But unlike the last time, there was no enticement to join her, no invitation to bathe. At long last, she waded back to the bank and climbed out. After brushing off the excess water, she dressed and sat down beside him.

"I never give it much thought, bein' scared, when I was married. I loved my husband, knew he'd pro- tect me no matter what…but he never had thet chance. After the Crow took me away, I thought about it a lot. At first, I was scared they was goin' to kill me, and after a while, I was scared they wouldn't. After we got to the village, I was treated like the lowest thing on earth, lower than anythin' I could imagine, until all I could think about was killin' them all, to take revenge for what they did to me and mine. It reached the point that I had to shut it out to make the pain go away. Then them buffers started it all over again when they took me from the Crow.

"Anton was more like a brother—treated me like his little sister. He never once touched me, not even when I offered. Then one day you showed up, and the old fool got it in his head thet me and you oughta git married."

"He was right. We shoulda."

"No!" she cried. "No. No. No… That's why I'm afraid of you— yer just like Anton. You make up yer mind and ya don't hear another word. I told him over and over thet I wasn't ever gonna leave this valley, but after you showed up, all he could think of was gittin' me outta here… And you weren't no help, makin' promises ya couldn't keep."

"I'm listening now. Why wouldn't you go with me? Nobody had to know. Even if they had found out, they wouldn't of thought the worse of you."

"I knew… I knew what happened wasn't my fault, but it did happen, and nothin' was ever gonna make things different."

"I figured what with us making love every night…"

"I know, I did too, but every mornin' I was scared, more and more, til I knew you had to leave or I'd go crazy. I loved you much as was humanly possible—I guess I still do. You finished what Anton started— you give me back my dignity…" Once again, her tears flowed, and once again, McPherson reached out to her. "Don't… Please. About a month after you left, a bunch of white men come in, lookin' for whatever it was Anton was protectin'. I kilt one, but they was just too many. It was like the buffers all over again, ceptin' there was more of 'em."

"I don't need to hear any more…"

"You said you wanted to help," she moaned as she continued to relate the events since he had ridden away. "In the beginnin', they tried to be nice—they thought Anton was still alive and I guess they was hopin' I'd tell them what they wanted to know—but once they realized I was alone… They played cards to see who got me fer the night, but when I tried to gut him, they held me down and took turns. After thet, they din't bother to pretend. I was a woman and from their way of thinkin', women was meant fer one thing.

"Mid-winter, it was, when the Nez Percé got here. The snow was comin' down pretty hard and they just all of a sudden appeared out of nowhere. They had broke away from thet hell-hole the army called a reservation and was just lookin' for a place they could live. They rode right up to the cabin, thinkin' Anton would greet them like he always did. The whites panicked and started shootin'—killed two before they could get away. The Injuns made camp down by the lake and kept watch and waited for the whites to stick their nose outside. By the time winter was over, all of 'em was dead—the Injuns picked them off one at a time.

"We made a deal of sorts and it worked out fine. I live here and they live up to t'other end of the val- ley. We visit, they bring me meat, and they seem to know when strangers are comin' down from the ridge." Molly could see McPherson's puzzlement—and defined it before he could ask. "They're as decent as any white man, more so if you ask me. They be polite and they treat me with respect—they don't hold what happened up for me to see." She laughed. "I even had an offer of marriage. I been happy, given the circum- stances—til today. I hold a special love for you and I always will, Jess McPherson, but you wern't s'pose to come back."

"But I did." His words, though not intended as such, had struck like a thunderclap, effectively silenc- ing her. "I told you, Molly, I didn't come back to argue with you. I had planned to stay a week or two and then move on. But if you'd rather, I'll leave in the morning."

Molly jumped to her feet and ran toward the cabin, leaving McPherson to wonder if she could listen calmly and rationally to anything he said. As he got to his feet, he also began to wonder if he had made a serious mistake in returning to the valley. On the other side of the pool stood two of the Nez Percé. A thou- sand consider- ations raced through McPherson's mind as he bent to gather up the rifle he had leaned against a tree. He was out of his element and he knew it. In the nearly four years he had spent in the West, his deal- ings with Indians was limited to the previous spring in Arizona, and even that had been unexpected. Now, he was faced with the possi- bility that these friends of the old man would see anything he did as being harmful to Molly and turn on him. On top of that gruesome thought was the reality that Molly was about as stable as the weather. In less than an hour, she had gone from fright to childlike glee to philosopher to near panic, and every one of the emotions was tied to the same thing—his presence in the valley.

Keeping his movements deliberate, he nodded to the Indians and walked slowly back up the hill to the cabin. He was greeted by a billowing cloud of dust as he stepped on the porch. Molly had been franti- cally sweeping the accumulated dust from the cabin floor into a pile against one wall, but had changed her mind and aimed it out the door. He tried to dodge but the cloud caught him full, turning the thin film of sweat on his face into a mask and his attempts at breathing into a momentary impossibility. Molly heard rather than saw him choking from the dust, but when she came outside, was con- vulsed by gales of laughter at the sight.

"Ohhh, Jesse," she whooped, unable to control her laughter. "I'm sorry. I din't know you was there." She tried to wipe some of the caked dust from his face, but only succeeded in making things worse. "You are a sight."

Molly's laughter was infectious, despite his instant irritation. McPherson hemmed and hawed in a vain pretense at anger but was quickly sitting on the porch edge, trying to get the dust out of his eyes, and laughing almost as hard as she was. She encouraged him to pull off his shirt while she grabbed a cloth and the pail of water from inside.

"Lean forward," she ordered, pouring most of the water over his head as soon as he did. Still chuck- ling, she began wiping the black streaks from his face, neck and chest. "Teach ya to sneak up on me."

"I'll holler next time...from somewhere up on the ridge."

"You do thet." She took a final swipe across his face and gave up. "Best ya try and wash down at the creek."

"Not too sure I want to do that. A couple of your friends were looking on with great interest from the other side right after you ran back to the cabin."

"Yer makin' them nervous, bein' here," she explained, sitting down beside him. "I ain't exactly comfortable with the idea myself."

"Mista McPherson... I ain't changed my mind about things, but I apologize fer how I been actin'. When I sent you away, it was like you had died—I never figured to see ya agin. Watchin' you come off the mountain and then seein' you inside the cabin was like...like seein' a ghost."

"I'm no ghost."

"No, yer no ghost, and I ain't laughed fer what seems a lifetime. Considerin' thet yer here, we might as well visit fer awhile."

"I'd like that. What about...?" he gestured toward the woods.

"I told them you were a respected friend. Once I tell 'em you won't be stayin' on, they'll give me a wide berth until yer gone."

"Why don't you do it now. I'd like to get clean but I don't cotton being in the creek naked and having to explain myself."

"I could be an hour or two." She gathered up the reins of the Appaloosa. "Just be sure. I don't figure me or them want any surprises."

THIRTY ONE

The moon was in its final phase, and an increasingly larger portion of the yellow circle was missing from the sky each night. Also in danger of disappearing was the relaxed atmosphere that had come to char- acterize McPherson's stopover. He knew at best he had no more than three to four days before he would have to be on his way, and while neither he or Molly would admit it, the thought of him leaving was creat- ing problems. Despite comments to the contrary, he would have preferred to delay his departure, but the presence of the Nez Percé precluded that possibility. The Indians might have been friends with the old man, but they didn't know him from Adam, and after the bitter lessons of Arizona, he knew that trust was something earned over a long period of time—not over a few short days.

The first week of his stay had passed quickly, more quickly than McPherson would have preferred. True to her word, Molly had returned within a couple of hours with the news of her visit to the village. As expected, the Indians had expressed concern at his presence, as much for their own safety as for hers. She reiterated that he was an honored friend, both of herself and of the old man, a friend whose counsel she respected and valued. She went on to explain that he would be leaving before the new moon, some ten or eleven days hence. The time limit seemed to satisfy the Nez Percé, and it allowed Molly to relax for the first time since his return.

The two had quickly settled into a pattern, beginning each day with hot coffee and then setting off on a long walk. The walks allowed them to relive the long winter months McPherson had spent in the valley, to laugh at the many and constant arguments with Schlesinger, more often than not triggered by some inconsequential incident, and remember with fondness how much he had meant to them both.

There was an unspoken pact to indulge in the moment, to disregard those things they had no control over. The walks evolved into a requisite swim, at first in the lake further down the valley, then in the creek below the cabin; and despite half-hearted efforts to the contrary, the sexual tension between them resur- faced, increasing slowly and inexorably until by the third day, they had surrendered to the primeval instincts they had shared in the past…

For the third continuous night, Jess and Molly had indulged in the pleasures of the flesh. They hadn't bothered to go inside until late in the evening, choosing the grassy creek bank and the darkness of the night to bear witness to their lovemaking. Once, twice, a third time they intertwined as the thin sliver of the moon made it way across the visible sky, moving inside the cabin only when it had disappeared behind the trees. They fell into an exhausted asleep, to be awakened at daybreak by a pounding on the door. McPher- son was quick to grab his Peacemaker, snapping the hammer back in anticipation of trouble, but the firm pressure of Molly's hand on his arm caused him to pause. After wrapping a blanket around her shoulders to cover her nakedness, she went to the door and opened it wide. An Indian filled the opening and was obvi- ously agitated, speaking quickly and excitedly. After listening for a moment, she turned to McPherson.

"We got problems… He says bluecoats."

McPherson started to question her, but she had gone outside and was already deep into conversation with the Indian. He jammed the pistol back in the holster, pulled on his trousers and boots and joined them on the porch.

"(…He brought them,)" the warrior gestured violently at McPherson.

"(He did not know you were here,)" she patiently explained, trying to calm him down. "(I do not believe that. If we must die, then so will he.)"

"(No one must die, Little Feather. Return to your people. We will send them away.)" "Molly?" McPherson interjected. "Ask him how many soldiers there are."

"(He asks the number of bluecoats?)" She listened for a moment and repeated it to McPherson. "He says they saw a dozen, maybe more."

"Where?"

"Just comin' over the ridge."

"Then we've got plenty of time. Tell him to warn his people… I just wish there was another way out of the valley."

"There is. Anton kept it a secret. Even from me." "Do they know about it?"

"Yes."

"Then tell him to get his people up there just in case I'm wrong." "He don't trust you."

"He ain't got a lot of choice at the moment. Tell him." "(He asks that you trust him.)"

"(That is difficult.)"

"(I know, but it is the only way. You must ready your people to flee. There is little time.)"

Little Feather hesitated momentarily, then leaped astride the Appaloosa from the porch. "(Take care, little sister,)" he called out as he disappeared from the clearing.

Molly's shoulders visibly sagged as the Indian vanished from sight. McPherson welcomed her embrace as she unwrapped the blanket from her body and pulled it around the both of them.

"I'm scared, Jess. Them soldiers ain't here just to be sociable."

"No, I don't expect they are, but we'll do what we can to turn 'em around." "Little Feather and his people just want to be left alone."

"Don't know if that's possible anymore," he reasoned, "although I can't for the life of me figure out how they would know the Indians are here."

"Why else would they be comin' to the valley?"

"Guess we'll find out soon enough. You best get dressed…and maybe get some coffee on. I'm gonna ride down to meet them."

•　•　•

McPherson stood to one side of the trail to await the arrival of the army, the events in Arizona weigh- ing heavily on his mind. Under other circumstances, he might have been better off to take the attitude of the old man and warn them off with a couple of well placed bullets. He had learned that the army wasn't prone to under-standing—or predisposed to forgiveness—when someone decided to shoot at them. The best he could hope for was to find out their reason for being there and try to convince them it was a waste of time. But he wasn't overburdened with illusions. The few encounters he had with the military had left a dis- tinctively bad taste in his mouth, and he thought it unlikely that this meeting would have different results.

The pace of the blue-coated men was such that McPherson had an opportunity to look them over without being noticed; and he was disturbed by what he saw. They were aniother rag-tag bunch, and with the exception of the lieutenant leading the column, none of them was wearing a complete uniform. More- over, the complement of men he had anticipated was shy at least three from the dozen the Indian had men- tioned. McPherson waited until they were almost on top of him before stepping into the middle of the trail, startling the lead horse and rider.

"Good morning to you, Lieutenant."

McPherson felt a certain amount of satisfaction as the silence of the woods was broken by the ner- vous sounds of horses and of weapons being drawn and cocked. His winchester cradled in the crook of one arm, he continued to block the trail as the lieutenant settled his horse.

"Mister, that's a good way to find an early grave," the officer snarled. "Relax, Lieutenant, no one's looking to die."

"That remains to be seen. Who are you, and what are you doing here?" "My name's Jesse McPherson, and I might ask you the same thing." "Lieutenant Walker… Out of Fort Washakie."

"You've come a fair piece, Lieutenant. Hard to believe you rode all that way just to drop by for a visit."

"We've had complaints about men being shot at, or just plain disappearing."

"Oh? This is a big country, Lieutenant. What makes you think these men were shot at or disappeared around here?"

"It's where they were headed."

"Somebody's pulling your leg, Lieutenant. The only folks that been shot at around here were tres- passing, and that's a fact. But as far as I know, ain't nobody disappeared."

"You're admitting you shot at people?"

"Ain't admitting nothing, Lieutenant, but since this valley belongs to me, I'd be inclined to shoot if I thought I was being threatened, especially after somebody'd been warned off and didn't listen."

"And what about us, Mister McPherson. You planning on shooting at us?"

"Now that you mention it, I ain't give it a whole lot of thought," McPherson answered with a grin. "You got plans on threatening me?"

"None that I'm aware of," he said with visible restraint.

"Then I guess you got nothing to be worrying about," he declared, the grin widening. "Can you suggest a location where we can bivouac for a day or two?"

"Well, now, Lieutenant, that's another story. If'n it's up to me, I'd just as soon you turn around and ride outta here."

"You're a mighty inhospitable man, McPherson. Mighty inhospitable." "Depends on your perspective, Lieutenant."

"My perspective, Mister McPherson, is that me and my men are mighty tired and to be honest, I'm not convinced you're telling me the whole truth."

"You calling me a liar, Lieutenant?"

"Not at all, Mister McPherson. But you've failed to mention the woman…or the Injuns." "What Indians?"

"Don't fence with me, McPherson. There's some breakaway Nez Percé living in this valley. They were seen last year."

"That's only partially true. The Indians were passing through to visit the old man that was here before me. They stayed the winter and moved on with the snow."

Just as McPherson's words reached Walker's ears, a commotion rose from beyond the rear of the col- umn. The remaining men were accounted for. Three Indian scouts rode to the front of the line. The lieu- tenant listened attentively before directing his attention once again to McPherson.

"Well now, Mister McPherson, seems you do tend toward lying. My scouts tell me there's fresh sign down by the lake. Injun sign. They say it can't be more than a few hours old. Sergeant?"

"Yessir!"

"Looks like we'll be here awhile. Set up camp at the lake. We'll begin the search in the morning. And Sergeant? Leave me two men. Mister McPherson might try to warn them."

"I'm not planning on warning anyone, Lieutenant, but it'd be better for everyone if you'd just ride out.

Hunting down a few Indians that've done you no harm will serve no purpose."

"There you go with that perspective stuff again. Suppose we wander up to your cabin. I'm most inter- ested in seeing what else you've lied about. Oh, and maybe you should hand over your weap- ons. Just never know what a liar's gonna do next."

"Your funeral," McPherson muttered under his breath.

Molly watched the procession as they came into the clearing and saw that McPherson was unarmed. The old man's words rang loud and clear as she cocked the Winchester laying across her lap: "If you're forced to shoot into a bunch, shoot the leader." As they approached the porch, she calmly swung the busi- ness end of the rifle toward Lieutenant Walker.

"Thet's far enough."

"No need for the rifle, Ma'am," Walker said as he reined up. "No? Coulda fooled me. Git yer guns, Jess."

"Mister McPherson will get his weapons back in due time, Ma'am." "He'll git them now or you're a dead man."

"You're no more hospitable than he is."

"I ain't in the mood to be neighborly to the likes a you. Now hand them over."

"Be reasonable, Ma'am. You can't kill us all. The other men will come running at the first shot." "Everbody dies sometime," she said resolutely, her rifle never wavering. "What's it gonna be?" Resigned that she would indeed shoot him, Walker gave the order. "Give him the weapons."

"I tried to warn you, Lieutenant," McPherson smiled as he returned the Colt to its holster. "She don't listen to me either."

"She's gonna get you killed, Mister."

"Not today, Lieutenant. Now suppose you step down and join us on the porch. There are things you should understand before you go making a mistake you'll regret. And send these two back with the others. Might as well have them all in the same place."

"You can't seriously believe you can hold me as a hostage?" Walker asked as he dismounted. "Not in the least. But…"

McPherson didn't get the chance to finish his remark. All hell broke loose: Molly screamed as the three scouts rode into the clearing, bringing the Winchester to bear on the nearest of them and pulling the trigger. He never had a chance as the bullet caught him full in the chest. He was dead before he hit the ground.

"Molly! No!" McPherson yelled as she levered another round into the chamber. She fired a second time, missing wildly as the others dived from their horses. She was struggling to cock the rifle a third time before McPherson grabbed it out of her hands.

"Why'd you stop me?" she screamed over and over, trying to wrench the rifle from his grip. "They're Crow. They killed my family. They killed me…" She went limp in McPherson's arms before he shoved her inside and turned to face the drawn guns of the three soldiers.

"Funny way you got of explaining things, McPherson." "Is it true? Them scouts Crow?"

"The Crow have scouted for the army for years."

"The Crow killed her husband and children and held her captive for over three years." "Makes no never mind to me, McPherson. Get the woman. She murdered one of my men." "Can't do that, Lieutenant."

"Then you'll have to die…"

For the second time in as many minutes, bedlam took over as shots came out of the trees behind the cabin and the two soldiers still mounted fell from their saddles, mortally wounded. Walker slowly raised his hands as a half dozen Nez Percé warriors appeared out of the trees.

"Would have been easier if you had turned around, Walker." McPherson disarmed him while the Nez Percé trussed up the remaining scouts. "Now it's gonna get a little complicated."

"What are you going to do?" Walker asked.

"We're gonna sit here and wait for the rest of your troop to show. And when they do, you best tell them to hold fire. If you don't, the odds on you and them surviving are gonna go down real quick."

"You're interfering in army business, McPherson."

"Damn it, Walker, you don't learn too good. I'm trying to save your life. I don't know what your real reason is for being here, but in case you ain't figured it out yet, I'm the only thing between you and a slow death. Molly?" McPherson yelled through the door. "Molly? I need your help."

He was shocked by the change in her appearance. Once again, her eyes were filled with a wildness, dominated by a glassy stare that bordered on insanity. "Molly? You've got to get out of here. The others will be coming." The stare never changed. "Do you hear me, Molly? Tell Little Feather to get back in the woods."

"Little Feather understands. Make the Bluecoats go away or they will die. (Come, Little Sister.)" McPherson watched in astonishment as they blended into the trees as quickly as they had appeared, Molly and the two Crow scouts in tow. Not once had she hinted that any of them spoke English. Maybe she didn't know, he mused.

"I'm gonna get us some coffee, Lieutenant. I'd recommend you sit tight. The Indians are close enough you won't get too far. Funny thing, Walker," he observed as he returned with the coffee, "I was down Arizona way last year. Had the chance to see how the army handled things down there. They tended to shoot first and not bother with the questions. That how you feel?"

"I've got my orders. These people left the reservation without permission. They have to go back." "I wonder about that. What harm were they doing, living here?"

"You're not blind. They killed two of my men. No White is safe."

"Uh huh! White men steal their land, shoot them when they object, holler for the army when they fight back. How many of them were killed when you made war against them? Seems to me, the army's not blameless in all this. and it seems to me the Indian's getting the short end of the stick."

"I'm not going to sit here and debate with you, McPherson. You're going to jail for aiding and abet- ting this bunch of renegades, and the woman's going to hang for murder."

"I see. Are you going to punish the Crow that killed her family in cold blood? Are you going to pun- ish those that raped her and held her captive? Or doesn't that count? I'll give you some advice, Lieutenant. Before you start dreaming up punishment for me or for Molly, best you consider how you're gonna get yourself and the rest of your men out of this valley in one piece. The Nez Percé haven't gone away, and in case you haven't figured it out, they outnumber you. If you don't leave, you will die. Pure and simple."

THIRTY TWO

McPherson shook his head in disbelief. Once again, he was a prisoner, but this time, his situation was considerably more tenuous. After the attack, he and the lieutenant had sat on the porch sipping coffee while he had attempted to explain, even justify Molly's reasons for shooting the scout. Walker had countered that the Crow were now more civilized, many of them now in the employ of the army and not responsible for the actions of others in the tribe. All the while they were arguing, the remainder of Walker's patrol, ever mindful they might be walking into an ambush, had been working their way toward the cabin. Their arrival brought the discussion to an end.

"About time, Sergeant," Walker commented getting to his feet. "What took you so long?" "Sorry, Lieutenant, we were tryin' to be sure."

"Understood. Place this man under arrest. If he so much as twitches, put a bullet in him." "Yessir. He do this?"

"No, but he could have prevented it. The Crow was shot by his woman. The others were killed by the Injuns he lied about."

"Yessir. What are our odds?" "They could be better." "Where you want this one?"

"Tether him to the corral. Maybe a few hours in the sun will help him decide to help. Worst comes to worse, we can always use him as bait."

"My pleasure, Lieutenant," the sergeant growled as he shoved McPherson off the porch.

Time slowed to a snail's pace as McPherson continued to mull over his situation, as well as that of the others in the valley. He was disarmed and outnumbered, his wrists bound with leather thongs to a lower crossbar of the corral, his chances of escape uncertain. But the circumstances for the remaining soldiers was for all intents the same. There was a sense of the inevitable—men had died, and others would join them before it would end. This small band of Nez Percé had decided to ignore his advice and take on the army. It was, at best, an unfortunate decision because it was a fight they couldn't win. Even if they killed these few men, eventually they would be found out and the price would be high.

The remaining soldiers, led by a young officer that knew little or nothing about a tactical retreat, were preparing to disregard the fact that the two Crow scouts were prisoners of the Indians, ignorant as to why they were taken. It would have served little purpose for him to mention past alliances between the Nez Percé and the Crow, to explain that the Nez Percé had fought beside the Crow against the Sioux.

The lieutenant was hard pressed to believe that the Nez Percé harbored considerable resentment toward the Crow, that instead of coming to their aid just two years past, the Crow had acted as scouts for the Army in their pursuit of Chief Joseph's people. Moreover, the lieutenant could not accept the fact that memories and a hatred of the Crow provided a common bond between a white woman and a small band of Indians, both of which wanted nothing more than to be left alone. Understandable, he muttered under his breath. If it hadn't been for people like Schlesinger and d'Iberville, he would have had trouble believing it himself.

Left unguarded by the soldiers while they buried their dead, McPherson worked his wrists in a vain attempt to loosen the thongs, but the manner in which he was tied prevented movement to any extent. He realized he was going nowhere fast, but the thought of being left to the elements was unsettling. He had watched as the billowing tops of thunderheads moved along the western rim, swinging along a southern arc until they were headed in a dead line for the valley. Normally, he wouldn't have been concerned, but now that he could see them fully, he knew if he didn't get loose, he was in for a pounding. He had been caught in the path of clouds like these once before—it wasn't an experience he relished repeating.

Steel grey in color, the clouds were layered in various thicknesses, the entire mass rotating slowly around a wide central axis. As the leading edge moved overhead, McPherson felt the beginnings of rain riding the wind, and within minutes, he was soaked to the skin. Frantically, he continued working the thongs, hoping against hope that the moisture would be enough to stretch the leather, but just as suddenly as the rain began, it stopped, leaving McPherson frustrated and still bound to the corral railing. The sky brightened as the clouds moved off, but the patch of blue quickly disappeared behind the white cloud of ice pellets that trailed the thunderhead.

The first wave of hailstones was more an annoyance than anything else—they were large enough to sting but too small to do any damage. But as the beginnings of the next wave lightly peppered the ground, McPherson's worse fears were realized. The stones rapidly increased in size, and there were more of them—lots more. The ground was quickly covered in white, and the stinging turned to real pain as McPherson slipped into unconsciousness.

McPherson's bare face and hands were a solid mass of bruises beneath the sunlit sheen of blood. He didn't see the remnants of the storm move off to the Northeast, was oblivious to the fact that Little Feather had cut the thongs and was draping him across the buckskin. He did not see Molly standing at the horse's head, reins in one hand, a cocked Winchester in the other. Wandering in and out of consciousness, he was only faintly aware that he was no longer tied to the railing. It was not until long after they had reached the village that he fully comprehended he was free, and even then, he was unsure as to where he was or how he got there. Not until two days later, when he was once again up and around and back at the cabin, was he told what had taken place after the passage of the storm.

McPherson relaxed in the fading light and warmth of the setting sun, his chest, arms and face a col- orful variety of yellows and blues and purples. He was sore beyond anything he could imagine— the pain was a constant reminder of the beating he had taken from the hailstorm. But the pain was minor compared to the despondency he felt. The story was sketchy, part logic, part embellishment, but it would haunt him in the months ahead…

"(Is he dead?)" Her question was obvious as she and Little Feather came out of the protection of the trees near the cabin.

"(It is possible, Little Sister. The white stones are many.)" "(If he still lives, we must free him.)"

"(The long-knives may return…)" "(Then we should hurry.)"

Without another word, Molly bolted toward the corral, and after a moment's hesitation, Little Feather followed, chagrined by the rashness of the woman. They would die quickly if caught by the soldiers. But luck was with them as they frantically went about their rescue. After checking McPherson for signs of life, Molly put a bridle on the buckskin and stood guard while Little Feather cut the thongs that bound McPher- son to the railing and hoisted him to the horse's back. They quickly fled the clearing and returned to the Nez Percé village where she spent the remainder of the day and a good part of the night bathing him in cold cloths.

While Molly tended to McPherson, the small band of Nez Percé warriors prepared to make war on the soldiers, determined to end the threat or die in the attempt. Their only other choice was to return to the reservation—an option they dismissed outright. In the mean-time, Lieutenant Walker, instead of searching out higher ground they could defend, returned to the lakeside bivouac, confident his men could deal with the renegades the next day.

By early evening, the first vestiges of a rare summer mist began to creep through the trees. Slowly, the valley was enveloped in a thick blanket of fog, providing the Nez Percé warriors with unexpected cover. The Indians moved quickly, surrounding the encampment by the time darkness was complete. Once started, the attack was swift and deadly, reminiscent of a similar event at a Nez Percé encampment years past. But this time, it was the army in the middle.

With Molly translating, Little Feather described the attack to McPherson in elaborate detail, speak- ing of the fight with the Blue Coats before they were overrun. He spoke with pride of the bravery of his own people and of the two who died in the assault. But he caught McPherson by surprise when he con- ceded that McPherson was not responsible for the presence of the Blue Coats. Nevertheless, Little Feather was adamant that McPherson must leave the valley and not come back. They, the Nez Percé, would see that the woman was cared for. In return, McPherson would lead the two remaining scouts out of the valley and deliver them to the army they served…

A sticky point, that last one, thought McPherson as Molly brought him coffee. Since returning to the cabin, he had persisted in trying to make conversation with her, to help her deal with what had transpired since the arrival of the small party of soldiers, but he was beginning to accept the fact that his efforts were a lost cause. Although she had continued tending to his cuts and bruises, bustling around him and the cabin like a mother hen, there was an aura of madness surrounding her. He had seen the wildness in her eyes the first day back, but there was little or nothing he could do about it. Had she gone with him the first time, she might have been able to overcome the events of her past. But the fact that she had crossed an invisible bar- rier was something he couldn't ignore. Like it or not, the choices available to him were limited: He could force her to leave—assuming the Indians would allow it—and hope he was wrong; or he could leave her in the valley and hope for the best.

Once again, McPherson tried to talk to Molly, looking for a way to solve his dilemma, but she simply ignored him except to periodically look at his cuts and bruises or bring him coffee or food. He had little doubt that the appearance of the Crow scouts was the catalyst that had finally pushed her past the point of sanity and had heard that many Indians honored madness as a spiritual manifestation, but that made his decision no easier. Nevertheless, he concluded in spite of his misgivings that the best decision was to say a prayer for Molly and leave her to the care of the Nez Percé.

The scouts were another matter. He had no desire to spend a week shepherding them back to an army post, considering the situation. The Nez Percé had decided to send a message back to the Crow for turning their backs on allies, and had brutally blinded them and cut their tongues out. They would never again scout for the army. *Better they were dead*, McPherson reflected, *for them and for me. Explaining this to the army without telling them anything won't be easy.*

For another two days McPherson allowed Molly to mother him, avoiding the inevitable, but the deci- sion to leave was made for him by the sudden appearance of Little Feather and the two scouts.

"(Why are you here?)" Molly bridled. "(He is not healed.)"

"(You have made him well, Little Sister. It is time for him to leave.)" "(No! You are wrong,)" she said defiantly. "(He needs more time.)"

"(There *is* no more time. He must take this vermin from the valley before the moon rises. Tell him.)" Since he understood nothing of what was being said, McPherson only suspected the direction of their con- versation, but the tone of Little Feather's soft spoken voice was clear. "(Tell him!)"

"He says you gotta leave," she told McPherson reluctantly. "And you don't think I'm fit to travel?"

"Not today."

"I see. How long before you figure I'll be healthy?" "Soon."

"There's something else bothering you," McPherson gently challenged. "What is it?" "You saved my life after thet ol' coot died."

"I s'pose I did," he acknowledged. "But I couldn't just let you die, now, could I?" "Why? Why'd you do it?"

"Damn it, Molly," he exclaimed, "I tried to tell you before. You can't just up and quit living. A per- son's got to go on." He hedged momentarily. "Your friend here is right. It's time for me to leave. Only thing is, I been puzzling about you and these Crow scouts. I don't especially want to take them out. And I don't want to leave you behind again."

McPherson's remark was like a slap, and it triggered an unex- pected response. Molly raced into the cabin, returning seconds later with the rifle, levering a shell into the chamber as she came through the door. In the same motion, she aimed and fired, the force of the bullet knocking the unsuspecting Crow from his horse. Before McPherson could react, she repeated the motion, killing the second Indian. Swinging the bar- rel around, she aimed it at McPherson.

"Now you don't have to take 'em. They be dead. Now pack yer gear and go afore I shoot you too."

McPherson stared for a long minute before getting to his feet, first at the scouts, then into Molly's face. There was no longer any question of Molly's sanity. Her eyes left no doubt about that. He put his few belongings into the saddlebags, belted on the Peacemaker and checked that it was loaded before returning it to the holster. Loading the pack horse and saddling the buckskin took a little longer, but within an hour, he was ready to ride.

"Jesse?" Molly was standing behind him, the sacks of gold they had buried two years before cradled in her arms. "Here. Now you got no reason to come back," she said as she handed him the bags. Once again, her eyes had calmed with no evidence of the madness.

"I can't take this. It's yours."

"I got no need fer it, Jess. I don't want it. It ain't good fer nothin' but trouble." "But if you change your mind…"

"I won't. Just take it. Please?"

Conceding it was an argument he wouldn't win, he added the gold to his saddlebags. "I'll never forget you, Molly."

"Better if'n you did. Go home, Jess. Find yerself a woman and settle down. This life out here ain't fer you." Standing on her tiptoes, she kissed him softly. "Ride out, Jesse McPherson. Ride out and don't look back. There's nothin' here fer you ceptin' grief." She turned and walked away.

McPherson stood atop the ridge and scanned the length and breadth of the valley, looking for any sign of Molly or the half dozen Nez Percé braves that had followed him until he cleared the treeline. But the valley had swallowed them up completely. If they were lucky, their presence would go unnoticed. But the army had a way of looking for missing soldiers, and it was inevitable that another patrol would come to investigate the disappearance of Lieutenant Walker and his men. Mounting, he gathered in the pack horse and glanced a final time into the valley below.

"Goodbye, Molly," he whispered, and spurred the horse toward the East.

THIRTY THREE

McPherson climbed out of his bunk, stiff and aching after being thrown the previous afternoon by a cantankerous horse that took exception to having a rider on his back. He'd been lucky, considering the fact that nothing was broken, but his body felt as if he'd been dragged through a field of stone. He grimaced as he slide into his boots, vowing under his breath to do the horse in if he ever got the chance. It was a rare morning on the *Broken J*, one of the few he could remember when he had nothing to do. He had called the Montana ranch home for better than a year, but he could count on one hand the number of days the old man that owned the place had given hands time off to while away. Most days, it was a routine of rising at dawn, filling the stomach with ham, biscuits, sawmill gravy, and hot coffee, and then spending the day in the sad- dle chasing ill-tempered cattle.

But even with the current aches and pains, McPherson was grateful to be alive. The old man had intervened in one of the many arguments he had instigated since leaving Molly's valley, dragging him kick- ing and screaming out of a Boseman saloon after he tried to pick a fight with a bunch of blue-shirted sol- diers. He was outnumbered, but copious amounts of whiskey had supplied him with a bravado guaranteed to get him beaten to within an inch of his life if not killed. McPherson grinned as he recalled that evening. The old man had listened patiently to McPherson's drunken objections, but when he tried to return to the saloon, the old man laid the barrel of a pistol alongside his head and tied him across the buckskin. It wasn't until hours later, when he sobered up, that his benefactor was prepared to allow him the privilege of riding upright in the saddle.

All things considered, however, the year had been a good one. Other than an honest day's labor, the old man hadn't asked for much, and in return, McPherson was given a place to live and three squares a day. There were no questions about his past, which was probably a good thing. More than once over the year, McPherson thought back to Arizona and remembered how the Colonel at Fort Apache had laughed when he suggested that d'Iberville and the band of Apache had been murdered. And while McPherson was clear in his own mind that Captain Reinhold deserved to die, waiting in ambush and then shooting him down made him no better than the man he had killed. He had avenged *René's* death, but at what cost?

Wyoming was a different matter. The valley had once again lived up to its reputation as being a val- ley of death. By heading away from Fort Washakie, he had hoped to buy them time, but as he had expected, the relative peace of the valley was short lived. He heard about the attack when he stopped for supplies at Fort Laramie. Ambushed by a few of the Nez Percé as they came down from the ridge, an army patrol returned fire and then proceeded to scour the valley, wiping out the small band of Indians. The account said a white woman was also killed in the attack, her death blamed on the Indians.

The news of her death had both saddened and angered him because it was so unnecessary. All she and her Nez Percé friends were trying to do was live out their lives. Why that lieutenant couldn't understand and leave them alone was beyond McPherson's comprehension. But then, he couldn't understand why the Nez Percé had insisted on remaining in the valley either. It was never a matter of whether the army would return, just when.

McPherson shivered as he wandered over to the cook shack. The snow line on the mountains sur- rounding the ranch was a thousand feet lower than the previous week and the wind carried a chill that cut to the bone. He wondered if he could handle another winter like the previous one when he spent many of his days fighting through waist deep snow drifts to feed the cattle. Just remembering was enough to setoff another round of shivering. The cook shack was empty except for the old man and his Chinese cook.

"Mornin', Jesse," the old man greeted him. "You don't look too happy."

"Morning, Mister Gallatin. Just not looking forward to winter's all." McPherson pulled a tin cup off the rack and filled it from the coffee pot Wing Lo kept on the stove.

"Figured as much. You been starin' at them mountains fer the last week or so." "Seems early for snow."

"S'pose it is, but they ain't much we can do about it." "Guess not."

"I'm s'pectin' the change in weather ain't really what's on yer mind, Jesse." The old man studied McPherson for a long minute. "I figure yer thinkin' about movin' on."

"You don't miss much," Jesse said, laughing.

"Humph. A man don't live long as me an not learn somethin'. When you plannin' on leavin'?" "Next day or so, I imagine. Like to get further south before that snow gets here."

"Makes sense," he agreed. "Look, Mister Gallatin…"

"Ain't no need to explain, boy. You more than earned yer keep." "I appreciate what you've done."

"Never had reason to regret pullin' you outta thet Boseman saloon. Where you headed?" "South… Denver maybe."

"Well, thet's thet… See me afore you go. Wing Lo here'll see you got plenty of supplies." The old man got to his feet. "I never much been one to hand out advice, mostly cause them thet needs it don't listen. But I'm of a mind to give you the benefit of the doubt. Best you take a real good look at yerself. You ain't no gunfighter—any fool with a lick a sense kin see thet—but the day'll come when thet Peacemaker'll git you hung. Go home. Nobody there knows 'bout the valley."

"How'd you know?"

"I may be gittin' old but I ain't deaf. And it's best you remember them army boys you tried to pick a fight with in Boseman heard the same stuff I did. Yer damned lucky they din't put two an two together. But one of these days you'll fergit an say the wrong thing to the wrong person an yer luck will run out."

"Maybe you're right," McPherson allowed. "I'll give it some thought." "You do thet," Gallatin said approvingly as he turned and left.

McPherson refilled the cup he had been nursing and sat back while the cook filled a plate for him. He felt a momentary twinge of regret—it seemed like he was always saying goodbye to people he cared for. Maybe it *was* time to go home and try to make amends for the hurt he had caused when he left. It would be good to see the family again, even Jacob. Of more immediate concern, however, was getting packed and a lot further south. If he was still in Montana when the snows hit, he would be there for another winter. Win- ter was one thing he'd had his fill of.

•　•　•

McPherson was visibly tired. Since leaving the warmth and pro- tection of the *Broken J* ranch, he had been running just ahead of one storm after another. Twice he had been stopped in his tracks—a month in Denver, another two weeks in Southern Kansas. When the storms broke, however, he returned to the trail only to have a resurgence of bad weather dogging his tracks. He finally crossed the Oklahoma territory into Texas, but he couldn't escape the ravages of winter. With temperatures plunging well below freezing, McPherson was forced to break through an increasingly thick layer of ice each morning to get to the water. Each day, he was faced with riding beneath the slate grey clouds that hung low in the sky. Slowly and steadily, he worked his way south and east to Texarkana, at last giv- ing in to the unavoidable fact that he couldn't outrun the cold and snow. The River's Edge Saloon became his home while he waited out the win- ter. Christmas and the New Year passed, and the weariness of seven years on the trail weighed him down, draining him of the constant vigilance that had been his companion for almost as long.

Now, after three months of inactivity on the frozen banks of the Mississippi, his daily routine had become predictable. Upon rising each morning, he dressed, scraped the light stubble from his face, and when he remembered, strapped on the Peacemaker that had been so instrumental in his survival. He would then stroll down to the livery to check on the buckskin before returning to the saloon and to eat a late breakfast. Afterward, he would settle in at a table near the back with a cup of coffee and a deck of cards to wait for his companions for the day. It was a time devoid of purpose.

As the month of March began, however, the change in the weather brightened his spirits. And while he continued the routine established since arriving in Texarkana, his thoughts were elsewhere. It was the nearest he had been to home since leaving that day in the fall seven years past, and the pull to return there was getting stronger as each day passed. After picking up the freshly dealt hand, he glanced around the bar- room before turning his attention to the cards.

"My Pa wouldn't appreciate this," McPherson mused to no one in particular. He failed to take notice that the stranger standing just inside the door was staring directly at him. All he heard was the shrill, pene- trating voice.

"Mista McPherson!"

BOOK 5:

We are as one;
Living within frameworks
Sculptured by the winds of time, and
Tempered by self-imposed moralities.

I feel the caress of your mind;
Massaging emotions run rampant
With hearts desires.

Your hands are electric,
Creating excitement;
Stirring passions lying
Dormant within the soul.

I reach out to touch
The elusive butterfly;
Seeing in it the dreams of ages,
An evolving metamorphosis
In a static world.

Thirty Four

Jess McPherson woke with a start. He was bathed in a cold sweat, the shrill accusatory voice of James Picquett again ringing in his ears. Unconsciously, he reached across the bed to touch the woman he had claimed as his own, the widow of the late Mister Picquett. Easing from beneath the covers, he slipped into his trousers, trying his best not to disturb her, but despite his efforts, she called out.

"Jess? What's wrong?"

"Nothing, Hatty. Go back to sleep. I'll be back to bed in a few minutes."

McPherson went outside, letting the nighttime chill clear the remnants of the dream from his head. The dreams were nothing new; explaining them away was another matter. Try as he might to ignore them, they continued to be disturbing. The gunfights were a part of his lessons in survival, costly lessons paid for with his blood, and with the blood of others. He had lost count of the number of times he was forced to defend himself, but the images of the men that had died at his hands were forever etched in his mind.

"You shoulda stayed in bed," he said, sensing Hatty behind him.

"You're out here," she responded, handing him a shirt. "I don't look after you, you'll catch yer death of cold."

"Ain't exactly winter, Hatty," he said dryly.

"Mister McPherson!" she scolded gently, helping with the buttons. "I don't recall asking the time of year."

"I s'pose you didn't."

"You were dreaming again." "More like a nightmare."

"Don't you think it's time you told me about them, Jess?" "I told you before you didn't want to know."

"That's for me to decide." She wrapped her arms around his waist and laid her head on his shoulder.

"If'n I'm gonna sleep beside you whilst you're thrashing around, I might as well knowwhy." "Maybe in the morning."

"No!" she exclaimed. "No more maybe in the morning. Tonight. Now."

McPherson imperceptibly shook his head, a soft chuckle escaping from within. He was never going to get his wish—that of finding a woman without a streak of stubbornness. Schlesinger was right; a man can't live with a woman on his own terms and ever find peace.

"You win, Hatty. But don't say I didn't warn you."

The faint baying of a hound on a dawn chase could be heard in the distance by the time he had fin- ished. He had touched on it all: the gunfights; Angéline Dubois and René d'Iberville; Schlesinger, Molly and the Nez Percé; the ambush in California; the attack on the Apache and the subsequent goading of an army captain into a gunfight; a repetition of the events leading up to the death of her husband. There was little rhyme or reason to the narrative as he skipped back and forth over his seven years of wandering, his emotions providing an intense coloring to the telling. As he talked, he began pacing the cabin, his footfalls contributing to cadence of the story. Eventually, McPherson grew silent, his recitation at an end. But his pacing continued.

At first, Hatty had listened with eagerness—it was a chance to share Jesse's experiences—shunning the occasional need to question why he had chosen a particular path. But as the minutes turned into hours, she began to wish she hadn't pushed the issue. Although much of what he conveyed to her seemed reason- able under the circumstances, there were other details to which she would have preferred to remain in the dark. She had never felt the pangs of jealousy with regards to her deceased husband—anger, but never jeal- ousy—but the mere mention of Angéline and Molly set off a churning ache in the pit of her stomach. Sometime during the night, she had added wood to the embers in the fireplace, and now, huddled in a rock- ing chair with a quilt wrapped around her shoulders, she stared at the flames and tried to make sense of the many revelations.

"I'm sorry, Jess" she apologized suddenly. "I shouldn't have put you through it agin."

"Ain't your fault." McPherson stopped his pacing. "You got a right to know what kind of man you're marrying... Maybe you'll change your mind."

"I know what kind of man you are," she whispered, "and I ain't changing my mind. I'm just sorry we didn't meet a lot sooner. Maybe we'd have both been spared some of the grief we been through. 'Sides, this baby I'm carryin' needs a daddy..."

Her announcement came as a shock. The few times McPherson had visualized himself as a father during the long hours on the trail had been dismissed as nothing more than daydreams. The unexpected news, however, sent shivers of exhilaration to his very core. He pulled her to her feet and enveloped her in a tight embrace.

"When?" he asked excitedly.

"In the spring, if'n you don't squeeze me to death afore then."

"I'm sorry," he exclaimed, almost flinging her backward in his haste to turn her loose. "I mean..." "You're a dangerous man, Mister McPherson," she teased. "Maybe I *should* reconsider."

"I didn't hurt you?"

"I ain't gonna break jest cause I'm carrying a baby," she laughed. "Now, you want to try that hug again?"

Any doubts in Hatty's mind disappeared as they stood arm in arm for long minutes watching the flames sporadically flare up and then die away into the bed of coals. She had hesitated for more than a week in telling him about the child, and after hearing about other women in his past, she wondered even more, but his reaction to the news washed away the jealousy and doubts in an instant.

"I really do love you, Hatty."

"I never doubted it, Jess, but it's nice to finally hear you say it." "We can't put off getting married any longer."

"I s'pose you're right. But there ain't that big a hurry. I want to get ahold of both our families wind invite them to be here."

"You're asking a lot, inviting Jacob here."

"I know, but it's important for you to make peace with him."

"I don't know if that's possible, Hatty. Even if it is, I ain't too sure about leaving you alone for that long."

"You're forgetting that I took care of myself just fine afore you come along." "Just don't want anything to happen to you," he said with concern.

"I promise nothing'll happen," she vowed. "Let's fix something to eat and then you can ride across the ridge and talk to the preacher over to Farmer's Grove. Ask him if'n he'd marry us here at the farm."

"Isn't he the one I chased off?" "Uh huh."

"What make's you think he'd come back?"

"He'd never pass up the chance to preach. We'll even invite Sheriff Rainey… Okay?" she asked ten-

derly.

"All right, Hatty. I'll ride up to the Gap and talk to Jacob, and we'll ask the sheriff, but I think the one's a waste of time and the other is a mistake. I'm telling you one thing, though. If either one…" "Shhhh," she touched his lips. "Don't be thinking that way. It'll be fine."

Despite her assurances to the contrary, however, McPherson wasn't so quick to let the matter drop. The foreboding he sensed back in the springtime was stronger than ever; and riding off to invite relatives to a wedding was near the bottom of things he considered important. For two solid days, he tried to persuade Hatty that their being together was the only thing that mattered, that neither his brother or Rainey were worth the effort. But the hurt in her eyes convinced him that continuing to argue the point would cause more harm than making what he thought was a futile attempt at peace. Nevertheless, after meeting with the preacher and then riding over to Clinton to drop in on the Sheriff, he had to concede he could be wrong. The preacher was more than willing to perform the ceremony and Rainey seemed to have forgotten—or at least put aside—their confrontation back in the summer. Even so, the uneasiness lay in the pit of his stom- ach like a green apple just short of being ripe as he rode out the gate. McPherson shuddered and spurred the buckskin into a gallop.

• • •

Once again, Hatty Picquett watched as McPherson disappeared across the rise, but on this occasion, there was a difference in his leaving. He would be returning within the week to get the crop in and two weeks after that, they would be married. She understood his relunctance to leave—she wasn't all that eager to see him go either—but she wanted one last time alone before they became one. She knew it was a silly thing, but it would give her a chance to daydream about their life together. And there was much to dream about. She and Jesse shared a love she had thought impossible, and the child she carried was living proof of their feelings. She stood by the gate long after he passed out of sight, basking in the warm inner glow she felt.

Late that afternoon, she was surprised to see the sheriff riding across the field. She waited on the porch while Rainey tied up his horse outside the gate and crossed the yard.

"Afternoon, Miz Picquett," he said, tipping his hat.

"Good afternoon, Sheriff Rainey. What brings you out this way?"

"Just paying my respects, Miz Picquett. I told Mista McPherson I'd stop by and check in on you." "Well, that's real kind of you, Sheriff," she acknowledged. "Jess must've forgot to mention you'd be around. Would you like to sit for a spell?"

"Don't mind if I do. Wanted to talk with you anyhow." "What about?" she asked guardedly.

"This ain't easy fer me, Miz Picquett, but I guess there ain't no use beatin' around the bush. It's McPherson. Folks here'bouts are wonderin' how you could take up with the man who kilt yer husband."

"Yes, I can see where they might be concerned."

"We ain't ones to be castin' stones," he hurried on, "but..." "But you all believe I'm making a mistake?"

"Yes ma'am," he replied nervously. "It's plain as night and day this McPherson's got ahold on you." "Oh? What makes you think that?"

"Well, you bein' a bereaved widow an' all… Understand, Miz Picquett, I've tried to look the other way. We all have. But there's some things can't be hidden away."

"You do take the cake, Sheriff. You all do. None of you has spend mor'n ten minutes at a time with Jesse, but you're prepared to pass judgment on him *and* me. Seems to me that casting stones is exactly what you're doing. I'm wondering what gives you that right."

"It ain't a matter of havin' to pass judgment. He's killed more than once, and who's to say he won't kill agin."

"I'm curious, Sheriff. Did you fight in the war?"

"Yes, ma'am," he answered, pride creeping into his voice. "I was with Polk and the 1st Tennessee at Stone's River. Why?"

"Did you kill anyone?" she asked softly. "There weren't much choice. It was war."

"From what he's told me, Jess didn't have a lot of choice either." "That's different."

"Is it? It troubles Jesse to this day that he was forced to shoot Mister Picquett. I believe that in spite of how he feels about me, if he could bring my late husband back, he would. Does that sound like a mur- derer, Sheriff?"

"No, ma'am," he replied, now on the defensive, "can't say it does. But yore husband was just the last of many."

"I expect that's truer than you think. But is that wrong, trying to stay alive?"

"Miz Picquett, it ain't so much a question of right or wrong as it is havin' a known killer livin' in the county. Folks are concerned with yore well being, myself included."

"Now that is truly interesting," she declared. "In all the years I've been here, I can't remember anyone being concerned about anything but Mister Picquett's gallivanting 'round the countryside."

"It's a failin' we'd like to make amends for."

"Best way to do that is to accept Jesse at face value and quit worrying about what might be. If them folks that are so concerned would just open their eyes, they'd see that Jess McPherson is a good, caring man."

"Well, I kin see where you'd feel thet way, Miz Picquett, but you know well as I do thet folks are slow to change their thinkin'."

"Then I guess this is one time folks'll just have to break with old habits," she whispered defiantly before softening her tone. "Look… I know you mean well, but nothing you've said is gonna put off us getting married."

"I didn't think it would," he admitted, heaving himself out of the chair. "I best be goin'. Be supper- time afore long."

As the sheriff rode out of sight, Hatty returned to the few chores that had to be done before dark. The sheriff's visit had left her with a lot of questions, mostly unanswered. She hated being suspicious about Rainey's motives—it was not part of her nature—but some things didn't add up, beginning with his sudden unexpected appearance. Considering Jesse's feelings toward Rainey, she couldn't imagine him asking the sheriff to look in on her; and the more she thought about it, the more she wondered about the sheriff's tim- ing. By the time she had finished with the chores, Hatty had worked herself into a full-fledged state of ner- vousness and was quite happy to be inside the cabin with the door barred shut.

Much to her relief, the sheriff failed to return the following day or the day after that and the time passed without incident. Nevertheless, she once again carried a rifle as she went about her daily chores. Late on the night before McPherson was expected back, her peace was shattered by shouts outside the cabin. Wakened from a deep sleep, Hatty was momentarily unsure of her surroundings, but the distinctive crack of rifle fire brought her to the window in a rush. What she saw chilled her to the bone.

The night sky was brightly lit by flames that were quickly consuming the barn, illuminating as well the men on horseback that were pulling down the split-rail fence she had labored over for so many weeks. Anger overwhelmed common sense as she flung open the door, rifle in hand, and fired erratically at the shadowy figures bent on destroying her farm. Pulling the trigger as fast as she could lever rounds into the chamber, she sensed a grim satisfaction as one of the bullets found its mark, eliciting a cry of pain. It was only when a couple of bullets slammed into the wall beside her did she realize how much danger she was in. Retreating inside, she barred the door, expecting an attack on the cabin at any moment. But all that came was a voice out of the darkness.

"Miz Picquett? You hear me, Miz Picquett? We don't mean you no harm." Hatty strained to put a face to the hidden shout, but try as she might, she couldn't recognize the voice. He called out again, but instead of answering, she reloaded the rifle and sat down at the table facing the door, intending to shoot any and every person foolish enough to make himself visible.

"I know you can hear me, Miz Picquett, so it don't make no never mind if'n you answer me or not. You tell McPherson we don't want his kind around here. You tell him this is just a taste of what'll happen if'n he don't move on."

Consumed by the fear that someone would attempt to enter the cabin, Hatty waited for the inevitable, fighting back the occasional urge to reply to the threats toward her man. But as the shouting diminished and hoofbeats faded into the distance, a cold dread washed over her as she realized this was only the begin- ning—Jesse McPherson would refuse to let the issue die.

For the remainder of the night, she sat at the table with the rifle cocked, expecting those who had burned the barn and destroyed her fence to return at any moment and finish what they had started. She was prepared for the worse, aware that she might never see McPherson again, that he might never see the birth of the child she carried. But even as the terror of the night continued to dominate her thoughts, she was unwavering in her resolve to strike back.

At length, the crowing of a rooster on the prowl announced that morning was near. She knew that for the moment she was safe, that the nightriders would not reappear without the cover of darkness, but even so, she hesitated to relax her vigilance. When at last she felt ready to face what awaited her on the other side of the door, the sun had cleared the treetops. Steeling herself against a welling fear, she lifted the bar from across the door and slowly pulled it open, half expecting someone to be standing on the other side. Seeing movement beyond the porch, she brought the rifle to bear.

THIRTY FIVE

It was a day short of a week when McPherson topped the rise behind the Picquett farm. The sun was high in the sky, intensifying the panorama of color that marked the fall of the year. He was in a light-hearted mood, minutes away from the end of a ride he wouldn't have believed could happen. Jacob seemed genuinely happy that he was getting married and even though he was in the middle of haying, he promised to attend the wedding. Maggie had insisted that she and her husband would make the trip early so she could help with whatever needed to be done. But the light-heartedness vanished when he pulled up in sight of the farm.

The cabin stood alone, surrounded by utter devastation. Streamers of smoke spiraled up from the pile of charred and blackened logs—all that remained of the barn and outbuildings. Most of the split-rail fence was strewn around the yard. The crop they had tended so carefully over the summer had been trampled into the ground. The carcass of a horse lay beside the remnants of the barn. Yanking his Winchester out of the saddle holster, he spurred the buckskin into a slow walk.

He dreaded what he would find below, but if Hatty was still alive, another five minutes would make little difference. As he inched closer to the cabin, the instincts built up over seven years kicked in. He scanned the edge of the woods, looking for anything amiss; a splash of color that didn't belong, movement to indicate someone was in hiding, anything, but he was greeted with silence. The hound that spent his days on the front porch was missing, and even though there was a definite chill in the air, there was no smoke from the chimney. As he angled up to the porch and stepped down, the door inched open. He levered a round into the Winchester as a shadow came from behind the door, but let the barrel drop as the missing dog ambled onto the porch and curled up in his usual spot. Caught unawares, he had little time to react as a gun barrel was poked through the door and fired.

McPherson hit the ground rolling, seeking a target as the all-too-familiar heat of a bullet burned throughout his shoulder. But instead of spraying the cabin with random shots in the hopes of hitting some- thing…someone, he held fire, ignoring an impulsive need to strike back.

"Hatty?" he called out as he got to his feet. "It's Jesse." "Jess?" she cried. "Jesse?"

Hatty burst through the door and flung herself into his arms, so overcome with relief she didn't per- ceive he had been wounded. Her face buried in his shoulder, a nervous laugh turned to sobs and then to tears as the tension of the past few days was released.

"You all right?" he asked with obvious concern.

"I am now," she whispered. "Hold me, Jess. Hold me tight." "We'd better patch me up first," he said softly.

"Patch you up?" she echoed. "Good Lord, Jess, you're bleeding."

"That's the usual effect when a person gets shot." "Shot? When did you…?" The tears started again.

"Hatty, this bleeding ain't gonna stop without some help." "But I could've killed you…" she argued hysterically.

"Unless you learn to shoot better, it's not very likely," he corrected with a grimace. But despite his attempt at bravado, the shock of the bullet and subsequent loss of blood were beginning to have an effect. His arm and shoulder were beginning to go numb, and he knew from past experience that if he didn't sit down soon, his legs would fail him. "Best we get inside and get this shirt off."

Once seated at the table, he took comfort in the fact that Hatty had set aside her hysterics to tend the wound. She pulled a small jug of whiskey off the shelf, adding as an afterthought as she poured the liquid over the wound: "This is gonna hurt."

"Do me a favor, woman," he said between clenched teeth. "If you ever decide to shoot at me again, just kill me. It'll be easier on both of us."

McPherson leaned back in his chair and sipped the whiskey while she scurried around, first building a fire in the cookstove, and then putting on a pot of coffee and water to clean the wound.

"Hatty? You see who burnt the barn?"

"All I could see was shadows. But one of them's carrying a bullet." "Then he'll be easy to find."

"And then what?" she asked, unable to conceal her alarm.

"That's up to him," he answered determinedly. McPherson's dread at the possibility of finding Hatty dead was replaced by anger—as much with himself as at the men who took advantage of his absence to ter- rorize Hatty. He had been right about the sheriff and right about leaving her alone; and while he was not given to jumping to conclusions, the message they left was clear enough.

"Jess… Maybe it'd be better if we leave it alone." The words rang hollow even as she said them. "You know I can't do that," he replied, surprised by the suggestion.

"Jesse McPherson!" she cried out. "If you hunt down the ones that did this, you'll have to leave. And I don't want you to leave ever again."

"Woman," he said softly, "that's enough of that talk. I'm not going anywhere, but you know as well as I do that if I don't make my… *our* displeasure clear, they'll come back, and next time it might not be the barn or the crop. It'll be you… or that child you're carrying. I'm not gonna let that happen."

"I s'pose," she agreed, shivering involuntarily, "but I can't believe my neighbors would intentionally hurt me."

"A week ago, you wouldn't have thought they'd burn the barn," he said dryly. "Hatty, folks that are afraid are liable to do most anything."

"For the life of me, I can't see what they're afraid of."

"The Sheriff's been running around talking his fool head off 'bout how I'm a killer, and more's the pity, these self-righteous neighbors of yours have been listening to him."

"What're you gonna do?"

"If you're through with that bandaging, I'm gonna have a cup of that coffee you made. Then we'll see if we can't clean some of this mess up, though you'll have to do most of it. Can't have folks coming to a wedding with the place looking like this."

"That's not what I was asking about."

"I know that, Hatty, and it'd be easier all round if I had an answer. If I was the killer they think I am, they might have gotten rid of me. Most gunfighters don't stick around once they're found out."

"We been through all that. You ain't that kind."

"Hatty, darling, your faith amazes me. Once you've made up your mind, it be easier to deal with that mule of yours."

"Too bad my neighbors never realized that. I might still have a barn."

"It's a lot more than the barn, Hatty," he said soberly. They've put us 'tween a rock and a hard place.

Nothing's standing but the cabin. Crop's gone. Garden too, near as I could tell." "That was our food for the winter."

"We'll make do."

"My neighbors never seemed the kind," she said, a sudden draft of air chilling her. "Gives a body the impression they're not wanted."

"What amazes me is that nobody bothered to threaten you."

"Maybe someone did," she surmised, remembering all too clearly the sheriff's last visit. "Sheriff Rainey dropped three days back. Tried to explain the errors of my ways."

"He *is* persistent," he reflected. "Hatty, do you want to leave?"

"I have no intention of going anywhere. This is my home. And soon as we're married, it'll be yours as well."

"Well, that should be clear enough, even to someone as dense as Rainey."

A wave of dizziness hit McPherson as he got to his feet, but the lightheadedness passed after a moment. He took down the belt and holster that had been hanging by the door since back in the summer and after a couple of tries, asked Hatty to help buckle it on. After she had tied the thongs around his left thigh, he drew the Peacemaker and checked the load before returning it to the holster.

"I'd rather have it on and not need it," he mumbled, as he sucked in air to clear the dizziness that had struck again. "Okay. Let's go take stock. Maybe some of it can be saved."

The damage couldn't have been worse. The garden had been trampled into the ground, as was the tobacco crop they had labored over for so many hours. Ready for harvest, the delicate leaves were now a part of the earth which had nurtured them. All that was left were a few chickens that had not been in the hen house when it burned. Surprisingly, the horse was still alive. It had obviously escaped the fire only to be shot down as it came out. The mule was nowhere to be seen.

"How could they do that, shoot a horse?"

"Some places I've been, it'd be a hanging offence," McPherson commented, shaking his head. He drew the Peacemaker and ended the horse's suffering. "Mule probably didn't get out."

The two continued poking around the ashes, realizing quickly that the effort was a waste of time. Other than the cabin, everything above the ground had been destroyed; nothing of any consequence remained to salvage.

"Some warning." she whispered, subdued. "They might as well have burned down the cabin too.

They said they didn't want to hurt me, that this was just a warning for you to move on." "You talked to them?"

"It's what they were yelling. Listen…" The echo of a soft whinny bounced off the hill behind them. "Somebody's coming."

By the time they had reached the front of the cabin, they could see the sheriff working his way across the field, Hatty's mule trailing close behind.

"He's got nerve, this one," McPherson mumbled as he unseated the Peacemaker ever so slightly, "More'n I gave him credit for." McPherson waited patiently as Rainey rode into the yard and stepped down.

"Miz Picquett…" Rainey greeted her. "Rode out soon as I heard about yer troubles. You all right?" "I s'pose I am, Sheriff, all things considered. How'd you happen to come by my mule? We figured he was in the barn."

"Found him wanderin' just this side of the Yarnell's place." He turned to McPherson, acknowledging his presence for the first time. "Surprised to see you, McPherson."

"I just bet you are," McPherson snapped.

"Thought you was up to the Gap," Rainey remarked, ignoring his sarcasm.

"I was. Got back this morning." McPherson gestured toward the barn. "You know who's responsible for this?"

"What makes you think I'd know anything?" McPherson fought back the urge to strike out. The fact that Rainey was hedging convinced him even more that the sheriff was behind the previous night's attack.

"Cause you're the only one I told I was going to the Gap."

"The ones who did this knew he wasn't here, Sheriff," Hatty interjected.

"Miz Picquett, you of all people should understand thet folks hereabouts are close-knit. Been thet way since the war. There ain't much thet happens in this county they don't eventually find out about."

"Knowing about something's one thing, Sheriff. Destroying my property is something else entirely." "More'n once I've tried to warn you how folks felt about this man," he explained, "but you seem determined to listen to him instead of yore neighbors."

"I guess I've missed something along the way," McPherson mused. "I always thought a person had the right to live their own life."

"Rights is somethin' thet disappeared with the war," Rainey sneered. "Folks ain't comfortable with outsiders around, and thet includes me. Long as yer here, feelin's ain't likely to change."

"I gather you have no intention of doing anything about this?"

"Yer sure a piece of cake, McPherson," Rainey said in amazement. "Just what is it you expect me to do?"

"Considering it might mean you'd have to arrest your friends and neighbors, I don't expect you to do anything. By the way, you know one of em's carrying a bullet?"

"Best you take a hard look at yerself, McPherson. Appears to me you been shot too. I'll be honest. It's no skin off my nose one way or the other, but if they were pushed, there's some might suggest it was you thet set fire to the barn."

"You know better than that," McPherson replied disgustedly.

"Well now, I don't know if I do. Miz Picquett, could you identify any of these people you claim did this?"

"No…" she answered, shaking her head. "I didn't see them up close."

"You can see my problem, McPherson. Without somethin' more than her word to go on, there's not much I can do."

"I can see you think you got it all figured out." "Thet's true," Rainey agreed with smug satisfaction.

"It's time you understood that this land belongs to Hatty, and she plans on staying put. That should be clear enough, even for someone like you."

"Got no problem with thet," he shrugged.

"Thing is, I ain't much for running scared so I expect I'll be doing the same." "You might be regretin' thet decision."

"The only thing I'm regretting is that we keep having this conversation," McPherson replied angrily. "But since your hearing appears to be failing, I'll repeat a couple of things. First of all, in two weeks, Hatty and me'll be getting married. Second, we plan on living here and raising a family, with or without the bless- ings of you and your friends. Now if folks around here want to drop by and visit, they're more than wel- come. But the next man that steps foot on this land intending to do harm would do well to reconsider."

"Folks here abouts don't take kindly to threats, McPherson."

"So you've mentioned," McPherson coldly acknowledged. "But if you've learned anything in all your prying, you know I'm not given to making idle threats. Your so-called *friends* destroyed just about every- thing last night, and I'm not of a mind to be forgiving and forgetting. Now if you'll excuse us, we've got to clean up this mess."

THIRTY SIX

Turning his back and walking away from Sheriff Rainey turned out to be the easy part of the day. Attempting to help Hatty in the clean up became difficult and then impossible as the wound in his shoulder and the heat of the afternoon sun depleted what little energy he had. Running on adrenalin was fine for a while, but even the adrenalin eventually disappeared, leaving him pale and drained. He argued, weakly to his way of thinking, when Hatty insisted he quit trying to prove she didn't know what and just sit on the porch and rest. He was of no use to her or himself if he wasn't healthy. So while he relaxed in a rocking chair with a Winchester across his lap and soaked up the afternoon sun, she continued to drag the split-rail fencing that had been strewn around the yard back into position.

Much as he would have preferred to be helping instead of sitting on his backside, his wound gave him the chance to take stock. The havoc visited on the farm was bad enough, but it wouldn't mean starting from scratch. True, the crop was history—and no big loss to his way of thinking—but the buildings could be replaced. The gold lying dormant in a Denver bank had for the most part been waiting for just such a sit- uation. But there was the matter of the sheriff and his nightriding friends. He had little doubt that their fear would lead to another attack, especially following the conversation with Rainey, but it would take time for them to build up sufficient courage to try again. The only difference was that the next time they showed up, he would be waiting.

His attention drifted toward more pleasant thoughts as Hatty continued to struggle with lengths of rough hewn fencing that were twice as long as she was tall. Watching her work was a diversion he had enjoyed time and again, if for no other reason than to admire her from a distance. She was not one to put on an air of pretentiousness. Instead, there was an unforced manner as she went about her business that he had seldom encountered—a simple take me as I am attitude that he dearly treasured.

As she continued to drag the fencing into place, she occasionally looked his way, as if to see that he was still there. McPherson smiled as he recalled their very first meeting and the image of her calmly aim- ing a rifle at the middle of his chest, quietly grateful she wasn't prone to shooting without first asking ques- tions. The amusing part of it all was that he had been so taken with Hatty that he never really paid a lot of attention to the gun. Most of all, he remembered thinking that she was the kind of woman a man could look forward to spending the rest of his life with.

McPherson grew drowsy from the warmth of the sun and nodded off just as Hatty started toward him. The last image he had was of her unbuttoning her shirt as she neared him. Now dream- ing, he watched as she opened the top of her pants and removed them to stand naked in front of him. She jumped back, teasingly, as he reached for her, a cloud of red blossomed suddenly from her chest as the sound of a weapon reverberated out of the hills. A second shot tugged at his shirt as he threw himself to the ground in a futile attempt to protect Hatty. The hills fell silent as he searched desper- ately for the gunman, the quiet slowly replaced by a growing moan as he verified what he already knew—Hatty was gone, killed stopping a bullet meant for him. A shudder ran through him as a voice pene- trated the veil of sleep.

"Wake up, Jess," Hatty called, "you're dreamin'. Jesse!" McPherson woke, startled to see Hatty standing in front of him, still dressed, and still very much alive.

"My God, Hatty, I thought you were dead."

"Well, that's a fine how do you do," she teased in mock serious- ness. "I'm out there workin' an you're asittin' here asleep an dreamin' about me bein' dead."

McPherson suddenly lunged out the chair and pulled her inside the cabin just as bullets slammed into and through the back of the rocking chair.

"Stay here and bar the door," he ordered.

Slipping out, he ran to the rear of the cabin and climbed onto the bare back of the buckskin, riding out of the yard at a full gallup toward the road running the length of Wolf Valley. A half mile down the road, he pulled up and dismounted, tying the horse back in the trees just past a trail that came off the hill. If he had guessed right, the shooter would be coming down the trail and he intended to be waiting for him if he did. His wait was short. Within ten minutes, a lone man picked his way down the trail atop a mule, seemingly without a care in the world.

"That's far enough," McPherson snapped as he blocked the trail. "Drop the rifle."

"How do, Mista McPherson," the man greeted McPherson as he leaned the rifle against a tree. "Fig- ured you was long gone by now."

"I don't take kindly to people trying to kill me."

"Sit up thar fer better'n an hour," he replied. "Coulda shot you anytime I took a mind to, if'n I wanted."

"Then why?"

He shrugged. "Jest tryin' to throw a scare into ya." "I don't scare easy."

"No, I s'pose you don't," he said easily. "You ain't too good at takin' hints, neither." "Damn it to Hell," McPherson muttered, exasperated. "Will you people never learn?" "'Pears to me it's you thet ain't too quick at learnin'. What are you gonna do?"

"Ain't decided."

"If'n yer gonna kill me, I just as soon you do it now an git it over with."

"You're not getting off that easy," McPherson declared as pointed toward the road. "Let's go." "Whar we goin'?"

"To the farm. It's time Hatty found out who one of her well intended neighbors is." "Cain't say I'd care to do thet, Mista McPherson."

"That's real unfortunate, seeing as how you don't have a lot of choice. Now move."

Hatty almost laughed when she saw the procession across the field. A tall, lanky man, bare-foot as near as she could tell, dressed in bib overalls and a floppy hat was leading a mule, with Jesse riding close behind, a pair of rifles across his lap. As they neared the cabin, her hand went up to her mouth to stifle a cry as she recognized the man.

McPherson swung a leg over and slide off the horse, letting the reins drop to the ground. "I gather you know this fool?"

"Uh huh," she answered, nodding. "Mose Harrison. Lives about two mile up the valley." "Seems he's taken up shootin' at folks."

"Din't shoot at anybody," Harrison corrected. "Shot at the chair." "What'd the chair ever do to you?" McPherson asked sarcastically. "Told you, jest tryin' to throw a scare into ya."

"You could have killed Hatty."

"Nosir!" Harrison was indignant. "I'd never shoot Miz Picquett. She's" "You burn my barn, Mose?"

"Yessum, I was here."

Neither one of the men was prepared for what followed. Hatty suddenly became possessed, assailing Harrison both verbally and with her fists. Harrison stood his ground but offered no resistance. By the time her anger had run the gamut, she was in tears, but there was one last explosion.

"You're beneath contempt, Mose, you and all the other *brave men* who burn barns and destroy crops at night, not to mention the fact that you scared me out of my wits."

"Miz Picquett…"

"Don't! Don't you dare apologize. I can't for the life of me imagine what you all were thinking, to presume to tell me how to live or who I should live with. Where were you when Mister Picquett was still alive?" For the first time, Harrison visibly reacted to her tirade. "That's it, isn't it? He weren't worth knowin' when he was alive, but that he's dead, you're gonna protect his honor. Well it's time you under- stood something, Mose Harrison. My late husband was a cheat and a liar. He didn't know the meaning of honor."

"Sheriff Rainey was right. Yer blinded to the truth."

"Ahhh, Mose," Hatty said disgustedly, "you wouldn't know the truth if it bit you. Has it even once crossed your mind that the sheriff might be wrong about Jesse?"

"Got no reason to doubt him."

"Well, Mose, on the way home, maybe you should think up one. Jesse, will you escort this defender of truth off our land? And Mose, don't you ever come back… For any reason."

Once Harrison was gone, Hatty helped Jesse out of his shirt and peeled off the bandage. "Is it hurt- ing?" she asked.

"Not too bad, considering. Be pretty sore in the morning." "You think I'm a bad woman, acting the way I did?"

McPherson laughed. "I think…you are a picture of loveliness. But you sure know how to stir up a hornet's nest."

"Will it do any good?"

"I doubt it, but you never know. Don't think he was expecting you to react that way." "I think I surprised myself."

"Well, it should give us a breathing spell to get a few things done. Tomorrow, we'll ride into Knox- ville and see about supplies for the winter."

"Takes money, Jess."

"Remember that gold I told you about? I've still got some of it deposited in Denver. Just be a matter of getting it transferred and we'll have more than enough."

"Why not use the bank in Clinton? It's a lot closer." "Guess I'm not feeling too trusting at the moment."

• • •

The trip into Knoxville went well, considering it took them two days longer to get into town than McPherson had anticipated. The bank questioned the validity of the tattered voucher McPherson had car- ried for more than four years, but after wiring the Denver bank, the questions ended abruptly. Hard coin in hand, Jesse and Hatty embarked on a whirlwind tour of most of the shops and stores in downtown Knox- ville, a circuit that left them both exhausted. Their first stop after the bank was to find a replacement wagon and new harness, a decision the mule took as a personal affront the moment the harness was on his back. Hatty recoiled in horror as the mule suddenly kicked out, the hooves narrowly missing McPherson as he bent over to attach the traces.

For the remainder of the day, they wandered back and forth between Gay Street and Central, twice venturing over to Market, adding to their purchases until the wagon was near brimming. In addition to the tools and hardware he would need to rebuild the barn, McPherson insisted that Hatty buy a new dress for the ceremony. It was an expense Hatty argued was extravagant and unnecessary, but the argument was short-lived. From the moment they ventured across the Gay Street bridge spanning the East Tennessee, Virginia & Georgia Railway, Hatty had been like a kid in a candy store. It was the second time she had even been in Knoxville—the first time had been with her family to attend a camp meeting when she was twelve—but other than in her imagination, she had never expected to be able to go into one of the fancy stores, much less buy anything.

It was well after dark as they turned down the valley road beside the Yarnell place. McPherson would have preferred to stop along the way and return the following day, but Hatty seemed indifferent to the fact they were easy targets. Even though there had been no further problems since the unexpected visit by Mose Harrison, McPherson was prepared for, even expected, an ambush anytime after they topped the ridge that paralleled Wolf Valley. But no attack came, and in fact, they met no one on the road. By the time the cabin was in sight, however, McPherson became as nervous as a cat.

"Whoa up," McPherson yelled softly, reining the buckskin and mule to a halt. Although he could see no evidence of horses in the dark, a lamp was burning inside the cabin. "Appears we got visitors, Hatty."

"At least they're not shooting."

"Small consolation," he muttered, handing her the reins. Pulling the Winchester from beneath the seat, he jumped down before levering a round into the chamber. "Give me a minute or two, and then nice and slow."

McPherson covered the ground to the cabin in short order, aware of the wagon's creak as it bounced unerringly toward him. Stepping gingerly upon the porch, he crouched, his focus on the cabin door, ready to shoot the moment someone, anyone came through it. By the time Hatty had reached the fence, the sounds were loud enough to be heard inside. When a muffled voice inside announced that someone was coming, McPherson grinned and released the hammer on the rifle. Maggie and her husband had arrived.

THIRTY SEVEN

Peace of a sort returned to the Picquett farm. Saturday was fast approaching as Hatty and Jess made final preparations for their marriage, and now, less than a week from the wedding, the farm was as ready as it could be under the circumstances. Time had passed quickly following the arrival of McPherson's sister and her husband, but there had been little opportunity for sitting around and visiting as they were pressed into service to help with the clean-up; but it wasn't until the fence was back in place that Hatty was pre- pared to declare the farm ready for visitors.

To McPherson's delight, Hatty and Maggie became fast friends, and although it turned out that Jona- thon Morgan was not a relative of Hatty's after all, McPherson's initial appraisal of him—that his sister had chosen well—was confirmed over and again. While McPherson scoured the county for a new horse, Mor- gan had worked the mule steadily, clearing away the charred timbers, then harrowing the ground to work the ashes in. After two days of looking, a chance remark turned out to be fortuitous as McPherson ended up crossing the ridge into Racoon Valley. He'd overheard talk that a sawmill oper- ator there had a young roan just broke to harness that he might be willing to part with. Not only was he able to purchase the roan at a reasonable price; he was also able to hire out a portable sawmill and a couple of men to operate it. All he had to do was supply the timber.

On Wednesday, McPherson and his brother-in-law were able to get in a full day of snaking logs out of the woods, but Thursday was a write-off as Hatty—over McPherson's objections—dispatched Morgan to invite most every neighbor in the valley to the wedding. The possibility that a few of those invited had very likely partici- pated in the night raid did not faze her; come Saturday afternoon, she was getting married and she wanted everyone to share in her joy. Even more disturbing to McPherson was her insistence that he go into Clinton to shop for things he thought unnecessary, a trip he felt endangered both her and Maggie since Jonathon was gone as well. But he finally threw up his hands and saddled the buckskin when he real- ized if he did not go to Clinton, she would.

Friday morning was spent snaking additional logs out of the woods, and when the sawmiller showed up at midday to set up the mill, there were enough logs piled to keep his men busy for a full week. Late in the afternoon, Jacob finally put in an appearance, and despite his gruff and unfriendly manner, was quickly won over by Hatty. Nevertheless, by the time everyone had settled down to the supper table, the long exis- tent tensions between Jesse and his brother threatened to erupt at any minute.

To the amazement of Maggie, Hatty kept them both in check with relative ease, steering conversa- tions away from anything that might cause rancor. Any sense of civility disappeared, however, when Jacob casually mentioned the last meal the family had eaten together, the night Jesse had informed their father he was leaving, for all intents accusing Jesse of being the cause of Zebadiah's death.

"What'd you say?" Jesse asked coldly.

"Don't see no reason to repeat myself, little brother, just statin' a fact. You hadn't gone gallivantin' round the countryside, Pa might still be alive."

"That cuts it," Jesse growled, getting to his feet. "I'm tired of your accusations. Outside." "Alright, little brother."

"No!" Hatty cried out, but realized she had lost control.

Jesse yanked the door open and stepped through, Jacob hard on his heels. The two brothers faced each other in the yard, Jacob relaxed, Jesse rigid with anger, his left hand resting on the pistol grip.

"Well, Jess, you figger on shootin' me, or you just gonna stare me to death?"

Jesse glared for another moment before untying the leather thong around his thigh and unbuckling the belt. Jacob didn't wait, unleashing a roundhouse that knocked Jesse off his feet.

"Git up, *little brother*. You been wantin' to hit me since you was a snot-nosed kid. Now's yer chance.

Or do you need thet gun to do yer fightin'?"

Jesse wiped the trickle of blood from the corner of his mouth, throwing himself at his brother's mid- section. The impact staggered Jacob, causing him to miss with a second roundhouse. Jesse's momentum slammed Jacob into the ground with Jesse on top, swinging wildly—and connecting—as Jacob struggled to regain his footing.

Now back on their feet, the two brothers circled warily, each of them looking for an opening that would allow them to end it. Their eyes smoldering with hate for each other, they didn't see Hatty run back into the cabin and return with the Winchester, didn't hear her screaming at them to stop. Not until she had fired into the air a second time were they even aware she was pointing the rifle at them.

"Stop it, both of you! The shame of it, grown men actin' like children," she said disgustedly. "I'll not have it, you two ruinin' tomorrow."

"Hatty…?"

"I ain't interested in explanations, Jesse. You ain't in the wild west anymore. You can't be flying off the handle every time you turn around."

"Miz Picquett…"

"And as for you, Jacob McPherson, it's time that you realized your brother's grown up, and come tomorrow, he's gonna be my husband. Now either this nonsense stops here and now or I'll just shoot the both of you and get it over with. If'n my life's gonna be ruint again, I might as well do it myself."

The brothers continued to glare at each other, but their private squabbling took on a new face. Jacob wasn't sure what to make of Hatty's threat, but Jesse had no such doubts. He knew if they resumed fighting, she just might up and carry through with her warning out of spite.

"I'm sorry, Hatty," Jesse's shoulders visibly relaxed. "We had no right to impose the ills of our family on you."

"Good of you to realize that," she gently chided. "Now do you suppose you two can get cleaned up so we can finish supper, or do we have to watch over you to keep you apart?"

"We'll mind our ways, Miz Picquett," Jacob responded sheepishly. "I never meant to bring offence…"

"I know you didn't, but still I'm pleased to hear you say it." She paused while Jesse picked up the pis- tol and holster he had discarded and wandered over to the wash stand. "You know, Jacob, I'd forgotten the meanin' of family til one night when Jess was reminiscin' about you and your Pa and your brother Aaron. But I'm thinkin' he was wrong about some things. He may never see the reasonin', but I surmise it was you that gave him the strength and resolve to survive all those years he was wanderin'. And I'll be eternally grateful to you for that."

"Don't know I'd agree with that. More likely, it was his pig-headed stubbornness."

"Seems to me stubbornness runs deep in your family, Jacob. It ain't somethin' he's got a monopoly on."

"No," he readily agreed, "I s'pose he don't. I'll wash up."

• • •

The day had been a long one, one of the longest McPherson could remember for a very long time. Saturday morning had dawned as perfect as a wedding day in late fall could be, the woods ablaze with bril- liant reds and yellows, the colors heightened by a light rain that had fallen during the night. No one had gotten much sleep—the excitement of the occasion had infected everyone, himself included— and once the sun was up, the number of last minute chores that needed doing before folks began arriving seemed end- less.

Given a choice, he would have preferred that he and Hatty had just gotten married and been done with it. He was uncomfortable in gatherings of any sort, no matter how well-meaning, and he could not rid himself of the nagging feeling that this one would prove to be another tragedy just waiting to unfold. But Hatty's happiness was paramount, and misgivings or no, he was determined to set aside his

288

concerns and make the best of the occasion. But even as neighbors arrived in twos and threes, smiling from ear to ear and filled with good intentions, he couldn't get the thought of a snake in the woodpile out of his head.

The ceremony turned into an ordeal—the preacher was even more long-winded than most. His ser- mon was interminable and boring, an opportunity to chastise them both for sins both perceived and imag- ined. Everyone was worn out long before he got to the I do's and the inescapable pronouncement that they were indeed husband and wife.

The ceremony over, they were subjected to a constant stream of congratulations and cool appraisals. Although Hatty knew most of the neighbors from her dealings at one time or another, it was the first oppor- tunity for any of them to get a look at the outsider that had ridden into the valley back in the spring. Jesse could have done without the fuss, but he had to concede that Hatty was glowing; the anticipated trouble had not happened; and if anything, their guests had gone out of their way to avoid asking questions that might lead to harsh words.

As final congratulations and goodbyes were being said, he was beginning to relax and enjoy the feel- ing of being a married man. But the feeling was short-lived as he noticed for the first time a lone rider crossing the field from the rise overlooking the farm. The rider was astride a mule, a rifle laying across his lap. Despite Hatty's warning, Mose Harrison had decided to pay a return visit. Excusing himself from a group of admiring women, McPherson went into the cabin and strapped on the pistol. Whatever the reason for Harrison's sudden appearance, Jesse could see no good coming of it.

Back on the porch, McPherson became curiously detached as he watched the scene unfold before him. Standing beneath the overhang, he studied the reaction of others as they became aware of Harrison's slow progress across the field, at the same time keeping the rider under a watchful eye. As near as he could determine, everyone seemed surprised to see him, but he could only guess. Once Hatty spotted Harrison, however, it was another matter. She searched about frantically until she saw him standing in the shadows, her eyes widening when she saw the gun on his hip.

Jacob had also seen the rider, and after seeing Hatty's reaction, first toward the rider and then to the pistol on his brother's hip, presumed the worst. Hurrying over to the porch, he instructed his brother to stay put, insisting that *he* could deal with the unwelcome guest. Jesse nodded his agreement and remained in the shadows as Jacob crossed the yard to confront Harrison. Standing to one side of the mule, Jacob's conver- sation appeared to be animated, and at times heated, the occasion word drifting across the yard. But after a moment or two, Harrison apparently lost interest in anything Jacob had to say.

Instead, his eyes wandered from person to person, coming to rest on Hatty. Digging his heels into the mule's flanks, Harrison started toward her, but pulled up short as Jacob grabbed the reins. Twice more Har- rison tried to pass around Jacob, but Jacob was having none of it, determined to prevent him from proceed- ing any further. Frustrated, Harrison levered a round into the rifle's chamber and pointed at the center of Jacob's chest.

Realizing that things were quickly getting out of hand, Jesse stepped out of the shadows, intending on distracting Harrison, but his gesture was too late as Jacob grabbed the end of the barrel and attempted to yank it from Harrison's grasp. Whatever the reason for Harrison's unwelcome appearance, it was lost in the confusing aftermath as Jacob was flung backward by the force of the bullet when the rifle exploded.

The resulting bedlam gave McPherson the opportunity to close the distance between himself and Mose Harrison to within a few feet as Harrison levered in a second round and brought the rifle to bear. Jesse's hand was a blur as he drew and fired at the same instance as Harrison. McPherson heard the screams as both bullets struck home, but he ignored them as he thumbed back the hammer on the Peace- maker a second time and then a third, methodically pulling the trigger and grunting with satisfaction as each round slammed into Harrison.

As Harrison slumped forward and the rifle slipped from his grasp, Jesse turned his attention to his brother, even though his own legs were beginning to fail him. But one look was enough. Jacob was crum- pled on the ground, his head cradled in the Maggie's lap, a dark redness blossoming across the front of his shirt. Jesse realized, however, that whatever the consequences his brother was facing, his own situation might well be just as bad. Although it didn't show, Harrison's bullet had done considerable damage—his insides felt as if they were on fire. He stumbled over to Jacob and fell to his knees beside him.

"Stupid," Jacob mumbled behind a grimace, "grabbin' thet rifle. Ain't gonna make it, am I?"

"I've seen worse," McPherson quipped, but his reassurance was a lie. He had seen stomach wounds before and knew his brother wouldn't make it back to the farm, at least not alive.

"Din't figure to die just yet, Jess. The farm…"

McPherson sat back on his haunches as Jacob breathed his last, realizing that Hatty was standing behind him as he felt her hands resting gently on his shoulders.

"Come on, Jess," she said through her tears, "we got to get you looked at." "Got to tend to my brother first…"

"Maggie and Jonathan'll take care of him," she sobbed. "Come on, now." Jesse struggled to his feet, leaning heavily on her as he made his way into the cabin. Each step was like a knife cutting through him.

"Ain't much of a wedding day, Hatty. Guess this is one of them paybacks the preacher was talking about."

"Don't talk that way, Jess. Jacob told me he was glad to be here."

"Maybe so, Hatty, but I can't seem to find much comfort in knowing that. There was times when I was a youngun that I hated Jacob. I can't remember a time when he wasn't yelling at me or beating on me.

He was wrong, blaming me for Pa's death, but there ain't much doubt I'm responsible for him getting shot. Didn't do much good for myself either. You best send for a doctor."

"Already done, McPherson." Sheriff Rainey interrupted, his voice tormented. "Should be here pretty quick."

"If he isn't, it won't matter. What I can't figure is what Harrison was doing here." "I can answer thet. He come to see Miz Picquett."

"My name is McPherson now, Sheriff," she corrected, as she helped Jesse out of his shirt. "Best you get used to it."

"Sorry, Miz…McPherson. Not thinkin' straight, what with all thet's happened." "Why *did* he come back here? He was warned to stay away."

"Don't know thet I can explain, leastwise not so it makes any sense." "Then don't. Hatty? Would you get Maggie? The sheriff'll stay with me." "I don't want to leave," she said fearfully.

"Just for a minute. I'll be all right."

"Look, McPherson," Rainey said as soon as Hatty was outside, "Mose Harrison's pa was a friend for as long as I kin remember Took a bullet meant fer me at Stone River."

"What's that got to do with anything?" "Promised I'd look after his boy."

"Well, Sheriff, you didn't do a particularly good job…" McPherson doubled up, racked by a fit of coughing. "And my brother's dead because of it," he added when he got his breath back.

"So's Mose…" Rainey said defensively.

"I don't give a damn about Mose Harrison!" McPherson whispered. "He was looking for a bullet and he found one. I never should have let him walk away the last time he was here."

"Why did you?" Rainey asked, his curiosity getting the best of him.

"That doctor better hurry," McPherson muttered, racked with another round of coughing. "You may this hard to believe, Sheriff, but I never took pleasure in ending a man's life, even when it was justified."

"I wish I could believe thet."

"It's the truth. Well? What's it gonna be? Does it end here and now, or are we gonna have to do this all over again? Assuming I pull out of this."

"Depends on you," Rainey offered. "Ain't nothing happened to change my mind."

"I'd be disappointed if you did. Tell the truth, if it was up to me, I'd be done with the lot of you; but for some reason, Hatty wants to stay, and unless she changes her mind, stay we will…" The words died on his lips as he lapsed into unconsciousness.

"Doctor's comin' cross the field now," Hatty announced as she and Maggie came through the door. "Is he…?"

"No, ma'am. He's still with us… Miz McPherson," Rainey took a deep breath, "I'm not askin' you to believe me, but for yore sake, I hope he makes it."

"Thank you, Sheriff. Would you see to the doctor?" "Yes ma'am."

· · ·

The night was late, and the guests were long gone. Hatty was mentally and physically exhausted, as were Maggie and Jonathon, but other than gazing quietly at the fireplace and adding the occasional chunk of wood, no one was inclined to move. The doctor had spent the better part of an hour fishing the bullet out of McPherson and then attempting to repair some of the damage that he and the bullet had caused. When he had finished, he left instructions for keeping the wound clean and the suggestion that a prayer or two might do more good than he had been able to. But despite the doctor's pessimistic outlook, Jess McPherson clung to life with a tenacious stubbornness throughout the night; and by the time the doctor returned the next morning, had responded, although weakly, to Hatty's touch.

Reluctantly, Maggie and her husband departed for Cumberland Gap—Maggie hadn't wanted to leave until she knew whether Jesse would make it, but she was the only one left that could represent the family at Jacob's burial. The sheriff, to Hatty's surprise, had volunteered to contact the Gap and make arrangements for his burial on the farm. And suddenly, or so it seemed, Hatty was left alone with her husband and her thoughts. Once again, fate had dealt her a terrible blow—it was all she could do not to fall apart com pletely—but feeding on her own misery was not her way.

Hatty's life became a narrowing circle of existence; one of checking Jesse's bandage, bathing his face, and occasionally pressing a damp cloth against his lips. Hour after hour she sat by the bed, reading to him from one of the many books she had accumulated, focusing her entire being on him and willing him to live, waiting for the moment when he would wake. Nevertheless, she had no misconceptions about his con- dition. The doctor had been very clear that his chances of surviving the wound were somewhere between slim and none; and despite the fact that he seemed to be holding his own, his skin had taken on the pallor of death.

The hours stretched into two days and then three, but little changed, except that Hatty was reaching a point of exhaustion. The lack of sleep, coupled with the constant worry that each breath Jesse took would be his last, began to take its toil. Hatty became pale and haggard, and although the doctor had added the Picquett farm to his rounds, he made it plain that he was not doing so out of concern for her husband but because of her.

The doctor was no happier about the events of the last couple of weeks than anyone else in the val- ley, an opinion he was more than willing to explain. He had seen Mose Harrison come into the world and like all the children he had delivered over the years, had looked upon him with a certain amount of pride. But there was where he began to run into difficulties because he had also delivered Hatty's two children and had rejoiced in her elation at their birth. When they fell ill with influenza, he had done his level best to save them. When she lost those two children, it had been like losing his own.

There were no such illusions, however, concerning the man she had taken for a husband. From the doctor's perspective, McPherson's presence in the valley had caused no end of grief. He fervently wished— and said as much—that Hatty had never met him, believed she would have been much happier in the long run marrying someone from the valley. But he conceded that wishing for such as that didn't make it so.

"…It's beyond me how he's holdin' on, Hatty."

"That's cause you never took the time to find out who he is." She sighed deeply, Jesse's ultimate fate weighing heavily upon her. "*Nobody* took the time."

"That may well be the case," he conceded, "but you of all people should know folks hereabouts are slow to take to anythin' new."

"My God, I'm so tired ahearin' about my neighbors and their fears. Try tellin' me my husband's gonna be well again…" she cried. "Tell me his child's gonna have a father."

"Yer expectin'?" he asked, her announcement catching him by surprise. "Yes," she answered defiantly.

"Be damned if'n the Lord don't work in mysterious ways," he mused with a shake of his head. "Don't He now," she said bitterly. "Sent a fool on my weddin' day to kill my man."

"Whatever Mose's reasons for showin' up, I can't believe that was his intention. But dwellin' on it won't change nothing. What you've got to do is get some rest."

"Jesse needs me."

"Hatty, listen to me for just a moment. Yer not doin' you or yore husband any good sittin' here day after day. If he comes out of this, that's when he'll need you. Right now, your first duty is to that child yer carryin'."

"But…"

"No buts, young woman. I've already talked to the Widow Hicks and she's agreed to spell you off.

She don't live far and it'll give her somethin' to do." "But I don't want any…"

"Right now, it don't matter what you want," he interrupted. "You recall, I helped bury yer two youn- guns. Don't intend to do the same with you." He picked up his bag and turned to the door. "She'll be here this afternoon… And no more arguing."

The whisper was so low, that for a moment, neither one of them heard it, but when it came again, it was like a fingernail on a blackboard, sending uncontrollable chills down their spines. They turned back toward the heretofore motionless McPherson, shocked to see his eyes fluttering ever so slightly.

"Jess?" she cried out, racing back across the room. "Jesse…?" "Thirsty…"

The End

AFTERNOTES

The origins of this story are many, most of which would fall under the category of a love for history, and a firm belief that we can learn much from the lessons history offers if only we are prepared to open our eyes to them.

My lessons started on Saturday afternoons at the now defunct Lee Theater, which was located on Tennessee Avenue, in the Lonsdale community of Knoxville, Tennessee, where I was enthralled with the multitude of good guys prepared to defend the rights of settlers against marauding Indians and along the way, fall head over heels in love with virtuous school marms who were always young and pretty.

The list of six-gun heroes were many: Hopalong Cassidy; the Durango Kid; Lash LaRue; the Cisco Kid; Gene Autry; Roy Rogers and that masked rider of the plains, The Long Ranger. Each of them had a horse identified with just them, and a companion who played second banana to the horse opera star. And that was just the A-list.

And I would be remiss to omit the folk heroes that also played a role in my early education, many who were often on the wrong side of the law. Individuals with names like Jesse James, Wyatt Earp, Doc Holiday, Kit Carson and Custer; and aboriginals such as Geronimo, Cochise, Sitting Bull and Chief Joseph all played a role in my education.

The part that Hollywood left out, however, was that the good guys and the bad guys were often indis- tinguishable, and every now and then, the same person; that wearing a white hat did not automat- ically sug- gest a halo; that Indians were more often than not defending their land and their right to exist.

Nevertheless, I developed a love of the old West through the eyes of Hollywood, and that love has never died. What changed was my perception of it. Thanks to an obsessive need to read (and myriad books that catered to the obsession), I discovered that much of the history relating to the old West (and to other matters as well) was written from the perspective of the winners.

Settlers moving West were fulfilling a "manifest destiny" and the fact that more than a few of them were unscrupulous thieves and murderers mattered little in the big picture. Land was routinely occupied without regard to the actual owners—the aboriginals that had been there for centuries—who were seen as Godless heatherns, savages to be subjugated or killed, whichever was most convenient at the time.

In writing this story, I made a sincere effort to make my characters believable and to give them cre- dence with respect to the times they were placed. I trust that if I have erred, you the reader will allow me some leeway.

The Widow Maker began as a few paragraphs written for a friend, Yoanna West. It was at her insis- tence and with her encouragement that it grew beyond those few paragraphs, which, strangely enough, mostly disappeared in the rewrites and editing.

I would like to express my thanks to the following people (ca. 1990-92), who unfortunately must remain nameless due to my carelessness in preserving files:

The historian/archivist at Tulane University for her help regarding the Natchez Trace and New Orleans.

The historian/archivist at the Mesquite Public Library for information relating to Mesquite, TX in 1879.

The historian/archivist at the Public Library in Cottonwood, AZ for her help regarding the Verde Valley and the Mogollon Rim.

In addition, I want to thank Dr. Paula Mitchell Marks, who's brilliant work: *And Die in the West: The Story of the O.K. Corral Gunfight,* gave me invaluable insights into the times I wrote about.